A.S.R. Gelpi is a master at painting with words. This author's world is enchanting and whimsical, with a dash of suspense! As you read through their journey, you feel closely connected with the characters and almost feel their experiences. This story is an entry to a faraway place with lands and creatures you could only dream of, but despite the fantastical details, the message in the story is relatable. Whether it is an escape to another world or you take away a life lesson, I believe there is something in this book for everyone.

— MARGARET POLING, AUTHOR

The plot was incredibly unique and original. Truly unlike anything I have read before, and fantasy is my top genre, so it was nice to read something new and imaginative.

— ROBIN DEGAN, AUTHOR

I was in love with the relationship Kharis and Saya had. They are the best part of this book. Kharis's' ferocity to protect, her slight vicious edge, and her trouble-making tendencies were incredible.

— GABRIELLE, BETA READER

The world-building is spectacular, so rich in lore, and the best backdrop to a refreshing fantasy story.

— NICK, BETA READER

The story grabbed my interest from the beginning
and held me with an original and compelling story-
line. The story kept me turning pages, and I read the
whole story in one sitting.

— EVEREN, BETA READER

A LAND OF SHADOWS AND MOSS

BOOK ONE

A.S.R. GELPI

Book cover design by germancreative
Cover images: DepositPhotos
Other images: Canva
Map by Cartographybird Maps
Fan Art Illustrations by @colouranomaly, @saramirza_art, @jemeny69, Duy Phan, and Sam Balgruuf

Silver River Publishing
P.O. Box 1272
Santa Maria, CA 93456

E-book ISBN: 979-8-9895382-0-1
Paperback ISBN: 979-8-9895382-1-8
Hardback ISBN: 979-8-9895382-2-5

First Edition: May 2024

A LAND OF SHADOWS AND MOSS

To every girl who ever felt misunderstood, unappreciated, or feared— know that you are the author of your story, and every page holds the promise of a brighter tomorrow.

AUTHOR'S NOTE

A Land of Shadows and Moss is the first book in *The Dandelion Chronicles*, a literary high fantasy series about Kharis, the curse that enslaves her, and her desperate wish for freedom. Set in a richly imagined secondary world, the series weaves an intricate magic system with its own mythology, prophecy, and cosmological stakes.

The narrative spans empires and even the spirit world, unfolding through multiple POVs across kingdoms, races, and timelines. Themes of war, betrayal, ancient curses, and divine forces shape the fate of nations and characters alike. With sweeping arcs divided into multi-part volumes, *The Dandelion Chronicles* offers readers the full scope of high fantasy worldbuilding and the grandeur of epic storytelling.

This book also draws inspiration from Polynesian cosmologies, particularly Māori traditions of sea and fire deities. While the names and details in this story are original to its world, I wish to acknowledge those traditions with gratitude and respect.

To enhance your reading experience, a brief glossary of pronunciation is included in the initial pages; a more comprehensive glossary of terms, along with detailed explanations, is provided at the end of the book. If you are reading on Kindle, the X-Ray feature is enabled.

The Empire of Zahar is an inclusive world where same-sex couples are a regular aspect of this society.

The story contains references regarding graphic violence within a fantasy framework (using magic or medieval-type weaponry); death during childbirth; suggested torture; abuse and assault, including against a minor; suggested stalking; content of a sexual nature, although scenes in this book are "closed door." Readers, please take note before embarking on a journey through Zahar.

Thank you for selecting this book. I sincerely hope you'll enjoy this wondrous, fantastical, coming-of-age tale and join Kharis as she searches for her truth.

GLOSSARY OF PRONUNCIATION

A more thorough list of terms used in this book is available at the end of the book. However, here's an initial list of words to get you started. How you sound the letters in your head will be close enough, so don't sweat it. Go forth and confidently read *A Land of Shadows and Moss*. Welcome to Zahar.

- Aghet Mendi - A-ghet MEN-dee
- Akumi - A-koo-mee
- aljaicin - al-ha-ee-SEEN
- Almarim - al-ma-REEM
- Andaheimur - an-HAEE-moor
- Arjun Ghan - AR-joon ghan
- Aroha - a-RO-ha
- Ataahua - a-ta-a-HOO-a
- Atarangi - a-ta-RAN-ghee
- Djinnshirukh - GEEN-shee-rook
- Götrid - GHO-treed
- Gutxi - GHOOT-chee
- Hala - HA-la
- Hröld - rold

- Ibaia - ee-BA-ee-a
- Jordha - JOR-da
- Kahurang - ka-hoo-RAN
- Kahurangi - ka-hoo-RAN-ghee
- Kharis - ka-REES
- Kiwa - KEE-ooa
- Koa - KO-a
- Mahabhal - ma-ha-BAL
- Mahaluika - ma-hoo-EE-ka
- Nikau - NEE-ka-oo
- rahuitia - ra-hoo-ee-TEE-a
- Rangatira - ran-gha-TEE-ra
- Rawiri - ra-WEE-ree
- Regiazenka - re-jee-a-SEN-ka
- rewera - Re-OOE-ra
- Saya - SA-eea
- Sorukhipa - so-roo-KEE-pa
- Taika - ta-EE-ka
- Tanganokai - tan-gha-RO-a
- Tawhiri - ta-WEE-ree
- Teppe - tep-pe
- tohunga - to-HOON-gha
- Tung - toong
- Urrun - oor-ROON
- Välissa - BA-lees-sa
- whānau - wa-a-NA-oo
- xakea - cha-KE-a
- Yuna Chantarasang - YOO-na chan-ta-ra-SANG
- Zahar - sa-HAR
- Zahar-Ghak - sa-har-GHAK
- Zahar-Homa - sa-har-HO-ma
- Zahari - sa-HA-ree
- Zahar-Katea - sa-har-ka-TE-a
- Zahar-Regia - sa-har-RE-jee-a
- zaldun - sal-DOON (singular)
- zaldunak - sal-DOO-NAK (plural)

Quick Explanations:

- **The Zahar-Regia** is the imperial walled enclave within Zahar-Ghak, the capital of Zahar. It consists of an inner, middle, and outer ring.
- **The Sendatorsum** is the royal compound at the heart of the inner ring, encompassing the imperial palace and royal residences. The term may appear in its shortened form, the Senda.
- **The Ghak** is the shortened name locals give to the imperial capital.
- **Bhiksun/bhiksunim** - Singular/plural genderless term that refers to monks, nuns, priests, and their acolytes.
- **Expletives** - The most sedate are "blasted" and "fires burn me." Then come "txakurra" and "txakurri." The worst is "spear me and gut me, too," often shortened to "spear me." This book does not use modern expletives.
- **Tavah/Mavah** - informal terms for father and mother used in the private/familiar sphere.
- **Asurûn / Arisûn** - formal terms for father and mother used in the public/court sphere.
- **The Hesharat** is the escort of the imperial king, comprising highly trained White Guard officers.
- **The Velathari** is the escort imposed on the Djinnshirukh, consisting of twelve highly-trained White Guard officers.

THE COMMONWEALTH OF NATIONS

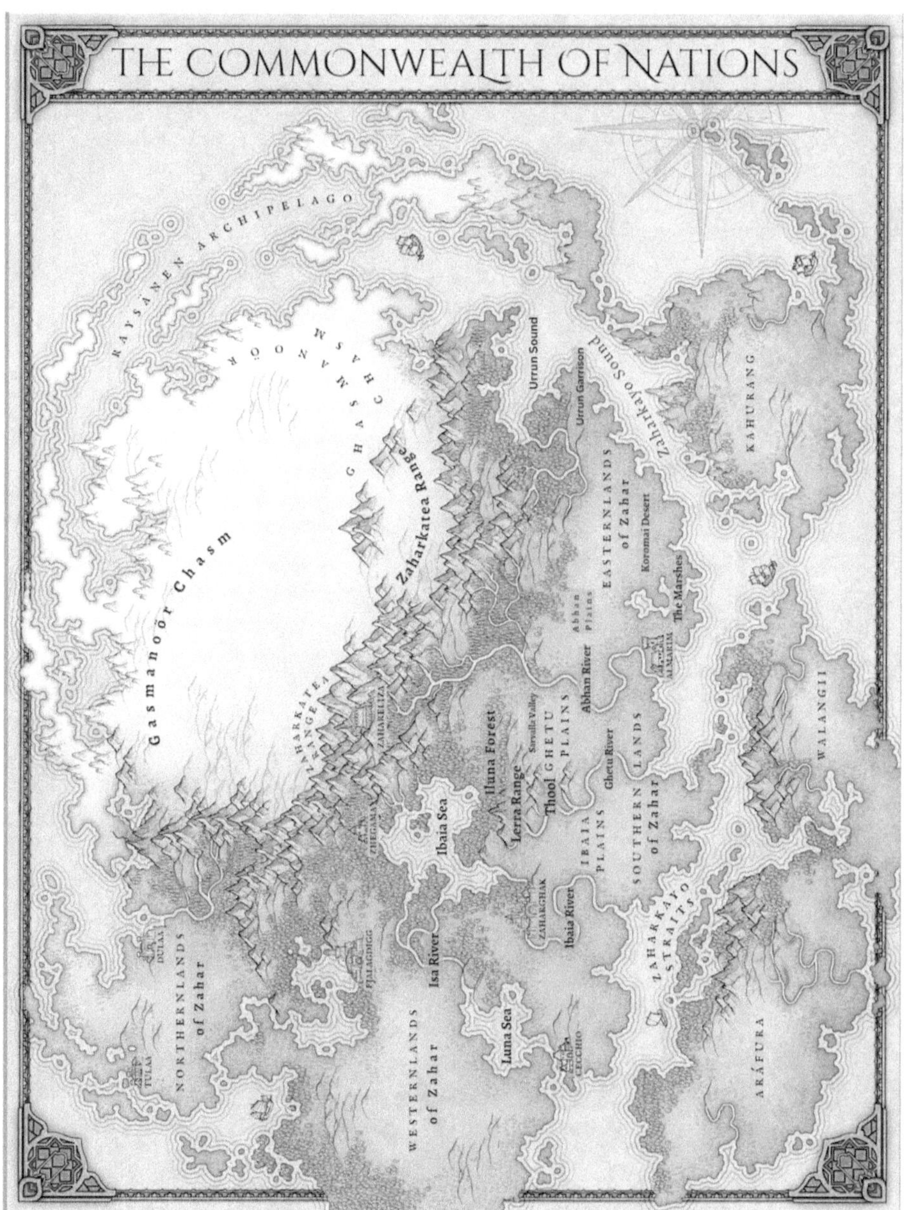

ZAHARKATEA RANGE
Zaharkatea Range
N
E
S
W
FJALAGDIGG
ZHEGAMA
ZAHARELIZA
Ibaia Sea
Iluna Forest
ZAHARGHAK
Ibaia River
GHETU PLAINS
IBAIA PLAINS
SOUTHERN LANDS of Zahar
ALMARIM
EASTERNLANDS of Zahar
Koromai Desert
Urrun Sound
Urrun Garrison
Zaharkayo Sound
ZAHARKAYO STRAITS

PROLOGUE

In shadows cast, my story gleams,
A dream embraced in woven seams.
A tapestry my hands have made,
An epic tale in threads I've weaved.

With this final fate, my journey ends,
As I knit the last of my yarn, my soul wends,
I am unfolding brilliance, a masterpiece,
A unique song, a boundless tale.

In every twist, a chapter unfolds,
The past and future, and the secrets they hold.
Each thread is a choice, a destiny's trace,
The paths I've chosen, my life's intricate lace.

Through storms and stars, I've found my way,
In moonlit nights and the light of day.
The colors blend in my heart's design,
A vivid mosaic, like my life, divine.

With every stitch, I've faced despair,

But also joy and love beyond compare.
I've worn my scars like precious jewels,
My strength and resilience, the finest of fuels.

In shadows cast, my story gleams,
A dream embraced in woven seams.
A tapestry my hands have made,
An epic tale in threads I've weaved.

—Poliormos, Weaver of Tales and Fates

PART ONE
THE WILL OF THE OCEAN GOD

CHAPTER 1
THE PORTRAIT

Kharis wasn't supposed to be here—skipping her lesson, slipping past guards, breaking palace rules—all for a stolen glimpse of her mother's portrait.

She sat tall on the throne, proper and regal. Oils and mineral pigments had captured her imposing presence—Queen Aghuti Ghan of Zahar, from the ancient and revered House of Ghan.

The twelve-year-old studied it, no other portraits catching her attention. This one, though, was worth the trouble of ignoring warnings, dealing with endless lectures, and potential punishment.

Queen Aghuti was outstandingly gorgeous, with olive skin and amber eyes that, even from the canvas, appeared to probe the world. A bloodred rose adorned her glossy brown curls, framing her delicate features. Her crown looked heavy, brimming with glistening gemstones and ornate golden filigree. The luxurious ermine cape cascaded down to the floor, where it flared. Her right hand held onto the royal scepter—a long, bejeweled metal staff that some said was a thousand years old. Her other hand rested on the elaborate armrest of the opulent Zahari throne.

Behind her stood King Hröld, a rose fastened to his lapel. His hand lay on her shoulder in an adoring gesture. Their love story drifted in the air, sweet and heady like the roses they wore for each other. To Queen Aghuti's right side was Crown Prince Hala, seven years of age at the time of the painting. Prince Khator would've been five. Princess Götrid, to her mother's left, was three years old. Helena, perhaps one, sat by her mother's feet with a toy.

Fifteen years after this portrait was made, Kharis was born.

But the woman in the portrait was front and center. Her face drew Kharis in, and everything else seemed to disappear. The artist had captured her beauty, presence, and the otherworldly power she exuded. *Her Imperial Majesty, Queen Aghuti Ghan, Daughter of the Sun.* The other individuals were required additions.

But the one thing that stood out as a truth in Kharis's mind was that she didn't look like anyone in the portrait—at all.

Kharis sported hair so black it sucked all light and glimmered blue when the sunlight hit it just right. The members of the House of Ghan were tall. She was small. And her eyes weren't amber or brown. A ring of gleaming silver encircled her pupils and radiated into brilliant sapphire.

How can I be their child? A question she'd been pondering lately.

"There you are." That voice snapped Kharis out of her ruminations. Golden-colored eyes stared at her, orbs shining like the Zahari sun. "I had a feeling I'd find you here."

Joy blossomed on Kharis's cheeks.

Saya, her twelve-year-old adopted sister, looked more like the people in the portrait. Kharis's gaze returned to it, confirming it—amber eyes so light they were gold, cascading chestnut curls, lovely olive skin, and... *A head taller than me.*

"You missed your morning lesson," Saya said.

Kharis shrugged. Tutors hated her. They'd rather she weren't there.

Saya arched her eyebrows but didn't utter a word, and Kharis knew why. *My reprimand will come later.* Her brother Hala would lecture her. Nana Yuna would defend her. Her father, His Serene Imperial Majesty King Hröld, Son of the Sun, would sit silently, listening.

"Come." Saya's smile brightened the world and made Kharis's that much better. "Food should be ready."

That perked Kharis up (and her stomach, too). "Well. Let's go."

CHAPTER 2
THE KAHURANGI DELEGATION

Prince Rawiri studied the waves, and their sight reminded him of his beloved Kora, the scent of salt and brine infusing that memory. Even in death, her spirit lingered in the ocean's perpetual dance. He leaned over the ship's rail, watching the waves crash against the bow, their spray cool and refreshing on his face. It felt like a sweet caress, and that sensation made the journey tolerable.

He loved the sea. He hated it.

The ocean had blessed him, but it had also taken from him.

The voyage from Kahurang to Zahar-Ghak would be long, nearly a month, but the Kahurangi, famed seafarers, thought nothing of it. Despite the original agreement to meet in the southern city of Almarim, halfway between the Zahari capital and the island continent, the Hāhona kept its course. The mighty royal ship sailed the choppy southern seas and maneuvered the coral reefs, shoals, and narrow straits like a graceful lady, her naval escort following.

"*Ka peke koe!*" King Kiwa shouted as he waved goodbye to the port city of Almarim. They cruised past it on their way to the giant mouth of the Ibaia Delta.

Rawiri laughed. Kiwa and his three sons propped against the taffrail, their wild eyes full of sea and salty brine, shouting with the same passion while defiantly raising their fists.

"*Ka peke koe!*" *Screw you.*

Rawiri sighed, resigned.

This morning, up and taut sails gobbled the prevailing breezes and moved the vessel over the dark blue waves. Dolphins greeted them, prancing and jumping in the ship's wake.

"Look!" Taika, the youngest of Kiwa's sons, gestured to the mammals while Koa, the middle prince, whooped excitedly.

"A good omen," Nikau, the oldest son, said. "Signs of hope and pleasant weather."

"Tanganokai is sending his messengers to protect us," Kiwa said, turning to his brother. "See? Our god sees this journey with good eyes."

The Kahurangi weren't supposed to go to the capital. Almarim was the designated spot for the historic meeting, but that wasn't how it would go, because no one could deny his brother a visit to the renowned capital of Zahar—Almarim be damned.

And so, the Hāhona sailed forward at King Kiwa's orders, disregarding all agreements and plans with the Empire of Zahar.

The crisp ocean breeze kissed the men's faces as Almarim became a distant spot. The naval cavalcade enjoyed glorious weather, perfect currents, and strong winds. Tanganokai, their god of the sea, bestowed his blessings for a successful journey.

The king and his sons laughed wholeheartedly, arms gesturing at the immensity of the waters they loved.

Rawiri simply smiled.

Queen Ataahua lounged on the deck with a book in hand, outwardly appearing to agree with Kiwa's plan, but couldn't resist an amused roll of her eyes. While he deliberated and strategized, she had already formed a meticulous plan in her mind.

Ataahua looked at her sons with pride. At nineteen, Nikau, her eldest, would rule Kahurang one day, and the hunt for a worthy wife was on. Koa, seventeen, and Taika, fifteen, were the perfect ages to enter betrothal agreements. Her envoys had mentioned that the king of Zahar had two lovely daughters, both of whom were soon to be thirteen. According to them, King Hröld of Zahar, a widower, was a healthy man of fifty-six with a face easy on the eyes.

And so Queen Ataahua brought her widowed sister along.

Suppose the King of Zahar were to marry Aroha. And if the Zahari princesses were to be engaged to her youngest boys... *Oh!* Ataahua drooled at the possibilities, tapping her chin as she planned and plotted.

The queen had questioned her husband's choice to sail past Almarim, worried about the implications and consequences. As she studied Kiwa, his decision satisfied her.

At forty-six, Kiwa was a mighty Kahurangi warrior—broad-shouldered, with solid arms and feral eyes. His intricate face tattoos danced when happiness parted his lips.

I married well.

Her heart pulsed lustfully, her gaze moving slowly from his broad shoulders down to the narrow waist she wanted to hold, the glutes she craved to squeeze, and those legs with perfectly carved muscles. Heat flooded her core. Perhaps she should lead him to their cabin, where she would shower him with her gratitude.

We've sailed past Almarim. The nerve. But she loved her Kiwa the most for it. In two more weeks, they would arrive at Zahar-Ghak.

She returned to her book, occasionally peeking over the pages to ogle at her man.

CHAPTER 3
THE DJINNSHIRUKH AND THE KAHURANGI

Kharis did her best to behave as the Zahari royal retinue waited on the Ibaia Harbor's platform, next to the dock where the Kahurangi royal barge would lower its anchor. But mostly, she blew air through her lips, bored out of her mind.

At the last possible moment, the Kahurangi had headed straight for the Ghak, what the locals commonly called the capital city. Not stopping in Almarim meant snubbing her sister, Princess Götrid, who ruled the Southernlands with her husband. Kharis didn't feel sorry for her, but her husband was a different story. Prince Bikram was kind and didn't deserve it.

Götrid had left the capital after Kharis's birth and never visited. She sent letters and essential reports to her father and brother, and whenever gifts arrived for the girls, Kharis knew they were from her husband, Prince Bikram.

Princess Helena, Kharis's other sister, oversaw the Northernlands from her palace at Fjalagdigg. The northern seas were rough, so travel by land was safer this time of year. Since it would take Helena an eternity to reach Almarim, the Crown didn't expect her to join them.

Why am I thinking of them?

The women were busy running kingdoms on their father's behalf. One day, Kharis would understand the burdens placed on adults, or so people said, but said people had been wrong before. Marna, her last nanny, had once hinted at the age difference to explain their aloofness. The sisters were twelve. Götrid was twenty-nine and Helena twenty-seven. Despite what Marna said, neither sister acted as if Kharis or Saya existed.

Sisters only on gold-rimmed parchment paper.

Prince Khator, their other brother, a man of thirty-one, would be arriving from the west. He oversaw the Western-lands from the harbor in Cecchio, the jewel of his kingdom. Commerce had made it an affluent city.

Khator.

He visited the capital regularly and dined with Hala and her father to discuss various issues with them. Still, he would seek every argument, pretext, and excuse to avoid visiting her. He would briefly chat with Saya if, and only if, he ran into her during his visits, but Kharis was a line he didn't cross.

Kharis couldn't shake the feeling that the three siblings blamed her for their mother's death.

Hala, their older brother, raised the sisters. He was over-protective, perhaps compensating for Götrid's, Helena's, and Khator's absences in her life, and Kharis did her best to rein in her resentment. *They are incidental relatives—names on royal family trees and nothing else.*

Kharis huffed under her breath.

She hated waiting.

Waiting forced her to think.

❧

Saya glanced at her sister.

Kharis stood, not tall and proud as expected of a Zahari

princess, but blowing on the strands that had already come loose from her hairdo. She was utterly bored and uninterested in the pomp and circumstance connected to the arrival of the Kahurangi royal family and their delegation.

She yawned loudly, and Saya elbowed her in the ribs, earning a nasty glare from Kharis. Hala pivoted his head and glowered at them. Both sisters squared their shoulders, back to paying attention and behaving.

Kharis stuck her tongue at Hala's back and blew more hair strands off her face. "They are taking their time, aren't they?" she whispered, curling her fingers over Saya's ear.

"Hala won't allow us to travel on the river. I don't know what would cause such delays."

Kharis exhaled. "Why can't we travel on a river barge? Khator does it every month."

"You're under a water prohibition."

Kharis wrinkled her nose. "What does that even mean? It doesn't save me from taking baths."

"Stop getting into fights or rolling in the mud with the dogs, and you won't need daily baths."

Kharis groaned in annoyance. "I don't get into fights. They come looking for me."

Saya rolled her eyes, shaking her head, but deep down, her sister was right. Noble-born children were calling Kharis names. The quiet grumbling in shadowy corners turned into bold grimaces and not-so-silent curses when she walked past them. "Raven Spawn" was their favorite.

"As for rolling in the mud," Kharis said, "I didn't do it on purpose. One of the guard dogs jumped at me. What can I do when their puppy eyes beg for my attention?"

"Puppy eyes?" That didn't convince Saya. Those hounds were taller and heavier than her sister.

A loud trumpet blare echoed throughout the quay, interrupting the conversation.

"They're here," Saya said with a warm smile.

"Finally!" Kharis threw Saya a glassy stare.

Kharis gaped as the Kahurangi king descended the ship's plank.

Complex tattoos adorned his face with curved shapes, geometric designs, and spiral patterns. Their design intricacy was mesmerizing and terrifying, putting the famed Kahurangi warriors in context. Meeting such a face in battle would've frightened soldiers and a few Zahari generals.

Her narrowed gaze swiveled to the imposing High General, Arjun Ghan. *I bet he was scared.*

Another choir of trumpets shoved Kharis out of her ruminations.

The Kahurangi queen's imposing beauty stole her breath. Even from afar, this woman exuded power. It curled around her like an invisible cape. Kharis fixed her gaze on the symmetric, tattooed lines and swirls that decorated her chin and continued down her neck with graceful fluidity, hidden under her elaborate choker necklace.

The king and queen wore magnificent black-feathered cloaks decorated with opalescent shell pieces that draped gracefully over their shoulders. The feathers shone blue against the sunlight while the shell pieces glinted in a rainbow of iridescent colors. Artisans had meticulously crafted the cloaks, with the exquisite black feathers arranged in intricate patterns. The extravagant embroidery and beading on their clothes showcased the Kahurangi's close relationship with the land and the sea, displaying vibrant shades of blue, green, and earthy reds.

Both genders wore long hair, but it seemed that roles determined the style of their hairdo. The warriors let theirs loose. The king wore his hair tied atop his head, secured by an ornate guan headdress made of gold and mother-of-pearl. The queen sported detailed braids adorned with pearls and a cascade of silky curls.

Despite the peaceful goal behind this historic meeting,

both royals were armed to the teeth. Baldric belts crisscrossed their chests, sporting daggers with lavishly carved hilts.

Kharis grinned. It was a blatant show of power.

Yes, she liked them.

The Djinnshirukh eyed High General Arjun Ghan, who shuddered at the sight of their weapons and the implied symbolism with an unfriendly, narrowed gaze. She smirked, enjoying his distress. *Serves him right.*

Behind the king and queen, three equally armed young men wearing kilts swaggered past the soldiers lined up to protect Their Majesties.

Curiosity lit Kharis's mind as she turned to Saya. "Their sons?"

Saya shrugged, unsure.

"Notice they have no escorts." Kharis's expression soured.

"I bet they behave," Saya countered.

The Djinnshirukh huffed with an eye roll.

There was much activity as the Kahurangi soldiers lined the dock while the royals leisurely stood across the plaza.

"Ugh, back to waiting." Kharis's gaze wandered, officially done with all the formalities adults imposed on life.

A glint of iridescent green seized her attention—a lovely hummingbird dancing through the air. It lingered nearby, almost as if vying for her to notice. A smile graced Kharis's lips. Hummingbirds were never far from her, though the reason remained a mystery. *Maybe I'm a flower to them.* She giggled at that idea.

Her gaze followed the tiny bird until she spotted three boys past the gathered crowd, harassing a young girl, pulling on what appeared to be her doll. Worse, the child sobbed, tears spilling out as she tugged on her toy while the nearby adults ignored the scuffle—the historic moment capturing their attention. By the identical hair color, one of the boys had to be an older brother—not protecting but pestering her. He seized the doll with a forceful yank and threw it at the other two, while the poor child desperately ran between them to retrieve her toy. When the cackling threesome ran away with it, the young girl chased after them.

Kharis gave it her all, genuinely striving to behave and stay put, but what she'd witnessed got her hackles up. Her fingers clenched, and her nostrils flared as the injustice fed her anger. The Djinnshirukh limbered her neck and shoulders and quietly retreated from the stage, disappearing from view.

CHAPTER 4
THE DJINNSHIRUKH
AND THE TUTOR

Hala took a deep breath.

Arjun Ghan's armor gleamed in the sunlight. He wore it to show *he* was the High General, supreme commander of the Zahari armed forces —should anyone need a reminder.

Even in this blasted heat, he wears his helm.

Hala shook his head. Ghan would be a thorn in his side. With the armies under his thumb, he could become a dangerous foe, and the arrogant man knew it, wielding his power with civil war as a silent threat. Hala wished him a quick death, hopefully before he ascended the throne. Yet, at fifty-five, the general was the epitome of health. And despite his various run-ins with death on the battlefield, the man was alive, with the blessing of a long life upon him.

The Kahurangi delegation was fast approaching. Hala hoped Ghan would behave—temper his mouth, remove the scowl from his face, and perhaps be a gracious host. *I'm asking for the impossible.*

The high general's hatred for the Kahurangi was well known, and the Kahurangi, in turn, hated him back with equal force. That dynamic would cause friction at the palace. *Almarim was the best location for this meeting. Why couldn't they stick to the plan?* Hala grumbled silently under his breath and took a deep breath to calm his nerves.

After all, essential trade agreements hung in the balance.

Hala took another cleansing breath and turned his attention to the group.

The king, his three sons, and a selected group of fierce-looking warriors settled halfway between the ship and the royal stage. King Kiwa was tall and wide and wrapped in so much muscle that it appeared his clothes could rip if he flexed his arms. Upon his command, they began a loud chant in their language, stomping their feet and slapping their bodies in rhythm as they sang—the power in the lyrics evident to all.

Hala recognized it immediately—Kahurang's anthem. It displayed national pride, strength, and unity, a well-crafted symbol of Kahurangi ethos for the Zahari. One more announcement that they'd arrived. And although Kiwa and his retinue danced, every Kahurangi present chanted in unison with their king.

"It's a powerful visual, don't you think?" Hala casually said.

Ghan scowled. "He who succumbs to the allure of fleeting appearances often discovers a dagger at their back."

Well, then. Hala barely masked his smug expression. The high general seethed at the display, gritting his jaw into a grimace. *Good. Now keel over and die.*

When the dance was over, the Kahurangi clamored loudly. The Zahari clapped, unsure of what was appropriate for this performance.

Amusement tugged at the corners of Hala's mouth. *Let's get this started.*

He and his father descended the platform's steps and met the delegation midway. Both kings leaned in, noses and foreheads pressed together, sharing the breath of life. When they straightened, King Kiwa laughed.

"The Zahari king knows our greeting."

Satisfied, Kiwa held Hröld's forearm—the Zahari greeting. "Blessed are the gods who made it possible to greet this day," Kiwa said.

"May they sustain us," Hröld said. "Welcome to Zahar."

And upon a loud command, the rhythmic thunder of taiko drums filled the plaza. Hala and his father led the Kahurangi delegation toward the quay's royal platform.

❧

Saya noticed the empty spot beside her, where her sister should have been standing. *Blessed Mother, where has she gone now?*

Saya's searching gesture tipped Hala off that Kharis was *not* on the stage.

Blasted.

Her brother glowered at her, yet her father spoke to the Kahurangi monarchs as if nothing were happening. Calm. Collected. The epitome of diplomacy and gracious welcoming.

Using hizkuntza, a signed language, Hala asked, "*Where's your sister?*"

"*Washroom,*" she signed back. A white lie. A big one.

Hala grimaced. "*Couldn't she wait?*"

"*Apparently not.*"

Angry, he signed an expletive as well.

Saya gulped, her eyes scanning the crowd again. *Blasted. Where are you?*

She closed her eyes and slowed her breathing to calm down.

A bond like no other, the crimson thread of destiny connected the Djinnshirukh and the Sorukhipa. Some said it was light like the wind but heavy like iron chains.

Saya quieted the world to focus on reconnecting to Kharis through this bond and hail her back.

The Sorukhipa released a wave of magic to search for her sister. Invisible to the human eye, translucent tendrils of diaphanous golden magic unfurled from her body, fluttering in the wind like gossamer ribbons. They combed through the crowds, slithering to the river shore and past the quay toward the alleys that lined the harbor's neighborhood until they found Kharis and wrapped themselves around her like a velvet caress.

૪

Kharis, who'd followed the kids to an alley, felt the call and grinned.

"You're lucky I must take my leave."

She wiped the blood off her nose, cracked her knuckles, and lunged at the tallest of the three boys, landing one more stinging punch in his face. The boy, much taller than her, crashed to the ground. The other two never had a chance to take action and help their friend. With an agile jump, she kicked the second boy in the head, who careened toward the third, both slamming against the wall and slumping to the ground.

They moaned, not moving much.

Kharis picked up the doll, dusted it off, and handed it to the girl.

"Here you go," she said as the child gazed at her hero with adoring eyes. "You should get going. Otherwise, you'll miss the show. I hear the Kahurangi are a sight to behold."

"You're missing it, too," the girl said, taking Kharis's hand. That gesture warmed the princess's heart.

"What's your name?" Kharis asked.

"Mira." Her voice was soft and sweet. "I'm five years old."

"Nice to meet you. Would you like to watch from the stage? It offers the best view."

Mira bobbed her head excitedly, not knowing who this

brave girl was. One hand clasped Kharis's, and the other held onto her beloved doll.

The Djinnshirukh princess turned to the three boys, issuing her warning. "In Zahar, we protect those who can't protect themselves. Use your strength to defend our homeland, its subjects, and the freedom we hold dear, for many died to secure it. Do *not* harass those smaller than you. Uphold our Zahari values. Don't stain them with your cowardice."

The tallest boy, Mira's brother, grimaced as he sat, clutching his stomach. His face paled as if he were ready to vomit. Blood trickled from his nose. With a shaky voice, he said, "We promise."

"Good." Kharis offered a confident grin, then pulled on Mira, and they ran toward the plaza. The Djinnshirukh weaved through the multitude when Mira halted, blinking rapidly as they approached the platform.

"What is it?"

"That's the royal stage," Mira said. "We aren't allowed—"

"Oh, yes, we are." A grin spread across her face. "Come!"

The crowd parted to let the two girls through. The soldiers stepped forward, their spears crossed to bar their approach. Kharis stood tall, meeting their stern gaze. Her grip on Mira's hand was firm. One soldier recognized the princess and mumbled to the other. Both raised their weapons and moved to the side.

Saya exhaled, relieved.

Hala didn't, aggravation wrinkling his face instead.

Everyone on the stage stared at the two girls climbing the quick steps and settling beside Saya.

A frightened wail broke through the crowd. "Mira!"

The young girl waved back, excited as any five-year-old would be at being on the royal stage.

Hröld arched an eyebrow, assessing Kharis and Mira,

then subtly gestured to Hala, who understood the silent command.

"Lord Kiwa," Hröld said, "it is my pleasure to introduce you to my daughters. This is Princess Saya."

Saya curtsied gracefully.

The queen studied her, pleased. Anyone would be. Saya was exquisite and possessed exceptional manners. Her violet chiffon dress accentuated her mesmerizing golden eyes and lovely chestnut curls.

Her father then stared at Kharis, that look conveying something she hoped was amusement.

"And this one," he said, "is my other daughter, Princess Kharis."

Still trickling blood, Kharis wiped her nose using her sleeve and curtsied.

The queen didn't utter a word, mouth agape in shock.

Kharis couldn't blame her. Mud peppered her dark blue chiffon gown, now torn in places. Her face was dirty, and she reeked of alley refuse. Blood smears stained her dress, and her hair looked like a cuckoo's nest. Given the burning and throbbing under her left eye, it appeared she would soon be sporting a black eye. Yet joy bubbled inside her.

"Welcome to Zahar." Pride sang in Kharis's voice. "Just as the prevailing winds blessed your journey forward, may good weather and less heat bless your stay, Your Majesties." Then Kharis turned to the little girl, who gazed at her with eyes full of worship. "This is my friend Mira."

The child gazed at the royals in awe, pressing her doll against her chest. "Nice to meet you."

Kharis puffed her chest, a toothy grin parting her lips.

The queen remained speechless.

The Kahurangi king laughed loudly and gleefully. "It appears intrepid spirits dwell in Zahar."

"She could write a book on the topic," her father said, a gentle smile spreading across his face.

"Good," King Kiwa said. "Then the time is right to introduce my brother, Prince Rawiri."

A man, tall and massive as a northern bear, stepped forward. Tattoos adorned his face—a mesmerizing swirl of symmetrical designs. Unlike King Kiwa's markings, Prince Rawiri's softened his features, giving him an almost surreal presence.

The sides of his head were shaved to show off how the sea snake designs wrapped around it. His hair, tied atop with a lavish hairpin similar to the Kahurangi king's, framed the intricate black tattoos on his tanned face. He wore his warrior uniform, a black-and-red embossed leather jerkin with segmented pauldrons and vambraces, a long cape, and the weapons his position required—a set of daggers on a baldric belt, a sword strapped to his waist, and a longer dagger fastened to his left thigh. His narrowed brown eyes studied the three girls on the stage.

Mira cowered behind Kharis with an audible whimper.

Saya pursed her lips.

Kharis scowled at the prince, her neck tipped back to take in his imposing height. She planted her feet firmly on the ground in a protective stance that made it clear she would not hesitate to protect Mira and Saya.

Prince Rawiri stepped forward as if testing her resolve, but Kharis didn't retreat. Not even half a step.

CHAPTER 5

TANGANOKAI AND THE KAHURANGI TUTOR

Rawiri took another step closer, but the defiant princess kept her intense gaze, brilliant sapphire encircling molten silver, and those eyes sucked him in. An metallic tang invaded his mouth, and a crushing wave overtook him, pushing him out of his body and into the ocean's depths.

Tanganokai, the god of the seas, was calling—again.

The vision came to him abruptly, and Rawiri remembered every detail as if it had happened yesterday, not fifteen years ago.

"Rawiri!"

A woman's shout caught his attention, and he lowered his spear, looking behind him toward the balcony wrapping around his mansion.

"She's seizing again."

The urgency in her voice sent a roll of shivers down his back, and he ran, leaving behind the soldiers in the training arena. His pregnant wife had taken ill, and when this odd fever seized her, the convulsions wracked her body.

He sprinted down the mansion halls, pushing people out of his way, ragged breaths in rhythm with his frantic footfalls. He flung the doors open and found the healers and women holding onto his beloved wife as she spasmed uncontrollably.

"Kora!"

His cry broke the spell, and Kora's body stopped jerking. She opened her eyes, but the bronze in them shone. An otherworldly power had possessed her. This Kora's gaze fixed on Rawiri with authority. He exhaled, aware of the silent command, and sat on her bed.

"I'm here," he said.

"Rawiri," she said in a low, resonant voice that wasn't hers, "the gods have destined you to meet the Child of Prophecy. Lead the child to Tanganokai, for they took her from him, and he demands her return."

Rawiri stared at his wife, then at those assembled around her.

The servants exchanged glances, some confused, others apprehensive. "Tanganokai." Awe and fear hid in their whispers. "He speaks to the prince."

A stern shush quieted the murmuring.

"The Child of Prophecy?" Rawiri asked.

"Lead her to Tanganokai," this Kora insisted. "When the time comes, you shall meet the child with his stamp." She let out a long, painful groan as if whatever had possessed her body was leaving it. "You must return her." Her eyes stopped glowing, and she slumped, her body limp in Rawiri's arms.

Rawiri glanced at everyone with deep concern. "What did she mean?"

Atarangi, a Kahurangi healer—a tohunga—broke the silence. "Princess Kora has the gift of sight, and this you know. Through her, Tanganokai has spoken to you. He blessed you at birth for a task he has revealed to you. Speak to him and request his insight and wisdom. Ask him to lead you, for he has come to remind you of your duty to him."

The men and women bowed to Rawiri with renewed reverence and left the room. When they were alone, the tohunga spoke once more. "Kora is Tanganokai's vessel. When the time comes, he will also demand her return."

"No." It came out harsh and full of anger. "Kora's *my* wife. I'm not giving her to Tanganokai or anyone else. She stays by my side, and that will be the law."

Atarangi gave him a rueful smile. "Displease Tanganokai all you want, Your Highness, but he will bend you to his will. You cannot stop what is, and if the gods—"

"Damn the gods."

Atarangi gasped, shocked by Rawiri's defiance.

"He keeps taking my children," Rawiri said. "He isn't taking *my* Kora."

Kora had lost every pregnancy so far—seven. Her health faltered with each, and despite the tohunga's warnings, she ignored them all, determined to give her beloved Rawiri an heir. She suffered in silence with each loss, ashamed that she'd failed him in this, the most expected of the female arts.

Rawiri loved her, wrapping his arms around her as the tohungas took each stillbirth away for burial. His tears were bitter, and his heart shattered with her wails. Rawiri didn't care if Kora gave him an heir or not. All he wanted was to have her by his side—seeing her smile, sing, and dance like she used to.

But with every loss, Kora sank further into a darkness he couldn't dispel.

"Damn the gods," Rawiri said. "What do we owe them, anyway?"

The tohunga didn't reply.

Prince Rawiri embraced his wife. Atarangi bowed and quietly left the room.

It was another stillborn, the eighth one, breaking Kora for good. She stopped eating, talking—living.

"Eat," Rawiri persuaded her in the softest voice possible. His gentle hand brushed a few hair strands off her face. "You must eat, my love."

But Kora, her eyes lost to a distant place in her mind, didn't respond. She didn't speak or move, and when the spoon brushed her lips, she didn't eat.

Rawiri never gave up. "My Kora is lost in a storm," he told Atarangi, "but eventually, the clouds will disperse, the churning sea will return to its soothing calm, and the sun will shine. With patience, the light will return to her eyes."

He picked flowers for her and filled her chambers with garlands of fragrant jasmine and sweet tiare. He gently brushed her long hair with her favorite mother-of-pearl comb and sang the many love songs he'd used to court her. At night, he nestled her in his arms, afraid that Tanganokai would snatch her if he closed his eyes.

The weeks turned to months, and the tohunga checked on Rawiri, worried.

"Is the prince eating?" he asked one servant.

"He understands that to care for the princess, he must care for himself."

"Not good enough." Atarangi pinched his lips. "Let there be joy in this household. Gloom has lurked for too long, and the time has come to dispel its power. Slaughter the fattest pig and prepare a feast—a grand celebration to invite the gods and their blessings back onto this house."

The servant nodded and left.

Atarangi, the wisest of the tohungas, sighed, saddened.

"We can't leave the gods waiting, or else they put a pause on the living."

The celebration was joyous. Every imaginable dish rested on the lavishly decorated tables, and a succulent pig turned on the spit. Musicians chanted as they drummed, and their vibrant music floated in the garden. The winds kept the foreboding thunderclouds at bay in the distance, allowing the cobalt sky to drape over the festivities.

When Kora flashed a soft smile—the first in months—Rawiri's soul danced with the stars. He sang to his wife as joy filled every inch of his body.

The men joined his spirited dancing, their laughter blending with the rhythmic claps of the women. Rawiri's heart swelled with an ineffable feeling of happiness. His joy transcended words, making his feet as light as air and his heart flutter like a delicate butterfly.

He moved to the infectious harmonies, his graceful foot-work weaving intricate patterns on the ground. His arms swayed in unison with the other men's, all moving in fluid synchrony with the melody. As he stepped and turned, he couldn't help but steal glances at his beloved Kora.

The cheerful laughter filled the air, claps marking the tempo. The songs came, one after another, and the dancing became an endless parade of bliss.

The music finally stopped. Rawiri, panting, faced the chair where Kora sat, but she wasn't there. He froze, arms limp by his sides.

"Where's Kora?" Fear heightened his senses.

A roll of thunder rumbled in the sky.

A lightning bolt streaked across the ashen skies, briefly illuminating the storm clouds as its luminous tendrils danced in the darkness. More thunder rolled, making its presence known, and weighty raindrops pelted the ground in a relentless, staccato drumming, soaking everyone and everything. People sought shelter, rushing to pick up dishes, chairs, rugs, and musical instruments as the downpour intensified.

The wind gained momentum, unleashing a fierce howl.

Rooted to his spot, Rawiri tilted his head and stared at the sky. He tasted the brine in the raindrops, and frantic thoughts encircled his head. *Salt.*

"You won't get her." The force of his voice burned his throat. As if pushed by phantom hands, he sprinted toward where the ground ended and the wild ocean began—the Pango Cliffs.

He ran as desperate thoughts enveloped him, dashing through the jungle on his way to the bluffs. The rain bombarded him, intent on stopping him. Its drops plunged from above like sharp needles, and the clouds dumped their weight with impunity, but Rawiri raced.

"Kora," he yelled.

Enormous rubber plant leaves slapped his face. Exposed roots tangled with his feet, and ferns and fronds conspired to slow him. The ominous lightning above warned him to stop and turn around. His wet clothes clung to his body. Hair plastered to his face as he protected his eyes from the watery onslaught with his arms. His feet sank into the mud, and when he slid, he lost his balance, falling into the sludge. Yet, determined, he reached the cliffs near his estate, where Kora stared at the stormy seas, the wind tugging at her hair.

"Kora!"

She didn't hear him over the loud swishing of the wild waves. The ocean, awakened by the storm, roared like a lion, and its giant swells crashed against the cliffs, pounding incessantly like watery hands demanding Kora.

The ocean opened, for Tanganokai's wait was over. Kora turned to Rawiri and smiled. Her eyes were soft, and her face was at peace.

"Kora, no!" Rawiri yelled at her again, his throat raw with the effort. "Come back!"

Kora opened her arms and dove into the maelstrom, giving herself to Tanganokai, and the sea swallowed her whole. Rawiri jumped in after her, but the waves shoved and thrashed him, displeased with this human. Determined, he broke the surface each time, screaming her name, and dove to find her, but the currents, like fists, battered him against the coral reefs. Caught in the undertow, his body swirled, powerless to fight the mighty Tanganokai.

When he opened his eyes, he lay on the sandy shore. His cuts and scratches, soaked with salty water, stung and throbbed. The sky was ashen, but the clouds had cleared. The angry ocean gray had returned to its dark blue. The sunset was turning bloodred on the horizon.

His people called for him, searching for their prince. Their lanterns fluttered like fireflies in the evening air.

"Your Highness! Your Highness!"

A choir of concerned voices drifted with the warm breeze. Among them was Atarangi. Perhaps the most worried of them all. Rawiri didn't reply. He lay on the sand, coughing salty water out of his lungs—defeated.

His Kora was gone—turned into sea foam.

§

"Rawiri?" Kiwa asked.

The prince blinked. He was back on the stage, facing the child before him.

"Are you well?" Kiwa whispered.

Rawiri ignored his brother, for before him stood a young girl with mesmerizing blue-gray eyes. Those feral, enigmatic orbs commanded his attention, rendering everything else in the periphery insignificant. The scent of wild seas enveloped her as if Tanganokai himself hugged her. He locked eyes with this extraordinary presence, his chest expanding with an inexplicable mix of wonder and awe.

He faced the child of a god. The aura of power she exuded was undeniable.

After fifteen years of wondering, Rawiri finally stood before this child wearing Tanganokai's stamp—blue-gray eyes and the scent of untamed seas—pleased to have been so thoroughly assessed by one so young. Rawiri quivered, yet he tried to conceal it from the others. Tanganokai's godly prickle was still upon him.

He had not forgotten, even if Rawiri had.

Fifteen years since Tanganokai took Kora.

The prince didn't know whether to accept his duty or be mad at the god who had taken his eight children and, unsatisfied, demanded Kora as well.

When he met Princess Kharis's gaze, he knew he would enjoy teaching this child with fierce eyes and a spirit shaped by the indomitable power of the ocean. He took a deep breath and yielded to the gods. *I can't stop what must be.* He dropped to one knee and bent his head to her.

❧

Kharis shifted her weight, trying not to fidget. Why was the Kahurangi prince kneeling before her? To save the moment, and probably wondering the same thing, Princess Aya, Hala's wife, stepped forward on his behalf. *Another speech.* Kharis schooled her face into something vaguely solemn and respectful.

"Prince Rawiri," Aya said as he rose, "your presence and willingness to tutor my sisters-in-law in Kahurangi history and traditions honor us. I also look forward to your lessons so our countries may grow stronger by understanding each other."

Saya curtsied once more. "The opportunity delights us. Please light our paths with your wisdom."

Queen Ataahua smiled at this girl.

Kharis blinked, her brow furrowing. "Wait. He's our tutor?"

Queen Ataahua's smile vanished.

"Kharis?" Hala waited for a woman who approached the stage with a White Guard escort flanking her. "This mother would like her child back."

Kharis scratched her head, chuckling nervously. "I almost forgot." She turned to Mira. "Did you enjoy yourself?"

Mira bobbed her head a few times, her eyes sparkling with innocent enthusiasm. "Thank you for helping me and letting me meet the Kahurangi."

"The pleasure was mine," Kharis said.

Mira gave Kharis a tight cuddle, bid her farewell, and, with a radiant grin, clasped her mother's hand. Kharis caught the flicker of fear on the woman's face—her over-the-shoulder glance, her flinch, as if she'd touched hot metal. The mother spoke softly to Mira as they descended the stage, but Kharis heard it. "That's the Djinnshirukh. You must never approach it."

Prince Rawiri frowned in their direction. He'd also heard it.

CHAPTER 6
THE UNWELCOMED GUEST

Early the next day, Hala walked the length of the table with his seneschal. The crown prince studied the table settings and decorations, exhaling with satisfaction.

Servants had decorated the Grand Hall, adding touches to make the Kahurangi feel welcome. Blue was the themed color. Ocean motifs—shells, dolphins, and colorful fish—decorated everything, from the dishes to the flower vases. They displayed the Kahurangi banners next to the Zahari ones. The coiled fern frond stood proudly against the Zahari sun as if it enjoyed the other.

"Given the short notice," Hala said, "I'm impressed with the work."

"Zahar always rises to the occasion, Your Highness."

"Will there be any delays?"

Tacit implications loaded his question. Would there be challenges or distasteful posturing? Unwelcoming gestures? Dissent? Mutiny?

The seneschal paused, thinking. "We've never had a Kahurangi royal delegation visit our city. However, the envoys have been forthcoming and diligent in explaining and correcting our assumptions regarding their customs and etiquette. The desire to put one's best foot forward is clear on both sides."

Hala exhaled, relieved to hear. Yet he still worried about how the evening would go.

"May I review the guest list and seating arrangements once more?"

"Of course, Your Highness. We revised them as you requested."

"Perfect."

Hala wanted Arjun Ghan seated as far away from the Kahurangi as possible. He wished he could even bar the man from attending. This banquet—the entire visit—had to be perfect, and only one person could ruin it all.

To Hala's chagrin, Arjun Ghan was coming.

Almarim was the perfect venue since Ghan couldn't attend it. Hala had seen to it. But the blasted Kahurangi sailed past the southern city and came to the Ghak instead.

Thinking about it, he almost cringed but forced himself to stay calm and collected—unperturbed.

Trade agreements, he reminded himself. *I depend on those.*

CHAPTER 7
THE RANGATIRA

Why now?

Fifteen years ago, Tanganokai had claimed his beloved Kora. Rawiri had engraved that memory into his heart. The sea raged that day, demanding its child. Kora had gazed at him with such love and devotion—a silent promise that she would always be with him. After that night, Rawiri often sensed her dancing in the salty ocean spray, constantly reminding him how much she loved him.

My Kora.

He loved the sea. He hated the sea.

"Rawiri?"

His stream of recollections halted. "Good morning."

Kiwa frowned. "Are you well?"

"Yes." Rawiri smiled softly. "Just tired from the journey."

Kiwa narrowed his eyes, unconvinced. "What happened?"

His brother knew him too well. "Nothing. It was memorable to meet the children."

"Memorable's an understatement." Ataahua returned a

vase to the table and ran her fingers over another, testing for dust. "That *rangatira paru* will keep you busy."

Kiwa burst out laughing at his wife's clever use of the term, eyes tearing up. "Never seen a princess so gloriously muddied."

Rawiri didn't chuckle. That nickname, *grimy princess*, bothered him.

"They are children," he said. "And they'll do what children do." He scratched his cheek, looking for ways to stop the *rangatira paru* conversation. "Have the servants unpacked everything?"

Ataahua raised an eyebrow. "Changing the subject doesn't become you." Her intense gaze bore into him as an owl caught sight of a ground mouse. "I echo Kiwa's concern. What happened? The ocean was awake, Rawiri. What did it want with you?"

Rawiri heaved a long exhale. "Nothing escapes your tohunga eyes." He couldn't fool her. And yesterday, her nose had picked up the potent scent of the sea in the air.

"Tanganokai has touched one princess," he said.

"The pretty one?" Ataahua brightened at the idea.

"No," he said. "Your Rangatira." He couldn't help but hint at sarcasm. He truly disliked the moniker.

Ataahua hummed. "Be careful. Do *not* play with Tanganokai's toys."

Rawiri frowned at her. "She's a child, not a toy."

"To the gods, such distinctions don't matter. Be wary. I'm not warning you as your queen but as the daughter of the two most powerful tohungas in Kahurang."

Rawiri exhaled, frustrated. "I'd never forget you have the sight."

Ataahua lifted her chin. "The reminder stands."

"We must get ready." Kiwa rose. "The Zahari will be holding a banquet in our honor."

Rawiri was glad Kiwa had moved the attention away from him.

Ataahua sniffed, unimpressed. "A celebration *indoors*, hidden from the gods."

"Zahar's a different country," Kiwa said. "Therefore, unusual customs. We must adapt."

"Adapt?" One of her eyebrows lifted. "We can't invite the gods to a celebration when there's a roof over our heads. I'll tolerate this for now, but if adapting means giving up on something so sacred to us, my answer is no. I won't comply."

Kiwa grimaced. "Hröld means his word to—"

"I worry not about the king of Zahar but his high general."

Kiwa's face darkened at the Butcher's mention. Aroha cringed, gesturing to spit on the floor.

The war between Zahar and Kahurang had been brutal. Stories abounded of High General Arjun Ghan's viciousness during the conflict, killing the wounded and unarmed. He survived the thick of it, even captured, but the grievous wound on the left side of his face caused considerable swelling, altering his features to such an extent that the enemy failed to recognize him. That wicked-looking scar became his shield, concealing him from adversaries who would've summarily executed him had they discovered him.

"So, this banquet." Ataahua broke the dark spell. "What do Zahari women wear to these things?"

❧

Ataahua tapped her fingers against the armrest during breakfast as she listened to Lady Rua, one of the Kahurangi envoys.

"There will be pomp and circumstance," Rua said.

Ataahua groaned at that. "How much of it?"

"The banquet will follow Zahari and Kahurangi protocol, Your Majesty." Rua faced them with a sharp smile and cunning gaze. "The Zahari have requested our assistance to ensure the banquet is a welcoming gesture that includes Kahurangi practices."

"We'll see about that." Ataahua waved her hand flat over her head, still angry about holding it indoors—under a roof.

Kiwa heaved a resigned sigh.

Rua explained the most common customs. "The Zahari often toast with wine."

Ataahua wrinkled her nose. "Why?"

"The Zahari prefer fermented drinks at their celebrations. In this case, wine."

"Fermented." Ataahua's appetite waned. "How is it made?"

"Grapes are collected and stomped by foot—"

She raised her hand. "We aren't drinking anything touched by feet."

Rua didn't press the subject.

"What else must we know?" With breakfast over, Ataahua signaled the servants to clear the table.

"Their common greeting is quaint," Rua said. "'Blessed be the earth and sun' is the most common refrain. We respectfully request that you refrain from discussing specific topics. The war, for example, is one of them."

Ataahua's mouth twitched, aware the comment was directed at her.

"One more thing, Your Majesties. The Zahari don't allow weapons at their banquets."

Loud grumbles drifted from the end of the table.

"Bite your tongues," Kiwa told his three sons. "You will abide. Honor Kahurang by honoring our hosts."

Nikau, Koa, and Taika still groaned at the order.

Ataahua squeezed Kiwa's shoulder. "I'll speak to them. Don't fret. This banquet will go well. We, the mighty Kahurangi, will shine so brilliantly that distinguishing between Kahurangi and Zahari will be impossible."

Kiwa rose from his chair, pressing his forehead against

hers, his hands clutching her hips. "The gods gifted me the most beautiful and wisest woman in Kahurang."

"They led me to you." She dragged her nose over his neck, immersed in his scent, and then gently bit his earlobe.

"Then remind me to pray to them often." His lips brushed the skin on her neck as his arms curled around her waist.

Ataahua hummed, pleased, tilting her head slightly to allow Kiwa's slow journey from her ears to her mouth as he murmured words of adoration for his wife. Their eyes met, longing and desire riding in that intense gaze. She wrapped her hands behind his neck, pressing her breasts against his chest. His kiss was soft and demure—a sweet pressing of lips that came with tender nibbling. A gesture that also asked for consent. Her response was hot and demanding, her tongue parting his mouth to accept what he had to offer. His hands fanned down her back, squeezing her buttocks as her hips ground against him.

The envoys didn't need any instructions. They bowed and quietly left the room.

Aroha and Rawiri did the same.

As the eldest, Nikau nudged his brothers out, not before turning to his parents. "We have a banquet to attend. Make it quick."

The vase Ataahua threw crashed against the wall, missing Nikau's head. He flicked a wet flower off his shoulder, bowed smugly, and closed the door behind him.

CHAPTER 8
THE BANQUET

The evening banquet unfolded gracefully. Speeches soared, toasts followed, and each side thanked the other in a carefully choreographed dance of diplomacy and lofty words.

It had taken an entire year to plan and coordinate this visit, and after thirty years since the war had ended, Ataahua finally sat at the Zahari king's table. She hid her satisfied smirk behind a gorgeously etched glass goblet filled with this tasteless swill the Zahari called wine, while studying every face at the table, considering gestures and quirks. She wasn't happy with her sister's seating arrangement, next to some Zahari noble whose name she couldn't bother to remember. Her gaze flitted between Aroha and the Zahari king.

Such a marriage would be ideal.

Her eyes moved to the two other tables. One table accommodated the royal offspring, while the other hosted older children from noble families. To her satisfaction, her three sons sat with the two Zahari princesses. Ataahua beamed, proud of her sons. *They are chatting and laughing—all good signs.*

Taika and the Rangatira appeared to get along, laughing the most. Nikau and Koa listened to the pretty princess. Koa was certainly mesmerized by her. The queen's heart thumped with satisfaction. The envoys had told her that both girls would soon turn thirteen. *I'll need confirmation. The Rangatira looks like she's ten, the pretty one, sixteen.*

She could envision Koa marrying the tall princess when she turned eighteen. *The people will receive such a marriage well.* Taika and the Rangatira laughed so hard that the Zahari crown prince sent frowns their way. *What could they be talking about?* Seeing those two together warmed her heart. *They genuinely like each other.* Ataahua could see the ink drying on the betrothal agreements. *Weddings in five years.* She couldn't wait to start planning.

The second table for the other children struck her as peculiar.

The reason became evident soon enough: a subtle glimpse from one of the noble children toward the princesses. Any other set of eyes would've missed it, but her tohunga gaze didn't. Those children disliked one princess— intensely. Ataahua had a good idea of who.

She exchanged a glance with Aroha, who understood her sly eye flick. Aroha turned discreetly to study the two tables for a long moment. A quick nod to the queen signaled the silent agreement to chat later. The sisters would gather all the colors they had collected from the evening and paint a better portrait of the Zahari court for Kiwa and Rawiri.

Ataahua kept her polite smile but occasionally glanced at her brother-in-law, who'd mainly kept to himself. Rawiri listened to those seated around him and, when needed, shared a comment. Otherwise, he seemed preoccupied, his gaze lost. Then he threw the noble children's table a furtive glance, quietly observing them. It appeared he'd picked up on the subtle disapproving glances and scowls directed at one girl.

Children are honest. They don't hide these things as adults do.

Kiwa's laugh brought Ataahua back. He was doing his best to be a gracious guest, laughing at the crown prince's comments. The twitch at the corner of his mouth told her how he wanted this event to end.

The rhythmic clinks of a spoon against a wine glass quieted the crowd. All eyes shifted to the Zahari king as he rose to provide the last toast for the evening. Servants rushed to fill all glasses with the finest Zahari wine the land had to offer. Ataahua and Kiwa half-smiled their thanks.

"Blessed be the earth and sun," Hröld said.

"May they sustain us," the Zahari replied in unison, their voices echoing across the chamber.

He raised his glass toward the king and queen of Kahurang with a warm smile. "I would give anything for my beloved Aghuti to be here tonight and witness what she started. Hers was an impossible dream, but she believed in it and made it a reality. I knew she would achieve the unimaginable, for she was a force of nature. She was fearless—a woman with an inspiring vision." He drew in a breath. "This evening, we welcome King Kiwa and Queen Ataahua into our city, homes, and hearts. Let us raise our glasses to remember the one who made this evening possible."

The crown prince, visibly moved, said, "To Queen Aghuti."

Everyone repeated it and drank, some of them emptying their glasses.

Ataahua stiffened as realization dawned on her, and one of her plans crumbled into dust. Hröld would never remarry.

He's in love with a ghost, like Rawiri.

Kiwa rose with a look on his face that hinted at an idea. The servants hesitated, but Hröld gave his approval with a subtle nod, and they refilled everyone's goblets.

Kiwa said, "To His Imperial Majesty, King Hröld, and his son, Crown Prince Hala, we extend our gratitude for such a warm welcome. To the brave people of Zahar, we give our thanks. Our gods watch with pride, marveling at what we've achieved. They smile upon us, blessing the peace that shines on the Commonwealth of Nations."

Kiwa gazed at his three sons and the two Zahari princesses, raising his glass in a toast to them. "Long live the pledged alliances and those yet to be made."

Prince Hala froze, eyes darting. A few at the table coughed. Others glanced away. Ataahua, who never missed a thing, understood straightaway.

Hröld, unfazed, raised his glass at Kiwa. His eyes sparkled with joy. "To Queen Aghuti," he said, "and the alliances yet to be made."

Everyone stood, echoed the king's words loudly and reverently, and drank.

Only one person remained seated at the end of a long table with his glass untouched—the Butcher, High General Arjun Ghan.

CHAPTER 9

ARJUN GHAN AND AGHET MENDI

Arjun Ghan fumed as he marched back to his palace wing, seething over King Kiwa's toast. "Alliances yet to be made." His fist struck a wall, his anger unleashing ragged breaths. "We'll see about that."

Alliances. That word revolted him. He struggled to exorcise the fastidious image and erase the sour taste that word triggered in his mouth. When sentries spotted him, they moved to the side, and Arjun Ghan flung his doors open, only to find Aghet Mendi in the sitting room, immersed in a book.

Even at forty-eight, Aghet was gorgeous to look at, with a well-balanced yet darkly handsome face, a long, straight nose, full lips, and olive skin. Silky brown hair cascaded past his shoulders. Adoring brown eyes turned in Ghan's direction.

"My prince—"

"Do not 'my prince' me." Ghan arched an eyebrow at his lover, slamming the door shut, and glowered at him. "You didn't attend the banquet. Why?"

A playful pout framed Aghet's face. "I'm not cut out for such events."

"I wanted you there."

Aghet cocked his head, a subtle frown wrinkling his perfect skin. "My prince, it wouldn't be proper—"

Ghan scoffed. "Proper?"

"For me to be there. I'm the son of a tailor, and you're a high—"

"My two sisters married below their stations, one choosing a commoner, that Anong. Why would it be different for us?"

"Well," a slight smirk adorned his cheeks, "the behavior one must maintain at such events grates me. Such containment... It goes against my nature."

Ghan huffed. "You knew, didn't you?"

Aghet's brow furrowed as if pondering how much to share. His eyes sparked with curiosity, studying Ghan with the intensity one expected of a lover.

"Know what?" Aghet closed the book and got up in a fluid motion, like a snake moving toward their prey, quietly yet dangerously.

Ghan met his gaze, unfazed. "That the Kahurangi intended to enter betrothal agreements."

Aghet shrugged. "One hears things." His brown eyes feigned innocence, but his mouth curled into a sly smile.

Ghan clenched his hands.

"My prince, why bother with the things you can't change? The Kahurangi can ask for the moons, but your imperial king can't give them away."

Ghan's brow furrowed.

Aghet closed the distance, leaning into him. "The Djinnshirukh and the Sorukhipa don't belong to him."

"The Regiazenka—"

"The Djinnshirukh doesn't belong to the Regiazenka, either." Aghet placed a gentle finger on Ghan's lips. "She belongs to you." He tenderly caressed the ugly scar on Ghan's face, studying every detail of the angry red line that crossed the left side from forehead to jaw. "It's sublime."

Loving fingers hovered over it. The black spark that often slumbered in Aghet's gaze flashed again. His smile turned greedy. "Magnificent."

Ghan's eyes narrowed in thought while allowing Aghet his moment of adoration.

The Djinnshirukh.

The training he provided her kept her Akumi monster sated. The immortals had created the Djinnshirukh as the ultimate weapon against the Akumi. When unleashed in battle, this creature would decimate the enemy. The idea of possessing such power was enticing. Then, his thoughts drifted to an ancient prophecy the palace had concealed for centuries.

All that was wrong will be righted,
When the immortal vessel dies.
Tear asunder the seals that contain it.
Let its flames roam with might.
Let it all be destroyed so freedom finds its light.
Let the world revel in fire.
Let it be consumed again,
So the spirits join and transcend,
And all the writings end.

As the human vessel to the soul of a formidable demon, the Djinnshirukh possessed the power to raise a terrifying army and end the world. And a thousand years ago, the Akumi king led his horde to do that, unleashing an ocean of fire that burned everything in Zahar. The end of the world now rested in the hands of an unruly twelve-year-old.

The thought of that insolent child possessing such magic roiled his stomach. *It should've been mine.*

"My prince?"

Aghet's voice pierced Ghan's turbulent mind like a sudden lightning bolt amid a storm. All images disappeared, and the outline of brown eyes with glimmering black flecks materialized before him.

"Allow me to help you forget." Aghet traced the tip of his nose along Ghan's neck while kisses traveled the length of his throat. "Grant yourself a reprieve from the thoughts that distress you," he whispered in Ghan's ear.

His warm breath sent a shudder down the high general's back.

"I'm still angry at you," Ghan said.

Aghet lifted his heavy-lidded eyes, filled with seductive promises. "Allow me to make it up to you."

"Then bring me the Djinnshirukh."

"As you wish." Aghet's hands moved down Ghan's chest, feeling his athletic body under the clothes. He slowly slid his fingers under the trousers' waistband, where tender digits curled around hard, velvet skin as if waiting for Ghan to give the order.

Ghan's core clenched at the touch. His anger melted as the sound of Aghet's hum overpowered him. When Aghet's hand stroked him, his hips bucked in response.

"Forget everything, my prince." Aghet's voice took on a seductive timbre, and it rolled inside Ghan's body the way thunder traversed the sky—ominous yet sensual. "Let me fill you with dreams better suited for someone like yourself." His lips brushed Ghan's, then roamed the length of his scar, kissing it from forehead to chin. "Let me in." Aghet's hand kept its teasingly slow stroking rhythm as he murmured and bit an earlobe, enticing Ghan to surrender and give his body to him. "Let me show you."

Ghan wrinkled his nose and yanked Aghet by the collar, slamming his body against a wall. He opened his mouth to say something, but the way Aghet gazed at him, full of desire and lustful assurances, dissolved the last of his resolve.

Aghet grinned at him, deeply satisfied with the silent

answer. His mouth went for Ghan's, his tongue parting lips apart to taste and devour.

CHAPTER 10

THE WARNING

With the banquet officially over, Ataahua huffed on her way to their palace wing.

Kiwa, Aroha, and Rawiri did their best to keep up with her intense pace while Kahurangi soldiers flanked them. She marched ahead, silently seething in frustration. The sentries barely had the time to open the doors for them.

"Leave us!" Ataahua commanded.

The servants bowed without argument and scampered off.

Kiwa frowned. "What's going on?"

"Those girls are *rahuitia*."

Kiwa blinked. "Forbidden? Why do you assume this?"

She exhaled slowly, dangerously. "The crown prince stiffened at the mention of alliances yet to be made. His eyebrows raised ever so slightly."

Kiwa furrowed his brow.

"A few of their so-called nobles hid their coughs behind their hands like I wouldn't notice," she said. "They hoped the earth would swallow them. Tension blanketed that table, clear as day."

"But the king—"

"Hröld saved our face, husband. Nothing more. He did what any wise and graceful host would do—spare his honored guests the embarrassment of having uttered foolish words."

Aroha, whose gaze spotted things others didn't, nodded in agreement with her sister.

"Now what?" Mortified, Kiwa blew air through his nose. "The crown prince wouldn't stop talking about trade agreements. He clearly wants them."

Rawiri crossed his arms. "There are divisions in the Zahari court. Before the imperial king, they act as a unified group, but I'm curious about what happens behind closed doors."

With her mind deep in political machinations, Ataahua faced Kiwa. "You must speak with Hröld and learn if his daughters are *rahuitia*. Use any excuse during our visit to bring up the matter of marriage—but only when you find yourself alone with him, out of any other's hearing. Ask whether he's made any promises. If he hasn't, make the offer before another nation does. Should they press for trade agreements, tie them to the betrothals. Persuade him—show him what such unions could mean for both our lands, and how they would fortify the Commonwealth."

"Why can't I simply ask—?"

"The Butcher didn't stand during the toast, brother," Rawiri said.

"May his death be slow and painful." Ataahua made a spitting gesture. "Kiwa, that man is our enemy—always has been. The war ended for everyone but him. The line at the banquet was unmistakable, and he stood on the other side."

"I wouldn't be too quick on that assumption," Rawiri said. "While the nobles sided with the king in a palpable show of loyalty, the Butcher chose to defy him publicly by not standing or joining in the toast. Therefore, the general must sway considerable power in the Court if the king didn't reprimand him for the transgression."

"A few glared in the Butcher's direction, so there must be a division." Ataahua turned to her sister. "We must speak to the ambassador tomorrow morning to learn who the guests were. We will gather information to earn their support."

Aroha's eyes lit up. "We could invite them to a private event."

"Precisely." Ataahua flashed a smug smile. "We'll thank them for their welcoming gestures and, in the process, discern where they stand. We'll earn their support, and they'll push for these marriages on our behalf."

"You speak as if this is war," Kiwa said.

"This is insurance," Ataahua said, "so there's no more spilling of Kahurangi blood. My father and brother died in that war. No one else is losing fathers or brothers."

Kiwa's smile reached his eyes. "Then I'll gladly do whatever it takes to make it happen."

Ataahua's gaze was once again focused. "Never again." She held her chin high. "I stand with my promise to our people. I'll be excessive with pretty words to strengthen our place in the Commonwealth, to ensure our men and women will never face the Butcher again."

Kiwa leaned in. "I'm glad you're my wife. My enemies may recoil in fear on the battlefield, but you're far more dangerous. A flick of your eyes makes the entire world rumble."

❧

Exhausted, Rawiri was heading for his chambers when the pungent scent of rotten eggs and molten metal invaded his nostrils. A sweltering phantom wind hit his face like he'd opened the door to a smelting oven. Before he could call for help, swirling tendrils of black smoke rose from the floor and enveloped him. An invisible hand took hold of him and yanked him away.

The smoke dissipated, and Rawiri found himself at the shore of a giant lake of fire. Its intense heat rose in gusts of scorching wind that blurred the blackened horizon. He protected his face with his arms and swallowed hard. The sky was dense with smoke, filling his nose. The sizzling and hissing of fire and steam, along with the flaming explosions in the distance, flooded the otherworldly silence.

Rawiri waited, rooted to his spot by the massive lakeshore in a place that only existed in myth and legend. Or so he'd thought.

Dread squeezed his heart. *The lake of fire in the Netherworlds of Ifran.*

The lake's surface rippled, flames parting, and a woman rose from its fiery depths. Her crimson eyes glowed with the power of multiple suns. Her hair cascaded down her shoulders like flows of lava. Her body appeared to have been dipped in molten metal, with swirls of bronze, silver, and gold adorning it. Flickering flares shaped her long nails.

"Rawiri." Her penetrating voice made his insides shake.

He dropped to one knee, afraid to glance at her. The blistering sand burned a hole through his trousers where his knee met it, but he gritted his teeth to curb his need to scream in pain.

"Mahaluika," he uttered with reverence, his heart racing as the goddess of fire addressed him.

"Look at me." Her voice thundered all around him, echoing inside his mind.

He raised his head, and the goddess met his eyes.

Mahaluika, imposing and formidable, captured his attention. Eyes made of blazing embers spelled him, and all else disappeared from his periphery. His conflicting emotions vanished, clarity striking him like a lightning bolt. The pain that had tortured him dissipated.

Mahaluika lifted a flaming finger at him. "Beware the Mate-Mate, Rawiri. Be careful, for he has seen your arrival."

The Mate-Mate? Fear surged through him in a paralyzing rush. The Mate-Mate, a shadow demon—a rewera—was the most dangerous.

"His claws are upon you," Mahaluika continued. "Falter on your steps, and he will feast on your entrails before you know you are dead. The Mate-Mate stains everything black, and whatever he touches will rot. Alabaster and gold will not contain him. Never turn your back on him or allow his hands on you, or he'll rip your mortal flesh and swallow your soul."

Rawiri gulped for breath.

"Heed my warning, for you must fulfill your task." Her voice resonated like an earthquake's reverberations before a volcano erupted. "You must return his child."

Orange flames burst high, jumping out of the lake to lick the embers and sparks that flew in the dry air. The heat was intense. The crackle of fire and the hiss of steam thundered in his ears. Thick, sooty columns of smoke rose from the scorching ground, blotting out the sky and blurring Rawiri's vision. With a wave of Mahaluika's hand, a scorching wind blew in his direction.

Rawiri braced for it, shielding his face with his arms. *This is where I die.*

The oppressive gust swirled around him. Floating ash coated him. Grit collected in his mouth. Soot and charcoal encased him. He coughed and hacked, the scratchy pain burning his throat like he'd swallowed glass.

"Remember, Rawiri. Return his child." Those last words echoed in his mind like a warning branding itself into his flesh.

His world turned black.

ॐ

A cool breeze caressed his face, and Rawiri opened his eyes with slow blinks. Ataahua and Aroha hovered over him, fanning him. Kiwa shook his shoulders, trying to wake him.

"He's coming to." Aroha bolted up, running to the doors and shouting, "We need water. Now."

"Rawiri!" Kiwa patted his cheeks. "Rawiri, speak to me." Panic made his voice high-pitched.

The servants' footfalls sent faint tremors on the flooring. The acrid sulfur scent dissipated. The world took shape. Rawiri propped himself on his elbows, and Kiwa helped him sit up. Aroha brought him a glass, and he cautiously sipped, observing how Kiwa, Ataahua, and Aroha exchanged concerned glances.

"What happened?" Ataahua's eyes were unrelenting.

Rawiri shook his head as he organized his thoughts. "I'm unsure." His throat throbbed relentlessly, the sensation of his windpipe being on fire lingering. Each breath stung his lungs. His mind was a chaos of swirling black smoke and dancing flames.

"One moment, you were up, and the next, you fainted," Kiwa said.

"Rawiri, what happened?" Ataahua's voice lowered, now an octave more dangerous.

He blinked rapidly, piecing together the images in his head.

Aroha took the glass with a gentle hand. "I'll bring you more water."

Rawiri nodded, thankful, and met Ataahua's intense stare. "Mahaluika gave me a warning."

Kiwa's breathing caught. The glass slipped from Aroha's hand and crashed on the floor, scattering hundreds of tiny shards across the surface.

Ataahua's frown deepened. "What did she say?"

"Beware the Mate-Mate—"

She gasped. "The most powerful of all the Kahurangi

reweras?" Fear widened her gaze, and she quickly cradled Rawiri's face. "What else did the goddess say? You must tell me."

Bile burned his throat. "That he saw my arrival and his claws are upon me, that if I falter on my steps, he'll feast on my entrails and swallow my soul."

Ataahua held his stare as if she couldn't believe her ears. "The Mate-Mate has already marked you?"

Rawiri sucked in a ragged breath. "I must never turn my back on him."

"Him?" Ataahua's head drew back. "The rewera is a 'he'?"

Rawiri nodded.

Frozen in a corner of the room, Aroha released a labored whimper.

Ataahua's eyes darted. "Rawiri... This means the Mate-Mate has already ensnared someone at the palace. This rewera devours hopes and dreams. It drains any hint of happiness. To survive and thrive, it needs a willing vessel, one who's angry and desperate. Then it torments them by always showing what they could have achieved if only they'd tried harder. If Mahaluika came to warn you, the rewera already has a willing host."

Myriad thoughts assailed Rawiri like a mob of crows pecking at his head. The Mate-Mate was the least of his concerns. Returning the princess to Tanganokai meant sacrificing her to the sea, the way Kora had sacrificed herself.

His insides grew icy, and shivers gripped his body.

Kora, an adult, had chosen her fate. The princess was still a child. That thought roiled his stomach, and unable to hold his nausea any longer, he turned from Kiwa and vomited.

Ataahua yelled at the shocked servants. "Bring the tohunga! Now!"

Rawiri retched and gagged, his body swaying with the effort. When he saw what came out of his stomach—soot and bile—he silently cursed the gods.

CHAPTER 11

KHARIS AND SAYA

Back in their bedroom, Kharis and Saya recounted the night's events. The candles' soft glow lit the color-rich bedding and plush pillows on their four-poster beds. Their laughter drifted as the sisters reminisced, their chambermaids working diligently to get them out of their gowns. The girls' exuberant antics often interrupted their efforts.

"Oh, Saya, can you believe that banquet?" Kharis's body buzzed with excitement, images of the night parading in her mind like sparkles. "I hope there are more. It's so rare for us to participate in any. Tonight was magical." She opened her arms and twirled.

A maid sighed.

"I agree," Saya said. "The Kahurangi princes were delightful."

Kharis nodded vigorously. "Absolutely! I've never laughed so much in my life. Taika had me in stitches."

The maids exchanged tired glances as they struggled to unfasten buttons and lace up nightgowns. Kharis didn't care, floating high on hope and bliss. "They are so carefree and free-spirited, as if they could do whatever they wanted.

I wish it could be like that for us—to experience their freedom."

Saya paused, biting her cheek, and turned to the maids. "Leave us."

The women stopped, perplexed by the order, but curtsied and exited the sisters' chambers.

Once Saya heard the doors close, she turned to Kharis. "You must be careful about what you say in front of them. From your mouth to their ears, sister."

Kharis groaned, jumping onto her bed and fastening the ties on her collar. "I bet the brothers don't have to worry about wanton gossip."

"Theirs is a country with a unique culture."

"Well." Kharis reflected on the night. "I want *that* if that's the case."

Saya crossed the distance and perched on Kharis's bed. "They do seem to live life to the fullest, don't they?"

Kharis's heart swelled with longing. "Yes, they do. I envy them for the freedom that colors their life. Don't you want the same? To sail the oceans and roam the world like they do?" Kharis gazed at the window, hoping she could fly away. "To be free."

Saya poked Kharis's cheek in jest and grinned. "It's late. We must go to bed."

"If we were free, we'd sleep whenever we wanted."

Saya arched an eyebrow. "Is that so?"

Kharis made a grumbling sound. After blowing the candles out, the sisters settled into their beds, but Kharis's mind whirled with the memories of the event.

"Saya?"

"Yes?"

"I truly want us to be free. Free of the palace and the Regiazenka, of being the Djinnshirukh and the Sorukhipa, of the rules and obligations, of the ridiculous expectations. I want us to live a life of our choosing. If we make mistakes along the way, so be it because those will be *our* mistakes."

Kharis wondered what such freedom would be like. She envisioned everything she would do: walk through the markets and try her hand at all the treats she craved to eat but couldn't, cross the Zahar-Homa gates, and explore all the neighborhoods in the capital. She would visit the open gardens, stroll the streets, head for the orchards on the northern hills, and even help during apple and pear-picking season, just like the other kids.

The moments ticked by in the darkness.

"I also wish for the same," Saya finally whispered. "A life of our choosing, mistakes and all."

The sadness that coiled around those words tugged at Kharis's heart.

CHAPTER 12

LET THE PLANNING BEGIN

Rawiri focused on his breakfast—or tried to, pushing the steamed spiced cabbage and potatoes around with the fork, the scent of roasted garlic and ginger not tempting him like it always did. Mahaluika's words had lingered like a bitter aftertaste.

Aroha and Kiwa exchanged worried glances, slowly chewing their food. Ataahua's eyes glowed as if exploring every inch of his soul about the secrets he concealed, as if she already knew. Rawiri sighed, aware of how concerned they were. Even the servants were jumpy. His nephews kept to themselves, aware of the tension at the table, and everyone ate in uncomfortable silence.

"Your Majesty." A Kahurangi soldier walked in. "The ambassador and his envoy are here."

"Excellent." Kiwa put his fork down, clearly glad to be done with breakfast. "I look forward to what they have to say."

Rawiri took his last bite and got up, thankful to walk away from Ataahua's intense gaze.

The envoy was brilliant, and the satisfied smirk on Lord Kauri, the Kahurangi ambassador, confirmed it. *Lady Rua is impressive*, Rawiri concluded.

"Invite *only* the wives," she said. "Allow them to bring their spouses if they wish. A few will come out of curiosity. Make it a gathering organized by the queen of Kahurang to thank the noble Zahari women for their welcoming advances."

"And this will keep the Butcher away?" Ataahua asked.

"Yes," Lord Kauri said. "He's known to despise these events. If he learns Her Majesty planned it, he won't attend. However, inviting the wives is the best strategy to avoid offense."

Ataahua smiled, seemingly pleased. "How do we invite the princesses?"

"Allow the women to bring their children to meet the princes," Rua said. "A few will jump at the opportunity since some seek alliances with Kahurang through marriages."

Ataahua scoffed. "Not with my boys. Are the princesses promised to anyone?"

Lord Kauri shook his head. "We've heard of no such betrothals. In Zahar, news like that would be cause for pride and celebration—we would've known if it were true."

"What about the king?" Ataahua asked. "How do we get him to attend?"

Rua's lips curved. "Invite the princesses, and he will come. He adores them, Your Majesty," she said. "When they receive invitations to social events, which is rare, he comes with them. This event also allows the sisters to experience Kahurangi customs and meet their tutor."

Kiwa frowned at that. "Are the invitations infrequent?"

"Yes, Your Majesty. The Zahari princesses lead a sheltered life and rarely leave the palace grounds."

The revelation surprised Rawiri. The palace was a sizable structure at the center of what the Zahari called the inner ring, the heart of the Zahar-Regia, the royal city. The neighborhoods where nobles and generals lived shaped the middle ring, while the outer ring housed the scores of soldiers and servants working in the imperial city. An ancient wall encased it, protective of what lay inside.

Past the ancient wall, the Ghak, as the Zahari called their capital, spread endlessly like a tapestry of people, colors, towering structures, and the bustling hum of life. Rawiri couldn't imagine princesses of the realm being denied the opportunity to explore the vast and intricate labyrinth of human achievement that was the capital of the Empire their father ruled.

"The king comes to all the events they're invited to?" Ataahua asked.

Lord Kauri nodded. "There's one catch. Prince Hala will come as well. He's the king's shadow."

"In a good way?" Kiwa asked.

"I can't read the crown prince," Kauri said. "He cares for the girls and is protective of them, but as the Zahari crown prince, being near his father appears to be expected."

"Very well," Ataahua said. "So he comes. Would he oppose marriage agreements between the sisters and our princes?"

"We're unsure." Rua drummed her fingers on her armrest. "The Zahari practice is to wait until their girls turn fifteen to start these discussions. Marriage is allowed by Zahari law once they turn eighteen."

"I've discreetly inquired with a few Zahari nobles," Lord Kauri said. "I'm trying to glean how the Zahari Crown leans in this respect, but they are careful with their words. Our spies have confirmed that the princesses rarely leave the royal compound, and on sporadic occasions, when they venture into the Zahar-Regia, they're heavily escorted. We also know that the crown prince is an ambitious man."

"Like his mother?" Ataahua asked.

"No Zahari could ever be like Queen Aghuti Ghan of

Zahar, Daughter of the Sun," Rua explained. "The Morning Star, as the Zahari call her, was beloved by all."

"The crown prince desires similar accolades," Lord Kauri said, "but he lacks the Morning Star's authenticity."

Ataahua rested her head on her hand, elbow on the armrest. "How do we pull him away from his father? My husband must have a moment alone with the Zahari king."

"We could devise a diversion." Rua tapped her lips. "Something that gets the crown prince's attention while allowing both Majesties a few moments without interruption."

Kiwa asked, "Can we trust you with this task?"

Rua gave her king a dangerous smile. "Consider it done, Your Majesty."

Lord Kauri rose. "We'll do anything to make it a reality." He bowed and left with Lady Rua.

Rawiri leaned back in his chair, a whirlwind of thoughts racing through his mind. He sensed Ataahua's intense gaze boring on him once more and exhaled, lifting his own. The queen of Kahurang stood tall, chin high, assessing him with a soul-probing stare, giving him the "we're talking about this later" look. Rawiri offered her a weak smile.

She sniffed at him before joining Kiwa and their secretaries. Ruling a kingdom never paused, even when abroad. Soon, Zahari mahazenka leaders would arrive with the crown prince, hoping to forge trade alliances and secure a foothold in the Kahurangi market. After that, the king and queen would draft letters, orders, and decrees.

Pride played with Rawiri's smile upon seeing the couple.

Kiwa had decided who his consort would be when he met the fierce Ataahua. *I'm going to marry her*, he'd said back then. Rawiri thought capturing Taniwha, one of the feared Kahurangi sea monsters, would be easier. That memory made him grin.

My brother chose well.

His thoughts drifted to his beloved Kora. Sailing

would've soothed his aching heart, but the ocean was far from the Zahari palace—not even a distant, thin blue line on the horizon.

Bridges, docks, and canals dotted the capital, built on the banks of the impressive Ibaia River. Water flowed through this city, fueling its prosperity, its arms winding everywhere as if seeking the child that Tanganokai lost. Rawiri walked over to an enormous bay window, observing the sights and pondering his next move.

Since everyone was busy with their assigned chores, he decided today was a good day to stroll through the Zahar-Regia and get acquainted—a chance to walk the empire's pulse and see what truly made it move.

CHAPTER 13
THE GARDEN'S PICNIC

Within weeks, the garden picnic came to life. Rawiri studied the activity with curiosity. The Kahurangi always organized banquets and festivities outdoors—the polite way of inviting the gods to partake in the festivities—while the Zahari held them indoors.

Hröld had agreed to Ataahua's request for an outdoor gathering and now strolled the celebration with Prince Hala. The princesses followed them, unnaturally obedient. The king, wearing a richly embroidered velvet doublet in vibrant spring colors, fine linen trousers, and leather boots, greeted everyone and graciously engaged in conversations with guests, exuding an air of regal charm and hospitality. Regiazenka ministers, on the other hand, saluted the king and queen of Kahurang, some pausing to chat.

The White Guard discreetly lined the garden's walls, while the Kahurangi warriors did the opposite, never far from the royal family. *Ataahua's plan is progressing nicely.* A swell of pride took root in Rawiri's chest.

Servants had decorated the expansive garden with sumptuous adornments and intricate embellishments.

Plush chairs, cushions, rugs, and tables lay throughout the space. Garlands and pennons with Zahari and Kahurangi motifs flapped in the wind.

Servants walked around with trays of finger foods and beverages. Younger children cheered and clamored as they played games the royal nannies had planned for them. The older children huddled in small groups near the crowd, chatting and laughing among themselves. A few young adults gathered at the end, sitting under the shade of trees.

The day was perfect. The gentle breeze kept the humidity at bay. The sun shone brightly in the clear blue sky, and instrumental music drifted through the air to seal a successful event—violins, flutes, and a harp strummed in unison to create exquisite melodies.

Kiwa stifled a yawn; the sedate tunes bored him. "This music's so different from our drums."

Rawiri chuckled. "This is music for conversation, not dancing."

"The Zahari don't dance."

Rawiri raised an eyebrow. "What makes you think that?"

"We've been here two weeks, and I've seen plenty of eating and drinking. Dancing, not so much."

"Not at the palace," Rawiri said, "but in the city, they do. All sorts of dancing, brother."

Kiwa scrubbed his face. "Then why doesn't anyone dance here?"

Rawiri shrugged.

"And how did you manage without being spotted?" Their facial tattoos were a novelty in Zahar.

Rawiri flashed a playful smile. "I used a rather sizable hood."

The king shook his head, amused, and squeezed Rawiri's shoulder. "How are you doing?"

Rawiri knew he was asking about his encounter with Mahaluika. "Never better." He lied.

"Well, I'm glad, then." Unlike Ataahua, Kiwa wouldn't

press him. Instead, he surveyed the crowd and flicked his head toward his wife. "Look."

Ataahua, draped in a flowing cerulean silk gown trimmed with intricate embroidery and lace, reclined in a plush chair beneath a grand umbrella. Beside her was Crown Princess Aya, Prince Hala's wife. Aroha remained with her sister and engaged in lively conversations with the women. Adorned in their most exquisite attire, the Zahari women encircled the queen, finding a place on chairs or padded cushions, their collective *oohs* and *aahs* drifting through the air.

"They are eating from her hand." Kiwa's eyes sparkled.

Rawiri had to agree. The event seemed to have taken months to plan, yet it came together remarkably quickly. Ataahua was shrewd, convincing the mahazenka leaders to dazzle her. "Allow me to view what you offer," she'd told them. "Convince me of its quality and your commitment. Surprise me," she'd dared them. "If you're successful, I'll encourage my people to enter trading partnerships with you."

And so, gorgeous table linens draped the tables. Outstanding fruit decorations adorned porcelain dishes with elaborate designs. Delicate flower vases rested on exquisitely carved teak tables. Rugs in bright, jewel-like colors—sapphire, ruby, and emerald—lined the ground. Artful wind chimes hung from nearby trees, their soft clinks adding to the comforting sounds in the garden.

The merchants had provided everything to impress the Kahurangi queen. Each mahazenka leader had committed time and effort to secure one of those coveted Kahurangi trading and export agreements. They would show this finicky monarch what her people could quickly procure if she would only allow it. Given what Rawiri saw, they'd outdone themselves.

My cunning sister-in-law. When he saw Hröld and Hala were approaching, Rawiri patted his brother's arm. "Be ready. They're coming. Remember. As we planned it," Rawiri whispered.

Kiwa gave him a crisp nod.

As the envoys had shared, the princesses did follow the king and crown prince, not participating in the children's games. It struck Rawiri as odd.

"Good morning," Hröld said.

"Your Majesty." Kiwa bowed. "Thank you again for allowing us this opportunity to pay forward the hospitality provided."

Rawiri gave the girls a mischievous wink. Their grins crinkled the corners of their shining eyes. Suppressing his eagerness to engage with them, he remained mindful of his primary mission: to support Kiwa in securing a few precious moments with the king.

While Hröld and Kiwa exchanged a few more pleasantries, the Zahari crown prince glanced over his shoulder. Taika had waved at the princesses from across the garden, and the girls walked away to join him. Hala's face displayed no overt emotion, but his slight finger tic signaled he was anxious about his sisters stepping away. *Why is this?* The crown prince wavered as if deciding whether to stay with his father or follow after his sisters.

Time to get started. "Your Highness," Rawiri said, "May I take a moment of your time? I wanted to share some thoughts and obtain your approval."

"Of course." Hala forced his smile.

"Please, walk with me," Rawiri said. "My legs could use it on this pleasant day."

Hala's lips twitched with a polite smile. Unfazed, Rawiri pulled Hala away from his father. "Your Highness, are there traditions or customs I must remember when teaching your sisters?"

"What do you mean?" Hala strolled uncomfortably straight, his hands clasped behind his back. He discreetly looked behind him as if itching to return to his father's side.

"Girls in Kahurang receive specific instruction, including martial arts. I've wondered if the same was true in Zahar or whether I should stick to subdued topics."

Hala laughed at the idea. "It appears my sisters' reputation precedes them."

"I taught three rather creative young men." Rawiri glanced at his nephews. The headaches they caused him often came with joyous laughter as well. "They weren't the first, nor will they be the last."

"If only subdued topics could temper my sister." Hala sighed like an older brother dealing with a beloved sibling who was a handful. "My father wishes them to be confident in the Kahurangi language and customs to represent the Royal House properly. It was my mother's vision for us to learn from the other kingdoms, and I'm grateful my sisters can partake in such lessons."

"The honor is ours," Rawiri said. "We appreciate Zahar's gesture. Can I cover various topics or limit my tutoring to approved ones?"

Hala tightened his mouth, thinking. "What would you teach them?"

Rawiri tapped his chin as though pondering the question with a deliberate pause to buy his brother the time he needed to speak with Hröld. "What about science and philosophy, astronomy, sailing—?"

"No sailing. That, I'm afraid, is a forbidden subject." Hala was ready to return to his father, smoothing his heavily embroidered long-sleeved kurta. The gold brocade glinting against the fabric's dark green.

"Your Highness, what about sailing mustn't I cover?" Rawiri had to delay Prince Hala as much as possible. He discreetly glanced at Kiwa and Hröld. The two kings were deeply engrossed in their discussion, neither of them smiling.

"What do you mean?"

"May I teach theory?" Rawiri asked. "Wind and ocean

currents, marine life, perhaps even the architecture behind ship design?"

"Theory is fine, as long as it doesn't encourage them to climb on an actual ship."

Eh? "How would I teach theory without stepping on one?"

Hala hummed, the sound signaling mild annoyance. "You may visit the royal shipyard and show them around. High General Ghan teaches them naval warfare. Rounding off that education could be useful."

Naval warfare? Rawiri's eyebrows flicked even when he did his best to hide his astonishment.

"Sailing on the river or the ocean," Hala said, "is out of the question."

"A lake, perhaps?"

"No open bodies of water. Theory is all they'll get."

Rawiri's lips twitched into a smile. Hearing he couldn't teach them to sail was disappointing, given it was integral to Kahurangi culture. "I'm glad I can ask these questions, Your Highness." He faked his gratitude. "I wish to provide them with an excellent education while adhering to Zahari standards."

Another furtive glimpse revealed that the kings were still talking.

A little more. "Besides sailing, is there something else I shouldn't teach?"

"I can't think of anything." Growing impatient, Hala fixed his stare on his father and turned to leave, but Rawiri gently touched his arm.

Not yet. "Your Highness, do the princesses have female tutors?"

Hala frowned, irritation and confusion wrinkling his face.

"Do they receive training in the female arts?" Rawiri explained.

"Female... arts?" Hala raised an eyebrow, bewildered.

"I understand that the Zahari will consider them as adults at eighteen. Therefore, are the sisters trained on what Zahar expects of them, not as children, but as women and princesses of the realm?"

The question visibly flustered Hala, who scraped a hand through his hair. "No. There's no need for those. The subjects you present are appropriate. If they require tutoring on these... female arts, Monk Yuna will provide it."

"Very well, Your Highness. Could I meet with Monk Yuna—?"

"She's the royal physician," Hala said tersely. "I'll arrange an audience with her. If those are your questions, let us return to Their Majesties."

Rawiri bowed at the crown prince, noticing over Hala's shoulder that Hröld and Kiwa no longer talked. Instead, they stood with their hands clasped behind their backs, smiling at passersby with the masks they wore in public.

The conversation—Kiwa's marriage proposals—hadn't gone well.

CHAPTER 14
THE GARDEN'S THORNS

Kharis had promised to stay out of mischief, but the unnerving sensation of eyes watching her followed her everywhere. She did her best not to look, aware that the Zahari nobles viewed her with disdain. A few hadn't forgotten about Rudra, and women nudged their children away from the princesses—gestures that irked Kharis.

Rudra deserved what he got. Why would I punch anyone else?

Kharis promised to behave, and *Blessed Mother above*, this event would proceed without a hitch. But she couldn't shake the feeling that someone was observing her—eyes that, like icy spiders, crawled all over her skin. The uncomfortable tingling made her twitch, and she curbed the urge to roll on the grass to rid herself of it. Looking around, her gaze locked on the tall tower rising from the palace. *Were they there?*

Kharis bristled with a pronounced shudder, and Saya turned. "Is everything all right?"

"Everything's fine." Kharis mustered a reluctant smile, aware that Saya wouldn't fall for her deceit. *Stupid bond.* It revealed all her emotions to the Sorukhipa.

On cue, Saya held onto Kharis's hand to provide support. Kharis did her best, but following her father and brother while trying to ignore that awful prickling on her skin was torture.

When they approached the Kahurangi king and prince, Kharis perked up. At least they were interesting people, especially the prince. She couldn't help but stare at Rawiri's facial tattoos and wonder whether he would allow her to touch them. Questions were already dancing in her head: How were they made? Why did they cover their faces? What did the designs mean? Why were women's tattoos different? Did it hurt?

Yuna had mentioned needles, but that fueled more questions for Kharis.

Kharis curtsied, and Rawiri winked at her with a conspiratorial twinkle. A grin bloomed on her cheeks just as quickly. While the men spoke, Kharis caught movement—the blur of a curious emerald hummingbird. It hovered, suspended mid-air as if waiting for her, then bounced from tree to tree. Kharis followed the tiny bird until she spotted Prince Taika waving at them, beckoning the sisters to come over.

"Shall we?" Kharis asked Saya.

Saya glanced at the four adults engaged in conversation. "I see no harm in being polite to the rest of the Kahurangi delegation."

Kharis beamed, squeezing her sister's hand. "Then let's go."

"Good morning!" Taika ran over, sporting a broad grin. "I didn't think you'd come. We were about to request our leave." He leaned in closer, eyes flicking behind him. "That group is as dull as weeding a garden."

Kharis laughed. Taika's brothers swiftly joined them.

"I'm pleased you waited," Kharis said. "Saya took her time getting pretty so that you may feast your eyes."

Saya glared at Kharis, pink coloring her cheeks.

"She's beautiful no matter what," Koa said.

Saya's face went from pink to red, and Kharis worried it would become permanent like the princes' facial tattoos.

"He-he!" Kharis twirled for the princes. Her rose-and-mauve chiffon skirt flared as she spun. "What about me? I had to sit still so my attendant could do my hair." An intricate black crown braid accentuated her uncommon blue-gray eyes. Lovely pins adorned with pearls decorated her hair.

Nikau said, "Both of you look lovely, Your Highnesses."

Kharis put her hands up. "We are all equals, so when it's us, I'm fine if you use my given name. I prefer it. It's stuffy using titles as if we didn't know who we are."

This time, Taika laughed. "Fine by me."

Koa turned to Saya, his eyes wide with eagerness. "What about you? Could I call you by your given name?"

Saya's ears turned as red as her cheeks. "Yes," was her almost whispered answer.

"Come," Nikau said. "Let's join the rest."

When Saya saw who "the rest" were, she halted, judging the young men and women cautiously. She gripped Kharis's hand, tugging on it to stop her.

"We shouldn't go," she murmured.

Kharis clicked her tongue, visibly annoyed by the group's presence. "I don't run from challenges." Ignoring her sister's warning or the unfriendly stares, she pulled Saya along.

CHAPTER 15

KHARIS AND THE ZALDUN

"Look who we found in the garden." Prince Nikau gestured to Kharis and Saya.

Kharis knew it would be a trying moment. The young nobles mumbled, all eyes fixed on the lawn. She gritted her teeth, doing her best to behave as promised, but this group tested her resolve.

Nikau's nostrils flared. "Last I checked, the Zahari bow to their royalty, do they not?"

There was fire in his voice, and Kharis liked it. *Why can't he be my brother?*

The young men and women bowed or curtsied, some barely hiding their displeasure. The women took their leave, one flicking her hair over her shoulder, and headed toward the dessert tables without a word exchanged with the princesses—a very public slight.

Saya grimaced slightly and lowered her head.

Something dark roared inside Kharis. No one shamed her sister and lived to speak of it. Saya squeezed Kharis's hand to remind her to rise above it.

The men—nobles around Nikau's age—glared at the girls, viewing them as an unwelcome intrusion. Unlike the

White Guard officers, who earned their posts through merit and skill, the *zaldunak* were nobles appointed to their ranks, a relic of King Aram's reign. Her father had since abandoned the practice. Dressed in leather armor embossed with heraldic crests, the *zaldunak* were meant to embody courage and justice. This group was the opposite—cowardly and corrupt.

"Don't you have to run to your brother?" one of the zaldunak said. His face flashed a smirk that lessened his handsome features.

"What do you mean, Lord Korshak?" Nikau asked.

"Your Highness," Korshak said, savoring the moment, "they can't mingle with us."

Nikau raised an eyebrow. "Why not?"

Korshak's brown eyes danced with vengeful delight. "Why don't you ask them?" His voice dripped with vileness. "Better yet, why don't you ask *her*?" He jerked his chin at Kharis, his purposeful omission of her royal title a disrespectful display. "Ask her about my brother, Rudra."

"You're speaking to a high princess of the Zahari realm. I'd swear titles are a must in Zahar." Nikau's hand clenched the hilt of his sword. "You should temper your words."

Korshak caught Nikau's gesture and raised his hand appeasingly. "We want no quarrel with you, Your Highness, especially since you don't know what the Djinnshirukh is capable of. Take this as a gift of goodwill toward Kahurang. Stay away from *that one*." His smirk had turned into a scowl.

"Then take this advice as a return courtesy." Nikau stood tall, fiercely staring at Korshak. "It would be best to apologize to Her Highness for your remark *now*."

"Are you joking?" Korshak huffed, defiance lining his eyes. "Apologize... to *that*?"

"Enough!" Kharis stepped forward, releasing Saya's hand. "Insult me all you want, but when you're rude to the crown prince of Kahurang, an esteemed guest of Zahar, and an honored member of the Commonwealth of Nations"—

her voice went lower—"or offend *my sister*," a dangerous growl built inside her, "you'll deal with me."

Wide-eyed, the men with Korshak backed away, trembling hands going for their hilts as fear spread. Wrath twisted Korshak's face. His stare flitted to the White Guard officers lining the walls nearby. No eyes turned his way.

Fury welled inside Kharis. "Always a coward, I see."

"My brother still has nightmares." Korshak's glower could light fires.

"Rudra got what he deserved for insulting *my sister*." The memory of that day intruded into her mind. The cruel slur he threw at Saya burned every inch of her soul. Tension surged through her muscles, poised to strike like a coiled serpent. "His barb was an affront to the Crown and Empire."

"You broke his jaw—"

"And I'll break yours if you keep talking."

"Kharis." Saya pulled on her sister's sleeve with an imploring tone. "We promised Hala—"

"Yes." Korshak sneered at them. "Run to your brother and hide under his robes, raven spawn—"

A dangerous blur of pink and mauve dashed past everyone. It happened so fast that no one had a chance to react. Her fist, hard as a ball of rocks, landed on Korshak's face too late for anyone to stop it, sending him crashing to the ground.

Korshak spat blood, fixing a seething glare upon her. "You... *txakurra*." His voice was deep and restrained. The expletive, *filthy bitch*, heated the air. A few of his men grimaced at the epithet, but Korshak no longer cared, his anger twisting around the word to make it grittier. He slowly rose, his eyes twitching with rage.

A few White Guard officers looked their way. One was about to approach when a man as massive as a northern bear appeared out of nowhere.

"Boys, stand down." Rawiri's voice was pleasantly

modulated but penetrating. Its cautionary tone held a warning that the men didn't ignore.

Kharis stood still, her hands fisted and ready for round two. She bared her teeth, her magic bubbling beneath her skin. "I dare you to repeat it," she growled at Korshak. "Show me how brave you are."

He scowled at her, wiping the blood off his split lip, then studied the imposing Kahurangi prince beside her.

Rawiri's facial tattoos appeared to glow. The bear was about to pounce.

Korshak dusted his pants, grinding his teeth. "It appears I tripped." He bowed low from the waist, uttering with pointed sarcasm, "My apologies, *Your Highness*."

His friends sneered as they followed Korshak without a glance at Kharis.

"What happened?" Hala asked.

Kharis flinched, startled that he was standing behind her.

"Nothing," she said, struggling to control her ragged breathing.

"I didn't ask you," Hala said.

The four Kahurangi men bristled at his unkind tone.

Ignoring Hala, Nikau knelt and smiled warmly. "Are you well, Your Highness?"

Kharis bit her bottom lip to keep it from quivering. She nodded, unable to speak. Fury swirled inside her chest, and angry tears pooled in her eyes. Her magic poked her insides, itching to come out. Her anger wanted to explode and burn everything, including foolish Korshak.

Saya took Kharis's hand. "All is well, Khiri."

Her sister's sweet voice quenched the fire within her, and her magic, like a wild beast, returned to its slumber.

Saya faced Prince Nikau, her golden gaze glistening. "Please don't hold this against Zahar. Even among the privileged, foolishness abounds. Accept our apologies."

"Why would you apologize for his behavior?" Nikau asked.

"Because as princesses of this realm, we bear the injuries caused by our subjects. We are responsible when they step out of line."

"Even when the injury is directed at a princess of the realm?" he asked.

"Yes." Saya lowered her head, embarrassment flushing her face.

Those idiots made my sister cry. Anger's arms wrapped tightly around the Djinnshirukh once more, whispering in her ear, and tempting her with promises of revenge—if she let it out. The slurs Korshak threw at her—txakurra and raven spawn—bounced inside her head like thorny burrs.

She knew that Lord Athon had sported raven-black hair and had kept ravens in the pigeon loft above the Keep, turning the insult to his benefit. However, after his death, the palace removed all portraits of the previous Sorukhipa, and such absence fueled her curiosity. She didn't look like any of her family members. Did she look like Athon?

Rawiri asked his nephews, "Must Kahurang apologize to Zahar?"

Nikau's gaze landed on Korshak, already at the other end of the garden. "No, Uncle. It appears Zahar must apologize to Zahar."

Rawiri raised an eyebrow, approached the sisters, and dropped to one knee. Kharis saw the pride in his eyes.

"If it happens again," he said, his eyes never leaving hers, "I'll gladly join the fight."

Kharis sniffled, almost lifting her sleeve to wipe her nose. "Even if they throw us into the Netherworlds of Ifran as punishment?"

Rawiri offered her a wicked grin. "Even if they send us to Ifran and beyond."

❦

Hala had seen the exchange from afar, but what could he do? Grudges against Kharis lingered, and she kept them alive with her sharp tongue and defiant ways.

His eyes locked on the Zahari zaldunak across the garden, rallying around Korshak with pats on his back. *The Regiazenka must not learn of this.* He groaned silently, aware that he would have to speak to the young man and smooth things over to avoid any issues. *Why can't she behave?* Everyone else appeared to enjoy the event, ignorant of the latest scuffle involving his sister. *Good.*

He frowned, not looking forward to lecturing Kharis again, and strode forward, ready to pull her out of the event, when Saya jumped into his field of vision.

"Are we in trouble?" She stared at him with begging eyes, the three young princes standing behind her.

Hala brought his hand down. Kharis's punishment would have to wait. "No, not at all." He patted Saya's head. "No one, Zahari or Kahurangi, is raising a concern. Therefore, why would I think you are?"

Prince Rawiri got up before Hala could utter another word. "If it pleases His Highness, I'll stay with the princesses."

Prince Nikau said, "We'll also escort them. Nothing will happen to them."

Hala rubbed his beard, pondering the offer. For his plan to succeed, the girls had to come to him, rather than seek help from others. However, accepting the Kahurangi gesture could help secure the trade agreements he coveted, even if common sense told him to remove the girls from the event.

It was a bet worth making.

"The Crown appreciates the suggestion and accepts it." Hala nodded to Rawiri and faced his sisters. "I must take my leave and see to Father. Until then, Prince Rawiri answers for you." He made firm eye contact with Kharis. "Do *not* disappoint the Crown."

Saya sighed in relief and grinned, curtsying. "Thank you, Your Highness."

Kharis curtsied, but no smile graced her face.

When Hala walked away, Kharis searched the crowd for Korshak, scrunching her nose. Her fingers curled as a fresh wave of anger washed over her. Lightning flashed in the storm brewing in her mind.

"Patience is the best ingredient for successful revenge."

Kharis jumped out of her angry spell and faced Rawiri.

"Wouldn't it be better if, one day, he had to kiss your boots?" Rawiri's eyes had a wicked gleam. "Fate has a peculiar way of manifesting itself when least expected, Your Highness. You could punch that face and break his perfect little nose, but it'll get you in trouble. Then you'll be the one groveling at his feet. However, if we turn things around and he's the one who gets scolded, he'll have to kiss yours—maybe even lick them clean." A dark chuckle bubbled out of him. "Ensure your boots are as dirty as possible. I encourage walking on horse manure."

The three princes laughed loudly.

Kharis, however, kept her frown. "How do I get him in trouble?"

"You don't have to do anything. His mouth will do it for you, Teppe."

Kharis cocked her head, her brow furrowed. "Teppe?"

Rawiri tittered. "It means little badger in Kahurangi, and it fits you. Come, sit down. Let me tell you a story. You, too, Nikau. You're as hotheaded as this princess."

Nikau rolled his eyes. His brothers cackled.

"Hey, maybe after this, you can teach me xakea." Taika's attempt to lighten the mood met Rawiri's approving nod.

"My sister cheats," Saya said with a mischievous glint in her eyes.

Kharis glared at her. "No, I do *not*."

Koa had the biggest laugh. "Taika cheats, too. No wonder you two get along."

Taika lunged at his brother, and the two tumbled across the grass, with Koa laughing hardest at Taika's failed attempt to shut him up.

CHAPTER 16

TANGANOKAI'S DRAGON

While Rawiri shared the story about a humble sheepherder and an arrogant prince, Taika picked up Kharis's scent in the soft breeze—citrus and the sea—and his heart almost jumped out of his chest. Words fled his mind as wild emotions coursed through him. Like a rogue wave, it seized him, dragging him into the deep with its irresistible force.

Is she the one?

His grandmother's voice echoed in his mind: "*One day, you'll meet the one destined for you; when you do, you'll know.*" His breathing quickened, taken by this otherworldly power that drew him to Kharis like a magnet. Her scent, reminiscent of sweet oranges and stormy ocean waves, invaded every inch of his nose. He couldn't get enough of it.

Sitting across from him, Koa stretched loudly with a satisfying groan. It jolted Taika back to attention.

"I'm hungry." Koa slapped his thighs as he sat up. "Who's with me?"

"I tell you what," Nikau said, getting up. "I'll fetch us something and bring it over."

"Wow, such service, brother," Koa chimed in.

"Keep that up, and I'll send *you* to fetch my food." Nikau gave his brother a playful wink. "I'm the crown prince, after all."

"I'm going with you." Koa got up and extended his hand out to Saya. "It would be an honor if you accompanied us, Your Highness."

Saya's cheeks reddened again, and a shy smile tugged at her lips.

Kharis bumped shoulders with her. "Ensure servers provide them with nothing but the best."

"Are you not coming?" Saya asked.

Kharis drew her knees to her chest. "Nah. You know it's better if I stay away."

Concern creased Saya's forehead.

"Go," Kharis insisted, wearing a broad grin. "And bring me one of everything."

Koa helped Saya up, offering his arm. Saya blushed.

Taika snorted and shook his head.

"What about you?" Nikau asked Taika.

"I'll stay with her," he said, feeling protective. "You go and get Saya something sweet." He gave Koa a wide, knowing smile. "I'm starving, but not as much as you."

Koa cleared his throat and looked away. Rawiri studied the crowd, narrowing his eyes. "I'll go with you." Like that, he uncrossed his legs and got up, agile like a cat. "Taika, you know your duty."

Taika patted the daggers strapped to his chest. "Her Highness is well protected, uncle, although I suspect she may be protecting me in the event of a commotion."

His brothers didn't argue that point.

The group walked away and soon blended in with the crowd. Realizing he was alone with Kharis, Taika became nervous. His mind wandered, scratching his cheek as he searched his inventory of jokes. *Peke! I forgot them all.*

He gulped, pondering what to say to fill the awkward silence.

Kharis hugged her knees, her gaze lost in the distance. Taika's blood boiled at the memory of that *zaldun* and his vile remark. He'd insulted her, and the looks on the other *zaldunak's* faces made it clear it had been something obscene. Taika bit his lip, fighting the urge to hit the man. What troubled him even more was her brother's reaction—the Zahari crown prince had stood by, as if she were the one to blame.

He caught his brothers laughing with Saya, and the sight warmed his heart.

"My brothers enjoy your sister's company," he said.

Kharis, who rested her chin on her knees, lifted a shoulder. "Everyone likes Saya."

Taika regretted his comment. "I—I enjoy your company." He clamped his mouth, nervous about how she would react.

Kharis lifted her gaze, and surprise made the silver in her gaze sparkle. Her eyes reminded him of the ocean, and her scent bewildered him as if the sea, not blood, flowed through her veins. Her lips pulled into a quiet curl. "And I enjoy yours." She searched for Taika's brothers in the crowd. "I enjoy their company, too. You... You treat us differently."

Taika cocked his head. "Should we not?"

"No, not at all. We're princes and princesses of our realms, children of kings and queens. You regard us as equals. That's what I meant."

A lovely smile parted her lips, and Taika thought it was the most beautiful sight in the entire world.

"If it were decided, I wouldn't mind." His words came out without thinking, and heat flushed his face just as quickly. *Curse the gods.* He rubbed the back of his neck, wanting to bite his tongue.

"If *what* were decided?" Kharis locked her eyes on the people parading before the Kahurangi and Zahari Majesties, yearning for even a fleeting glimpse of their attention.

"My mother has high hopes for betrothals and has made

her intentions clear to us," Taika said. "If they selected you as my betrothed, I—I wouldn't mind."

Kharis's gaze went from unfocused to focused, and she observed him with an intensity that startled him. Her astonishment was genuine. "You wouldn't mind?"

Taika shook his head, his lips pressed tightly. His neck became hot, and he massaged it, moving it from side to side. "I—I would enjoy your company on a more... permanent basis." He breathed in to calm down. "If you agree, that is. I'll wait until you're of marrying age, and when the time comes, perhaps you could ink the last design on my face."

Kharis cocked her head. "What do you mean by that?"

His cheeks heated furiously. "Our tattoos are sacred and personal. Allowing you to ink my face implies," he swallowed hard, "intimacy." He scrunched his lips to keep his heart from bursting out of his mouth.

Kharis cast him a look, pondering this. "May I touch them?"

Taika's breathing caught. "Yes."

Her sapphire gaze shone with curiosity as she gently traced the tattoo patterns on his skin. He closed his eyes, and all distractions disappeared. Her fingers were on his face, and it was divine. He let that sensation fill him, taken by currents he couldn't control.

"Do they mean something?" Kharis hugged her knees, resting her head on them, eager to learn.

"The gods drive the inspiration, and our tohungas bring it forth to awaken our spirit and tell the world what resides inside us."

"Like a message from the gods?"

He nodded. "The designs reveal my power, noble status, and position among the Kahurangi. Some are wards to protect me, but I don't know which." A nervous laugh escaped him. He felt like pinching his leg to stop being such a peke fool.

"Why do they only cover your left cheek?"

"I'm the third son," he explained, "So only one-third is covered." He traced his forehead with his forefinger. "One." Then he poked each check, "and these make two and three."

"Hmm." Kharis turned to the crowd, then returned to him. "Your mother's tattoo is different. Why is that?"

"Ah! The power of women needs little to awaken it, whereas ours... It requires more gentle prodding." Taika chuckled at the idea. He feared his mother, especially when her eyes sparkled with her otherworldly intensity. Having seen Kharis land a punch on an idiot, his heart soared. *She's fierce like her.* He wondered what her tattoo would be and whether she would allow him to ink it. That image sent a surge of heat rushing through his body.

A melancholic aura settled in her eyes, and that stumped him. "Is everything all right?"

She studied the grass for a moment, lost in thought. "If the betrothals became a reality, would we live here or in Kahurang?"

Taika swallowed hard, twirling a rock between his fingers to steady himself. His heart was beating so hard. "Wherever you wish."

"Kahurang," she said. "I choose Kahurang."

He raised his eyebrows, surprised.

"I've never been." Then her playful smile vanished. "Taika, I enjoy your company and value our friendship, as new as it is. The future is uncertain, but promise me we'll remain friends, no matter what lies ahead."

He nodded, glad that a relationship was possible.

Kharis studied the clear, blue sky as if pondering something. Her rueful expression tugged at the strings in his heart. *What is she thinking about?* He looked for the zaldunak, who had already left. He would tell his father of the incident so he could speak to the Zahari king and ensure that the young man was punished. *He insulted her.*

Before wrath enveloped him, Kharis exhaled softly. "What design would the gods choose for me?" she asked.

Taika gave her a long, sideways glance and tilted his head to feel the sun's warmth on his face. He took her hand and traced a spiral on its back that swirled up her arm, past her shoulder and neck, until his fingers brushed against her lips. Kharis stood still, barely breathing, her cheeks flushing pink.

"A dragon," Taika said, his gaze intense. "A long, sinuous, and mighty sea dragon."

CHAPTER 17

THE PROMISES GODS MAKE

Ataahua hummed, pleased with herself. The garden picnic had been a tremendous success.

"Queen Ataahua is delightful," was the most common remark. Zahari women gradually filed out of the venue, planning to invite the queen and her sister to tea during their stay in the capital. The race to win the favor of the Kahurangi royals had officially begun, their eyes on three remarkable prizes: the Kahurangi princes.

Ataahua smirked. *These women will soon be telling me everything.* That idea engendered a dark chuckle.

Her curious gaze roamed the garden, observing a few servants gracefully gliding through the space, almost blending into the background. Her boys were nowhere to be seen. The Zahari king, the crown prince, and their daughters had also departed. Even Kiwa had taken his leave. *Where did he go?* An eyebrow lifted in mild annoyance.

Suddenly, icy fingers pricked her skin, triggering a shuddering breath. Every nerve in her body fired in alert. Out of the corner of her eye, she caught the blur of a shadow melding into the darkness of a stone corridor. *What was that?* Ataahua turned to her sister. She'd noticed the same, but fear had widened Aroha's eyes.

"Did you see *that?*" Aroha's voice shook, fear clinging to every word she uttered.

"There you are." Rawiri closed the distance.

"Where's Kiwa?" Ataahua asked.

"He left earlier with Lord Kauri."

"Did he?" He usually involved her in all discussions.

"He requested a private meeting with the ambassador," he added. "He's waiting for us now, so perhaps whatever they discussed is connected to his summons."

"I should lie down." Aroha rubbed her forehead with a shaky hand. "I—I'm tired."

Ataahua didn't press her sister. Whatever they'd seen unnerved her enough, and the color had yet to return to her face. She gently wrapped her arm around Aroha's shoulders. "It was a long day, sister," Ataahua said. "I'll walk you to your chambers. Rawiri and I can meet with Kiwa." Ataahua's gaze sharpened. "However, it isn't good when the king *summons.*"

Rawiri's exhale signaled agreement. "Let's see what he has to say."

❦

After leaving Aroha in her chambers, Rawiri marched with Ataahua.

Her smug smile conveyed the satisfaction of a day well spent. Triumph shaped her grin and fueled the sparkle in her amber eyes to the point that she ignored the glares they received from Zahari sentries. Rawiri glanced at her, observing how she savored victory, and inhaled quietly, keeping his opinions to himself.

What does Kiwa want to tell us? The image of him standing stiff and uncomfortable beside the Zahari king replayed in his mind, and a hollow sensation grew in his chest.

As the sun set slowly over the western horizon, the Zahari sky turned magenta. When they entered the king's chambers, Kiwa sat in darkness, lost in his thoughts.

Rawiri halted. "Kiwa?"

The king kept his gaze unfocused, bt his voice was stern. "Sit."

Ataahua sighed, sitting beside Rawiri, her fingers impatiently tapping on her knees. "Very well, we're all ears."

"There won't be a betrothal."

"What?" She sprang to her feet.

Kiwa raised a hand, silencing her. "There won't be *any* betrothals. The princesses *are* rahuitia."

Ataahua's face blanched as all her plans dissolved in an instant. "Why? Are they promised to others?"

"No."

"Then, why?" Her voice surged, palms up into an angry shrug. "Is it because we're Kahurangi? Tell me, what reason were you given?"

Kiwa groaned. "Hröld won't allow it due to a curse."

"A curse?" She blinked once. Then twice. "Is this a joke?"

Kiwa drew in a breath. "The Regiazenka must approve anything related to the girls."

"Hröld is their father," she said. "He's the king."

Kiwa glared at her. "I'm not done."

Every muscle on Ataahua's face tightened. The silence between them hung heavy for a few noisy breaths. Rawiri lowered his head, hoping for the ground to swallow him.

Ataahua sat and crossed her legs, the glow in her eyes betraying the storm brewing within her. "Go on."

"One girl is the keeper," Kiwa said. "The other protects the keeper. This curse binds them together, and no one can unravel it. As a result, they can't marry *anyone*. There's little he can do."

"Their father has *no say* in this matter?" Ataahua muttered.

A million thoughts whirled in Rawiri's head, all sharp as blades. "I don't understand. Why would the Regiazenka be responsible for them? Queen Aghuti created it to temper the monarchy's authority and ensure a balanced approach to ruling. King Aram was a mediocre man who wielded absolute power—"

"Regardless of their practices," Kiwa said, "this curse terrifies them. Lord Kauri confirmed it."

"He knew?" Ataahua spat, her gaze a searing glare.

"In his defense," Kiwa said, "he thought it was idle gossip. He was as shocked as I was." His shoulders dropped. "It's unfortunate, for without this, Hröld would've agreed to the betrothals—"

"Wait." She rose slowly. "Without this curse, he would've?"

"Yes."

Ataahua's eyes glowed, an idea already taking shape. "Then we get rid of the curse."

Kiwa frowned. "Have you lost your mind?"

Ignoring the comment, Ataahua paced the room. "Think about it. We possess the most powerful tohungas in the Commonwealth. Yes, the Zahari have healing monks, but ours are much more than healers. Our tohungas speak to the gods. We'll break their curse, enter betrothal agreements, and in five years, we'll celebrate the most important weddings in the Commonwealth."

Ataahua waited for the only response she would entertain. Kiwa gazed at her in silence. "We've waited years for this opportunity," he finally said, a wicked smile outlining his face. "And we're done waiting."

"We can't break it," Rawiri said.

Ataahua glared at him. "And what do you mean?"

"It's not a curse." Rawiri clasped his hands on his lap,

resigned to share what he'd hoped to ignore. "It's a *herea*, an eternal binding involving one of the princesses."

Ataahua drew her lips into a thin line as if she knew the answer to her question. "The Rangatira?"

Rawiri nodded, and the fluttering in his stomach increased.

Ataahua tilted her head to the side, her eyes assessing Rawiri with a look that could kill. "You said Tanganokai had *blessed* her."

"I didn't know it was a *herea*," Rawiri said. "And I didn't realize *she* was the child he wants returned."

Ataahua's breath caught. "Returned?" She stepped back. "What do you mean?"

Rawiri exhaled slowly, not looking forward to her reaction. "She's the Child of Prophecy."

Ataahua stilled, her chest barely moving. Her smile grew bitter. "I knew you were hiding something from us because why else would Mahaluika come to warn you?"

Rawiri glanced away, an icy sensation spreading through his chest.

"So she belongs to Tanganokai," she said. "And he has tasked you with returning her, hasn't he?"

He didn't answer.

"This is why Mahaluika warned you." Her tone turned accusatory. "Because Tanganokai has commanded you."

Rawiri winced, unable to lie anymore. "Yes."

The pain etched across Ataahua's face twisted his heart.

"Breaking Tanganokai's *herea* is impossible." She rubbed her forehead. "Only a god can tear such a connection." She grumbled under her breath, then halted. "Wait." Her eyes widened with the spark of a dark thought. "She's Zahari. How can *she* belong to Tanganokai?"

Her tone irked him. "Why can't she?" Rawiri crossed his arms. "I can't wait for you to enlighten me."

His sarcasm stung her, and the glow in her eyes turned ominous. "Tanganokai's *herea* with Kora was powerful, turning her into his vessel. He gifted Kora with the power of sight, turning her into a bridge *to him*. She became Tanganokai's most formidable *toa*. Our pride and joy. Last I checked, the Rangatira isn't Kora."

"She *is* like Kora." Rawiri's voice boomed across the room. The anger that usually slumbered inside him surged as he rose slowly from his chair. "The child may not have the sight or speak to the gods, but Tanganokai wants her back, and Mahaluika, his sister, warned me of the one who could stop me. I can sense Tanganokai's power swirling inside the princess, and as much as it pains me to say this, she surpasses Kora." He cast a dismissive glance in Ataahua's direction. "Think whatever you want, but the Zahari know something, for they won't allow her near water."

"It doesn't matter." She raised her voice over his. "No one can change Tanganokai's will."

Rawiri's voice sharpened. "Then tell me how he plans to accomplish this because I, his *toa*, apparently don't know."

"Enough!" Kiwa glared at both of them, his face red with anger. "This bickering helps no one. The princesses are *rahuitia*, and nothing will change that."

"It's much worse, Kiwa." Ataahua slowly pivoted toward him. "Tanganokai wants Rawiri to fulfill his task, and when that child is returned to him, what do you think the Zahari will do?"

Kiwa's face turned pale as he suddenly understood, turning to Rawiri. "You can't do it. What Tanganokai wants will result in conflict, and we can't be plunged into another war."

"I don't intend to do a thing." Rawiri settled by the bay window, gazing at the stars twinkling in the Zahari night sky. "I begged Tanganokai. I pleaded with him, and yet he took my children and my beloved Kora anyway. Now that he begs me, I won't listen."

"What are you planning to do?" Ataahua almost whispered.

"I'll protect her as if she were *my* child. Tanganokai won't have her. I'll make sure of it."

Kiwa slumped in his chair, burying his face in his hands. "Defying Tanganokai will curse us, and obeying him also curses us. There's no way out of this." An expletive flew past his lips as he struck the armrest. "We're returning to Kahu-rang, and that is it."

Rawiri gazed at the stars, seeking a solution to the impossible challenge.

"You're both wrong." Ataahua broke the silence. "If Tanganokai wants his child back, no power on this earth can stop him. No one can defy his will, not even you, Rawiri. He's a god, and time is on his side. He'll patiently wait, and when the opportunity arrives, for it will, he will act. Do *not* toy with him because he will crush you."

She flexed her fingers as if attempting to rein in all the emotions whirling inside her.

"Then there's Mahaluika," she went on. "She warned you of the Mate-Mate, so be thankful for her aid. Tanganokai's sister wants you to succeed. Why else would the fire goddess bother with any of us? Yet she came to *you*." She lifted her forefinger. "The gods have singled you out for a task hidden in the shadows until now. Do not play with them, for they won't play with you."

"I'm not playing," Rawiri spat.

"You're Tanganokai's *toa*, his chosen one." She raised her voice. "Betray him, and you'll become his *kanga*, an empty shell holding nothing in your hands. He's testing you, Rawiri, and I can't do anything to help you."

And there it was—the source of her anger.

"No." She shook her head, fighting back the tears that made her eyes gleam with an otherworldly light. "It's worse than that." Defeat weighed her shoulders. "*We* can't help you. Tanganokai made you a part of his grand plan, and you can't back away without suffering his retribution. From this moment on, we must break away from you, for if you fail, your punishment cannot touch Kahurang."

"We're not betraying Rawiri," Kiwa thundered.

She spun. "As a monarch, you rise above men. The gods chose and have aided you, so now you owe them your loyalty. The husband I know will walk the right path, even if covered in hot coals. Rawiri must walk his."

She shifted, hands clenched at her sides.

"If I can't see my children married to Zahari princesses, they'll marry Kahurangi ones, and that will be it. If this door is closed, I will force open a window. And listen well. The gods have proclaimed that Kahurangi blood *will* sit on the Zahari throne, and you, Rawiri, will lead them to it. Nothing will change a divine promise."

With that, she walked away, slamming the door behind her.

Like a frigid swell building in the depths of a dark ocean, a dangerous sensation twisted Rawiri's insides. "What do we tell the boys? They expected betrothals out of this visit."

"Nothing." Kiwa sank his body even deeper into the chair, his head nestled in his hands, elbows propped on his knees. "Not a word until we're far away from this disturbing place."

The weight of silence hung between them.

"I stand by my choice," Rawiri finally said. "I'm staying to protect her."

Kiwa bobbed his head, resigned. "I won't stand in your way." His eyes glistened as he stared at his brother. "But I can't stand in Tanganokai's way, either."

"I'll never blame you for it." Rawiri returned his attention to the window. The swath of stars giving shape to the Silver River twinkled on men and gods alike.

CHAPTER 18
THE THIEF

Rawiri brooded in his chambers, unable to sleep, when soft, stealthy footfalls landed inside his room. Someone had jumped in through an open window. He quietly brought his daggers out of the belt hanging from a peg, and with his back against a wall, he took advantage of the shadows to hide and wait for the intruder.

"Taika?" said a small voice. "Are you there?"

Rawiri cocked his head.

"Taika?" A soft female huff filled the silence.

"Who do we have here?"

Startled, Kharis jumped back, hitting a table behind her. The items on it fell and crashed on the floor. "Blasted."

The spark of a flame lit Prince Rawiri's frowning face. "Are you aware of how dangerous it is to enter my chambers?"

"Apparently not." Her eyes fixed on one of the sharp blades he gripped while she scratched her head, smiling nervously.

Rawiri's frown deepened. "What business do you have with Prince Taika in the middle of the night?"

Kharis froze. "Um..."

"Explain yourself!"

She grimaced and slid a bag around her shoulder. "Taika wanted to learn xakea, but it's been challenging since people always push us in opposite directions. Look, here's the proof." She cautiously approached him, her bag open to reveal the checkered board and game pieces.

He glanced at what was inside before moving towards the window. His quarters were on the third floor. Windows lined the floors below his, but the stone walls provided little grip. It was windy enough to make the climb treacherous without ropes, which he didn't see hanging from the roof. The drop revealed how precarious and desperate any climb would've been. *Assassins would dare it, but a twelve-year-old?*

"How did you get here?" He glared at the princess.

"I climbed."

Rawiri choked on a cough. "You... climbed?" He studied the dizzying drop one more time and locked the window.

"Yes," she said, "but I miscounted the windows this time."

"This time?" He raised his voice.

She fidgeted with the bag's belt.

"Having you in my rooms is already an aggravating affair." Rawiri huffed loudly. "Sit."

Kharis swiftly dropped her body on the floor. "Please, don't tell anyone."

"Tell them what, exactly? That a minor was in my rooms at night without an escort or chaperones?"

She cringed and lowered her head. "I'm sorry."

"Your stunt impacts us equally, Your Highness."

She lifted her gaze. "Kharis."

"What?"

"You can call me Kharis."

He rubbed his forehead with a loud groan. "Did it occur to you that you could've asked any of us for permission to spend time with Taika?"

"I did, and it was denied. My brother refused the request."

"Why?"

Kharis squirmed with a nervous smile. "I—I got in trouble before you came and when you arrived."

"Ah, yes. The issue with the young girl and her toy." Despite himself, Rawiri chuckled. "I recall your dirty clothes and messy hair, but your grin that day was as bright as the sun, and that child held your hand as if you were her hero."

Kharis nodded. "That's one instance. Before you got here, my sister and I escaped."

"Escaped?" His mouth fell open.

"Yes, but my brother caught us before we could enjoy more of the Zahar-Regia."

"More of it?"

"Uh-huh." Pride beamed in her eyes. "We wandered the markets, saw a puppet show, and checked out a wedding, but when a few people saw us, we ran out of the pavilion—big mistake going out the front door—and bumped into our brother. That ended our adventure."

Rawiri pursed his lips, connecting dots. "Do you not go into the Zahar-Regia?"

Kharis shook her head. "We aren't allowed outside palace grounds."

"I see." He tapped his chin, pondering the many reasons children defied their elders. His nephews weren't different, but climbing walls on a windy night was never part of their repertoire. He sighed and sat before her. "This place could become pretty small for someone like you. I'll venture that your father forbade you from leaving your rooms, which explains why your brother denied your request."

Kharis confirmed his assumption with a quick nod. "I truly wanted to teach Taika before he returned to Kahurang."

Rawiri pinched his chin. "Would you consider teaching me as well?"

"I'll teach anyone." The silver in her eyes shone like the ivory moon.

"Then I'll arrange it. I'm sure my nephews will enjoy it. What about your sister? Does she play this xakea?"

"Everyone in Zahar plays it."

"Then it's a deal. You and Saya will teach us."

Kharis let out an excited whoop.

Rawiri put his hand up to temper her excitement. "It's late, and you aren't supposed to be here. How do you intend to return?"

She pointed at the window from which she'd entered.

"Absolutely not."

"I won't fall—"

"I won't allow it."

The bear had spoken. The cub conceded.

Rawiri crossed his arms. "Why aren't soldiers sounding the alarm?"

Kharis shrugged.

He huffed again. *This girl.* "What about your sister?"

"Sleeping. Saya doesn't even know I'm gone."

He dragged a hand down his face. "And when she wakes, and you aren't in your bed, she'll alert the guards."

"She won't."

His eyebrows shot up. "Is this night strolling a common affair?"

Kharis wore a guilty look. "Uncommon, but on occasion, needed, or else I'll explode."

Rawiri stared at her, shaking his head. They couldn't leave the palace and were under constant surveillance. *Any free-spirited child would erupt.* "Does your sister feel the same way?"

"Yes, but the cause is different."

He exhaled loudly. "Explain it to me."

The silly grin vanished. Instead, Kharis fingered the bag's belt. "I'm the source of my sister's anxiety. She tries to curb my impulsivity, but as you can see, she isn't successful sometimes."

Rawiri inhaled deeply, suspecting the correct word was "often." One thing was obvious. As her tutor, he had his work cut out for him. "Well, it's late, and you should be sleeping. How do I return you without alerting half the castle?"

"Take me to King Kiwa's chambers."

He blinked. "What?"

Kharis put her hands up to appease him. "The palace retrofitted a few ancient escape tunnels during the Unification Wars, you know, in case things turned for my grandfather. People have forgotten about them."

Rawiri frowned, not believing a word of it. "If they forgot, how is it you know about them?"

"I..." She glanced away.

He crossed his arms. "Teppe?"

"It's a secret." She averted his gaze.

He slowly shook his head while at a loss for words.

"A few bedchambers at the palace have them," she said with a grin. "Like the one His Majesty is using now."

He pinched the bridge of his nose. "Take you to my brother in the middle of the night?" An exaggerated groan escaped his throat. Kiwa's lecture would be lengthy. And if Ataahua were to be with him... *Gods above and below.*

"Maybe I should throw you out of the window."

"He-he!" Her toothy grin was broad. "Tell His Majesty that I have an important invitation."

CHAPTER 19
A GAME OF XAKEA

Rawiri liked this room—spacious and light. The company made it better.

The morning sunlight filtered through the translucent curtains. The open windows let the breeze dance with the drapery, bringing the fresh, sweet scent of garden flowers.

Prince Hala had brought the sisters, and now they sat cross-legged with the boys on the plush rug, surrounding a low table. Xakea boards lay on it while the princes listened to the girls' instructions. Ataahua and Aroha sat nearby, de facto chaperones for the group.

It was charming to watch Kharis, her eyes brimming with joy. Her body was in constant motion, announcing her boundless excitement this morning. Her laughter sounded like a happy melody, stirring conflicting emotions within him: his duty to obey Tanganokai versus his duty to protect this child. He settled beside her as she demonstrated how the pieces moved.

Kharis fidgeted with the xakea pieces, twirling one between her fingers. "The idea is to keep me from getting to your side of the board. These pieces move like an army, each with a task, and you must play them carefully." She uncrossed her legs to lean on the table. "I'll sacrifice a few to advance. Losing some may allow me to capture more of your territory."

"Like a bluff?"

"Yes." She crossed her legs and leaned back, resting her weight on her hands. "Sometimes, I'll make you fall for a particular move to fool you into losing an important piece. Other times, it'll be because I wasn't paying attention." A mischievous gleam curled her lips as she set her elbows on the table, her chin resting on her hands. "Either way, you won't know."

He raised a brow, stifling a laugh. "That's still a bluff."

The glimmer in her eyes was dangerous, and he liked it.

She gestured to random squares in the middle of the checkered board. "These have special markings. When you reach one of them, the rules for moving your piece change. Thus, my goal is to get to them before you do." She sat back, fingers drumming on her thighs.

"Why?" Rawiri asked.

"They make your pieces more powerful." She twirled a lock of black hair around her forefinger. "Able to move in more directions or advance more squares. It depends on the markings and whatever lands on them."

"Hmm." He tapped his chin. "This reminds me of a game we play in Kahurang. The concept's the same, but the board design's different."

The silver in her eyes sparkled. "You must teach it to me."

He chuckled. Too bad he couldn't share her excitement in equal measure.

Once in the king's chambers, the Rangatira had crawled through a small trapdoor hidden behind a fake panel. She had entered a tunnel, disappearing into its gloom. Somehow, she had reached her chambers, and no soul had found out about her midnight stroll.

Kiwa, displeased to learn that his chambers came with a secret passageway, had spent the night rearranging furniture with Rawiri, moving a rather heavy armoire in front of the panel in case others decided to pay the king of Kahurang an unexpected visit.

The next day, both men woke up with bags under their eyes while a well-rested Ataahua shook her head at them.

This morning, Ataahua watched how the Kahurangi and Zahari royal offspring shared laughs over board games. She also wore a smug grin whenever she met Rawiri's gaze, flicking her eyes toward the gaggle of laughter to remind him that no one could defy the gods.

Rawiri heaved a sustained sigh.

Kahurangi blood will sit on the Zahari throne. Given all the merriment around him, he had to agree with her.

⁊

Kharis couldn't stop smiling. The Crown had disbanded her circle of playmates at age eleven, no thanks to stupid Rudra, Korshak's younger brother. Since then, it had been just Saya and her. Today, three Kahurangi princes sat with them, undaunted by the Djinnshirukh.

The brothers got along well, telling jokes and laughing frequently, bumping shoulders, and rapping knuckles on their heads—their gestures a natural flow of how they cared for one another. Kharis found their physicality contagious and loved every moment. Even Saya beamed joyfully. *When was the last time I saw her this happy?*

Like his father and uncle, Nikau sported symmetric tattoos on his face. Depending on perspective, they made him look fierce or adorable.

Koa struck her as the most talkative of the three. Tattoos covered his cheeks, and when he smiled, they danced.

Taika was the loudest. Of the three, she liked him the best.

Queen Ataahua lavished her sons with affection and praise. It was hard not to envy them.

"Is it the three of you?" Kharis asked, curious about their upbringing.

The brothers stopped horsing around.

Nikau nodded. "Yes, just us, but back in Kahurang, a mob of thirty-seven cousins surrounds us."

"That many?" Kharis had never met her cousins.

Nikau nodded. "Mother has five married siblings. Father has six."

"It's quite noisy at the palace," Taika added. "With a lot of running and hollering."

Koa grabbed his brother by the neck, shouting, "Hollering!" in his ear.

Laughing, Taika shoved him away. "Here, we can sleep better. When you visit, you'll see."

Kharis thought it sounded magical. "Tell me about Kahurang."

"What would you like to know?" Rawiri asked.

Kharis was unsure where to start. "Everything?"

Ataahua cleared her throat, and all eyes turned to her. "Ours is a land of contrasts." Pride sang in her voice. "Fire and ice, and soil and sea define us. Verdant valleys, endless shores, a tall mountain range with ancient glaciers and azure lakes, deep fjords, and swift rivers bless Kahurang. It is also home to volcanoes, hot springs, and spectacular caves. We boast rainforests and deserts."

Kharis blinked. "How is it you have it all?"

The queen laughed elegantly. "When the gods created Kahurang, they couldn't agree on a blessing for our land. After much bickering, each god bestowed one, and as a result, we received many."

It sounded magical, like the stories nannies read to her when she was younger. "If you could only receive one blessing, what would it be, Your Majesty?" Kharis asked.

"Only one? Hmm." Ataahua carefully pondered her reply

as she glanced around the room. A satisfied smile curled the corners of her mouth. "My answer is always clear. My *whānau*."

"Whānau?" Kharis cocked her head.

All three princes answered in unison, arms up in victory. "Family!"

"Our concept of family is complex," Rawiri explained. "It refers to close and extended family, friends, neighbors—our tribe."

"Land without whānau isn't land," Ataahua said. "It lacks spirit. Whānau is the fire that keeps us warm, the ice that cools our passion, the soil that grows our blessings, and the ocean on which we sail toward our dreams. Whānau is everything, and without it, we don't exist."

Whānau. It sounded like a formidable incantation that could undo a sealing enchantment.

"What about you?" Ataahua gave Kharis a long, appraising stare. "What blessing would you request from the gods?"

A smile creased the corners of her eyes. "My answer is also clear, Your Majesty. Saya is my blessing, so I'd ask them to strengthen our connection further—to deepen its roots and stretch its branches high."

Guards opened the doors, and servants walked in with trays.

"Food!" the brothers yelled, fists up.

"Ah! Lunch is here," Ataahua said. "As a token of our thanks, we wanted to introduce you to Kahurangi dishes. Our envoys secured provisions for our stay in case Zahari food is..." She smiled politely. "It's our hope you'll enjoy it."

"I can't wait." Kharis got up with Saya, both about to head for the dining room.

"No. You stay seated on your cushions," Ataahua said. "The five of you will eat here."

Kharis and Saya exchanged confused looks.

"We're providing you with the full Kahurangi experience," the queen explained. "When possible, we sit on the floor to eat."

Nikau, Koa, and Taika whistled their agreement. They quickly put the boards away, and servants placed a parade of dishes on the low table. Kharis and Saya glanced at each other, astonished by the quantity and variety—some items unfamiliar to them.

"It's so much," Kharis said.

"The gods provide," Ataahua said, "so we can provide to them. This is food to nourish the body and the soul." With her clap, everybody stilled. Ataahua lowered her head in reverence and recited, "*Mauru'uru no to tatu kai.*"

"*Whakawhetai ahau ki a koe,*" the brothers replied.

Ataahua winked at the girls, saying, "We must *always* thank the gods for our food."

With that done, the young men took plates and started piling food on them. It was odd to see them serving themselves instead of having the servants do it, as was the custom at the Zahari palace. It appeared they ate what they wanted, selecting and ignoring items. *The freedom to eat what I want.* It was an experience she would ask for again. The vision of her brother's head exploding in confusion brought on a silent giggle.

Taika filled a plate with fried fish, roasted root vegetables, and watercress salad, then gave it to Kharis with a shy smile. "These are my favorites. I hope they'll be yours, too."

Kharis took it. When their fingers touched, it was electric.

Nikau argued with Koa over what to serve Saya. "She won't like that. Here, eat this instead." To annoy Koa, he added everything he liked to her plate while removing Koa's favorites.

"Would you stop that?" Koa barked.

"Boys!" Ataahua warned.

Nikau sat back, laughing while his brother stared daggers at him.

Everybody sat and dug in, but Kharis noticed that the queen didn't have a plate, and no one was rushing to get her one. *This isn't right. She's the queen.* Servants always served her father first.

Kharis got up with her dish and handed it to the monarch with utter reverence. Ataahua cocked her head, her brow wrinkled.

"We are whānau," Kharis explained with an honest smile. "You must eat with us."

Ataahua's eyelids fluttered with surprise. Her slow grin reached her eyes. "Yes." She patted Kharis's cheek with motherly affection. "We are family. Therefore, let's share this plate, yes?"

Kharis grinned with a nod.

CHAPTER 20

THE REWERA

Lunch with the Kahurangi had been a whirl of exciting anarchy. The young men had competed to grab their favorite foods, their forks and spoons everywhere, reaching for the various plates on the table. Kharis thought it had been magical, the mayhem whimsical, filled with affection and loving abandon, and without suffocating rules and prohibitions.

Even the food tasted better.

"I'm full." Taika stretched loudly, satisfaction softening his features.

Koa already lay on the rug, his arms folded under his head, drifting into post-lunch slumber. Nikau scratched his chin, got up, and started singing, his feet stepping in synchrony as he urged his mother to join him with beckoning arms. The queen did, to Kharis's surprise. She and Nikau pivoted in perfect synchrony. Ataahua's skirt swirled, accentuating the gentle sway of her hips. Their arms traced patterns in the air, mirroring each other's movements.

"*Noooo.*" Koa's complaint lasted the length of his breath. "It's rest time, brother. Why are you dancing?"

Nikau glanced over his shoulder, then cheekily spanked his glutes. "*Ka peke ahau.*"

Taika and Rawiri burst out laughing. Ataahua frowned. "Manners!" she warned.

Kharis failed to understand what was funny. "What does that mean?"

Taika suppressed a laugh. "You don't want to know."

"You missed a step." Koa, resting on the rug, whined.

"Then get up and teach it to him." Taika rapped his brother's belly.

Koa curled with an annoyed huff and glared at his younger brother.

"Come, baby," Ataahua said. "Show them how it's done."

Koa groaned and settled beside his mother. Both opened their arms simultaneously, and Koa began the chant, stomping his feet and slapping his arms and chest to the rhythm of his song. Ataahua joined him, their bodies moving in unison, turning their heads, raising their arms, and stepping together, as one. Kharis and Saya watched, amazed by their graceful agility. Nikau, Taika, and Rawiri sang loudly while the servants clapped.

Aroha sat beside the girls.

"This is the story of a mischievous god," she said. "He stole the fish from the ocean and the stars from the night sky. He fished and fished," Aroha explained as Koa and Ataahua mimicked the movement, "and then plucked the stars from heaven like ripe mangoes. Thinking it would be funny, he placed the fish in the sky and the stars in the sea."

"That sounds like something Khiri would do." Saya poked her sister's cheek.

Kharis grunted.

"Join us," Nikau said, and he and Taika pulled on the sisters.

Kharis swiftly withdrew her hands. "We don't know the steps, and I can't—"

"Just do what we do." Taika wore a playful smile. "Even Nikau messes up the steps."

"I heard that," Nikau said.

"Girls." Ataahua's voice boomed. "*You* mimic *my* moves." She gave her sons a nasty glare. "The roles of men and women in Kahurangi dancing are particular. Besides, it's better to follow the queen." She winked at the sisters.

"Do you dance a lot?" Kharis stood beside her, clumsily mirroring how the queen set her feet and swayed her arms.

Kharis twirled and bumped into Saya, both bursting into a peal of laughter.

"Dancing is an essential aspect of our culture, like breathing and eating," Ataahua said. "Our tohungas pass our history down through songs and dance. Our movements carry meaning and tell a story like this." Ataahua stepped forward, gave a short, sharp cry in her language, and started chanting a different song. She moved like a graceful leopard, ready to pounce on prey.

The ornate doors leading to a separate room flung open, and Kiwa entered, wearing a wicked smile. He replied with a similar shout, responding to the queen's dare. The princes whooped, fists waving, encouraging the dancing challenge.

"This is our creation story," Aroha told the girls. "The Song of Tanganokai and Te Anukai. In the dawn of time, Tanganokai and Te Anukai embarked on a celestial dance that gave birth to the world. Their movements shaped mountains and valleys, while their graceful spins gave rise to rivers and oceans. With each step, life emerged—forests bloomed from the land, creatures roamed the seas, and stars adorned the skies. Tanganokai moved with Te Anukai to craft the oceans and paint the sky. Their dance became a harmonious collaboration of divine forces as they became one. Tanganokai resides in the oceans and Te Anukai in the heavens."

The king's and queen's steps were elaborate and intense,

accompanied by fast, rhythmic arm gestures and sensual hip swaying—a fierce give and take of movement.

Kharis's body shook under the power of their dancing, urging her to join them—to imitate their steps. It beckoned her, lured her to move and twist, and begged her to step outside the invisible line others had drawn for her.

She turned to Saya, who beamed, equally spellbound, clapping and grinning. Seeing her sister truly happy made her heart flutter. It sealed her resolve. She would finish the map of the tunnels, find the one that took them to the royal quay, hide in their ship as stowaways, and leave Zahar behind. *World, here we come.*

Amidst the jubilant commotion, a servant walked in and whispered something to the others. Instantly, their expressions changed.

The doors opened, interrupting the impromptu celebration.

A bitter man stood at the threshold with his entourage of soldiers. Harsh, judgmental eyes added to the air of superiority, drawing a scowl across his face. He didn't utter a word, lips flattened with his usual disdain, but Kharis knew that High General Arjun Ghan would've called the Kahurangi savages if he'd spoken.

The magic disappeared.

The mood shifted.

Kiwa and Ataahua straightened, neither pleased with the general's presence. Rawiri and Aroha took their places beside their Majesties, their features hardened. Sheer hatred cast a dangerous glow in their eyes.

"Are you here to discuss how *your* soldiers got into an altercation with ours yesterday?" Kiwa said, his voice deep and dangerous.

Arjun Ghan stared at them first, lazily sizing the king with a bored look. His head didn't move, but his gaze traveled to the sisters. "I'm here to retrieve the princesses."

Saya heaved a whispered gasp.

Defiant, Kharis met Ghan's stern glare. "Our father permitted us to spend time with them, from breakfast until dinner. The day isn't over yet; when it is, they'll ensure our safe return to our chambers. We appreciate your interest in our well-being."

"Your well-being," Ghan said with sarcasm, "includes training—"

"What is so pressing that you must take them now?" Ataahua stepped forward, placing a supportive hand on Kharis's shoulder, almost nudging her to stand behind her.

Ghan arched an eyebrow, clearly annoyed with having to explain. "The princesses have a tight schedule, including instruction I oversee."

"What sort of training is this that it can't wait?" Ataahua's eyes narrowed into slits.

The general stared at the Kahurangi queen. His smile was soft and polite, but Kharis knew there wasn't anything kind about it. "Bladework, strategy, and defense, Your Majesty."

Ataahua shared a glance with Kiwa. His nod conveyed support. "Ours is a visit of historic proportions," she said. "The princesses' presence here provides them with an excellent opportunity to learn from one nation in the Commonwealth. Surely, there'll be time for training once we return." She waved her hand dismissively and sat. Kiwa did the same.

Kharis's eyes darted between Ataahua and Ghan, aware of how the queen wanted to sink every blade in the room into Ghan's chest.

"It is our understanding that His Imperial Majesty, King Hröld, wants his daughters to study Kahurangi and become acquainted with our customs and traditions," Kiwa added, picking at his nails. "Their presence today honors us." His gaze lifted, the icy softness of his voice in contrast with the fire in his eyes. "His Majesty agreed to our request to host them, and it would disappoint us to bid them goodbye when there's so much more we'd planned for them."

A deep line formed between Ghan's eyebrows. "I was unaware of such a change in their schedules."

"You are now," said another voice.

Hala stepped out of the adjoining room. His face remained neutral, but Kharis swore he wore a faint smirk. "I had business this morning with His Majesty." He tilted his head toward Kiwa. "I revised my sisters' itinerary and brought them myself. They'll resume their training under you soon enough. The Crown appreciates your work in educating *my sisters*. It's refreshing to see how committed you are to them."

Arjun Ghan's mouth twitched. "The Crown also punished them for their ill-guided decision to—"

"The king has allowed them a reprieve from their punishment," Hala cut him off, "given the magnitude of the Kahurangi visit."

A muscle feathered along Ghan's tight jaw. "Discipline is an important aspect of their training. Disrupting it could be detrimental to their education."

Hala pondered the comment with care. "I see your point. Prince Rawiri could oversee such training and ensure its rigor. After all, the Kahurangi visit is important to both nations. What better way to prove it than to start their lessons earlier?"

Ghan pinched his lips, visibly mortified.

"I'm curious to see the prince in action," Hala said. "I've been told that his battling technique is immaculate and that his nephews, whom he's trained, are well-regarded among the Kahurangi warriors." He tapped his chin, clearly enjoying every moment of Ghan's distress. "It'll be a rare opportunity for the princesses and certainly an effective way to expand their repertoire of defense arts."

Ghan offered a dry smile. "I agree that expanding their defensive knowledge is a good call." His voice went an octave lower. "Thankfully, poor techniques can be unlearned. After all, Zahar is responsible for the Djinnshirukh and the Sorukhipa."

He stared at Kharis, and she understood everything communicated in that glare. Ghan would make them pay for their public defiance.

The bond between the sisters went taut, and rage traveled through the magical thread connecting them. It tightened every muscle in Kharis's body and melted the gold in Saya's eyes, making them shine ominously.

"We plan to stay." Saya met Ghan's stare with such ferocity that the man swallowed hard, his Adam's apple bobbing up and down. She was supposed to be kind, loyal, and reliable—the obedient child—not the feral beast glowering at him.

Kharis smirked. Her sister had crossed her imposed line, and there was no coming back. The magic that bound the Djinnshirukh and the Sorukhipa kicked in, a relentless pull, and those invisible arms wrapped around the sisters protectively.

A spell so formidable there was no space for a third, much less Arjun Ghan.

Kharis joined hands with her sister, never breaking eye contact with the high general.

Ghan glared at the sisters. Arching an eyebrow, he shifted his attention to Hala. "Very well. I'll resume their training once the Kahurangi have departed." Then, locking eyes with Kharis and baring a malicious smile, he spoke in a soft yet lethal voice. "I eagerly anticipate instructing the Djinnshirukh," his gaze shifted to Saya, "*and* the Sorukhipa again."

A chill gripped Kharis's chest, now acutely aware of Ghan's veiled threat.

Hala gestured to Kiwa as if nothing had happened. "Shall we continue? We've made significant progress today, Your Majesty. All we have left are the trading agreements."

Kiwa glared at Ghan, his loathing palpable, and led Hala back into the meeting room.

&

The Butcher stared at the girls for a moment—an eternity to Ataahua—and exited the chambers with his men after a tense bow and a sour smile.

Black shadows, invisible to everybody but her, had enveloped him—a rise and fall of black mist as if a living thing had clung to the high general. A pair of glimmering onyx eyes emerged from that billowing fog and locked on the girls. Its hiss immersed the chamber in its rasping sound. It lingered, like a warning, then dissipated.

It can't be. Ataahua shook her head slowly. The Mate-Mate had coiled itself so tightly around the despicable general that they had melded into a single entity. With the *rewera* firmly in place in the Zahari court, she truly feared for Rawiri.

Wishing the shock to leave her body, she turned to the group.

Rawiri chatted with her sons, who were back to laughing and singing. Aroha settled between the girls, a gentle anchor steadying them until the rough waters calmed.

The Rangatira, however, stole a look over her shoulder, her intense stare fixed on the doors through which The Butcher had exited, but someone else was watching through those blue-gray eyes, its power rolling off her petite body in formidable waves.

Ataahua shuddered.

CHAPTER 21
THE WEIGHT OF DARK MEMORIES

Ghan stormed into his chambers like a wild tempest, the sound of his boots reverberating through the floor. His voice, a thunderous roar, sent vibrations trembling through the air as he bellowed his command.

"Out!"

Danel, this trusted servant, bowed and swiftly exited his chambers without uttering a word.

Ghan stomped around the sitting room, his rage mounting. His fingers closed around the first object within his reach, a vase adorned with intricate patterns of cobalt and gold, and smashed it onto the mosaic-tiled floor. Flowers flew in every direction. Water splashed everywhere. The porcelain shattered into a thousand glittering fragments, scattering across the floor.

"Blasted Kahurangi."

He paced like a caged beast, his boots crunching shards onto the floor.

The Kahurangi presence had changed everything, and now, with their confidence bolstered, the sisters were openly defying him before the enemy. *Aghuti's child and the bastard.*

He exhaled loudly, hands still fisted, and dropped onto a couch, his neck tilting back against the plush backrest, hoping for this wave of anger to recede. Was there a purpose to his existence? Was there a reason for living beyond this?

Am I a mistake?

His father had consistently disregarded him, irrespective of the relentless effort he'd invested to prove himself to him. For ten long years, the Unification Wars lasted. Arjun Ghan had brought accolades and territorial expansion. He had battled tirelessly and conquered. He'd forced the warring factions to their knees one after another, compelling them to pledge their loyalty to his father, King Aram.

With each hard-fought victory, the mighty noble Zahari Houses standing behind Prince Narayan in defiance of Aram's ascension to the throne fell. And with every fallen House, with every bent knee, his father's claim grew more secure, cementing his authority over the Empire.

"And for what?" Ghan shouted at the empty room. The recognition he'd sought from his father never came.

Aram respected Yuna's brilliance and leadership.

Aram adored his graceful and exceedingly stunning Aghuti.

But Aram, unsure of what to do with his son, simply ignored him, relegating him to a corner with expensive toys while he praised Yuna's intelligence and admired Aghuti's beauty.

Arjun Ghan scoffed at the memories. "They hated you, Father. Your beloved daughters loathed you. I bet they were the ones who sent the assassin to kill you."

His thoughts moved to his uncle, Prince Narayan, his mother's twin brother.

Narayan and Naya.

Aram made Naya suffer, directing his abuse toward her. He belittled and ridiculed her because, in the end, she couldn't persuade her brother to accept Aram as the imperial king of Zahar.

"My poor mother. Maybe she hired the assassin."

Ghan exhaled, angry that he hadn't plunged that dagger into his father's chest himself. Life back then was suffocating, as he hoped for something that never came: his father's approval. A bitter smile pulled at his lips.

"I need a drink."

Ghan went to the spirit's cabinet. His boots shattered the porcelain fragments, the resonant crunch satisfying, and he served himself the most potent liquor he possessed.

The door handle jiggled with a faint metallic rattle, the hinges creaked in protest, and the door groaned as it swung open, inch by inch. Ghan didn't even bother to turn. "Why are you here?"

Aghet Mendi remained silent, waiting until Ghan turned to face him. "Danel came to fetch me." His stare grew sharp, focusing on the golden liquid in Ghan's glass. "He was concerned." He cast a lingering, searching gaze around the room, his eyes absorbing every detail until they hit the floor. "That was my favorite vase—"

"Then get another." This would be the closest thing to his *I'm sorry*.

Aghet frowned, the pause between them heavy, and cocked his head with a sharp look. "What troubles my prince?"

Ghan exhaled, studying the contents of his glass. *How do I even answer that question?* "Tell me, why are you with me?"

A sly smile dimpled Aghet's cheeks. "I want to understand why I didn't kill you that day."

Ghan huffed, replaying the memories of the brutal war with Kahurang. "You've been with me for thirty years. Haven't you figured it out by now?"

Aghet's glimmering eyes locked onto Ghan with an intensity that would've iced anyone else's blood. He sauntered toward the high general with a piercing gaze, moving silently through the room, each step shrouded in a disquieting silence, then carefully removed invisible lint from Ghan's embroidered collar. "Shall I give you my answer, then?"

Ghan met his gaze. "To understand why?" He leaned in closer. "Is that the only reason you are with me?" Hope burned brightly that affection was the answer—that in this place, at least, Aghet loved him.

Aghet tilted his head sideways. "It was. Once. But you're different."

"How?"

"There's something about you that calls to me. That's what I can't figure out." Aghet drew closer, the tip of his nose tracing the column of Ghan's throat as he inhaled. "I often lie in bed thinking as I watch you sleep, wondering if today's the day I'll bathe myself in your entrails, and just when I think I'm finally ready, this essence of yours enraptures me again."

Ghan stared at him, pondering what to make of thirty years with him. Aghet made his life bearable. He didn't bring music or colors. He brought something sharp, dangerous, and so seductive to his life that he couldn't get enough of it. In a world blinded by the relentless Zahari sun, Aghet was comforting darkness. Ghan moved with him as if he were dancing with death.

And that was absolutely glorious.

"Why have you declined my offers of marriage?"

Aghet pulled back, arching one eyebrow. "Why are you bringing this up?"

"Why not?" Ghan drained the last of his drink, the swallow burning his throat. "What excuse will you use this time to deny me?" He hurled the glass across the room, and it crashed against a wall with a resounding clash.

Aghet didn't move; the distance between them never decreased. He looked askance at Ghan, possibly mystified, possibly aroused. Ghan couldn't tell and didn't care. Suddenly, nothing mattered anymore.

"My prince." Aghet's voice was low and seductive, with a tinge of menace. "That glass was part of a set. Two unique pieces of art, made at my request by glass artisans from Almarim." The black flecks in his eyes glowed, slowly swallowing his brown irises. "They were a gift *for my prince*."

Ghan grimaced and glanced away. He'd never seen Aghet this angry. *Did I cross a line?* Perhaps, today, Aghet would finally spear him to the wall.

A gentle hand caressed his cheek, its touch tender as it guided his face, coaxing him to meet Aghet's gaze again.

Ghan wasn't sure whether he was staring at a man or a monster.

Aghet cocked his head, ominous curiosity glinting in his eyes. He spoke slowly, endearingly, but this time the expectation of an answer was embedded in the way he enunciated each word, with a dark, addictive sweetness. "What vexes my prince?"

Ghan closed his eyes. There were so many ways to answer that question.

"You... You've kept yourself away ever since the Kahurangi arrived. You didn't join me at the docks or the banquet—"

"Is that what bothers you?" A playful grin bloomed on Aghet's face. "I've been busy."

"With others?"

"Jealousy?" Aghet tapped his puckered lips, surprised. "I would've never expected it from you." He beamed at the news, his adoring gaze drinking all of Ghan's features. "I'm going to let you in on a little secret." Aghet dawdled toward the bedroom door and opened it. "But first, I should make you pay for breaking my vase and the glass."

Ghan hated dares. "Then make me."

"Oh, I plan to. But knowing you don't want to share me

with anyone else is... adorable. I thought you only had eyes for her."

Her. The Djinnshirukh.

Aghet's smile dissolved. A creeping shadow cast an eerie, almost spectral glow upon his eyes. His voice dripped with ominous intent. "When you learn who visited the Kahurangi's chambers in the middle of the night, you'll find yourself on your knees, offering me the thanks you never thought you would."

Ghan digested that statement for a long moment, eyes darting nervously. Then his gaze bore into Aghet. "Who?" Frustration sharpened his voice, his anger simmering just beneath the surface. "Aghet, who?"

He demanded answers—needed them.

Aghet simply tsked, a wicked smile outlining his face as he entered the bedroom. "Punishment first."

The sound of his cape sliding to the floor hung in the air.

CHAPTER 22

THE VISIT

Kharis's head spun.

The Kahurangi delegation had toured every point of interest in the Zahari capital. Speeches about peace and collaboration were written and given. Endless meetings with important people and agencies—from hazenkas to charities—peppered the busy royal schedules.

At the height of the active month, the families visited the Tomb of the Unknown Soldier in the Royal Cemetery to pay their respects. Rose and gold hues painted the crisp morning sky as the sun began its ascent.

The monument was a colossal white marble structure. The statue of a nondescript soldier stood on the pedestal. A pennon hung from his hand, symbolizing the honor he protected. His other hand held a sword, a symbol of justice. His gaze, fixed on the Zahari sky, spoke of hope—the wish for this to be the last war and for him to return home.

Kiwa and Hröld, dressed in their finest attire, carried elaborate wreaths. The two kings settled side by side and bowed their heads in silent reflection. The wind whispered through the trees. The distant sounds of the capital faded.

A sense of history and honor enveloped the space.

Quiet weeping drifted in the breeze.

King Kiwa caressed the white stone, his cheeks damp with tears. "We haven't forgotten you." He tipped his head toward his group, and the Kahurangi soldiers blew conches, announcing their presence to the gods. A deep, anguished cry escaped the king, a raw expression of his grief.

In perfect harmony, the Kahurangi sang, their voices rising in a haunting, mournful cadence. Their arms and legs moved in graceful unison, singing of a land immersed in fire and ice, blessed by forests and deserts, land and sea, and valleys and hills—a poignant song that conveyed their deep sense of loss, for their loved ones were here, in Zahar, not in Kahurang.

Two words shone brightly in Kharis's mind: *whānau,* family, and *te kāinga,* home. Since these soldiers wouldn't be returning home, the Kahurangi delegation was bringing "home" to them.

The final stop took them to Queen Aghuti's mausoleum to honor the woman who had become a legend. Because of her vision, thirty years ago, the Commonwealth of Nations was born, and peace became a colorful thread woven into Zahar's tapestry.

The mother I never met.

Kharis stood unnaturally still, her gaze studying the elaborately carved words on the marble.

Wife.
Mother.
Queen.
Visionary.
Our Morning Star.

Twelve years had passed since the tragic night Aghuti died in childbirth. Although she was gone, her legacy transcended the capital's boundaries, becoming a legend that drew pilgrims from every corner of the Empire.

On this particular day, a children's choir sang a beautiful hymn, their voices woven with sweet clarity, paying homage to the indomitable spirit of the Morning Star. It was once sung in the poor neighborhoods of the Ghak. A melody hummed in defiance of King Aram's cruel reign. And today, Kharis's heart soared, wondering about this woman—this legend—that was her mother.

Her father was visibly affected, sobbing. One hand rested on the marble while the other pressed onto a bloodred rose to his chest. Theirs had been a love for the ages, the material with which poems and songs were written and legends spun.

Yuna kept her misty gaze down, lost in memories of long ago. Anong, her husband, wrapped an arm around her shoulders. They shared a glance filled with endless affection, and she rested her head on his chest.

It was odd to see High General Arjun Ghan decked in regalia as if to honor a fallen warrior. He remained rooted, a solitary figure amidst the crowd. He clasped his hands behind him, lost in recollections of the past, his eyes glistening with undeniable emotion. It was clear he'd loved Aghuti, too.

Kharis remained unsure of her feelings. After all, how did one love a person one had never met?

Saya grasped her hand as if sensing Kharis's turmoil, giving her sister a comforting smile. Kharis leaned in, letting the music wash over her.

"I love you," Saya whispered.

Kharis savored those words. "And I love you more."

By the time the remembrance ceremonies were over, the scent of incense lingered in the air. The Zahari sun shone fiercely on the world, its light filtering through the trees like a cascade of gold.

Surrounded by White Guard officers and nobles, the royal entourage remained under a sizable canvas canopy, waiting for the carriages to arrive. Kharis, aware of the fear she engendered in people, sat under the cool shade of a tree, watching a playful hummingbird. Today, shared grief had brought Zahari and Kahurangi together.

Seeing that degree of fellowship filled her with hope.

The soldiers, however, didn't share the same desire for closure. She picked up the tension and the nuanced glances. *This is why Father wants us to learn.*

One small step to heal deep wounds.

One small step to steer everyone onto a new path—a new future.

Her Nana had been right. His message was vital to the entire Empire: learning from the Kahurangi was a way to open Zahar's heart to understanding. It allowed for closure and flowers to bloom once more.

She sighed, her eyes following the gorgeous little hummingbird as it moved from blossom to blossom with graceful determination. A soft breeze blew the hair off her face like a loving caress, carrying an invitation for her to come. Following this odd pull, Kharis walked away from the group, heading into a different section of the royal cemetery.

Here, endless rows of identical marble headstones stretched before her. Each bore the name of a Sorukhipa—a thousand years' worth of them. The engraved royal seal, the Zahari sun with seven flares, adorned each.

She strolled through the rows, her fingertips grazing the stones as she read the names. "Vaha of Zahar. Arek of Zahar. Umbu of Zahar. Kia of Zahar." Only Zahar.

None listed their family name or parents. The Sorukhipas had no personal history; their role was to serve the Empire's Djinnshirukh with absolute commitment. Her gaze drifted to the palace, its outline visible from the cemetery. "All of them slaves to Zahar."

Her thoughts settled on Saya, the current Sorukhipa. The notion that her sister would one day be laid to rest in this nearly forgotten section, that her tomb would only read "Saya of Zahar," while the palace would inter her beside her parents at the farthest end, deeply troubled her.

"Is this why Father adopted you?"

Kharis craved freedom from being the Djinnshirukh—for her and her sister to live and die as they wished, making their own choices. Perhaps she didn't need a map of long-forgotten tunnels or to sail to Kahurang as a stowaway. She needed a spell to end the Akumi king's hold on her body.

"A spell to squeeze him out."

Without a Djinnshirukh, there's no need for a Sorukhipa.

She focused on the palace's outline. "Where in that place would I find spells?" Her eyes widened. "The Archives." And a particular tunnel map would take her there.

With a plan in mind, Kharis quietly honored each tombstone until she reached the end.

Two cloaked figures stood before the headstone of Lord Athon of Zahar, the former Sorukhipa. They were burning incense, their heads bowed in prayer. Sensing her presence, one of them turned, lowering their hood. Bouncing brown curls cascaded past her shoulders, framing a lovely face and eyes with a shade of deep, dark blue and a touch of mauve, resembling the colors of the evening sky at dusk.

Her male companion, much taller than the young woman, had a gaze brimming with bronze and gold. A tousled mane the color of roasted chestnuts framed his handsome face.

"I'm sorry," Kharis said, "I didn't mean to interrupt you."

The woman smiled. The power of that gesture could coax Sharan to rise again. "We came to pay our respects to

Lord Athon." Her voice was melodious, like a solitary flute playing in the wind. "Are you here to do the same?"

Kharis nodded.

"Then please, come and join us."

Kharis settled by them, lighting a stick of incense and placing it in its receptacle. "Blessed is the earth that sustains us," she said after a slight bow. "Blessed is the sun that rises to guide us. As you were blessed in this lifetime, may the gods bless you in the next."

The Zahari prayer felt empty compared to the Kahurangi, who sang and danced for their fallen comrades with their hearts and souls, honest and open in their vulnerability.

Since Lord Athon was far from his home in the mountains, Kharis considered bringing it to him. She didn't know any Zherik-Umea songs or ballads that spoke of the hero's journey and their endless bravery in the face of insurmountable challenges, so she decided on a song she knew by heart —the one about the One War, the genesis for the Djinnshirukh and the Sorukhipa.

> "A thousand years ago, our world was broken.
> A thousand years ago, they came.
> They burned our forests.
> They razed our land.
> A thousand years ago, our hope was stolen.
> But a thousand years ago
> Four warriors came with their armies.
> They fought his darkness.
> They brought the sun."

Tears streamed down her face with each verse, leaving trails that the breeze cooled.

Kharis surrendered to the mournful refrains, letting them dictate her steps. Enraptured, she forgot her dancing prohibition, allowing her body to sway gently to the haunting lyrics. Her dress billowed with her movements. Her feet glided across the grass. Her arms rose and fell, her fingers tracing invisible patterns as if weaving together all the memories the melody evoked.

"Four warriors came with their armies,
And the battle was won.
We mourned our losses.
We gave them our son.
And from that turmoil,
A weapon was born."

Magic awakened inside her, and Kharis's soul sang with it. Goose bumps traveled the length of her petite body, wrapping around her like early morning sunlight.

"Our lands, we reclaimed,
And life was golden.
We rose from our ashes,
Like the phoenix of old.
And a thousand years ago,
We feasted and sang,
Under a brilliant Zahari sun."

She dried her tear-stained cheeks when she finished her song.

"That was a beautiful rendition of Lady Poliormos's poem," said the young woman.

Her voice brought Kharis back from her rapture.

"Are you aware there's one more refrain?" the woman asked.

Kharis shook her head. "I didn't know."

"Could I sing it for you?" the woman asked. "Perhaps you wish to learn it."

When Kharis nodded, the woman parted her lips and sang.

"Four warriors came with their armies,
And the battle, they won.
We mourned our losses.
We gave them our son.
And from that turmoil,
A weapon was born.
But while our land recovered,
And hope was once woven,
The gods imprisoned the four.
And a thousand years ago,
While we feasted and sang,
The lands of the four were frozen."

Kharis grew still, allowing the final verses to settle in her heart.

"I'm Maia," the young woman said, "and this is Yuri."

Kharis refocused her gaze. "Nice to meet you. I'm Kharis."

Maia beamed. "We're honored to have met the one who weaves the tapestries of fate, and for her to recount her tale with us."

Both bowed to her with a degree of reverence that stunned her. Kharis then realized she was alone with two strangers. "What do you mean?" she asked.

"With you," Maia said, "all that is wrong will be righted, and on that day, all the writings will end."

"The end approaches," Yuri said in a clear tenor. "A new beginning awaits."

Maia craned her neck toward Yuri, the couple having a silent conversation. Then she turned to Kharis. "You have a lovely voice, and your body remembers the rhythms of the universe. Perhaps you wish to join us?"

The Djinnshirukh blinked. A million thoughts crashed into her mind, but one stood out above the others: "Only if I bring my sister with me."

Maia offered a wistful smile. "She can't come with us, for this is where she belongs."

"Then I stay." Kharis lifted her chin. "I'm not leaving Saya behind."

"We didn't think you would." Maia's eyes brimmed with infinite kindness. "But it was worth asking." She winked, and her playful laughter sounded like the chink of wind chimes.

"Did you know Lord Athon?" Kharis asked.

"We loved him, and he loved us." Maia's gaze was lost in the haze of memory.

"He guided my wife on a perilous journey so she could find me." Yuri wrapped his arms around her with affection. "He protected and aided her." He nuzzled her cheek. "When others would've walked away, he took her hand and led her to me."

"I didn't know this."

"There is much that the Lord Sorukhipa kept to himself," he added. "He was a member of our Court just as he was a member of yours."

"Your Court?" The sound of footfalls on cobblestones made Kharis turn.

"There you are." Taika wore a look of relief. "We've been looking for you."

Blasted. Only then did Kharis hear others calling out her name. *Another lecture is shaping itself.*

"I came to pay my respects to Lord Athon and ran into —" She turned, and her arms fell limp to her sides. "Where did they go?"

"Who?" Taika asked. "You were here by yourself. I heard you sing. That's how I found you."

Ice surged through her veins. Kharis surveyed the space where, not a heartbeat ago, a young man and a young woman had stood. *Did I imagine it?* Her gaze flitted across the Sorukhipa section, spotting a few White Guard officers but not the couple. However, three incense sticks still burned in the receptacle. Tears stung her eyes.

"You're crying." Taika dashed to her, his thumbs rubbing the tops of her cheeks to dry them. "Are you unwell? Are you hurt?"

She shook her head. "This day." Her voice quivered. "It was hard."

Her mother.

Her sister.

Loss.

Weaving tapestries. Righting wrongs.

Secrets hid in the dark recesses of her mind that she knew to be true.

"I didn't want to forget about Lord Athon," she said. "For anyone to be forgotten—to be truly dead."

Taika hugged her, and the warmth of his body exorcised the odd chill in her bones.

"Please, don't cry." Taika's kiss on her forehead—sweet, innocent, and affectionate—took her breath away.

"We won't forget them," he whispered, stroking her head. "We never will."

Half her face was pressed against his chest, and she felt his words rumble inside. His heart thumped against her ear in a comforting rhythm, and she realized it was the most divine sound—one she wished would never cease to entice her.

And so her thoughts wandered to the one place that held the key to her freedom.

The Royal Archives.

CHAPTER 23

THE ROYAL ARCHIVES

Kharis hurried through the secret tunnel, keeping her eyes on the map. Hidden doors and ancient wards protected these passageways, but to a highly inquisitive child like herself, these obstacles were puzzles to be solved. After several nights of testing different tunnels, this one had to be the right one.

An impenetrable darkness shrouded this tunnel, the air carrying a musty blend of dampness and decay. The rough walls seemed to close in on her, their texture biting at her touch. Cobwebs clung to every surface, wisps of silk whispering ancient tales of neglect. The occasional skittering of tiny legs on damp stone made her stop. The unsettling crunch of debris underfoot met her steps. She chose not to look.

Her lantern's flickering flame barely illuminated her path as she maneuvered this intricate web, stopping to check her map. Left, left, right, left, straight, right again. She navigated the narrow passageway, her footsteps echoing in the darkness.

Soon, she reached a dead end. Exhaling a huff, she placed her hand flat on the wall, frustrated by yet another failed attempt. Heat surged from her hand onto the cool rock, and well-defined cracks emerged, glowing as if filled with molten rock. The wall's glamour was concealing a small door.

"Yes!" Kharis lifted a fist in triumph.

With a grunt, she pushed on it, the hole revealing a narrow alcove. She crawled through and kicked a nearby rock to gauge the shaft's depth. A blink later, it hit the bottom. The drop was manageable, likely no more than twice her height.

Kharis stuffed the map inside her tunic, sat, scooted toward the alcove's edge, and jumped.

The oil sloshed inside the lantern, snuffing the flame when she landed.

"Great!" she griped. "Now I can't see a thing."

More deliberate prodding revealed another small door, this one metal. She pushed on it, the feeble moonlight revealing that the shaft was the interior of a sizable, hollow statue. The narrow hatch clicked open, and she skillfully squeezed her body through the narrow gap between the effigy and the wall, barely getting out.

Kharis brushed the cobwebs clinging to her hair and dusted her clothes as she entered the Royal Archives. Her arms rose in celebration, and a silent whoop sealed her victory. Finding matches, she lit her lantern again, ensuring the flame was as small as possible. The last thing she needed was to announce her presence to the guards on patrol.

The faint glow revealed the room's splendor. Towering shelves lined with leather-bound tomes and scrolls stretched before her like sentinels of forgotten knowledge. The scent of ink, parchment, and age thickened the air.

Kharis placed her lantern on a nearby table, rubbed her hands excitedly, and scanned the stacks, tiptoeing between the rows of books as her fingers traced the spines. She advanced deeper into the Archives like a seasoned explorer.

Her keen eyes searched, but she wasn't sure as to what. Would the spell be in a scroll, a book, or something else?

She scratched her head, wondering, "How do I find a spell?" She looked to her right and left, filling her lungs with air, and cringed. "Blech!" A few coughs escaped her. She couldn't imagine working in this musty air day in and day out.

"Maybe I need a spell to find a spell?" She was willing to try anything, even if foolish, with freedom on the line. She lowered her voice to sound like an aged wizard of old and recited, "Oh, ancient secrets, hidden well, reveal yourself. I implore you to give me a spell."

She stifled a laugh.

Her eyes darted, hoping for something interesting to happen.

"Hello?" Her greeting resonated, then faded into dissipating whispers.

"*Hello,*" said a soft, silvery voice.

Startled, Kharis nearly jumped out of her skin, half her heart pounding in her chest like a drumbeat, while the other half almost leaped out of her throat.

"Who's there?" she stammered, her voice barely above a breath.

She strained her ears. The sound seemed to swirl around her, echoing in her mind, not off the ancient tomes and dusty shelves. Her fingers trembled as she clutched the lantern and scanned the darkness.

"Who's there?" She asked again, her voice quivering. "I'm armed, you know." Her hand went for the dagger strapped to the small of her back, its hilt reassuring against her palm.

"*If you close your eyes, you'll find me,*" the voice murmured.

"Pfft. Like I would." Then Kharis stilled. *Wait.* Was the voice coming from inside her head? She shook it, aware of how ridiculous that sounded, and quickly snuffed the lantern's flame. The abrupt darkness swallowed the chamber. She crouched low behind a table. The pale moonlight filtered through the top windows, casting eerie, shifting shadows that danced across the space.

"*Close your eyes,*" the voice said again, unhurried—amused.

Kharis huffed. "Fine. But any funny business—" She didn't finish her sentence, mostly because she was unsure what she would do. Poke an eye or slash the face? Stab the chest? Run? The possibilities were endless.

"*Your eyes?*" the voice said.

Kharis rolled them, but when she closed her eyes, images of this chamber played in her mind. All sorts of books opened in it, their pages crackling with age, and their words, shimmering with power, danced before her. Their brilliance intensified, enveloping her in a burst of light.

She found herself inside a black void. Faint glimmers of magic, like gossamer tendrils, danced around her. And in the middle of all that activity, a single flickering flame, much taller than her, stood before her as if observing her.

"*Hello,*" it said.

"Who are you?" she asked.

"*Are you the Djinnshirukh?*"

"I am."

The voice's hum was deep. "*You are smaller than the others.*"

She narrowed her eyes in annoyance. The others had been adults. "And who might you be?"

"*What do you seek?*"

"I asked you first." Frustration honed her voice. "Who are you?"

Kharis didn't receive an answer. The Archive doors groaned as they opened, their hinges creaking like ancient bones. The magic that had enveloped her vanished, and she was back in the Archives. Distinct voices drifted in her direction.

Blasted. The night guards.

Pressing her back against the shadowed wall, Kharis strained to discern their patrol pattern. Would they go left first? Or right? Or perhaps go straight and run into her? A flicker of anxiety tickled her chest. Her clandestine expedition had just taken an unexpected turn.

Padding toward the massive statue, she pushed the hidden door behind it, squirming through the narrow gap while the guards chatted. She found it more challenging to squeeze in, her shirt getting caught on a metal protrusion. *Blasted.* She shoved herself inside it, ripping the fabric. The conversation stopped. Kharis chewed on her bottom lip. The conversation resumed, but the voices were getting closer. *Fires of Ifran. They are coming this way.* She closed the metal door, hoping its click would be soft enough not to be heard.

It wasn't.

"What was that?" one guard asked.

"What?" the other said, his voice loud and husky.

"Didn't you hear that? Ruk, someone's here."

Ruk groaned. "Argi, keep it up, and I swear I'll hit your head."

"I'm telling you. There's a ghost in this place—"

A slap reverberated in the chamber.

"Ouch! What was that for?" Argi whined.

"All that reading is messing with your head," Ruk said.

"It's not," Argi huffed loudly. "Ask the archivists in the morning. They'll tell you about it. A ghost roams this place at night."

Ruk grumbled. "You mean, ask the pretty archivist you've been ogling?"

"What? She *is* pretty."

Ruk's deep groan filled the air. "Let's do our round and get out. This place gives me the creeps."

"Ha!" Argi clapped. "You believe me—"

"Shut your mouth. I believe nothing."

The boot clacks dissipated as the guards walked away, bickering.

Relieved she hadn't been found, Kharis pressed her hands and feet flat against the statue's interior to gain leverage and shimmied up until she reached the ledge and sat on it to catch a breath.

"Next time, I'm bringing a rope."

She wiped her sweat, crawled through the hole, pushed the stone back in place, and soon returned to the tunnel.

A distant screech pierced the quiet, vibrating down the passageway.

"That's new."

She turned, squinting into the darkness behind her. A cold gust of wind blew past her, carrying the sound of yet another one of those ominous shrieks. "That doesn't sound like a rat."

The thought struck her all at once. She hadn't seen rats at all.

The sound rose again, a spectral wail that set the air trembling. Cold rippled along the passage as it echoed, signaling that whatever *that* was, it drew closer.

With enough common sense flooding her head, Kharis rushed back to her chambers.

CHAPTER 24

THE ZAHAR-HOMA

According to Kharis, the best stop was the last—a tour of the Zahar-Homa, the ancient wall. On their last day in the capital, Hala took the Kahurangi royals on a sunset stroll. The ancient rampart wall rose tall and impressive, now acting as the imperial city's boundary.

Beyond the wall, the Ghak spread into the valley and surrounding hills, hugging the mighty Ibaia River.

The skyline was bright red and dark orange. Eye-popping colors set the sky ablaze as the sun hid behind the western horizon. The breeze played with Kharis's hair as the evening's indigo and purple slowly quenched the fiery display. A few twinkling stars emerged, announcing the night.

The Zahari and Kahurangi retinues promenaded atop the Zahar-Homa's parapet, enjoying the cool evening weather while the royals were deep in conversation. The imposing wall impressed King Kiwa, Prince Nikau, and Prince Rawiri. Encouraged by their questions, Hala slipped into professorial mode, discussing all things Zahar-Homa—its history, the lore surrounding it, and the engineering that made such a structure possible. King Hröld added to his son's commentary here and there.

Contrary to the adults, the panoramic views enthralled the young princes. The last outbursts of sunset tinged the sky—a formidable performance for the Kahurangi. Koa flanked Saya, listening as she pointed out neighborhoods while Taika and Kharis rested their arms on the battlement, gazing ahead.

"I see why you love it here," Nikau told Kharis. "The evening lights come on, and the darkness gives way to an ocean of stars across the capital."

"It's a beautiful sight." Kharis relished the rare chance to stand on the wall, enjoying the cool air. "How do you like it so far?"

Taika cast her a quiet look. "It's bittersweet."

"How so?"

"It's a beautiful sunset, more so given the company." His gaze met hers, and her throat went dry. "This is also the last one I'll watch with you." Taika studied her hand for a long moment and clutched it as if he'd mustered enough courage. "Friends, then?"

Kharis gave him a crisp nod.

"Promise me you'll write."

She grinned. "Of course, but it means you'll have to write back."

He waggled his eyebrows. "I'll write in Kahurangi, so you must learn it."

"Ha! I can ask your uncle to translate—"

"No, don't do that." His cheeks turned beet red. "Or I won't write to you."

"Fine." She relented. "Does it mean I have to write in Kahurangi?"

Taika dipped his head with a playful smile. "Yes." He studied her face as if memorizing every detail. "And only in Kahurangi."

She scratched her cheek and glanced away. His eyes

made her heart jump up and down like a monkey. "I may need your uncle's help."

"Of course." His voice was low. "But I'm leaving you a book so you can put into words what you may not want to ask my uncle."

Suspicious, Kharis narrowed her eyes. "What exactly am I supposed to write to you?"

He shrugged, but that mischievous smile was still on his face. "Tell me about Zahar. Describe all the things you see and how they make you feel. Tell me about you." He pondered thoughtfully. "Tell me that you miss me." He winked at her. "Just write. Allow me to know you through our letters." He inched closer until their arms brushed against each other. His silence lasted a few heartbeats, but to Kharis, it felt like an eternity.

"We're only two years apart," he said.

"Yes. I'm almost thirteen. You are fifteen."

"I can wait until you are of age. Eighteen, right?"

She gulped, studying how he threaded his fingers through hers. Her heart jumped, too buoyant to stay inside her chest. She wanted him to hold her hand forever.

"I promise to write," she said.

Taika sighed in relief. "Five years will fly swiftly."

It made Kharis wonder. So many things could change in five years. "According to my brother, your tour was successful. The people of Zahar will speak of it for a long time." She caught her lip between her teeth, hesitant to hope or wish for anything. "Perhaps... Perhaps we'll visit Kahurang next."

"Good." His smile flashed, eyes sparkling. "I'll start planning."

A laugh escaped her. "Don't make it boring."

His intense gaze met hers. "I'll ensure you never want to leave."

Kharis swallowed hard. Her eyes wandered to his lips, and the sensation of them brushing her forehead at the cemetery ignited a fire she didn't know how to put out.

CHAPTER 25
THE FAREWELL

Early in the morning, people crowded the royal quay. Many came to see the Kahurangi delegation off— Regiazenka ministers, Zahari nobles, mahazenka leaders, and curious onlookers.

The taiko drums boomed across the grand plaza as if awakening the gods to ensure a safe journey down the Ibaia River. The imperial barge, moored at the dock, stood ready with its gangplank extended. The sails weren't up yet, but the breeze signaled the winds would bless them with a swift trip downstream.

Misty-eyed, King Kiwa landed a heavy hand on Rawiri's shoulder. "I dislike leaving you in a foreign land." He leaned in, their noses and foreheads pressed together to share the breath of life. "I'm going to miss you, brother. I..." Emotion kept Kiwa from finishing, and his hand squeezed his brother's shoulder instead.

Rawiri sighed sadly.

From this moment onward, he was alone, for he couldn't allow Tanganokai to punish his homeland for his defiance. "I'll miss you, too. I'll miss all of you."

Kiwa heaved a long sigh, choking on a sob, and straightened. "Even when far from us, our hearts will remain with you. You are in our thoughts, and we'll pray to the gods to keep you safe and guide your hand."

Ataahua approached, her brows knit in a frown. Rawiri didn't utter a word. He just stared at her, knowing.

She paused dramatically, her chin high, her amber eyes on him, then pressed her forehead and nose against his. "Rawiri." Her lips quivered, struggling as much as Kiwa. She pulled back and threw the Zahari sisters a furtive glance. "Don't attach yourself to the Rangatira."

Rawiri's smile flattened. "Your advice reached me too late, considering fate has already entwined me with hers."

Her stare intensified, and her voice lowered one more octave, soft enough for him to hear. "The rewera's watching you. If you ever face him, don't turn your back on him. Don't utter any words, for he will use them to trap you. Please be careful of those who dislike this peace, for they're as dangerous as Tanganokai."

Rawiri understood, his eyes flicking toward Arjun Ghan. He let her warning sink in, then wrapped his arms around her.

The gesture startled her.

"I love you, sister. Always keep your eyes on me."

Ataahua kept from uttering a wry remark, fighting the silver pooling in her gaze, and wrinkled her nose, settling by Aroha.

His nephews threw themselves at Rawiri, a mob of affectionate arms that teetered between sadness and excitement. They were ready for the salty water to spray their faces and the scent of marine brine to fill their lungs—to return home. Yet, leaving their beloved uncle behind broke their hearts.

Kiwa heaved a mournful cry. His sons settled beside him, and the four began a chant—a farewell song that spoke of a land with tall mountains, verdant valleys, and wild seas. Ataahua and Aroha flanked them, singing and dancing in unison.

Every Kahurangi present joined in song.

Rawiri stepped forward—one last dance with his beloved family before they sailed back home. He joined them as tears trailed down his face. He'd known this was coming, but now that the occasion had arrived, he was in denial. The haunting pain in his heart wasn't new. How many goodbyes had he uttered to dear friends on the battlefield? He'd lost count, but this grief was intense, and he feared his heart would explode.

He moved his body, each step precious, each chanted word louder than the previous one—pride and love in motion. He danced because he would drop to the ground and weep if he didn't.

The royal family gazed at Rawiri, and to his astonishment, Kiwa and Ataahua bowed low in reverence. This was one last tribute. One final gesture of affection and respect before their departure for the sacrifice Rawiri was about to make.

If Tanganokai doesn't kill me, the Zahari will.

The gesture surprised the princes, who weren't aware of its significance, but they emulated their parents nonetheless. Kiwa's shoulders shuddered, taking this farewell the hardest.

Rawiri watched in silence as they climbed the gangplank. The crew raised the sails, the men on the dock loosened the moorings, and the anchor groaned as it emerged from the waters. Rawiri's breathing hitched when the winds swelled the sails with a loud "whoop."

They're leaving.

Standing on the quarterdeck, his nephews lifted their right fists and shouted, *"Ka peke ratou."*

Rawiri laughed through his tears.

A small hand gripped his calloused one, catching him off guard. Kind blue-gray eyes gazed at him, her warm smile like a soothing gift to his heart. "Saya holds my hand when I'm sad," Kharis said.

This child.

His entire soul shook. He would give his life to protect her. Tanganokai had taken his children—all eight of them—so Rawiri would keep this one.

"What was it they yelled?" she asked.

He laughed as his eyes misted again. "You don't want to know."

The colossal bear stared at his wild cub and grinned.

PART TWO
THE THREADS OF DESTINY

CHAPTER 26
IDLIS AND CHUTNEY

Two weeks in Zahar, and it already feels like an eternity. Rawiri marched on, lost in his thoughts—two weeks to grasp and understand the Zahari Court.

It would be easier to tame a sea dragon.

The polished marble floors reflected the morning light. Lit by this radiance, floating specks lazily hovered in the corridor's emptiness. Intricate tapestries adorned the hallway, providing pops of color in the otherwise long, dark corridor that led to the crown prince's chambers.

He halted to study the lavish Tree of Life embroidery. The Mahabhal, as the Zahari called it, stood at the center of everything that defined Zahar.

Queen Aghuti, it appeared, had been obsessed with it.

Rawiri cast a quick look over his shoulder. His soldiers, an escort Kiwa insisted he kept, offered him the relief he needed. Their tattooed faces gave him a sense of familiarity in an unfamiliar place, but their hardened gazes conveyed apprehension. Thirty years ago, Zahar was *rahuitia.*

Once he turned the corner, the sentries spotted the Kahurangi prince and stood at attention, thumping their spears on the floor.

Their unfriendly stares carried thirty years of disdain. High General Ghan, who openly disliked him and his soldiers, used every opportunity to openly complain about the Kahurangi's presence: that it disrupted the Court.

Whining like a child.

Rawiri stood before the wooden doors. Inside, the crown prince waited. Curiosity gnawed at him, his mind brimming with questions. Whether he would get answers was another matter.

What does he want?

After two weeks in Zahar, he understood that the Zahari gave nothing willingly. There was a graceful dance to all exchanges, implying a tit-for-tat. They measured their words, and fake politeness coated their requests so much that it was confusing, even distasteful.

Rawiri braced himself for more of this annoying verbal dance as the imperial sentries opened the double doors and urged the prince to enter, yet they barred his bodyguards.

"You weren't invited," one barked.

"We go where His Highness goes," spat Tawhiri, Rawiri's general.

Rawiri lifted a hand to stop Tawhiri. "It'll be fine."

"But Your Highness—"

"Just wait here." A quiet smile tugged at Rawiri's lips. "*Ka peke ratou.*"

Tawhiri didn't smile. "*Hiahia ana koe.*"

As you wish.

It didn't help. The Kahurangi warriors fixed their surly eyes on the Zahari sentries anyway—a silent warning that spoke volumes. Thirty years would never erase the brutality of the war at the hands of their high general, Arjun Ghan.

"Blessed be the earth and sun," Hala greeted Rawiri as he entered the chambers. "Thank you for visiting me."

Visiting? Rawiri barely dipped his head, forcing a polite smile. *This was a summons.*

Hala gestured toward chairs and a round table set with what appeared to be a lavish breakfast: idlis, savory rice-dough thin flatbreads—a Kahurangi staple. One of Rawiri's eyebrows went up.

The crown prince wants something.

"Please, come in and make yourself comfortable."

Rawiri resisted the temptation to make a sardonic comment and took his seat. The absence of servants suggested an air of secrecy rather than comfort. To his surprise, Hala served him tea, handing him the cup. Its warmth was soothing in his hands. The heady scent—cardamom and cinnamon—was intoxicating. The other herbs hitting his nose spoke of indulgent luxury.

He really wants something. Rawiri's guard went up.

Hala served himself from the same porcelain teapot and sat across Rawiri, taking a long sip—a symbolic gesture to show the drink wasn't poisoned. To avoid offense, Rawiri sipped. Its flavor was sweet and decadent, with a warmth at the back of the throat that hinted at ginger and black pepper.

"I hope you're settled in," Hala said, a warm smile parting his lips. "Are your accommodations to your satisfaction?"

"They're spacious and comfortable. I'm most grateful."

"Your presence excites the Crown, even if serendipity played a role in seeing my mother's vision come to fruition."

Serendipity? It was a diplomatic way to explain bypassing Almarim.

"Tell me, what do you think of the princesses' readiness to start their lessons?" Hala asked.

Rawiri lowered his cup. "I'm assessing their current knowledge to determine the best course of action regarding their education."

"Fascinating." Hala took a plate and served Rawiri a few idlis. "Tell me, what does your assessment show?"

"That your sisters learn differently." Rawiri took the plate from Hala and set it down. "I should present the same subject differently so they grasp concepts better."

"Wouldn't that be too much work?"

"Educating children isn't *work*, Your Highness."

"Please, call me Hala. It's just the two of us. We can dismiss the usual palace conventions and enjoy a quiet breakfast. May I address you by your given name?"

Rawiri nodded with another polite smile to go along with... *Whatever this is.*

Hala studied his plate, fork in hand. "I'm unsure how to eat idlis," he said, "and therefore, I look forward to your guidance to avoid any violation of Kahurangi etiquette."

Rawiri sighed quietly, uncertain if Hala's comment was a ruse to level the field—to allow him the upper hand on something. He studied the different sauces on the table. Selecting the roasted red pepper chutney, he spread some on an idli, rolled it, and ate it with his hands.

"Ah!" Hala's eyes widened, pleasantly surprised. He emulated Rawiri, taking a bite of his, and moaned his approval. "Quite delicious." He finished his and readied another. "So, what are your thoughts on the girls?"

Rawiri tilted his head. "Both are bright and lean toward different subjects. Each presents strengths and weaknesses."

"Weaknesses? Are you referring to Kharis?"

"Oh no, not at all." That comment bothered him. "Princess Saya devours books. Her ability to retain information is spectacular. Princess Kharis is also an avid reader, but her choices differ. Our visit to the palace library was an attempt to understand their preferences." He chuckled at the memory of two twelve-year-olds pulling him in opposite directions. "Princess Saya is mathematically inclined. Her tastes are like yours, Your Highness."

"Hala, please."

For a moment, his annoying mask vanished, making Rawiri smile.

"She enjoys science and excels in architecture and engineering. Kharis likes history and philosophy and leans toward diplomacy."

"Diplomacy?" Hala almost choked on his tea.

Rawiri placed his cup on the table. "Given their interests, would the Crown permit me to take them out of the palace?"

"Why?" Hala's mask reappeared.

"The Zahar-Regia offers an opportunity to visit sites where Saya can experience the inner workings of mechanical devices. The capital has drawbridges and water gates. We could study those more closely to witness theory in action."

Hala tapped his chin. "It's a logical request." He sipped his tea slowly, his eyes on Rawiri appraisingly. "And Kharis?"

Rawiri beamed without thinking, but quickly schooled his face into neutral. "Her Highness's curiosity is perhaps her best asset. Museums and monasteries would let her expand what she knows. While Princess Saya has clear preferences, Princess Kharis is different."

"How so?" Hawkish brown eyes studied the Kahurangi prince as if looking for something.

But what? That gesture bothered Rawiri, but he kept his calm demeanor.

"Puzzles, Lord Hala. Princess Kharis enjoys them. Her mind has the uncanny ability to break things apart and put them together, as if she could reweave a complex tapestry, making it better and stronger in the process. The princess finds ways to solve complex problems."

"Yes," Hala said flatly, serving himself more tea. "We're quite familiar with her... problem-solving tendencies."

That faint, sarcastic tone rubbed Rawiri the wrong way. "The nature of the puzzle doesn't matter," Rawiri continued. "It challenges her to find a solution. Her eyes see the world differently, as if she could anticipate moves, her mind always steps ahead of—"

"My sister's like water."

Rawiri stiffened. A chunk of ice lodged in his chest. "Come again?"

"Water's stubborn," Hala said. "It goes where it wants to go. If one path is impossible, water carves another. Eventually, water always reaches the ocean." Hala took a sip. "Be mindful that, like water, my sister could slip through your fingers."

Rawiri mustered a soft smile, an essential bluff in this game. Hala gestured to Rawiri's empty cup. He agreed to more tea, watching the crown prince pour it and then serve himself another idli.

"What would you suggest next?" Hala studied the dipping sauces with curiosity.

"I'm partial to chutneys," Rawiri said. "But you may enjoy this one." He pointed to a dark sauce with the consistency of caramel. "Cooks make it with tamarind paste. It has a crisp, tangy flavor, but when paired with the right spices, it explodes in your mouth. Idlis are the best vehicle to carry such flavors."

"Hmm, how would it be done?" Hala asked.

"Spoon some on your idli, roll it, close your eyes, and bite. That's what I'd do."

Hala did, and while the flavor transfixed him for a moment, that aggravating mask disappeared.

"I would like permission to take them on tours of the Zahar-Regia."

"Both of them?" Hala asked.

The question struck him as odd. *Why would I bring one and not the other?* "Yes, both of them."

Hala chewed slowly, thinking. The spicy, sour-sweet flavor seemed to mellow his concerns. "Very well. I'll allow it under certain conditions."

"Name them."

"A Zahari escort, foremost. One of my sisters is as slippery as an eel."

Rawiri lifted his hand. "I agree to it. If I can show they behave and follow my instructions, may I eventually dispense with it?"

The mask was back on, and nothing would remove it this time. "We'll see how it goes first before agreeing to anything else. An escort will be necessary when *my sisters* leave the palace. Their safety is the Crown's primary concern."

"Of course." The emphasis on possession—*my sisters*—struck Rawiri as peculiar. It was as if Hala were trying to state something without saying it. *Typical Zahari.* Still, Rawiri dipped his head to show his agreement.

Hala stared at Rawiri silently for a long moment before his gaze returned to the array of dipping sauces. "So, which would you recommend next?"

Rawiri walked the hallways in a daze. He missed Kiwa, his confidant, and Ataahua, whose eyes didn't miss a thing. He wondered how they would've counseled him after this audience with the crown prince.

"Your Highness?" Tawhiri asked.

Rawiri blinked and turned to his general. "My apologies. Sometimes, I forget I'm not in Kahurang."

Tawhiri gave him *that look*. No confusion clouded his eyes. The men were tense, cautious, and observant, even assessing the shadows. The war had ended thirty years ago, but that ghost still haunted them. The hostile glares they received as they marched past Zahari sentries confirmed it.

"Let's go out," the prince said.

His men sighed in relief.

"I'm not expected to tutor the princesses until this afternoon. Therefore, a walk after that breakfast would clear my head. Besides, I'd like to visit a particular person."

"Who?" Tawhiri asked.

"One not expecting me at all. Yuna Chantarasang."

The cloaked figure entered the chambers, emerging from a side door. "Your Highness?"

Hala smoothed his kurta, a long green tunic with exquisite floret embroidery, and turned, studying the Shadow Walker with mild interest. *Our trained spies. Loyal and committed to the Crown.* He suppressed a grin. *Thank the Blessed Mother for that.*

"Walk with me," he said. "The servants are clearing the breakfast service, and our presence delays their work."

The woman nodded and followed the crown prince to his office chambers with silent steps. She wore the usual uniform: a long-sleeved black tunic with shiny black silk embroidery, leather armor, trousers, and boots, and, despite the heat, a cloak with a sizable hood. A scarf concealed half her face. In her line of work, her face was a commodity. Very few were allowed to gaze upon it.

Once in his office, the woman took a letter from under her cloak and handed it to him. "It arrived today. A letter to the Djinnshirukh princess from one of the Kahurangi princes."

Hala's frown replaced his surprise. "Have there been others?"

The woman shook her head. "Only this one. What would you like us to do?"

Hala scrutinized the doors, casting a discreet glance over her shoulder. His staff would arrive soon, and he needed the Shadow Walker gone before they did. But more than that, he wanted Kharis bound to him alone.

"Bring them all to me," he said. "Letters to her or from her. Do you understand?"

She nodded.

"As for this one," he said, waving it, "you never saw or received it and never gave it to me. Is that understood?"

"As you wish, Your Highness."

The woman bowed and exited the room.

Once he was alone, Hala crumpled up the letter in his hand.

CHAPTER 27
WATCH AND LISTEN

Rawiri took a deep breath as his eyes drank in the city sights.

The imposing Zahar-Homa enclosed the imperial city. The king's residence towered above all the buildings as its heart. In contrast, the middle ring held the mansions of noble families, generals, royal advisors, and the lofty homes of the imperial White Guard. Tall, skinny townhouses crowded the narrow, winding streets on the outer ring, where servants and soldiers lived. Beyond the Zahar-Homa, the glorious capital, Zahar-Ghak, or the Ghak, as the locals called their city, spread like a vibrant quilt.

The aromas wafting through the Zahar-Regia were different—exciting and refreshing. Hundreds of merchants and vendors crossed the gates daily to participate in the bazaars on the outer ring, selling items Rawiri had never seen: sultry spices, intriguing fruits and vegetables, aromatic oils, and fabrics.

Rawiri filled his lungs with this electrifying energy.

"Where to, Your Highness?" Tawhiri strolled beside him, his brown eyes fiercely assessing everyone near them. One hand gripped his sword hilt, and the other rested on the daggers strapped to his chest.

"I'm headed to the Royal Academy of the Healing Arts. You're more than welcome to roam the city."

Tawhiri protested, "Your Highness—"

"What's your concern? At worst, this monk will stick me with a needle."

"His Majesty left us with detailed orders—"

"And as your *commanding* officer," Rawiri said, "I'm telling you to wander. Enjoy the sights. Watch. Listen. Then tell me everything."

Tawhiri hesitated, unhappy with the idea of leaving the prince behind.

Rawiri's features eased. "There's a two-story tavern near the western gate. The Porcupine. It's a popular venue, and I've spotted a few Zahari nobles eating or drinking there. The food is good, and their ale is exceptional. Who knows? It might loosen a few lips." He squeezed Tawhiri's shoulder, handing him a coin pouch. "Be generous with the invitations, especially to the nobles."

Tawhiri understood the veiled command.

"Divide your men and send some to the bazaar by the southern gate. The palace servants often purchase their wares there. The zenka vendors are friendly and, as I've discovered, quite chatty when the opportunity for a sale is at hand." Rawiri smirked. "We could learn a thing or two."

Tawhiri nodded. "When are you expected back at the palace, Your Highness?"

Rawiri tilted his head, scratching his neck. "Come and fetch me once the sun is mid-point. The princesses will have lunch first, then their lesson with me."

Tawhiri offered a crisp bow and issued instructions to his men. Rawiri picked up his pace and approached the ornate doors to the royal academy.

Monks moved in and out, some nodding in his direction. A few wore long-sleeved tunics and trousers in shades of blue, while others donned wrapped kilts instead. They had kind faces and warm smiles, pressing their palms together as they uttered the usual Zahari blessing: "Blessed be the earth and sun."

A unique set of people. "May they sustain us," Rawiri replied each time.

He eyed the impressive building and, aware that he had no plan, went up the stone steps and entered.

CHAPTER 28
THE BEAR AND THE FOX

Yuna studied Rawiri as if he were a challenging patient. Her mouth thinned. She tipped her head back to take in his height. Then, she gestured for him to sit.

Rawiri sat, her sharp eyes still assessing him.

"I've been expecting you." Her eyes narrowed to mere slits. "And you're late."

Her bluntness startled Rawiri. The Zahari usually prattled on with the usual diplomacy and graceful vagueness that hid their agendas. "I can't be late for a meeting that wasn't on my itinerary."

She sniffed. "My time for idle chat is limited," she said coolly. "You must be here to ask about the girls. What do you wish to know?"

Well... That took him by surprise. "I've been told that the princesses undergo tutoring under you."

"Yes, both do." Yuna crossed her arms. "The healing arts is a required subject but not a choice connected to lofty ideals. I train them so they know what to do when injured."

Not if, but when they're injured. The remark struck him as odd. "I've noticed that Princess Kharis has difficulty reading."

"Yes, she does. She often transposes letters or reverses sounds, making reading and writing challenging. Please, be patient with her."

"What do you suggest?" His interest was genuine. Kharis was already so unique.

Yuna stared at him for a long moment. "You must have her full attention. She can't process what you say if you turn your back on her. Therefore, face her when speaking to her. Competing sounds will be challenging. Select quiet places for her instruction. If there's background noise when you talk, it impairs her ability to listen to you meaningfully. Worse, it'll aggravate her, bringing me to my last suggestion."

Rawiri nodded. "Please, go on."

"Certain noises are abhorrent to her. Her reaction to undesirable sounds is strong. Be mindful of the signs telling you she's about to explode." Yuna frowned at him, her voice taking a somber tone. "Do *not* ignore them."

Why would I? Still, he made a mental note of it. "What about memorization?"

"Kharis has an exemplary memory, regardless of her learning challenges. Her mind makes connections when allowed. Don't impose practices assuming she's like any other child, for she isn't. Laughter and joy will reveal her brilliance." Yuna narrowed her eyes. "I recommend not provoking her anger or fear at all costs."

He grimaced before he could master his expression.

Yuna's face remained unreadable. "May I suggest something?"

Rawiri shifted in his chair. "Please, do."

"Don't repeat former tutors' mistakes. She won't sit still and listen as Saya would. Theory isn't enough for her to comprehend and compel lessons to memory. She must *do*.

Allow her to put theory into action, to touch and move so she can process effectively."

Rawiri tapped the armrest, thinking. "Dancing may—"

Yuna raised her hand. "No dancing."

Rawiri blinked.

"Kharis is under two prohibitions set by the palace's Oracle. One forbids her from dancing."

Rawiri frowned. "Is this why there's no dancing at the palace?"

Yuna smirked. "You catch on quickly. The other forbids her from entering open bodies of water."

"I was aware of the water prohibition. Prince Hala had alluded to it vaguely. Why must she stay away?"

Yuna removed invisible lint from her sleeve. "Ignorance would be my answer. It sneaks into everything."

Rawiri clenched his jaw. "Why keep it, then? Forgive me for being blunt, but it's an absurd prohibition."

"And I agree. I'm merely explaining."

He did his best to calm down.

"The night Kharis was born," Yuna said, "the Oracle had a vision and wrote part of it down: 'As she steps to dance with death on the battlefield, the fire maiden must not touch the waters of the pure.' We don't know what followed the word 'pure.' The Oracle died that night, leaving a long, unreadable scribble instead. The interpretation is that Kharis can't enter open bodies of water."

"I don't follow," he blurted out. "Why does this keep the sisters from dancing?"

Yuna flicked a hand. "Some believe she invites death when she dances, so no dancing."

Rawiri clenched his jaw, dragging a hand down his face. "What about the fire maiden part?"

Yuna studied him with a sharp look. "What have you been told about Kharis?"

"Actually... nothing, save for the water prohibition."

Yuna groaned, rubbing her forehead. He pursed his lips. *Was it a mistake to talk to this woman?*

"Do you know what a Djinnshirukh is?" she asked.

"I've overheard the term." He offered a small smile.

"The Djinnshirukh is the human vessel of a powerful fire demon. Kharis is the current Djinnshirukh; hence, the fire maiden."

An unpleasant fluttering stirred in his stomach.

"A thousand years ago," she said, "the king of the Akumi led his army, destroying everything in their path. The Forest Kin and Spirit Kin clans used their magic to defeat this army and seal the Akumi king's soul into the human king's son."

The hairs on his arms lifted.

"Since then, the ruling monarchs have selected a human vessel, and the Akumi king is resealed. The Djinnshirukh is always the child of a monarch, for true blood seals the spell. An adult chooses this duty and trains for it."

She gripped the armrests with force.

"Kharis's selection, however, turned the world upside down. Her mother sealed the Akumi king as she gave birth. A newborn became the vessel. There was no choice, no preparation, no training."

Rawiri gulped.

"Since fire and water are opposing elements in our creation story, keeping her away from open bodies of water became an extension of this belief."

Rawiri lowered his head, pondering Mahaluika's involvement. "Could Kharis summon fire?"

Yuna flicked her hand. "I hope she never does."

He lifted his gaze. "Why?"

"Fire summoning signals the beginning of the madness that afflicts every Djinnshirukh."

Rawiri's eyebrows shot up.

"Humans can't wield such magic, Rawiri. Eventually, their bodies wither, and their minds unravel. The

Djinnshirukh and their sheath, the Sorukhipa, are wards of the Regiazenka. They decide on them."

The conversation Kiwa had with Hröld at the picnic now had context. "So King Hröld holds no sway over his daughter?"

"Daughters." She emphasized the plural. "Kharis is the Djinnshirukh. Saya is the Sorukhipa. Kharis is the weapon. Saya is the sheath."

Rawiri felt dizzy.

She exhaled. "Hröld adores them, but all he can do is watch."

A cold drop of sweat rolled down his back. Everything now made sense.

"Were you not told any of this?" Yuna asked.

He shook his head slowly, waiting for his shock to abate. Within this context, he understood why the Regiazenka would never allow the girls to marry. If Kharis were this fire maiden, the water prohibition made sense, too, yet... *Tanganokai wants his child back.* Mahaluika, who never meddled in Tanganokai's affairs, warned Rawiri of the danger in fulfilling this mission. *Both gods want her returned. But why?*

"Only Princess Kharis is under these prohibitions," she clarified. "However, since one sister can't do it, allowing the other is unfair."

That knowledge lit an angry fire under him. "No sailing. No dancing. Anything else I should know?"

Yuna furrowed her brow. "Why must you know?"

Rawiri scoffed. "If I'm to be their tutor, I should. Otherwise, how could I plan lessons that would interest them? Learning only happens when the topics engage them. I could force-feed Kahurang's history, but that wouldn't foster learning. To encourage them, I must understand what engages them."

Yuna studied him. "You aren't like the other tutors."

"I hope not." It came out without thinking, and Rawiri

regretted his lapse of judgment. "My apologies. I spoke in haste."

She waved her hand, unfazed. "The tutors I'm familiar with were always quick to impress the Crown until they ran away, tail between their legs, frightened by the prospects of teaching the Djinnshirukh. You're the first to show a genuine interest in instructing *them*."

Yuna steepled her fingers. "Tell me. What would you consider the most challenging aspect of their education?" Her steely gaze felt like an arrow aimed at his head.

That challenge had a face and a name.

"Arjun Ghan," he confessed. "I'm concerned about his influence over them. I've seen how Saya stiffens at the sight of him. I've caught the hatred in Kharis's eyes."

"You're not wrong."

He exhaled, glad to have passed her test.

The monk rang a bell, and a monk entered the office. "Suri, please, could you bring tea?"

"Yes, Your Excellency." Suri closed the door behind her with a crisp nod.

Yuna crossed the room and opened the balcony doors. The translucent curtains billowed in the playful breeze. "The city noise can be useful sometimes, especially when no one else should listen to our conversation." She gestured to two overstuffed chairs.

Rawiri moved, sitting in one.

"As the Djinnshirukh," she said, "Kharis possesses extraordinary strength and speed, two of the four gifts the Akumi king bestows upon his vessel. The third is her remarkable ability to heal herself. I believe he grants these gifts for a simple reason: if one survives, so does the other. There is, however, a darker facet to this bond: the magic that awakens her fourth gift. It's the sign everyone fears."

"Why?"

Yuna straightened in her chair with a sharp inhale. "Kharis's fearless, prankish personality worries the

Regiazenka. The ministers view her as an unpredictable child—a dangerous liability. Add fire to the mix, and the result could be explosive. Saya has started her bleeding, and it is a matter of time before Kharis does. The Regiazenka is anxious as the coming-of-age ceremony approaches, not knowing what puberty entails for a female Djinnshirukh. Unlike former ones, who were adults, Kharis is a child—a wild card."

Rawiri sat back, his gaze wandering. "I didn't know any of this."

Yuna sighed, and that soft breath tugged at Rawiri's heart. Outside Yuna's door, Rawiri picked up the soft murmurs of conversations and monks shuffling past on their way to their stations.

"Palace staff aren't careful when speaking of the Djinnshirukh," Yuna said. "Kharis's stealth is extraordinary, which means she most likely has eavesdropped on the palace rumors, gossip, and chattering while hiding behind curtains and tapestries, within fake walls, under tables, inside armoires, and storage spaces. People fear her, Prince Rawiri, and she's acutely aware of it."

"Do you fear her?" Rawiri asked.

She glared at him, offended. "She's been under my care since birth, and Saya since she was two. I adore them with all my heart and will do the unspeakable to protect them." The fire in her eyes confirmed it. "What about you?"

A breath escaped him. As a child, Kharis had no choice in the matter and couldn't fully understand what people asked of her.

"I've seen nothing that tells me I should fear her." A surge of bile gathered in his gullet. "What happens to the former vessel?"

"They die."

Rawiri's stomach clenched.

"There have been exceptions regarding the lifespan," Yuna added. "Her mother, Queen Aghuti, was the

Djinnshirukh for twenty years. The unraveling didn't touch her as it did the others." She read the questions on his face. "The queen never displayed symptoms of madness. She became the Djinnshirukh *after* marrying Hröld."

Rawiri shook his head, perplexed. "But I thought the Djinnshirukh couldn't marry—"

"That's incorrect." Her voice had a hard edge. "'Shouldn't marry' is more accurate. The Regiazenka refuses to compete for influence with a vessel's lover."

The sounds of merchants and traders drifted through the balcony doors, their lively yet distant chatter carrying a melodic cadence as they peddled their wares. The creaking of wooden wheels and the occasional clatter of a horse-drawn carriage filled the office's silence.

"Aghuti's was a resealment that went wrong. That's how the monks explained it. She broke every expectation about the Djinnshirukh as if that magic couldn't taint her."

Her gaze grew distant.

"Ironically, childbirth was her undoing." Yuna pressed a hand over her heart. "She was extraordinary, and her death came unexpectedly. Aghuti had selected Hala as the next vessel and oversaw his training, yet fate played with us. Kharis became the Djinnshirukh the moment she took her first breath."

Hala was the appointed vessel? That he didn't expect.

Kharis possessed Tanganokai's stamp and Mahaluika's blessing. She wasn't a god's toy but much more—*the child of a god.* The hair on the back of his neck stood on end. But something else bothered him. A Zahari woman was providing him with crucial information, and the Zahari never did anything for free.

There has to be a catch. "Why are you telling me this?"

"So you may understand what I'm about to ask of you."

And there it was—the catch.

CHAPTER 29
THE CATCH

Rawiri leaned back in his chair, speechless, a sudden coldness expanding in his chest.

"The Kahurangi visit took the palace a year to organize," Yuna said. "In that time, I've done my best to check on the man who would become tutor to my girls. The palace has spies everywhere, but my spies are equally skilled, if not more. I've been studying you to ensure you're the one."

Rawiri gaped, brows raised. "The... one?"

Her smile turned dangerous. "A prophetess once foretold of one who would come from a land birthed in fire and ice, destined to claim the Child of Prophecy."

His breath caught.

Yuna recited the prophecy.

"From a realm born in flames and ice's embrace,
One shall rise with a journey to trace.
He'll walk the path foretold by divine breath
to claim the one born of godly grace.
A Child of Prophecy, by gods, adored.
The destined heir's a story to resolve.

In hands that hold both frost and blaze,
The Child of Prophecy shall meet their fate.”

Rawiri felt dizzy, the world tilting beneath his feet.

Yuna's gaze was intense. “I've been told that you're one of Kahurang's *toa*, blessed by your ocean god since birth. You're the man mentioned in the divination, the one ‘who walks the path foretold by divine breath.'”

Goose bumps prickled across his skin.

“As the Djinnshirukh, Kharis is at a dangerous crossroads,” Yuna said. “She possesses endless empathy, with a heart so vast the universe fits inside it. Arjun is the complete opposite—bitter and dark. A void from which light can't escape. Worse, he has craved the Djinnshirukh role since he was young, but now it's out of his grasp. Given he can't have it, he'll destroy her. And when he does, the Djinnshirukh cycle will begin anew. Then he'll step forward to become it.”

Rawiri stiffened—seething and flexing his fingers. *Is this why Tanganokai demands her return? Is this why Mahaluika warned me? Are they trying to protect her?*

“What about Saya?” he asked. “You said she's the sheath.”

“While the ruling monarch selects the Djinnshirukh, the gods select the Sorukhipa. Our task is to find them. Usually, there are signs and omens, and monks often locate them quickly. In Saya's case, it took two long years, as if the gods wanted her hidden.”

Rawiri cocked his head again. “Why was it important to find her?”

“Because the Sorukhipa is the Djinnshirukh's eternal companion, housing the other half of the Spirit Kin queen's soul. The Ancient Writings tell us that the connection between the Djinnshirukh and the Sorukhipa is a permanent bond.”

“Is that why they can't marry?”

Yuna hummed. “Nothing would stop Saya from finding a

partner. However, the Regiazenka fears that the Sorukhipa could lose their focus on their task to guard the Djinnshirukh."

"What about Kharis?" He had to ask. "Can she get married?"

Hope burned bright in his heart, thinking of Taika.

"That's more difficult to answer. The Regiazenka ministers view her as a formidable weapon, so why would they relinquish their control over such power? Besides, we know that female Djinnshirukh have passed some of their abilities to their offspring with dire consequences since their children lack the protection the Spirit Kin queen bestows on the vessel."

"But Queen Aghuti was the Djinnshirukh. She had five—"

"Six, actually. The fifth birth was stillborn. If you listen to the palace's whispers, you'll learn many believe the baby died because the Akumi king collected on the queen's debt."

Rawiri sank back into his chair, his heart shattering into pieces. Kharis's fate cast a dark shadow over her future, and the prospect of Saya moving on with another Djinnshirukh added a poignant layer. A storm of thoughts blew through his mind.

"Why are you telling me this?"

Yuna smiled enigmatically. "Because I want you to take them far from the Ghak."

A jumble of words tangled in his head. "Huh?"

"What about my words is confusing?" she said. "Take them to Kahurang, Aráfura, or Walangii. Make it the Ghasmanoör Chasm. I don't care where, as long as they are away from a man who doesn't wish them well."

"Arjun Ghan," Rawiri uttered that name like a wretched curse—a word that rolled off his tongue with the bitter taste of bile.

"Then we understand each other." Yuna gave him a lingering look. "Can I count on your help?"

Rawiri drew in a slow breath. He understood the peril lurking in Yuna's dangerous plea. Standing at a junction, he weighed his options. Tanganokai's shadow cursed one path. The other promised to shield Kharis from harm but turned them into fugitives.

The prince took a deep breath, seeking the clarity he needed. Before him lay the only choice he would contemplate, bathed in hues of sapphire and silver. He would protect the girls at all costs.

"Yes," he said. "You have it."

"Good. I'll do anything to free my darlings from their enslavement, and you were the last piece I needed—the one who shall rise with a journey to trace."

The knocks on the door brought him back. Suri came in, balancing a tray.

"Ah! There she is," Yuna said. "I hope you enjoy tea, Prince Rawiri. I made this batch from a unique blend."

Rawiri's heart galloped like a stallion, his head spinning with the whirlwind of thoughts. He'd come to tutor the girls and had just agreed to kidnap them on Yuna's behalf. Tanganokai, who wanted his child back, would curse him, and Mahaluika would join her brother's retribution. He would become a fugitive of men and gods, and to avoid a war with Zahar, his brother would have to disown him or, worse, kill him.

Have I gone mad?

CHAPTER 30
THE LESSON

Rawiri left the Academy and marched back to the palace, still in a daze. He'd agreed to take the girls out of Zahar, and Yuna had plans for that. Tanganokai had tasked him with returning his child. Rawiri had no intention of doing it.

He took a long breath and headed to the girls' wing for their lessons. *No dancing.* This prohibition bothered him the most. *How am I to teach them our lore without it?* Dance, to the Kahurangi, was as essential as breathing.

"Your Highness?"

Rawiri jumped out of his rumination and turned his head.

"Is everything all right?" General Tawhiri asked.

Rawiri stared at the man, unsure how to answer. "I'm trying to solve a puzzle."

"Could I be of any help?"

Rawiri pursed his lips. "How do I teach dancing without dancing?"

Tawhiri tapped his chin as he marched beside the prince. "Defense arts? The foot-and-arm work required in hand-to-hand combat strikes me as similar. Teach one, and you're training on the other."

Rawiri halted. "You're brilliant." He clapped Tawhiri's back. "Absolutely brilliant."

The gray clouds in his mind dispersed, and he returned to his thoughts. This time, his gaze was clear, and he flashed a smile the rest of the way.

The doors opened, and a beaming Rawiri stepped in. "Your Highnesses, may the earth and sun bless you."

"May they sustain us," the girls chorused.

Kharis raised an eyebrow, eyes squinting. Saya smiled. "Why so happy, Your Highness?"

"Ah!" Rawiri rubbed his hands in anticipation. "I have a special lesson for you today, but we need space."

"How much?" Kharis narrowed her gaze, her hands resting on her hips.

"What about the southern garden?" Saya asked.

"Is it spacious enough to allow for movement?"

"What sort of movement?" Kharis's sharp eyes remained on Rawiri.

"Kahurangi defense arts."

Kharis kept her frown but cocked her head, perplexed. "No language arts?"

"Oh, we'll do that *and* defense arts."

"Huh?" Kharis stared at Saya with a skeptical look. "How do you intend to teach us both?"

Rawiri couldn't help his raucous laughter. "The 'how' will also be part of today's lesson."

⁂

High General Arjun Ghan found them in the southern garden, as the servants had shared. He lingered by the ornate wrought-iron gate, displeased with the change in location or with having to find them. Wasting time aggravated him. That a Kahurangi had caused it intensified the burning in his stomach. His eyes landed on Princess Kharis, and endless envy swallowed him. *That child has no business being the Djinnshirukh. None.*

He struggled to contain his rising ire, nettled endlessly by anger's insistent, sharp finger.

The sisters followed the Kahurangi prince's instructions, placing their feet and arms in a particular flow while he repeated something in his language. *Are they dancing?* That thought angered him. *That's it.* He threw the gate open and stormed in without a care for the flowers he was stepping on, directing a scowling gaze at Rawiri.

The Kahurangi guards, who had maintained their positions in the garden, swiftly assumed their battle-ready stances when they spotted the high general marching in.

Ghan ground his teeth. *This is Zahar. Why are they providing protection here?* He strode forward, nostrils flaring. "What are you doing?" His voice surged.

Rawiri stopped and turned. The confusion on his face evaporated when he realized why the high general was in the garden. "My lesson!" He bowed with an apologetic look. "My heartfelt apologies. I lost track of time."

"Obviously." Ghan's tone was harsh, and the sisters flinched, glancing at each other. "Your lesson ended a while back. You should've brought the girls to me." He threw Kharis and Saya a glare before refocusing on Rawiri. "As I asked, what are you doing?"

Rawiri's smile didn't falter. "The Kahurangi alphabet carries sound and numerical value. We also use it as a form of musical notation. So, to teach them the alphabet, I'm using movement—"

"They're under a dance prohibition."

"It's not dancing, but defense arts—"

"I teach them that," Ghan nearly shouted. His hands fisted, aching to punch Rawiri's face. "Your lesson has ended." He faced the girls with fire in his eyes. "And you are late for your lessons *with me.* Get going."

Wide-eyed, Kharis and Saya curtsied and dashed out of the garden. Ghan's escort quickly followed the princesses.

"Sticking to your schedule," Ghan hissed, "and keeping your nose out of what doesn't concern you is best." He leaned in closer, teeth bared. "Don't forget where you are."

Rawiri straightened his back, limbering his shoulders. "Providing them with the instruction King Hröld requested is *my concern*. However, if you disagree, we could discuss it with His Majesty."

Ghan gritted his teeth in response to the challenge. He hated dares with every fiber of his being.

Rawiri remained in place, wearing his annoying smile. His bodyguards settled by his side, all of them glowering. Provoked and frustrated, Ghan raised his chin, clicked his tongue, and left the garden. *You may be under Hröld's protection now, but I'll get you soon enough.*

CHAPTER 31

THE FIRE DANCE

Morning rain whispered against the window in Rawiri's sitting room. Kharis blew warm air, fogging the glass. The Royal Archives presented a puzzle: how to find an unbinding spell in the vast repository. Her midnight forays were unsuccessful, so it was time to ask an archivist. *Easier said than done.* Convincing Rawiri to take her would have to be her next step.

Deep in concentration, Saya stuck the tip of her tongue out as she completed the final strokes of her sentence, her quill moving gracefully over the parchment.

Kharis heaved a long sigh. "Why did it have to rain today?" The angry morning sky dumped water on the world. "It would've been nice to visit the Royal Archives and—"

"Young lady," Rawiri said from across the room, "you must finish your assignment."

Kharis grunted and slumped in her chair.

"Stop shaking the table." Saya glared at her.

"I can't help it." She threw her arms up. "Rawiri demands that I complete the translation."

"Girls, enough arguing." He closed his book and walked

over to them, taking Saya's paper to study it. A grin split his face. "Excellent job."

Saya smirked at her sister. Kharis wrinkled her nose in response.

"I want to see yours, Teppe."

Kharis harrumphed and handed her sheet over. He cupped his chin, reading her work carefully. His lengthy pause made her nervous. She fidgeted until she couldn't take it anymore.

"Well?" she asked, rubbing the back of her neck.

"I'm impressed with your work."

Kharis's eyelids snapped open. No tutor had ever complimented her work. Bright sunlight pierced through the dark clouds in her mind, and its warmth surged forth to envelop her. "You are?"

Rawiri nodded. "Very."

Kharis's chest swelled with satisfaction. "I used what you taught me—how the letters have a name that shapes their sound and directs the hands and body."

"Ah! So, you were paying attention."

"I always do."

He raised an eyebrow at her.

Kharis scratched her cheek. "Most of the time."

"You both did well," he said, "and soon enough, I'll teach the lessons in Kahurangi."

"Will you teach us curses?" Kharis asked. "You know. The *peke* one."

Saya stiffened.

"I won't," he said. "I'll teach you the language; what you do with it is your decision."

A giddy rush bubbled up inside Kharis. She could hardly contain her grin as she leaped to her feet, the thrill of possibilities electrifying her mind. Finger-pointing at an invisible person, she said, "May you fall down the stairs and hit your head."

"May the food make you vomit," Saya said amid titters.

"Oh, wait." Kharis's eyes widened with a gleam of mischief. "May a wasp sting your bottom so badly you can't sit for a week."

"It's hot," Saya said.

"*Sayaaa*, that's not a curse."

"No, it's sweltering." Saya got up, fanning her face with both hands.

Kharis, realizing her sister was right, eyed the door and gasped. "Rawiri?" She gestured to the smoke coming from under it.

He rushed toward it to open it and recoiled in pain, snatching his hand away from the metal handle.

"Get to the window. Now." His face had turned ashen. He pushed it open and peeked out, rain quickly plastering his hair to his face. The drop was dizzying, and the deluge made it dangerous to descend.

Soldiers sounded the alarm, a calamity of bells and trumpets blaring from outside the door. The pungent scent of smoke choked the air, acrid tendrils snaking into the room.

"Let's tie the curtains," Rawiri shouted his command. "We'll use them to reach the lower windows."

They got to work, grabbing and knotting curtains and sheets as fast as possible.

"Khiri, grab that tablecloth." When Kharis didn't bring it to her, Saya turned around. "Khiri?"

Across the room, Kharis watched as plumes of fire slithered through the ceiling in a mesmerizing display of oranges and reds, their heat soon overwhelming the chamber. Glowing embers appeared on the doors, and their faint crackle could be heard as they spread through the wooden surfaces, swiftly growing in size.

Panic gripped Saya. "Khiri, no. Get back!"

The warning didn't come fast enough. The doors exploded, and a dense cloud of fire slammed into the room. Rawiri wrapped his body over Saya, bracing for it, but nothing happened. Their clothes didn't get singed. Their skin didn't burn.

Saya wriggled out of Rawiri's shielding hold.

Kharis, still standing on the same spot, had raised her arms as if commanding the fire to stop advancing. The flames swayed like snakes, as if awaiting her instructions. They didn't appear to be burning the chambers anymore. The blaze sizzled and crackled all around Kharis as if whispering to her. Her sister seemed to control it, and that realization sent an icy shudder across Saya's skin.

Fire summoning. The fourth gift.

Kharis swayed her body, and the flames twirled with her to the rhythm of a melody only Kharis could hear.

Blessed Mother, she's dancing! Her fingers curled into her sleeves as the heat licked higher.

The fire yielded to Kharis's will, swirling as if she presided over it. The Djinnshirukh hopped and spun as fiery arms twirled with her like a willing partner in an enthralling dance. Her steps were graceful, and the flames embraced her as if full of affection for this child.

Saya couldn't stop watching.

Energy pulsed through the chamber in rhythmic waves, clearing the smoky air. A sudden gust burst all the windows open at once, letting rain pour in and soak the rugs. Outside, the wind howled and whistled through the dark.

Saya felt a shift in the air.

A swell of magic flooded the room. Sounds softened, their sharp edges blunted into something warm and melodic. Colors brightened, each one wrapped in a luminous glow that made them shimmer with life. The air grew lighter, sweeter, carrying a scent that reminded Saya of oranges mingled with sea salt.

Harmony, long hidden within the blaze, surged

outward, filling every corner of the space. And the Sorukhipa heard it at last: the music to which Kharis danced. Intricate, breathtaking—a melody woven with layers of sound, each building on the next.

Saya's tension melted. Her worries dissolved. She wanted the moment to last so she could savor this vision of movement and color.

Why can't she dance?

She shook her head slowly.

Why?

Saya's entire being thrummed to this sublime energy.

❧

Kharis twirled with open arms, given entirely to the experience—gone from the world.

"Hello?"

A silvery male voice caressed her mind. She halted and opened her eyes in slow blinks. The world had vanished, and darkness encased her instead. A tall, flickering flame caught her attention. That same flame had spoken to her at the Royal Archives. It stood a few paces away. The figure concealed in it assessed her.

"Aren't you afraid of me?" he asked, sounding perplexed.

Kharis shook her head.

"What are you doing?" he asked, his voice resonant.

"This music." She closed her eyes, allowing the rich, sultry melody to caress her senses like a velvet blanket. "It's magical." The ground beneath her feet provided little resistance when she spun around. Then she halted, a sudden ache tugging at her heart. "Nobody allows me to dance. Are you going to stop me as well?"

There was a long pause. A thoughtful consideration. *"No."*

"Good." A thrill made her heart beat faster. "Then dance with me."

And so, without a care, the Djinnshirukh resumed her graceful stepping. The flickering flame exploded into a kaleidoscope of crimson, gold, and silver.

That warm embrace confirmed she now had a dancing partner.

Rawiri shook his head. "What's going on?"

"It's the Akumi king," Saya stammered. "He's taking over."

Her protective instinct kicked in, and magic coursed through her veins like molten gold. Fine golden threads appeared before her, delicate like cobwebs. Mesmerized, Saya reached out hesitantly, her fingers barely brushing against the filaments. They pulsed in response to her touch, and for a tiny moment, the world stopped moving.

Startled, Saya withdrew her hand. Was this some trick of the light, or something extraordinary? And yet, a sense of the familiar spoke to her.

Hoping for the best, she seized a fistful. The flames halted their sputtering and flickering. Raindrops suspended mid-air. Rawiri was frozen in place. All motion and sound in the room had come to a standstill.

Saya, the Sorukhipa, had stopped the flow of time.

She released a massive wave of magic that shimmered through this expansive web, meeting Kharis's magic head-on. The blast rattled the walls and shattered the windows. It sucked the air out of the room, extinguishing all the flames. In its wake, gold dust floated in the air.

Saya let go of the threads, and time returned its forward journey.

Rawiri, as if awakened from a dream, seized Saya and Kharis by their waists, hoisting them like sacks of rice on each hip, and swiftly fled the chamber.

CHAPTER 32

THE APPROACHING STORM

When Hala walked in with Jordha, what he saw left him speechless.

The ceiling and flooring were charred, the walls blackened. The shattered glass from the windows lay scattered everywhere. In the intense heat, pieces had melted into the burnt floor. Realizing he'd stopped breathing, he inhaled, the lingering scent stinging his throat.

"Who did this?" He kicked a piece of rubble, his fingers flexing.

Jordha scratched his beard, turning around slowly. "Hard to tell. My men are questioning the servants and guards on duty. However, given how the fire moved, this had to be the epicenter." He gestured to what was left of the entryway—now a gaping hole in the wall. "Someone set the fire outside this door."

"How?" Hala took a few more steps into the chamber, fisted hands quivering. "Who did this without being seen by the number of sentries on this wing? Jordha, the girls were in a *well-guarded* palace wing." He rubbed his forehead as he took in the destruction. "This was the work of more than one person."

"We don't know that."

Hala huffed, the burning in his stomach flaring painfully, and gestured to the chamber. "Convince me otherwise. Tell me how the sentries saw no one."

"Let's think logically." Jordha raised his hands in a gesture of appeasement, and this irked Hala. "The first fact in the investigation is the most telling." He closed the distance. "The Djinnshirukh *was* in this room."

Hala's body tensed. "What are you suggesting?" The pause between words hid an old fear.

"In the annals of Djinnshirukh history," Jordha said, "we've had instances of vessels with fire-summoning power. The individuals who reached this stage were few, but historians have documented these cases and—"

"You believe my sister started the fire." Hala swallowed hard.

Jordha glanced away. "If she did, and I hope that's not the case, the news isn't good, cousin." He scraped charcoal off the floor with his boot. "Fire summoning announces the onset of the madness."

Hala's pulse spiked, sending a jolt through his body. This could not be happening.

"If Kharis did this," Jordha said, "it means she's unraveling."

That word stabbed his chest. "She's twelve, Jordha. A child."

An uneasy pause fell over them. Jordha exhaled, lowering his head.

"Listen. I don't have proof that she did this. And I lack proof that she didn't." He gave the chamber a long, assessing look. "Given the palace's gossip machinery, we must come up with some explanation swiftly, or the Regiazenka will decide for us."

Hala groaned loudly. "The Regiazenka mustn't reach the

same conclusion you have." Drops of sweat rolled down his back. "They just can't."

Everything was falling apart. Everything.

"Hala, calm down."

"How?" he shouted. "My father remains silent on naming the Djinnshirukh's replacement. For all I know, it could still be me. If the Regiazenka suspects she started this fire—"

"We'll bury any proof," Jordha whispered, squeezing Hala's shoulder, "and call it 'an unfortunate accident.'"

A tense quiet. "Will the Regiazenka believe that?"

Jordha gave the room another glance. "I'll leave the convincing to you. My job is to find evidence that this was a stroke of bad luck." He gave Hala a quick, tight smile. "If the Djinnshirukh did start the fire, no one will ever know."

Hala grumbled, pressing a hand to his forehead, not looking forward to the task ahead.

"However." Jordha narrowed his gaze. "If Kharis didn't do this, your sisters are in danger."

Hala grimaced, taking the damage once more. "Find me a culprit, but continue the investigation. Quietly."

"Will do." Jordha made to leave but halted, still for a moment, then turned around.

"What is it?" Hala asked.

Jordha rubbed his mouth, lost on a thought. "What if someone were interested in starting a conflict with Kahurang?"

Hala's eyes widened. He'd forgotten these were Rawiri's chambers. "An assassination attempt?" He lowered his voice. "Ghan?"

Jordha rolled on the ball of his feet, hands in his pockets. "Why not? Everyone knows he despises the Kahurangi prince. His opinions on the subject have been *very* public."

Hala crossed his arms, fingers tapping against his biceps. "It could convince my father."

"It could," Jordha agreed.

Did Kharis start the fire? Jordha believes she did. Hala kicked another sizable chunk of burnt debris.

A bitter chucke escaped him. "Fire summoning displays always start small," he said. "Inconsequential accidents that signal the awakening magic: flickering candles, exceedingly hot tea, a flaming quill, stray embers that appear out of nowhere. She hasn't displayed any of it."

He drew a slow, steady breath, grasping at whatever little hope he could.

"She would never jeopardize Saya's safety," he said. "Pranks are one thing, but starting a fire? She'd never put Saya in harm's way."

Jordha didn't comment.

"Besides, all three shared the same story: the fire began outside the door. The charring patterns confirm this. The scenario that makes the most sense implicates Ghan, who loathes Rawiri... But Ghan would never place the girls in danger." A wayward thought tensed his muscles. "Or would he?"

Jordha shrugged. "I believe him capable of anything."

"If Khiri didn't do it," Hala said, "they escaped by the Blessed Mother's grace." He rubbed his temples to forestall a wicked headache. "We must appease the Kahurangi, who believe this was deliberate arson against their prince. Their diplomats have been up in arms about it. And I must convince the Regiazenka that this was an accident."

Jordha bowed, sporting a tight smile, and left.

"Ghan..." Hala stopped. "What if someone else did this?"

CHAPTER 33

THE DRAWBRIDGE

"How did you arrange for this, Rawiri?" Kharis blurted, bouncing on the balls of her feet, unable to keep still.

He gave her a pointed glance. "It's Your Highness—"

"Saya, look!" Kharis ran toward the canal and leaned over the barrier to check the water flow and the gates that controlled its level. "This is so amazing!" she shouted.

Saya offered Rawiri an apologetic smile. "She sort of dislikes titles and authority."

"I can see that."

"Don't take it personally, Your Highness."

He laughed heartily, brimming with pure joy. "Call me Rawiri. Your sister does." He tilted his head at Kharis, who was jumping up and down, all grin and sparkling eyes, waving her arms at them, beckoning them to join her.

"Impatience should be her middle name." Saya sighed and walked over.

Still apprehensive after the accidental fire three weeks ago, Rawiri pondered how the blaze had started. Had it not been for Kharis's magic, they would've died.

Saya had called it fire summoning.

"No one must know," she'd told him. The trembling in her voice, the begging tone she'd used, haunted him. She had pleaded for his silence, holding back tears. The color had returned to her face when he had promised to keep her secret.

Rawiri looked behind him. His Kahurangi warriors had spread over the plaza's perimeter, keeping tabs on the crowd. Zahari soldiers weren't far. Their distance from the three royals gave them the illusion of being on their own. His eyes moved to the nearby roofs where archers were stationed. *The security is excessive.*

Three weeks ago, a fire had almost claimed their lives. After a thorough investigation, the palace had deemed it an unfortunate accident. A rusty torch bracket had given way, and wall tapestries had caught fire when the torch had fallen. Thankfully, no one had been injured or died. Carpenters and stonemasons were already working on rebuilding the affected chambers. The palace had relocated Rawiri to different quarters, and normalcy had resumed, except that the protection for the sisters intensified. That gave him pause.

Leaning against the canal's railing, Kharis and Saya eagerly chatted. *If they were my daughters, I would be extreme with their protection.*

He suspected the fire had been intentional and that the Crown was hiding something. *But what?* The imposing palace, a behemoth of alabaster, marble, and white granite was visible from this neighborhood. He grunted. *That place is disturbing.*

"Rawiri!" Kharis's shout pushed him out of his rumination, her enchanting excitement hard to ignore.

He exhaled, letting all worries leave his body, and closed the distance. "How do you like it so far?"

Kharis wrapped her arms around him. "Thank you." Her head tipped back, a smile lighting her face.

Saya hugged him, too. "Thank you, Your Highness."

Warmth bloomed in his chest. The sisters had carved a place deep within his heart. They were no longer merely his charges; they'd transformed into the children Tanganokai had denied him.

"You should be thanking the Regiazenka," he said. "They allowed it."

"Perhaps," Kharis said, "but you interceded on our behalf." An ocean filled with silver and sapphire gazed at him. "A lake's surface ripples when one throws a rock into it. Without it, the water stays still."

"So I'm a rock, eh?" He dropped to one knee and held Kharis's hand. "When did you become so wise?"

"I learn from the best." She flashed him a grin. "Will you ever teach me to sail?"

The prince tilted his head back and laughed. "Ah, Teppe. You're a handful."

Kharis frowned, puffing her cheeks.

Saya poked one. "You are, and don't deny it."

Kharis sniffed. "Two against one isn't fair." She faced him, eyes overly bright. "My question still stands. Will you?" she asked. "Teach me how to sail?"

Rawiri tightened his hold on her hand. "If you wish to learn, I'll find a way." With a wink and a nod, he got up. "Come. The drawbridge isn't far. The crown prince has arranged for us to visit the control tower and for the engineer to show you how it works." He studied the sky for a moment to check the time of day. "He may even allow you to pull a lever or two. A ship will be approaching soon."

Saya's eyes brightened at the thought. "We can do that?"

"Of course. It's a great opportunity to learn and view the mechanisms in action. I have a feeling you'll be pleasantly surprised."

Saya beamed, thrilled to no end.

"Will there be a test?" Kharis eyed him with suspicion.

"Three!" He thundered as he led the princesses down the street.

&

Yuna was about to start her rounds with a new group of apprentices when she caught the eye of a bhiksun in maroon robes waiting for her.

She walked over to the older man. The bhiksun pressed his palms together, bowed, and lowered his hood. "They are visiting Stoneberry Bridge. A sizable Zahari and Kahurangi escort is with them."

"And the girls?" Yuna asked.

"The field trip thrills them, and both are in high spirits."

Yuna smiled, satisfied. "Anything else?"

The man shook his head. "Everything is proceeding as planned."

"Thank you for keeping an eye out for them."

"It's an honor to serve you, Your Highness."

Yuna frowned at the title, but the monk bowed and walked away.

How she wished to see the girls' faces.

Stoneberry Bridge was a good start. With time, the allowable radius would increase, extending to the docks—inching its way to the goal where freedom awaited. Yuna and Rawiri would earn the Regiazenka's trust, and before they knew it, Rawiri and the girls would be so far away that no one would ever find them, least of all Arjun Ghan.

She beamed at the group before her.

"Good morning, everyone. Today, you'll care for actual patients, and I'll assess your knowledge and grit. Follow me."

Yuna marched, floating high on hope. *Today was Stoneberry Bridge.* That thought washed over her as she led her students onto the floor.

CHAPTER 34

THE PRINCE AND THE GENERAL

Rawiri couldn't contain his grin as he watched the sisters.

Despite her efforts to concentrate on Ghan's training lesson, Kharis wouldn't stop discussing the field trip, even when earning a disapproving frown from the high general. Every detail of the drawbridge, from its intricate cogs and wheels to the giant chains and how a tall sailship had glided gracefully across, sprinkled her animated conversation with Saya.

"It was magic," Kharis said.

"It was science," Saya countered.

"Girls," Ghan warned.

They returned to their drills, but the hand of hope caressed the sisters' faces, and that was enchantment enough for Rawiri.

He sat across the room, near the entry doors, following their training. Occasionally, Kharis turned and smiled at him—her eyes ablaze with an unfettered grin. The somber clouds that had haunted her after the fire were gone.

Today, the girls were part of a group of ten children training with wooden swords. The drills they undertook had been crafted to strengthen their arms and wrists while focusing on enhancing speed and agility. The kids, aged twelve to fifteen, were the offspring of noble families—future zaldunak of the Zahari armies enjoying the honor of training under High General Arjun Ghan. His commands bounced against the walls, his staff striking the floor with a rhythmic beat perfectly synchronized with the children's progress through the various sword positions.

Here and there, the general helped a kid with form or posture.

"Keep the sword up; don't lower it," he instructed one, lifting the child's elbow to demonstrate proper placement.

"Stance, stance. Maintain your stance," he reminded the others.

On this day, Ghan ignored Rawiri's presence, moving around as if he weren't there. Ghan directed no scowls or veiled comments his way. Rawiri frowned at the unexpected pleasantry and kept his guard up as he jotted down ideas on what to teach the girls next. *Metallurgy would interest them. We could first visit the palace's blacksmiths' stations.* He recalled seeing a few zenka forgers past the eastern section of the Zahar-Homa. *The glass blowers weren't far.*

It would also be a test. *If we can leave the Zahar-Regia and enter the city proper...* The imposed radius was increasing. The pace was glacial and deliberate, but with patience, the docks would be within his reach.

He closed his notebook and studied how the sisters sparred. They moved well, deflecting and attacking, equally matched in skill, even when one was taller than the other. Saya was precise and confident. Kharis shifted swiftly, moving in bursts like a hummingbird, bold with her assaults.

Kharis is the weapon. Saya is the sheath.

That thought made him wonder.

Kharis's speed and strength shone through in her moves. He found it odd that Ghan didn't train her with this in mind—that he muted her training. *Perhaps to protect the other children?* That made sense, but it wasted her talent.

How does Saya turn Kharis's power off?

Were they trained to be this way, or did their roles grant them this instinctive ability? He knew that the Akumi king gave Kharis strength and speed, but what power did Saya have? He returned to his memories of when the fire had engulfed his chambers. It appeared Kharis had stopped it from advancing. Then he blinked, and the blaze was gone. *Did Teppe do this? Or did Saya do it?*

Saya had to be endowed if she was the Djinnshirukh's sheath. *But what could it be?* He made a mental note to ask Yuna.

Two shadows standing behind the door caught his attention. King Hröld and Crown Prince Hala spied on the kids before protocol stopped the training. Like him, they were also assessing the girls' progress.

Clutching his notebook, Rawiri rose to greet them. "Blessed be the earth and sun, Your Majesty, Highness."

"May they sustain us," Hröld said, sporting a guilty grin. "We're waiting for an opportunity to enter the room."

Hala's brow had creased, narrowed eyes fixed on his sisters. "What's your assessment?"

Rawiri glanced back. "The princesses are agile and quick in their responses. Their defense arts class is paying off." It sounded more like a question, and he regretted the intonation.

Hala arched an eyebrow.

Rawiri offered a tight-lipped smile. *He doesn't miss a thing.* He had to be more careful around him. "I'm not an expert on Zahari technique," he said. "The training is slightly different from what we do in Kahurang. The princesses are adept with weaponry but should learn to defend themselves without them."

Hröld studied the hall. "What would you suggest?"

"In Kahurang, we teach our children hand-to-hand combat, on top of blade work, spear, and bow."

Hala pursed his lips. "Hand-to-hand combat?"

"And you teach it to your children?" Hröld's brows furrowed, then released. "Why?"

"To bring an enemy down when weapons aren't available," Rawiri said. "The training leads to enhanced mental toughness, increased range of motion, discipline, and control when under attack."

"Discipline and control." Hröld's gaze focused inward as if he were letting those words sink in before he shifted his attention to Hala. It was a subtle gesture—a silent conversation—and it piqued Rawiri's curiosity, for the quick exchange between father and son expressed more than mere interest. "I would enjoy seeing a demonstration of this art," Hröld said, throwing Kharis a glimpse.

Rawiri understood.

"I'll work with the crown prince to arrange it," he said.

"We would appreciate it." After a polite nod, Hröld entered the training room.

Upon a loud command, everybody turned and saluted the king—right fist to the chest, right foot stomping the ground.

"Father!" Kharis ran and wrapped her arms around him. "Look, I'm getting stronger." Proud, she flexed her arms, muscles tightening beneath the skin.

Hröld's eyes sparkled when he gazed at his daughters, his love for them evident.

"How come you are here?" Kharis asked.

Hröld tilted his head. "Do I need a reason to fetch my children?"

Kharis scratched her cheek. "No...?"

"Good. I'm glad to know." The king chuckled. "Let's go, then. Dinner awaits." Hröld held his daughters' hands, gave Ghan a quick nod, and they exited the training room.

Once in the hallway, Kharis stopped and spun. "Rawiri, come!"

"Young lady, you shall address him as His Highness."

Kharis lowered her head. "Yes, Father." She eyed Rawiri over her wrinkled forehead. "My apologies, Prince Rawiri."

Hröld heaved a sigh, resigned to this child. "Please, join us for dinner." It was an honest and heartfelt invitation—a genuine expression of gratitude.

Rawiri assented with a nod. "It would be an honor."

"Where might you go next?" the king asked.

"Today's outing to Stoneberry Bridge was a success," Rawiri remarked. "The princesses behaved admirably and were fully engaged in the lessons and demonstrations. The Royal Library springs to mind as the next place to visit."

"The Library's architecture is astonishing," Hala said. "And the rotunda's art is unparalleled."

"Could we go?" Saya asked, her eyes pleading with her father.

"Exemplary behavior deserves exemplary rewards," Hröld said, his gaze regal, his chin high. "Since the visit to Stoneberry Bridge went well, Prince Rawiri may take you."

"Yes!" Kharis's loud victory cry burst through the corridor.

❧

Ghan stood by the door, watching them walk away. Aghet, who settled behind him, whispered, "So, *that* prince gets to have dinner with them?"

The high general gritted his teeth. "Tell me, Aghet, how do we get rid of him?"

"Ah!" The ghost of a smile warmed Ghan's nape. "I have a gift for you."

Ghan craned his neck toward him, curious.

"A common thief, locked deep in the dungeons, with

interesting information to share in exchange for his life." A low sigh blew air into Ghan's ear. "Such a predictable fool."

"And?"

Aghet hummed seductively. "I have three words for you."

Ghan returned his gaze to the hallway. "Go on."

"Silver." Aghet's warm breath tickled Ghan's ear. "Moon." He nipped the earlobe. "Festival."

Ghan's brow furrowed, confused. "The Silver Moon Festival?"

Aghet nodded slowly.

"That's in six weeks," Ghan griped.

"Indeed." Aghet rested his chin on Ghan's shoulder. "And it gives us the time to plan and be ready."

"Why should I care?"

Aghet's voice turned sultry. "Because soon enough, what you want will be yours, and this festival is the opportunity you've been seeking."

Ghan's eyes widened. "The Kahurangi prince?"

"And the Djinnshirukh."

Ghan grinned wickedly. "Care to help me interrogate the prisoner after this?"

Aghet's voice deepened. "I can't wait."

CHAPTER 35

THE GUEST

Rawiri inhaled deeply, relishing the fragrant aromas that lingered in the gentle morning breeze—the sweet scents of primrose, peonies, and daffodils.

Birds chirped, flocking from tree to tree with energetic determination. Squirrels chattered playfully as they chased each other. New leaves were budding everywhere, replacing winter's gray with a dizzying array of green—light, dark, and everything in between. Flowers bloomed because competing for attention was something nature did well.

And with spring came the princesses' coming-of-age ceremony, a lovely celebration for the sisters.

The ritual is simple, Rawiri noted. The girls, now thirteen years old, chanted passages from their sacred book. A monk spoke of the transition from childhood to adulthood, wishing the sisters endless blessings colored by ancient wisdom. When the last benediction ended, the guests pelted the girls with aljaicin—symbolic wishes for a sweet life.

An odd yet endearing custom.

When Rawiri had entered the temple, the ushers had given him a few candies, but he'd eaten them, unaware of their intended use. Now he watched, slightly embarrassed.

Giggling, Saya did her best to hide behind Hala. Kharis dove head-on for the candies, collecting them with her skirt. She celebrated her aljaicin stash, showing it to her father, who beamed with pride.

When her eyes met Rawiri's, a grin lit her face.

Ah, Teppe. Her antics made him laugh.

A petite child, Kharis looked younger than her actual age. Saya, much taller, looked like she was already sixteen. Now that Rawiri studied Saya more carefully, he noticed facial similarities with Hala. Both had a well-defined jaw and the same dimple on their chins. Dark chestnut hair framed their faces. A glance revealed the same features on Hröld.

Kharis, on the other hand, had inky black hair and an oval-shaped face that framed blue-gray eyes. *Perhaps she resembles her mother?* Curiosity poked him. *I'll look for Queen Aghuti's portrait when I have a chance.*

A sumptuous meal followed the private affair. Rawiri sat beside Yuna, steering their conversation towards the guests, careful not to reveal their secret allegiance.

Kharis and Saya sat at the head of the table with their father and brother. No other children were present, and that threw Rawiri off. In Kahurang, a similar celebration would've been teeming with them. Their laughter would join their joyful shouts and delighted squeals, adding to the cacophony of happiness that, like a wave, crashed over everyone in his homeland.

Here, the celebration is dull, almost obligatory.

Deep down, he wished his nephews could be here and inject this monotonous event with their effervescent laughter. *I miss them.* His thoughts drifted to Kiwa and Ataahua. *I miss Kahurang.*

᠅

Kharis hadn't received a letter from Taika, but she hoped the one she'd written would make him laugh. Since Rawiri wasn't teaching her curses, perhaps Taika would share a few. She still wanted to know what the *peke* curse was all about.

Her gaze roamed the long table, worried that Prince Rawiri wasn't enjoying the evening. Then again, she was bored to tears and secretly hoped for a swift return to their chambers for a game of xakea with her sister and the Kahurangi prince.

Nana could stay, and we could have dessert in our rooms.

Her plans for a quick retreat deflated when the chef brought a lavishly decorated cake—Almarim cocoa with a raspberry mousse filling and a cascade of pink buttercream frosting. Glazed raspberries and strawberries adorned the top, with green fondant mimicking vines and leaves. Sugared flower petals added to the spring theme.

Everyone *oohed* and *aahed* at the spectacular display.

Kharis glanced at Saya, who had similar thoughts—dessert had thwarted their escape.

"We'll have seconds in our chambers," Kharis whispered with a wink.

Saya beamed. "That would be nice." She leaned in closer. "I don't know who these people are."

Kharis shrugged. "They are here to check I won't explode—"

"Never say that." Saya pinched Kharis's thigh.

Startled, Kharis jerked her knee against the table, earning a frown from Hala. She wrinkled her nose at Saya. Yet Kharis had to agree with her sister. *I must temper my mouth.* Her eyes swept the room, studying the unfamiliar faces. As usual, Khator, Götrid, and Helena had found excuses *not* to come with their families.

Selfish idiots.

"You don't need them."

That whisper furled her mind. Kharis straightened and

carefully looked around for the voice's owner. Everyone was involved in their conversations—not one head turned in her direction.

"*You require no one,*" the soft, silvery voice said.

This voice. It had spoken to her at the Archives and on the day of the fire. Now, it caressed her mind like a gentle morning breeze. Phantom arms wrapped around her shoulders like a plush blanket.

"*I wish you a happy day,*" he said. "*Spend it with those who make you smile.*"

What's going on? Kharis shrank in her chair, her gaze darting carefully. *Am I going mad?* She'd heard those rumors.

The voice didn't speak any further.

Where did it go?

The slice of cake before her snapped her out of troubling thoughts. Kharis turned to her father, wondering if eating it was acceptable. He grinned with a mischievous twinkle, nodding as if aware of the question on her lips.

"It's all yours," he said.

Hröld clinked his glass, capturing everyone's attention. The king stood and raised his glass.

"Today, we celebrated how two girls became young women now at the service of the Empire. I wish them all the happiness they so richly deserve and the time to treasure the memories that lie ahead. May wisdom pave your road, dear daughters. May the Blessed Mother shower you with her many blessings. Kharis, Saya, know that we love and cherish you. Blessed be the earth and the sun."

Everyone stood with their glasses raised and recited in unison before drinking, "May they sustain us."

Saya finished her juice.

Kharis sipped, touched partly by her father's words, but her mind was not on the cake, the inspiring toast, or his loving wish. She couldn't get over the sensation that a pair of eyes watched her—that someone hid in the shadows of her mind wearing a satisfied grin.

CHAPTER 36

A PIECE OF HEAVEN

The next day, Kharis strolled beside Saya and Hala down a private passageway lined with fragrant rosemary and lavender. A playful hummingbird fluttered over her head, its iridescent feathers glistening in the sunlight. It darted back and forth, its tiny wings buzzing with a mesmerizing hum.

"You have an admirer," Saya said amid giggles.

Kharis ignored the tiny bird, walking with slumped shoulders. She hated the sunny yellow tulle dress the attendants forced her to wear. *Ugh.*

Saya wore a similar one that complemented her chestnut curls. Kharis's dress clashed with her jet-black hair. Saya, much taller, wore it well.

I look like a yellow ball.

Her brother, a man with impeccable taste, wore his imperial leather uniform, complete with trousers and boots. *Lucky him.*

"Where are we headed?" Kharis lacked the patience to suffer secrets, and not when wearing a hideous dress.

"Ah! It won't be a surprise if I tell you, will it?" He winked at her, making them wait, building suspense.

Saya nudged her along. "We won't get there if you keep asking questions."

Kharis groaned. "At least give us one hint."

"Nope," Hala said. "No hints. It'll ruin everything."

Kharis grunted. "You're insufferable."

"And you're being difficult," Saya said. "Come on, keep walking. I can't wait to see what this is about."

Hala spun to face them, hands braced at his hips, a wicked grin carving across his face. "I bet you can't catch me." And like that, he took off running.

"Wait," Kharis hollered.

A gaggle of giggles in lemon-colored dresses chased after the crown prince.

The girls reached the iron gates of a walled villa outside the palace.

"We made it," Kharis said. "Out with it."

Hala chuckled. "It doesn't work if I beat you to it."

She grumbled. "Well, you clearly cheated. So, where's this surprise of yours?"

"It's inside. Let me show you."

The gate opened to a sizable three-story structure—a separate building on the eastern side of the royal compound, isolated yet connected to the palace by a private passageway.

"The first floor houses a kitchen and a spacious sitting room," Hala said.

Kharis rolled her eyes.

"The second floor holds the bedchamber, a balcony with a tall marble balustrade, a bathing chamber, a small library, another sitting room, and a private dining room." Then he turned to Saya. "The third floor is a projecting stucco tower with a mirador. The view from up there is breathtaking."

"Hala—"

He lifted a finger to stop Kharis's whining, prompting an even louder grumble from her.

"This is the garden," he said, "my favorite space in the entire villa."

"We already know this," Kharis muttered under her breath.

"As you can see," he ignored her belly-aching, "it's a considerable courtyard, sliced in half by a shallow pool. The lion-shaped fountains are the best feature. The engineers designed them to take advantage of gravity, so they are always on."

The jet's spray danced in the wind, creating ripples in the water. Saya walked over, noting the gentle, almost imperceptible slope that fed it into the plumbing.

"Don't go digging, Saya," Hala said with a smile. "Or you." He frowned at Kharis.

Flower beds bordered the courtyard walkways. Tall palm, lemon, and orange trees lined the walls. Huge bougainvillea shrubs in brilliant merlot and magenta draped the southern wall.

"Very well," Hala said. "Now, for the surprise."

Kharis heaved an exaggerated sigh. "Finally."

"To find it, open the entry doors."

Kharis and Saya sprinted for the doors and pushed them open. The foyer was empty, devoid of furniture, portraits, or wall tapestries. The marble floors were bare without the usual colorful rugs.

Both sisters turned toward Hala. Saya scratched her head. Kharis narrowed her eyes with an exasperated glint, waiting for an answer.

"Well, how do you like it?" He settled by them.

"Like what?" Kharis frowned, utterly perplexed. "There's no gift."

"Ah, but there is. Now that you are thirteen, Father and I have agreed that you might enjoy having a private residence *away* from the palace."

Kharis blinked.

Saya gaped.

"This villa will grant you a degree of autonomy," he said. "I can't provide you the freedom you wish for, but this is as close as we royals get to that. As you know, Aya's pregnant, so we moved to a larger residence, and the timing couldn't be any better."

Kharis, who'd heard nothing else after "private residence," couldn't even form a word.

Hala looked worried. "Don't you like it?"

The sisters stared at each other for a long moment. When it hit Kharis that it wasn't a dream—that Hala meant it—she squealed loudly and joyfully. The sisters wrapped their arms around their brother, and he lurched backward, pushed in part by their waves of spellbinding joy.

❧

Saya sat on a bench, wondering about their new residence. *It's away from the palace.* Her smile wavered, torn between conflicting emotions. She thought of her father and brother and their intended goal. *Are they trying to isolate her? Keep her away from palace gossip?* That sinking feeling in her stomach returned. *Some call her 'raven spawn.'*

Hala walked over. "Still thinking about how the fountains work?"

Saya pulled a forced grin, hiding her concerns. "Is she still inside?"

Hala nodded. "Running up and down the stairs, exploring every inch of this place."

Kharis's loud *woo-hoos* broke the otherwise pleasant garden tranquility.

"Is it safe to have the pool here?" Saya asked.

"Of course." He smiled. "It's shallow and contained by hewn stone, not an open body of water, like a river or a lake. Kharis will be fine even when she dips her feet on a hot day. If it were unsafe, I would've had it removed."

The fountains filled the garden with comforting burbling sounds. "I'm glad you didn't have to," she said. "It would've been a shame to destroy the engineering that made it possible."

Hala took the scent around them. "Why are you not inside, running with Khiri and shouting like a hyena?"

"I'm thrilled. Don't get me wrong." The corners of her lips curled into a hesitant smile, betraying her whirlwind of thoughts. Had the fire been an accident, and this move *just* a coincidence? Was there more they hadn't been told? "This was an unexpected gift." Saya took in the sights. "I'm still adjusting."

"I'm glad you're both happy." Hala drew in a breath, tilting his head. "Privilege comes with a heavy burden. If you ever wanted to talk about it, I'm here for the two of you." He took her hand and patted it. "You can continue your lessons with Prince Rawiri here without the interruptions you normally face. Plus, it's a quieter place. You know Nana has been vocal about your sister's need for less noise around her. The passageway connects this villa to the palace, which means we'll still see you."

"And the training with General Ghan?" It was worth asking.

Hala sighed. "That I cannot change."

Hearing it deflated her.

"The Regiazenka feels strongly about the instruction he provides you."

Saya exhaled, unhappy about it.

"This place will be good for your sister." He squeezed her hand. "Look, Khiri's doing much better. There are far fewer pranks and mischief in our midst, and we have Prince Rawiri to thank for some of that. And in case you were wondering, Nana wholeheartedly blessed this idea. I'm surprised she isn't here, running alongside Kharis."

Saya snickered, imagining both women sliding down the

stairs' handrail. "Thank you, Hala. This... This means a lot to us."

He hugged his sister. "I cherish the fact that I can dote on you two."

Saya understood what he didn't say—to dote on two girls cursed by an awful fate to handle more than any thirteen-year-old girl would ever face.

CHAPTER 37

THE ARCHIVES, AGAIN

The coolness of the metal door stung against Kharis's skin as she leaned against it to open it. The click it made echoed in the quiet chamber. The musty scent of ancient books and parchment teased her nostrils. She exhaled and twisted, ribs scraping stone as she wriggled out of the hollow statue. Once out, she scanned the space, blinking to adjust to the lack of light.

"Now, which row shall I check next?"

With their impending move to the villa, her access to the palace's secret passageways would be curtailed, adding to the challenge of finding a spell to undo the curse binding her to the Akumi king.

Shadows cloaked the Royal Archives, their towering shelves filled with ancient knowledge. The faint moonlight streamed through the tall, arched windows, casting a silvery glow across the rows of books. Kharis skulked among the bookstacks, her fingers brushing against the spines as she lifted her lantern to read their titles. The gold foil on some of them was long gone, making the titles more challenging to read in the feeble light.

She moved with determination, her eyes darting from

one text to another or skimming the contents of scrolls, searching for an unbinding spell. Yet, after nights of searching, there was no sign of written spells.

"Ugh. Where are they?"

Her heart raced as she rounded a corner, her boot heels barely clacking against the stone floor. She had to move swiftly before the patrol entered this space on their usual round.

A sudden rustle of silken fabric and the softest footsteps echoed in the chamber. Kharis, who knew no one should be inside at night, snuffed the flame in her lantern and crouched behind a shelf, swallowing hard.

An ethereal woman emerged from the shadows, pale moonbeams outlining her form.

Kharis almost gasped. *The ghost.*

The apparition carried herself with a regal air of formality that seemed out of place in the clandestine depths of the Royal Archives. A bejeweled circlet adorned her fore-head, and her silver eyes gleamed, reflecting the light of a thousand stars. Her long hair cascaded like a black waterfall past her shoulders. The indigo glimmers it released were hypnotic, much like her own hair. Moonlight appeared to have woven her elegant gown, shimmering as it billowed sideways with each step.

And she strolled directly toward Kharis.

"Hello." Her voice, soft like a breeze and sweetly melodic, carried the faintest hint of an accent. Kindness shaped her smile. "You wander off where you shouldn't."

Kharis heard the veiled question and thought of a hundred lies, but that intense gaze seemed to look as though it could effortlessly probe her mind and pick them out like ripe fruit on a laden tree, so she stuck with the truth... for now.

She rose slowly from behind her hiding spot. "I—I couldn't sleep."

The woman's silver eyes glowed as if expecting more.

Kharis bit her bottom lip and scratched her cheek. "I need an unbinding spell."

The woman regarded her with eyes full of ancient wisdom. "The spell you seek isn't housed in these halls." She pressed a hand to her chest, gazing affectionately at the space. "The Royal Archives safeguard prophecies and oracles, the histories of kings and queens, books on the magic of the Forest Kin, and atlases that chart the realms of this world. But what you desire does not reside here."

Kharis's eyes squinted. "And how do you know this?"

A lingering sadness clouded the woman's gaze. "I've curated every inch of this space. And I have even written a few of them."

Heat stung behind Kharis's eyes. "I've taken an enormous risk bypassing security night after night only to learn my quest has been in vain." The back of her hand wiped her damp eyes. "My sister's very existence depends on it." She wiped her nose with her sleeve. "I just don't know where else to look."

The woman closed the distance, gently tipping Kharis's chin up and offering a reassuring smile. "I could guide you down a different path."

Kharis regained her hope. "You can?"

"What you seek exists, but you must go to Hegra to find it."

Kharis had never heard of this place. "Hegra?"

"It holds the knowledge you require. Locate it, head north, and you'll find your answers." With a nod, she whispered, "May the Blessed Mother guide your way, Kharis."

Kharis's heart jumped. "You know my name?"

"Why would I not?"

The woman had a point. She got into so much trouble that even the garden birds knew who she was. "What about your name?"

A smile danced on her lips. "My name is Poliormos, and I couldn't sleep either."

Before Kharis could ask more questions, the woman gracefully melted into the shadows, leaving the Djinnshirukh alone.

"Poliormos?" Kharis called out, but silence was her response. She scratched her head, trying to remember where she'd seen the woman before.

"So I must go to Hegra?" She raised her arms in frustration. "Good luck with that. I can't even leave the stupid palace grounds." Before she headed for the map room, the sound of boot clacks and muffled voices sent her running to the statue. The patrol was back.

A *peke* curse floated on her mind.

&

Using the rope left inside the hollow sculpture, she climbed while pondering her next steps.

"Find Hegra and head north."

Not all was lost. Kharis would return to her bedchambers and find a way to obtain a map. She'd never heard of this place, but if it held her answers, by the Netherworlds of Ifran, she would find it and go there.

Kharis retraced her steps through the long tunnel. The walls were more oppressive than they'd been on her way in. It was colder, and the faint echo of her footsteps bounced against the walls. She hurried, her mind racing, when a sudden frigid gust rushed past her, carrying an eerie screech. Her heart almost leaped out of her chest. She stilled, figuring out where that sound had come from.

"The plumbing?" That made sense. "Wind drafts? Heating pipes?"

A tremor ran along the uneven ground, and she steadied herself against a wall. A low-frequency vibration hung in the air, making her slightly dizzy.

It became quiet once more.

Exhaling in relief, she turned, only for her eyes to meet the gaze of a giant creature beyond her worst nightmares.

The monstrous entity had a grotesque, human-like face, but distorted and ghastly. Its overly big, round, black eyes glimmered, observing her with ravenous hunger. They protruded from its face, transparent eyelids closing from the bottom up to clean the gunk collecting in them. Long, wet hair, thin in places, was plastered to the slimy head perched on a reedy neck. Like a four-legged spider, the gangly arms and legs held its body upright. Sharp claws stuck out from its spindly fingers and toes. It possessed a widened torso, every vertebra visible on its curved back. Ribbons of corded muscle strained against blackened, leathery skin. Dead plant debris coated its form, its skin oozing a foul-smelling mucus.

Kharis stepped back with a gag. Cold sweat prickled her skin.

The creature scrutinized Kharis. It grinned, revealing glistening rows of jagged black and yellow teeth. Its fetid breath, reeking of decay, slammed into her.

"What have we here?" The creature cocked its head, its voice a grotesque whisper.

She backed away with longer strides, building her distance.

"Mmm." The monster's eyes gleamed with a perverse delight. "You look scrumptious." It licked its lips with a disgusting smacking sound, drool trickling down the corners of its mouth. "Such a succulent morsel."

Before Kharis could react, the creature lunged at her. She jumped, her heart pounding as she narrowly evaded the snapping jaws that almost clamped onto her legs. Her scream tore through the darkness. The echo multiplied as if a thousand of her were screaming at once, each bouncing off the walls with relentless force. The monstrous creature staggered, emitting a pained moan. Its massive frame trembled. Seeking respite from the disorienting din, it dropped closer to the ground, cowering beneath the onslaught of sound. Its clawed hands shot up to cover its ears and shield itself from the assaulting cacophony.

Fueled by adrenaline and sensing an opportunity, Kharis leaped, her boots sinking into its slick, leathery skin. The monster's head slammed onto the ground with her weight, the sound of crushing bones resonating like a blast. She ran the length of its back, its bony protrusions and slippery skin challenging her balance. Breathing heavily, she hopped off at the other end and dashed down the narrow tunnel.

The enraged monster snarled. Its hulking form hindered its attempts to pivot, its body a mess of flailing limbs.

Kharis sprinted, aware that the creature would soon be hot on her heels. Her heart raced like a frenzied antelope, its rhythm thumping in her ears. Heat surged inside her, an internal blaze growing with each breath—wildfire spreading from her core to her arms and legs. Iridescent scales now adorned her arms, their faint glow dispersing the gloom. As she dashed down the tunnel, a luminous trail of stardust followed in her wake.

Blasted. I'm a running beacon.

A sudden flash of crimson filled her vision, nearly halting her in her tracks. Her sight expanded. The darkness dissipated, becoming daylight. Kharis simply ran faster.

The monster emitted a bone-chilling shriek, its haunting echo resounding through the tunnel as it drew closer. The rhythmic click of its claws on the stone created an ominous percussion. The monster surged forward, unwavering in its goal to get its meal. Its jaws clamped onto the back of her garments with a vise-like grip and yanked. The fabric tore as its teeth dug into leather and cloth, scraping the scales covering her back.

With the contact, tiny sparks erupted, igniting the shimmering stardust. Her silver mist burst into flames, and a massive plume of billowing fire surged through the passage.

The creature recoiled, releasing her from its grip. Her scream got lost in the creature's shrieks.

The monster howled in agony. Its skin sizzled and smoked. The slime bubbled and boiled. The creature slammed against the walls, struggling to extinguish the flames consuming its body. It slumped to the ground, its arms and legs thrashing wildly in a frantic, futile struggle.

Kharis ran in the opposite direction, still burning like a torch, charring the ceiling and ground as she hurried down the tunnel. The monster's piercing shrieks faded, leaving only the lingering odor of something foul and the inky maw behind.

The darkness soon swallowed Kharis as her fire dissipated. She dashed forward, turning left and right, almost slipping as she sprinted past bends and corners, and crawled through the fake panel, entering her rooms in a frantic rush, her chest rising with each ragged breath. Slamming the secret door shut, she locked it and pushed a heavy cabinet in front of it. Her body slid to the floor with a heavy thud. As if startled by a bad dream, she patted herself until she realized her skin and clothes were untouched.

She stared at her hands, turning them over in disbelief. "I'm not burned."

It was a statement, a question—a miracle.

❧

"Khiri?" A hand gently patted her face. "Khiri, wake up."

Kharis bolted up from the cushioned settle. "The monster!"

She blinked. Saya stared at her with a slight frown. "Another nightmare?"

Kharis's lips flattened, suddenly unsure. *And when did I fall asleep here?*

"Why didn't you wake me up?" Saya wrapped her arms

around Kharis. Her fingers caught on the torn fabric, and she sighed, resigned. "Another ruined uniform."

Kharis didn't know what to say.

"This is the last day we'll spend here," Saya said, referring to their palace chambers. "Tonight, we sleep in the villa." Excitement sang in her voice. "Come and get dressed."

Kharis slowly nodded.

"Breakfast awaits." Saya brushed a cobweb off Kharis's hair with a look that carried too many questions. Thankfully, she didn't ask any.

CHAPTER 38
A LINE IN THE SAND

A week after the move, Kharis lounged with Saya and Rawiri, enjoying the perfect spring weather of a Zahari afternoon, not visiting the Royal Archives as Kharis had requested (repeatedly!).

We're having a blasted nap.

"How exactly is this training?" she asked in perfectly intoned Kahurangi.

Rawiri kept his eyes closed and his smile soft.

"Shouldn't we be doing something?" she insisted. "Maybe go somewhere, like the Archives?"

"We're doing something," he answered in Kahurangi. "Rest is as important as action. A warrior knows when to pick up his blade and when to put it down. Balance is crucial in everything we do, and rest is an aspect of seeking it. Besides, when the body rests, the mind can work."

"How?" Kharis was only half convinced.

"Ah, Teppe. The mind creates extraordinary things when the body is at rest. Close your eyes and envision your act of creation. Visualize your body in motion. Play the scene from different angles, consider what you could do differently, and allow your mind to show you the endless possibilities.

Inspiration is possible when we let the mind do its work." Rawiri inhaled deeply. "It's a moment when not doing leads to doing."

"Hmm." Kharis chose not to argue. "Fine. Let's see what this not-doing can do."

Rawiri laughed.

Kharis breathed slowly and closed her eyes, allowing her body to relax.

The blanket under her was plush, but her fingers moved past it and fanned against the cool grass. A gentle breeze blew, carrying the scent of jasmine. It rustled through the lemon and orange trees, filling the garden with the jingles of wind chimes. Their soothing, inharmonic music helped slow down her breathing. Glimmers of bright light appeared behind her eyelids, sparkling in rhythm with the wind chimes. Soon, those sounds became distant.

When her nose picked up an unfamiliar fragrance, she sat up.

The shores of a lake greeted her. The soft wind caressed her face, gently tugging at her hair. The scent of pine and birch lingered in the air, and a playful breeze brought the sweet aroma of wildflowers. Like a mirror, the lake's still waters reflected the majestic peaks surrounding it. An endless, brilliant ribbon of dark teal forest framed the lake.

"Where am I?" She looked for Saya and Rawiri, wondering whether she'd fallen asleep and was dreaming.

In this piece of paradise, solitude was poetical and sacred, and the landscape invited her to sit under the shade of an ancient tree. It wanted her to linger and never leave. Kharis took it all in and meandered to the water's edge, curious about the open body of water. Her toes wiggled on the sandy shore, barely touching the water, hesitant to do more. The gentle waves beckoned her to approach—to enter their abode.

"*Come,*" a melodic whisper enticed her.

The voice drew Kharis's attention, and she lifted her gaze, scanning the waters.

Sunlight glimmered over the lake's surface in a glorious array of colorful twinkles. She felt an overwhelming urge to take a dip. Carefully, she took one more step into the water. It kissed her ankles, and the breeze blew past her wet skin, sending pleasurable shivers up her legs.

Why am I not allowed to swim?

The sensation that often simmered under her skin like a slightly annoying tingle quieted as if the magic of this place spoke to whatever magic resided inside her. Here, her mind was still enough that she could immerse herself in the experience. All the thoughts cluttering her head vanished. A calming sense wrapped around her, and she filled her lungs with crisp forest air.

Here, she could forget her worries. Or float like a flower offering to the gods.

"Kharasdir, come closer," the velvety male voice from the lake said again.

She took another step forward. Her fingers formed ripples on the surface, and she no longer suppressed a grin.

"Khiri?" Someone in the distance called out. "Khiri...?"

Kharis turned, searching for this other voice. It was familiar, bright like the sun, sweet and kind, and full of affection.

The forest was quiet. The lake remained calm and inviting, summoning her with a clear, pleasant sound.

Tendrils of gossamer light emerged from the lake, embraced her gently, and her eyes returned to the water. *"We've been waiting for you."*

Kharis beamed, satisfied with this world and this overwhelming sensation of being *home*. She forgot about the Archives, the Akumi king, and unbinding spells.

"Khiri," that other voice insisted, piercing the quiet in her mind. "Khiri, please, wake up."

Wake up...?

Saya patted Kharis's cheeks, her voice slightly shrill. "Khiri, wake up." Fear tensed her forehead as she shook her sister. *Please, please.*

Kharis opened her eyes in slow, lazy blinks. "Saya?"

Saya exhaled loudly. "Thank the Blessed Mother." A tear rolled down her cheek, and she wiped it off. Without another thought, she hugged her sister, stifling her sob.

"Saya?" Kharis patted Saya's back with a hesitant touch.

"How are you doing?" Saya pulled back, controlling the fear coursing through her.

Kharis leaned on her elbows. "I'm fine. I just fell asleep—"

"No, you didn't." Saya's frown deepened. "You entered Andaheimur."

Kharis squinted. "I don't think so. I can't enter the spirit world without you." She flicked her hair off her face. "You know this."

Saya stared. "How do you know you didn't?"

That question gave Kharis pause.

"It couldn't be Andaheimur." A soft smile bloomed on her face. "This... This was different, like a nice dream. There was a forest and a lake. Its waters were so clear, I could view the bottom."

Rawiri, kneeling beside the sisters, stilled, bulging eyes framing a ghostly white face.

"A voice invited me to enter it," Kharis added.

Rawiri listened with a fevered stare, his hands clenched.

"A voice?" Saya fisted her hands to keep them from shaking.

"I didn't want to go." Kharis closed her eyes. "I wanted to stay and go for a swim."

"You don't know how to," Saya nearly shouted.

"It was a dream, Saya." Kharis's face tightened. "I can't drown if it's *my dream.*"

"Get up, Khiri. We must head back inside." Saya turned to Rawiri. "Please, help me lift her."

"Saya, I just fell asleep—"

"I said, get up." Saya's voice strained, rising in pitch. She could barely control the quaking in her hands. "You must eat." It was the only thing she could think of to bring her sister into the house.

"Fine," Kharis huffed. "You're making a mountain out of an ant hill."

"Your Highness?" Saya leaned into Rawiri, mindful of Kharis. "Please have your most trusted soldier fetch Monk Yuna immediately. Only her. No one else must know what happened just now."

Before Rawiri could ask questions, Saya sprinted after Kharis, who stumbled and almost fell on a rose bush.

The heavy footfalls from the mirador's spiral staircase announced the person emerging through the trapdoor. Saya knew who it was without looking. "How's she doing?"

Rawiri approached the railing and peeked out, taking in the sights. "Yuna's seeing to her."

Saya and Rawiri watched soldiers change shifts amid a blare of trumpets and shouted commands. Merchants carted their products to the palace, the clatter of their wooden wheels adding to the sounds the wind carried. Swift-footed servants rushed to their afternoon stations. Beyond the Zahar-Homa, the capital stretched vast and endless.

"How are you doing?" Rawiri finally asked.

Saya was lost in the many thoughts swirling in her head, among them that Kharis had entered Andaheimur. Saya was sure of it, regardless of whatever Kharis had claimed. Her sister could summon fire, and although that power had saved them from the blaze, it also marked the beginning of the unraveling. And now, a voice had spoken to her, urging her to enter a lake. A chill settled in her chest, and Saya found it difficult to breathe.

The signs are there.

The madness would slowly consume her sister. Saya had to figure out how to slow it down if she couldn't stop it.

Her gaze focused on the Zahar-Regia's activity.

There must be a way.

"I can't help you if I don't know what I'm dealing with," Rawiri said.

His voice, soft yet deep like a canyon, brought her back. Saya lowered her head and gripped the rails, her knuckles whitening. She stifled her tears, taking in a sustained breath. "I lack the courage to face what comes next."

Rawiri wore a thoughtful expression. "What would that be?"

Saya gripped the railing so hard it hurt.

"My sister is hearing voices." The words were barely a whisper, as though speaking them aloud might make the dread real. "And today, those called to her, asking her to stay in Andaheimur, but staying too long in the spirit world is dangerous. Her soul could be trapped if led astray by pleasant visions, and that"—she squeezed her eyes shut—"means she would die here. I'm her guardian, yet I almost lost her today."

Rawiri's hand rested on her shoulder. "Focus on what you did well and not on what didn't happen."

She shook her head slowly. "I must keep these things from happening."

"And you did. Why can't you see this?"

Saya opened her mouth, but her words got caught in a vortex of emotions. Tears spilled from her eyes like frantic little lemmings jumping past a cliff of desperation.

"I can't stop the madness." She shook her head in denial. "No one can. I can slow it down, but she can't escape the fate that shrouds every Djinnshirukh." Her low, sustained moan clung in the air. "I'm useless."

Strong arms, full of tender affection despite their size, wrapped around her.

"No, you are not." Emotion choked Rawiri's voice. "You're a bright young woman who cares deeply for her sister and who will go to the ends of Ifran to help her." He paused, his own body shaking. "Never utter those words. You're Saya, a proud Zahari princess and the most powerful Sorukhipa who has ever lived." He pulled back, gazing at her. "Together, we'll find a way to save Teppe."

Saya stared at him, salty water pooling in her golden eyes.

"Together," he insisted.

Her chin quivered as she nodded. When another sob escaped her, the wail swelling inside her broke free at last.

CHAPTER 39

NOW OR NEVER

Yuna paused at the door, smoothing her kashaya as her emotions clashed. It was now or never. She contemplated what to reveal, grappling with the impending conversation. Heaving a sustained sigh, she entered. Rawiri rose and bowed formally. She regarded him with a curious look.

"I wasn't fully aware of your status," he said.

She huffed, displeased. "And it should've stayed like that."

Rawiri gave her a quizzical look. A noise rumbled in her throat. She couldn't escape explanations. "I gave up on the Zahari throne thirty years ago. That life would've never suited me." That memory, burned forever in her mind, came to her—the day she walked out on her raging father, her sobbing mother, and the Empire.

"Arjun, next in line, had thrown himself into the Unification Wars, hoping to impress our father. His eyes danced at the idea of triumph and welcoming parades, of returning home a hero that Father would celebrate. But Aghuti, without even trying, became the queen and the pen with which the gods wrote the fate of nations. My brother fought and spilled his blood countless times, but Aghuti achieved the impossible *with words*.

"My sister took on the role as if she'd been born for it. Lauded for her beauty, few paid attention to how intelligent she was... until the *Morning Star* became *Daughter of the Sun*. Aghuti learned how to listen from Hröld, and fate gifted her the power to conjure worlds with words."

Yuna took a seat, settling into the plush cushion. The memory of Aghuti's ascension to the throne always brought tears to her eyes. It had become a singular moment that changed Zahar's fate.

"I loved my sister dearly. She was unique, and even her birth was a unique event. I was a girl of fifteen when she was born—the cry that woke the Empire of Zahar. My brother never had a chance. He returned home from the war with Kahurang only to find Aghuti sitting on the throne."

Yuna took a deep breath to cool the sting of tears.

"I may command the Royal Academy of the Healing Arts, but that building was Aghuti's gift to me. She collected the stones and instructed me to give them life. Thus, I have amassed incredible knowledge and skill; my job is to share it with the world. But to do that, I couldn't be the imperial queen of Zahar. Besides, I loved Anong too much to give him up. Back then, the senate teemed with self-serving nobles who would've never entertained the notion of a commoner ascending to the throne as my consort. Thus, I eloped to marry the love of my life."

Yuna poured herself a cup of mint tea and sipped it, glad for its tingling sensation. Rawiri bid his time.

Yuna, far too wise, saw all his questions in how he held his cup, sipping with eyes that never left her.

"Thank you for alerting me," she said—an overture to start the conversation. Rawiri nodded, and she regarded him with a slight lift of her eyebrow. "I've sent all servants away, and the girls' bedroom is at the other end of a rather *long* hallway. We can sit here, enjoying the tea and scones, or discuss business."

Rawiri almost choked on his tea. A few coughs settled in his throat. The crease on his forehead deepened. "What happened to Teppe?"

Yuna set her cup on her lap. "It's happening faster than I thought."

"What is?" he asked.

"The madness."

Another cough rasped his throat.

Yuna set her cup on the table, hating every moment of this uncomfortable conversation. "When a demon possesses a human body, it exerts undue influence to inhabit it fully. Exorcisms work because we can extract and purify them. And yet, we keep the Akumi king sealed inside the Djinnshirukh."

She inhaled slowly, but it didn't steady her.

"My niece is one more sacrificial lamb in a long line of individuals sent to the slaughterhouse for the sake of a war the Crown has yet to see after a thousand years of waiting. The Spirit Kin queen was wise, granting the Djinnshirukh a companion, but this role isn't exactly what you think."

"Then explain it to me," Rawiri said. "Otherwise, how can I help the girls?"

An icy feeling settled in the pit of her stomach. "Take them away, Rawiri. Get them out of here."

"What's Saya's role in all of this?" His glare demanded the truth.

Yuna looked away. "Just take them away as we've planned."

"What is Saya's role?" His voice deepened.

She broke into a cold sweat, gripping the armrests to summon her courage. "When the time comes, the Sorukhipa becomes the Djinnshirukh's executioner."

The cup in Rawiri's hands crashed to the floor. Speechless, Rawiri sat back in the chair, arms limp by his sides.

"As short as it may be," Yuna went on, "my Gutxi must live her life freely. Saya will return the Akumi king to Andaheimur. No more resealment rituals or Djinnshirukh cycles. Saya knows what to do."

A pause.

"If that's all it takes," Rawiri raised his voice, "why hasn't it been done before? Why wait until now?"

She glanced away. "Yours is a good question. The Djinnshirukh has always been an adult. Further, a consistent detachment has existed between the vessel and the Sorukhipa, allowing the ritual to unfold unencumbered by emotion."

Rawiri fixed his gaze upon her, his eyes nearly piercing through her as uncomfortable heartbeats thudded between them.

Yuna swallowed a sob. "Kharis and Saya became the Djinnshirukh and the Sorukhipa at birth. My girls have been inseparable since they were two years of age, raised as sisters by Hröld's royal decree. Thus, the bond they've formed is far deeper and stronger than the one a Sorukhipa and a Djinnshirukh should ever have. And love, as Lord Athon used to tell me, is formidable magic."

Yuna pulled a handkerchief from her pocket, gently dabbing at her eyes. "I don't know how long Gutxi has to live since the madness is already manifesting—"

"She just turned thirteen," he shouted, the rage in his words burning like fire.

Yuna's mouth curled into a grim twist. "Hearing voices and fire summoning are always the start of the unraveling. The Akumi king's magic has begun corrupting her."

Rawiri pressed a hand to his mouth with a wandering gaze that didn't settle.

She took a shuddering breath. "We must forge ahead

with our plans. Nothing has changed. Take them to Kahurang. It's what Gutxi dreams of."

Rawiri's face paled.

Yuna clenched her jaw, thinking of her little butterfly. "The journey will be challenging. Once the palace realizes they're gone, they'll pursue you. Are you still willing to go through with this?"

Rawiri lowered his head, his gaze focused on his clasped hands. The silence between them was heavy and thoughtful. The curtains rustled in the soft breeze, lifting at times. When he raised his head, clarity infused his gaze.

"What must I do?" he asked.

That question released the vise clamped on Yuna's chest. "I've arranged for the girls' safe passage and ample discretion. Decoys will leave the Ghak simultaneously, leading White Guard officers on a wild-goose chase. My network is ready to end this folly. Gutxi has months to live if her fire summoning is this advanced."

"No." He struck the table, rattling Yuna's cup. "There must be another way. Let me speak to the king."

"That won't do."

He did a double-take. "Why?"

"Hröld walks a thin line," she said. "As the imperial king, he must never show favoritism toward any of his children. That's rule number one. Arjun controls the armies. That's rule number two. One misstep, and Arjun, who was denied everything he'd ever wanted, will plunge the Empire into another civil war. Hröld understands this."

Rawiri's eyes darted as he pondered. "Then let me talk to the crown prince."

"That won't work either."

He scrunched his face in frustration. "You're being unreasonable."

Yuna gave him a withering look. "I'm sixty-three, Prince Rawiri. I've lived an eternity under the shadows of this palace. You've been with us for mere months. Don't presume to know—"

"That's your mistake," he shot back. "Questioning opportunity when it knocks on your door."

She fixed him with a piercing glare. "Do you even know which door to knock on?"

Frustration etched the lines in his features. "Why won't you trust me to speak with Prince Hala?"

Her stare lingered for several breaths. "You're aware of the secret passages, are you not?"

Rawiri narrowed his eyes. "What about them? I thought we were discussing—"

Yuna lifted her hand to silence him. "More than a thousand years ago, the Forest Kin clan built this palace. This city was their stronghold, the center of their world, until the Akumi army appeared on the horizon."

"And your point is?"

Yuna exhaled. "The immortals built hidden passageways to ensure a swift escape should the events during the One War not unfold as hoped. The Akumi horde was advancing, coming here to burn the city to the ground and destroy the whole world. Over time, people forgot about the escape tunnels until my niece discovered them. Those allowed her freedom within the palace, enabling her to move unseen and eavesdrop on many conversations. I can only imagine what Gutxi has learned."

Her heart twisted at the thought.

She picked on her orange scone, chewing on a small piece. "Why do you think we gave them this villa?"

Rawiri poked his cheek. "It was a gift to celebrate their entry into adulthood. To provide them with a place of their own. A semblance of freedom."

"Freedom." She clucked her tongue. "My father, King Aram, had this villa built some fifty years ago. Therefore, it lacks the secret passages that riddle the palace. This *gift*"—

she almost choked on that word—"is meant to keep them isolated and as ignorant as possible."

Rawiri grimaced, staring at her. "Why?"

"Simple. Hala has figured out that Gutxi's been using the tunnels. I wouldn't trust him at all. Have you not wondered why my other nieces and nephews don't visit?"

Rawiri blinked. "They have other siblings?"

"Ah!" Yuna smiled smugly. "So, they haven't told you about Khator, Götrid, or Helena?"

He shook his head.

"Well, I'm not surprised. Khator handles the western Mahazenka from his palace in Cecchio. It's an affluent city far from the Ghak—so convenient, wouldn't you say? Helena manages the northern Mahazenka Court, her castle located in Fjalagdigg. I'm told it's a frozen wasteland most of the year. Götrid oversees the southern Mahazenka from Almarim. Khator got floods and mosquitoes. Helena ended up with snowstorms. Götrid acquired droughts and sandstorms.

"Hala keeps his siblings away. On purpose." Yuna's face hardened. "Oh, those positions were gifts, just like this villa was a gift. Don't underestimate my nephew, Rawiri, for he's ambitious." She narrowed her eyes into slits. "The Djinnshirukh and the Sorukhipa are integral to my nephew's scheme. He keeps them on a short leash. It's the 'why' that scares me. I know with certainty that everything has a purpose for him. Therefore, be on your toes."

Rawiri cringed. "But he loves them."

"Of course he does," Yuna said, her tone still sarcastic, "as much as he loves Khator, Götrid, or Helena."

He gulped, lowering his gaze.

Palace intrigue exhausted her. "A strong sense of justice moved my sister. Aghuti wanted to end the carnage my father started with the Unification Wars and bring peace to the Empire. Above all, she wanted to protect her subjects."

Her gaze locked on the large bay window and the sight

beyond it. "Visit the poor neighborhoods, and you'll find altars in her honor. There, many worship her as if she were the Blessed Mother."

Rawiri sat silently, not asking a single question.

"Without wars to fight, Hala lacks a backdrop. The Empire grows fat. Prosperity is everywhere. How is his name entering the history books if all is well and good in Zahar? Where is the glory he seeks, the immortality his mother achieved?"

Rawiri glanced at his hands, his lips pinched.

"Aghuti, Athon, and I laid the groundwork when my sister learned she was pregnant with Hala. She wanted to end the ritual that turned children into future Djinnshirukh, to spare her own and any others, and Athon sought the knowledge needed to accomplish it, sometimes traveling far to obtain it. Aghuti and Athon intended to be the last ones, having decided to free the Akumi, but both"—her hands fisted—"died unexpectedly."

Murdered.

One day, she would find the evidence to prove it.

"I've continued my sister's work," Yuna went on. "Slowly, carefully, deliberately. A token here. A chip there. It has taken me twelve years to accomplish this, and you're the last piece I needed to win my game."

She sat upright, smoothing her robes.

"Our plans remain the same."

Rawiri stiffened, gaze lifted.

"In four weeks," she said, "Zahar will celebrate the spring equinox. The Silver Moon Festival is particularly auspicious this year, as it coincides with the appearance of two full moons in the same month, an event that occurs only once every seven years. As a result, the crowds alone will be something to behold. The entire city will spill into its squares and streets, and the festivities will last well into the night. And on this night, in the ensuing mayhem I've organized, you'll take the girls on a ship headed for Kahurang."

Rawiri stared at her, the silence between them leaden.

"You're wrong," he finally said.

Yuna lifted an eyebrow. "About what?"

"You would've been a formidable queen," Rawiri said. "Probably dangerous, too."

The smile she gave him—the power behind it—made him shudder.

"Then it's a good thing I like you," she said.

CHAPTER 40
THE SILVER MOON FESTIVAL I

Kharis twirled in her lavender dress. She jumped and swayed her arms, humming to herself as excitement powered every cell in her body.

Saya threw her a glare. "You aren't supposed to dance."

"And what exactly, oh mighty Saya, will happen if I do?"

Saya tsked. "Fine, dance away, but don't let anyone catch you, or Hala won't allow us to go."

Kharis halted immediately, arms down and stiff by her sides. "I'm not dancing."

The possibility of being disciplined on this day was enough to make her behave. She would eat charcoal and shoot a thousand perfect arrows to visit the Silver Moon Festival. Saya practically laughed at her unnatural stiffness, but Kharis, undeterred, carefully smoothed her dress to remove any telltale signs of wrinkles.

"Rawiri is late."

"He's not," Saya assured her. "Nana and the prince will be here soon."

"What should we do first?" Kharis greedily rubbed her hands as she pondered every possibility. "Oh, moon cakes."

She was already drooling. "Let's buy lots of those." She smacked her lips, savoring the thought. "Filled with almond paste or chestnut puree or raspberry preserves. Wait, no." Eyes full of wonder stared at Saya. "With peach filling."

"We'll get one of each. Just don't complain of a stomachache."

"Curse my stomach." Kharis held a fist up. "I shan't be denied."

Voices, footsteps on cobblestones, and armor clacking announced the approach of a unit. Kharis dashed to the nearest window. "They are here!" She squealed with excitement and sprinted out of the room.

"Khiri, wait, lift your—"

But Kharis was gone, fast as lightning, rushing down the stairs until her foot caught the hem of her dress. She squeaked. Muffled thuds echoed through the stairwell as she tumbled down the last few steps.

Saya hurried downstairs, where servants fussed over Kharis and her gown, checking her for scratches and bruises and her dress for tears or rips.

"I'm fine," Kharis said, done with all the fussing, "and the dress is fine." She turned to Saya with a flashy grin. "Come! They are here."

"Wait, your hair—"

Kharis pulled Saya toward the broad entry doors and flung them open with a loud, "Ta-da."

Rawiri gaped, surprised.

Yuna didn't. "I won the bet," she said.

Rawiri narrowed his eyes at her. "How? We bet Teppe would dash to the iron gate before we reached it."

"Well, she did run to meet us. Let's call it a draw."

"Yuna, you lost."

She ignored Rawiri.

"How are my darlings?" She gazed at them with adoring eyes. "You look lovely, both of you." Then she cocked her head and studied Kharis's messy hairdo. "I won't ask. A brush, please." A servant provided one quickly. "This is an important occasion, and I won't repeat how you're to follow instructions. Rawiri will do it for me."

He made a grumbling noise. And so, while Yuna brushed Kharis's hair back into place, Rawiri went into lecturing mode. "You will *never* leave my side, no matter what. If I tell you to run left, you will run left—"

"Yeah, yeah, run left," Kharis said.

Rawiri threw her a mortified glance.

"Gutxi?" Yuna's voice carried a dangerous sweetness.

Kharis swallowed hard.

"We've spoken about your need *to listen*. Otherwise, events such as this one wouldn't be possible."

Kharis lowered her head. "Yes, Nana."

"Your protection is foremost in your father's mind." Yuna gently tipped Kharis's chin up. "The festival is a grand celebration, but also an opportunity for unsavory activity. Therefore, you must listen to Prince Rawiri's instructions."

With a remorseful nod, she turned toward him. "My apologies, Prince Rawiri. Please continue."

Rawiri glanced at Yuna, impressed. "My escort will flank us. I trust my men with *your life*. A Zahari unit will accompany us, but they'll be more spread out. If we are to be attacked, they will act as the first wall of defense for our protection, and if it falls, the Kahurangi will be our last resort."

Kharis nodded. "We'll run left or right, whichever way you tell us."

Rawiri gave her a proud pat on her head. "I know you will."

"I'm brushing her hair," Yuna grumbled.

Miffed, Rawiri rolled his eyes at her.

Kharis and Saya exchanged chuckles.

❧

When she descended from the carriage, the explosion of color struck Kharis. Crowds flooded the streets in garments made of cobalt and violet. Others wore ivory or silver, a reference to Sharan, the moon.

Banners and pennons fluttered in the wind like sentinels. Instead of the usual golden Zahari sun icon with seven flares, an embroidered silver moon in an indigo field adorned them.

The Silver Moon Festival featured vendors from all over the region, selling moon-themed items, including those tasty moon cakes covered in white powdered sugar that Kharis coveted. Books and talismans abounded, and moon-shaped jewelry and amulets were available for the right price. Ranchers brought their prized animals to the auction markets. Zenka booths lined the streets, peddling everything imaginable.

Kharis couldn't stop gawking at all the products on display, from elaborate wood carvings and textiles to flower arrangements and gorgeous portraits and illustrations.

Humanity had spilled into the capital.

And since such festivals also attracted a different audience—thieves, frauds, drunks, and pickpockets. Zenka soldiers flooded the streets.

"We'll be on foot from now on," Rawiri said. "Remember your promise. You must listen to my commands, no matter what."

Kharis noticed the unfamiliar edge to his tone.

"Stay here." Rawiri stepped away to discuss with General Tawhiri and Commander Sono, Tawhiri's Zahari counterpart.

"What are they doing?" Kharis asked.

"They're discussing the map," Saya said. "You did pay attention, didn't you?"

"Attention... to what?"

Saya's gaze flicked upwards. "Khiri, you were at the meeting. There's a sequence to how we'll walk the streets."

"There is?"

Saya slapped her forehead. "You were daydreaming, weren't you?"

Kharis's guilty side glance confirmed it. How could she not? They were going to a festival for the first time, and every book she read about it filled her with exciting images and ideas.

"Rawiri is ensuring everyone's aware and in agreement with the next steps," Yuna said. "Although I don't expect any spectacles or commotion, it's in our best interest that our escort knows where we are going and when. In this fashion, they'll easily find us if we're separated."

Kharis frowned. "It sounds like a lot of work."

"It is, Gutxi. The logistics to make this visit a reality are complex. Therefore, be grateful for the opportunity and *do not* squander it." Her eyes locked on Kharis. "Now, promise me again that you will always stay with Rawiri and your sister and not chase moon cakes."

Kharis squared her shoulders and gave the monk a confident nod.

"Girls, if you could go anywhere, where would it be?" Yuna's voice was soft, as if she didn't want anyone else to hear.

"The caramel apple booth?"

Yuna stared at Kharis with a raised eyebrow, a mix of amusement and something else coiled in that stare.

"We haven't been outside the palace, much less the Zahar-Regia," Saya said. "We wouldn't know where to go."

"Well, if you could go anywhere," Yuna said, "where would you go?"

Kharis thought for a moment. Taika was her favorite xakea player after Saya. Wanting him to hold her hand brought on a roll of internal butterflies. Then guilt squashed it when she remembered she'd only written two letters to him. His brother, Koa, was sweet on Saya. That was as plain as day. *Forget the letters.* She wanted to see them again.

"Kahurang," Kharis said. "I would go to Kahurang."
Yuna grinned. "Good."

CHAPTER 41

THE SILVER MOON FESTIVAL II

The festival was magical—dazzling and entertaining and colorful—everything Kharis had imagined and more.

Whimsical kites danced gracefully in the warm winds, their vibrant colors and intricate designs painting the sky above the city. Kites launched from rooftops and terraces soared triumphantly, their silhouettes casting playful shadows against the radiant sun.

Hoping for a sale, a kite vendor approached the group. The Kahurangi guard immediately fenced the princesses. Rawiri, however, gestured at the man to come closer.

"I have kites for your lovely daughters," the vendor said.

Yuna stifled a chuckle.

Rawiri frowned at her.

"My name's Foághlam." The vendor dropped to one knee, showing Kharis and Saya his inventory. "Would you like one?"

Kharis turned to Rawiri, who nodded his approval.

While Saya studied the array of kites, Kharis turned her gaze to the man. He was tall and lean, with long, glossy silver hair bound at the nape with a strip of black leather.

247

His eyes were striking—clear seafoam green, bright and watchful.

"Your eye color is rare in Zahar," she said. "As if green and silver had been mixed to make it."

Foághlam grinned. "So is your color, my lady. Silver and sapphire sparkling in perfect harmony." His smile was warm, with a tinge of mischief that spoke to Kharis. A familiar scent enveloped him, but she couldn't place it.

"I like this one." Saya showed Rawiri one that resembled a rainbow.

"And what about you?" Foághlam asked Kharis. "Have you made your selection?"

Her gaze swept the array, and one caught her attention. "I like that one." Kharis gestured to a bloodred dragon with open wings.

"Excellent choice." Foághlam's eyes glowed with delight. "It's perfect for you."

"Are you traveling from afar?" she asked.

The vendor's eyes gleamed. "You could say so."

"Are you from Kahurang, like Prince Rawiri?"

Foághlam tilted his head to the side, pondering how to answer. "I come from much farther." A mischievous grin brightened his face. "From so far away that it may not be on your maps."

Kharis's eyes widened at the prospect of a place farther than Kahurang. "I would like to visit your homeland one day." She knew she couldn't, but it didn't stop her from wishing to see the world and sail the open seas.

"Perhaps when you're older." Foághlam smiled with fatherly gentleness. "And if you do, do look for me."

A spark of curiosity ignited in her mind. "What's your country's name?"

"Hegra," he said.

Her mouth parted.

"How much for the kites?" Rawiri asked.

Foághlam winked at a stunned Kharis and rose. "No

charge. Consider it a gift—a token for them to remember this festival."

"I insist." Rawiri went for the small leather pouch fastened to his belt.

Foághlam grinned at Kharis as the air around him rippled, all the colors overtaking him until he vanished. Rawiri lifted his gaze, coins in hand, and scanned the area, perplexed. "Where did he go?"

"He vanished," Kharis shrugged, "through cracks in the air."

Yuna laughed, patting Kharis's head. "You have such a vivid imagination. The man's probably hawking his kites, blending into the crowd."

Kharis didn't think so.

"I'll have a soldier stow these in the carriage, so you won't need to carry them around." Rawiri gestured for one to approach and handed them over. "Are you ready to move on?"

Both girls shouted, "Yes!"

⁊⦁

Competitions for children abounded. Rawiri encouraged the girls to enter the archery competition. Kharis jumped at the opportunity. Given her royal status, the men moved the targets closer to her.

"No, no!" She waved her hands at them. "You must move mine further back, behind the others."

The helpers exchanged confused glances, but did it.

When her turn came, she took careful aim, inhaling deeply to center herself. She loosed her arrows, one after another, each finding its mark with pinpoint accuracy. Rawiri, Yuna, and Saya erupted in applause, breaking the crowd's stunned silence. A radiant smile graced Kharis's face.

"We have a winner," the organizer declared to the

crowd, now cheering.

"I appreciate it," Kharis said, "but it wouldn't be fair to the others."

The man was taken aback. "Aren't you interested in your prize?"

Kharis shook her head. "I cherished the opportunity to participate; that alone is reward enough for me. However, my sister can present the prizes if you want."

He didn't wait. "Ladies and gentlemen, Her Royal Highness, Princess Saya!"

Saya stepped in to hand out medals to five wide-eyed kids, brimming with joy at the prospect of receiving their awards from a royal princess.

On Bhajan Square, the unexpected royal presence honored the performers, who swayed and twirled in a spirited display for the girls. Their movements flowed harmoniously, forming a seamless line of vibrant colors and graceful motions. They enhanced the dance's visual appeal with ornate fans and feathered banners.

Next, the acrobats astounded the crowds with their gravity-defying leaps and twirls. They bounced off each other and executed mid-air flips, always landing safely in the hands of their expert partners. The audience *oohed* and *aahed*, wholly captivated by the spectacle.

Kharis applauded enthusiastically after each performance, secretly wishing the festival would never end.

Afterward, Rawiri bought mooncakes for the girls. Saya nibbled on hers to make it last. Kharis gobbled hers and asked for another, flashing a grin covered in powdered sugar and peach filling.

"I have a surprise!" Yuna said as she handed them white paper lanterns. "This is a popular tradition at this festival. You write your wishes on them, light them, and let them rise into the night." She gestured to the sky, showing them how they lit the night like ivory fireflies.

"Will my wish come true?" Kharis asked.

Yuna smiled. "Only one way to find out."

Kharis took one and quickly wrote her wish—freedom. Both sisters lit the small candle inside them and watched it float.

"What did you wish for?" Kharis asked Saya.

"If I tell you, it won't come true."

"You're mean." Kharis pouted, poking Saya's cheek.

It only made Saya laugh.

"Ready to keep moving?" Rawiri asked.

"I am," Saya said.

"Teppe, what about you?"

Kharis didn't hear Rawiri's question, captivated by the masks displayed at a nearby stall. Crafted with felt, fur, and feathers, they reflected every known animal. She turned to Rawiri with a wide-eyed grin.

"Could we?" Her eyelashes fluttered in quick succession.

He chuckled. "Of course, choose one. You too, Saya. Pick whatever you want."

Kharis studied them but was unable to make a selection. "You choose for me."

Saya, who knew her sister well, had already picked a white fox mask for Kharis and a silver owl for herself.

Commander Sono approached with a frown. "Is everything all right? This was an unexpected stop."

Rawiri nodded toward the sisters, now donning whimsical animal masks. "I couldn't resist," he admitted with a faint smile. "And you—have you any children of your own?"

"Four."

"Why not get them some?" Rawiri asked. "I'm sure they'll enjoy them."

The commander briefly eyed the stall, then gave Rawiri a piercing look. "It might be best to purchase them for your soldiers. It would make them less conspicuous." He turned and walked away.

Kharis stiffened, aware of the veiled insult, and it took everything in her to curb the urge to punch that man's face.

Rawiri balled his hands into fists, but Yuna swiftly grasped his arm, shaking her head.

"Prince Rawiri?" Kharis tugged on his sleeve.

Startled out of his dark mood, he looked down and smiled. After all, who could resist a giggling snow-white fox?

Rawiri took a deep breath, exchanged another glance with Yuna, then turned to the girls. "Ready?" he asked, his smile wide again.

"Where are we going next?" Kharis clutched Rawiri's hand.

"It's dark enough now," Yuna said. "The fireworks display will start soon. We should head for our viewing spot."

"You mean it?" The cute white fox bounced up and down, her excitement bubbling over.

Yuna confirmed it, and the fox and owl held hands, gleefully cheering.

General Tawhiri approached. His face split into a grin when he saw the giggling girls in their masks. "Where to next, Your Highnesses?"

"Fireworks!" The sisters replied quickly, arms up in the air.

"Let's check the map." Rawiri studied a few routes with Tawhiri and Yuna.

"We could take this street and turn a corner here," Yuna said.

Tawhiri shook his head as he rubbed his chin. "That route is roped off to control the foot traffic. We shouldn't use it."

"What seems to be the problem?" Commander Sono had settled beside them.

"The fireworks display will start soon." Yuna regarded him with a displeased stare. "We're discussing the safest yet quickest route to the main square."

His eyes darted between Rawiri and Yuna, and acknowledgment flared in them. The commander squared his shoulders, aware Queen Aghuti's sister had addressed him, and studied the map with sudden formality. "It's best to stay on this street, then turn east here. That's the most direct route to Karrakusi Square."

Yuna scrutinized the suggested route, shared a complicit glance with Rawiri, and offered Sono a dangerous smile.

"Perfect," she purred.

CHAPTER 42
THE FIREWORKS DISPLAY

The uncomfortable humidity had dissipated once the sun set behind the mountains. Festival lanterns hung from eaves, their golden light enveloping the stalls as dusk gave way to the evening. More people poured into the festival, and the crowds doubled in size.

Kharis and Saya twirled their sparklers, thrilled to watch fireworks up close. Hala had arranged special seating for them, and Kharis could hardly contain her excitement.

Ahead, a large crowd of onlookers blocked their path as they watched dancers perform. A few of the Zahari soldiers advanced to break up the unwilling gathering.

"Wait your turn," a voice in the crowd bellowed.

A few heads turned. Eyes narrowed with hostility.

The soldiers weren't having it.

"Move it!" they barked, shoving people aside. "Out of the way!"

Yuna nudged the girls closer to Rawiri. The Kahurangi retinue swiftly encircled the four of them.

More Zahari soldiers, including the commander, marched toward the group to aid the efforts. A few onlookers refused, and the pushing turned to shoving.

"Get moving," Sono yelled while his soldiers pushed people out.

An angry fist punched Commander Sono's face, sending him to the ground.

That started the melee.

Fists and kicks flew in every direction as the remaining Zahari soldiers surged forward. More fighters spilled into the street, emerging from every alleyway to join the fray. Groups clutching pairs of children scattered, darting down side streets. Still more people poured into the square, transforming the scene into a swirling mass of bodies, cries, and confusion.

Yuna grabbed Rawiri's arm quickly. "As we planned it." It was a command, a warning—a plea.

"What's going on?" Kharis asked, her heart ramming her ribs.

"You're coming with me. Now." Rawiri took the sisters' hands and ran, pulling them along. The Kahurangi guards heeled them, hands on their swords and daggers.

Kharis glanced over her shoulder, only to witness how the crowd swallowed Yuna, who didn't run with them.

༄

The shadows devoured the Kahurangi group as they ran down a narrow alleyway. It pleased Yuna to see them vanish. *So far, everything is going according to plan.* A young man wearing commoner's clothing stood in a corner. Yuna spotted him and grinned at the familiar face. *Now, let's finish this.*

"Please, forgive me," her apprentice said as he approached her.

"Well, make it count, then run like the Fires of Ifran are chasing you and get out of here. Understood?"

The young man hesitated, his eyebrows knitted. "Um... I..."

"Now!" she yelled impatiently.

A stinging punch landed on her face, and she staggered back. Her shoulder hit the cobblestones with a snap. *Blessed Mother*. Pain rippled through her body, her face pulsing with every heartbeat. The metallic taste of blood filled her mouth. *This will leave a nasty bruise.*

Then suddenly, the night was ablaze with fireworks, swallowing the chaos. Like giant flower blooms, their dazzling explosions painted the heavens with a kaleidoscope of vibrant colors. Each burst, punctuated by a resounding boom, sent vibrations through the air, rattling the windows of nearby buildings.

My girls didn't get to see them. Yuna spotted a zenka soldier dashing toward her. Hoping for the best, she let go of her regret, surrendered to the excruciating pain, and fainted.

CHAPTER 43

THE ROYAL QUAY

Kharis and Saya ran, the fireworks explosions drowning the yelling and screaming they were leaving behind. The group dashed down narrow alleyways, swiftly turning corners with dizzying speed—left, right, straight, left again. Out of nowhere, a lantern flickered in the alley's gloom.

"There!"

The group split.

"You know where to meet us," Rawiri said.

Five soldiers, including General Tawhiri, stayed with their prince while the others nodded and kept running.

Rawiri and his group rushed to a man who beckoned them to enter a narrow three-story townhouse. Once in, the man closed the door and gestured to two women—his wife and daughter.

"Quickly, Your Highnesses, you must change," one of the women said.

Confused, Kharis and Saya turned to Rawiri.

"Do as they say." He and his soldiers turned around. "We have no time to lose."

Kharis and Saya stepped out of their gowns, wearing

only their slips. The women pulled plain cotton dresses over their heads and draped black cloaks around them.

"I must take these," Rawiri said as he took the sisters' masks.

Kharis eyed her white fox mask, her forehead wrinkled. "But—"

"I'm sorry, Teppe," Rawiri said, his tone soft. "You must leave it behind, but I promise to buy you another soon."

"What's going on?" She was on the verge of tears. "Where's Nana?"

Aware that time was not on their side, Rawiri dropped to one knee and held her hands. "If you could go anywhere in the world, where would it be?"

Kharis didn't waver, even when she sniffled and sobbed. "Kahurang."

"And what about you?" Rawiri asked Saya.

"I'll go where Khiri goes."

Saya's answer didn't surprise him, and his heart swelled with affection. "Then we'll go to Kahurang."

"But why?" Kharis pleaded.

He fought the urge to share how Yuna had planned to make this happen, that her coming-of-age gift to the sisters was, in fact, freedom.

"Why not?" he said, his warm smile calming Kharis. "Once we're safe, I'll explain everything. For now, I beg you to trust me."

"Your Highness," one of the women urged, "you must leave."

Rawiri got up. "Is everyone ready?"

His men nodded, pulling their hoods over their heads.

"Burn the dresses and masks," Rawiri whispered to the wife. "Don't let anyone find you with them."

The husband pushed furniture away with the soldiers' help, moved a rug, and lifted a trapdoor on the floor. "This way, Your Highness," he said. "Stay on it. It will take you to the quay."

Rawiri went down first and helped the girls down the rickety stairs. "We're going to run," he said, "and we're not stopping until we reach the docks, understood?"

Both girls gulped but agreed. The trapdoor closed, and gloom enveloped the group.

Rawiri lit a torch.

Then they ran.

CHAPTER 44

THE IBAIA RIVER

Kharis ran down what felt like a seemingly endless, dark tunnel—a sight eerily similar to the ones that haunted her nightmares. An iron grate loomed at the end. She sighed in relief when they finally reached it.

Users had sawed off the joints long ago, but it still looked like a sealed tunnel, more so in the dark. Rawiri and his men grunted, straining as they heaved the heavy iron grate aside. They slipped through the opening one by one, emerging into the open air before sliding the grate back into place with a thud.

The river scent was strong, reminding Kharis she was in forbidden territory. The Ibaia was ominously close, mere marks from them.

"We've reached the docks," Rawiri said, pulling the sisters' hoods over their heads. "Tawhiri?"

Peeking past a corner, Tawhiri scrutinized the marina, focusing on the shadows. "It's safe, Your Highness."

"Let's go," Rawiri instructed.

Tawhiri led the group toward the quay. The Kahurangi flanked their prince, who held onto the girls' hands.

They crept past a few shacks under the cloak of darkness. Waves lapped softly against the boats. Sharan's moon glow illuminated their path, casting eerie shadows that seemed to reach out and grab at them.

Kharis's grip on Rawiri's hand tightened, her pulse hammering so loudly against her ears that it drowned out all other sounds. She took a peek, her curiosity consistently strong. The Ibaia River's presence was formidable, and the other shore was so far from them that it felt like a different world resided at the other end. The thought of arms reaching out from the water to grab her terrified her.

I can't be near water.

"*And what will happen if you do?*" the silvery voice asked.

"I don't know."

"Khiri?" Saya glanced at her. "Are you well?"

Kharis timidly nodded. "Just nervous."

"*Water is water,*" the voice said. "*There's nothing to be afraid of.*"

Water is water. Why did that expression resonate with her so strongly? Her water prohibition had never made sense, but now wasn't the time to find out what would happen if she ran toward the river.

The men, all tight-lipped, skulked from shadow to shadow. The occasional rustle of sails and the croak of a nearby frog sent a shiver down her spine. The gentle whisper of reeds bending with the currents and the murmur of water as it flowed uttered her name. Their call was melodious—tempting.

Why can't I? Being this close to the river, a different question danced in her mind. *What's keeping me from jumping in?* Her magic stirred, but it was different this time. Sparks didn't tickle under her skin, itching to turn into a blaze. The cooling sensation branched from her chest into her arms and legs. The murmuring started.

"*Kharasdir,*" the river voices called.

"*Kharasdir,*" they beckoned. "*Come.*"

"Why don't you go?" the silvery voice encouraged. *"Don't you want to know why they call you?"*

The splash of a fish jumping through the water made everyone crouch behind crates, breaking her spell. Tension draped the group. Boats rocked gently in their moorings, their thuds rhythmic. More fish jumped out, creating multiple ripples on the surface.

"The fish have gone mad," Akona said softly.

"Be quiet." General Tawhiri rose cautiously to survey their surroundings.

"It smells of the sea," Akona insisted, wrinkling his nose as he took a whiff.

The other men nodded.

"We are nowhere near the ocean," Manaaki, the youngest of Rawiri's men, said. "It's weeks south of us."

"Focus on the mission," Wiremu said. "We can talk later."

Manaaki clicked his tongue, annoyed.

The evening fog enveloped the area, carrying the scent of river water and rotting wood. The waves turned rough, and the vessels slammed against the docks, their sounds like erratic drumming.

Rawiri looked behind him, his eyes darting over the crafts.

"It's like the water's boiling," Akona said.

"The ocean's calling," Hōhepa, one of his men, added. "I can smell its strong, briny scent. It's like we're standing on its shores."

"I'm telling you," Manaaki insisted. "We're nowhere near the ocean."

Tawhiri shushed them.

Kharis had never seen the sea, but a tutor had once brought seashells and driftwood to class to show them. The driftwood's scent was salty and earthy, and the shells reminded her of the rotten fish used to make fertilizer for the royal gardens. Now, a similar fragrance infused the air.

Rawiri frowned, a *peke* curse escaping his lips once he picked up the scent of salt in the air.

"Tanganokai wants something," Hōhepa said, his voice tense.

"Nonsense," Rawiri said, visibly concerned. "Tawhiri, what's the hold-up?"

"Still waiting for the signal." The general scanned the ships ahead and shook his head. "Nothing so far." A flicker in the dark caught their attention. "There." Tawhiri gestured. "That's the signal."

"Then let's go," Rawiri said.

"*Don't go there.*" The silvery voice turned shrill. "*Avoid that ship.*"

Kharis halted mid-step.

"*Jump into the water,*" the voice said anxiously. "*It'll be safer.*"

"I can't," she told the voice. "I shouldn't."

Saya stopped. "Khiri, what's going on?" She tugged on Kharis's hand.

Kharis didn't budge.

"*Jump,*" the voice insisted. "*Tell everyone to jump.*"

"Khiri?"

Rawiri turned, realizing the sisters weren't following. "Girls?"

"We shouldn't go on that ship," Kharis said, fear thrumming in her chest. "It might be safer if we swim—"

"Teppe." The prince dropped to one knee, both hands clutching her arms. "You promised to follow my instructions. This isn't the time to question them. If you want to be safe, we must board that ship."

Her eyebrows tightened. "Something's telling me to jump into the water—"

"Sorry, Teppe." Rawiri flung her over his shoulder, held Saya's wrist, and ran for the ship with his men.

CHAPTER 45

BETRAYAL

The group climbed quickly, the gangplank wavering under their weight.

Rawiri dropped Kharis down next to Saya. "Wait here." He walked over to untie the ropes when cold metal grazed his neck.

"I wouldn't move if I were you," a sinister voice hissed.

"And I wouldn't want to be you." Moving swiftly, Rawiri's fingers latched onto the attacker's wrist with a vise-like grip. With a surge of momentum and using the element of surprise to his advantage, he twisted, sending the man hurtling over the ship's side. The body hit the stone quay with a dull bone-snapping thud and a resounding splash as the intruder disappeared beneath the waves.

Two more assailants emerged from the shadows, rushing at Rawiri, fists flying in a desperate attempt to overwhelm him. Rawiri moved, dodging a swinging punch, the fist passing through empty air. The prince delivered a quick blow that landed squarely on his opponent's jaw. The popping sound made the man wail in pain. He staggered back, crashing to the floor, moaning as he held onto his face.

The second attacker kicked Rawiri in the side. He lost

his balance and hit the rail, but he saw the second kick coming and evaded it with a swift dunk, leaving the assailant off-balance. Rawiri seized the man's leg and countered with a hard knee kick to the groin, sending the attacker stumbling backward, his face twisted by pain. He slammed against the ship's railing, and with Rawiri's shove, he went overboard.

Rawiri stood his ground, hands raised into fists, breathing heavily but ready for the other attackers approaching him, moonlight glinting on their weapons.

The whimpers brought him back, and he turned in their direction, only to witness two Zahari soldiers holding onto Kharis and Saya, both girls now limp in their arms.

Dread froze Rawiri. "What did you do?"

A few lanterns lit, and he gasped. A Zahari platoon stood on deck, with spears angled at his men. Tawhiri bared his teeth, gripping his sword even when a spear poked his ribs.

"Order them to stand down," said a low, gritty voice. "I won't touch your men." One more lantern illuminated General Arjun Ghan's face. "We're at peace, after all."

"What did you do to them?" Rawiri's eyes fixed on the unconscious girls, his ragged breath in unison with his quickened heartbeats.

"Ah!" The high general snickered.

Rawiri wanted to punch that smile off Ghan's face. "If you've hurt them—"

"That's chlorazim," Ghan cut in. "It induces sleep. It's what monks use on patients before surgery, one of Yuna's clever discoveries." He descended the quarterdeck, sporting a smug grin. "Tell your men to stand down, or I'll have the girls thrown overboard."

Rawiri curled his fingers, momentarily taken, and blinked. "You wouldn't dare."

"Oh, but I would." He jerked his chin at the two officers, and they got closer to the taffrail, positioning themselves to drop the sisters.

Rawiri's breathing hitched. "They're princesses of the realm."

"Hmm." Arjun tapped his chin. "Indeed, they are, and if they were to drown, I guess Zahar would declare war on Kahurang."

What? Rawiri's jaw clenched tightly, grinding his teeth, aware that someone had betrayed them. He scanned the deck for any weakness to exploit, but the Zahari soldiers outnumbered them. Worse, two held the sisters precariously over the rail, waiting for Ghan's orders to release them into the water below.

"What will it be?" Ghan asked, enjoying the upper hand.

Rawiri tamped down his surging rage. "Stand down."

Tawhiri snarled at the order, sour eyes fixed on the two officers holding onto the girls, but he was the first to drop his sword. The rest followed, the clang of metal resonating against the wood.

"See?" Ghan said, wearing an arrogant smile. "So easy. You, Kahurangi, are predictable and—"

A commotion below deck interrupted him, cutting his speech short. Ghan clicked his tongue in annoyance.

"Sir?"

Ghan's gaze turned sharply towards the men holding Kharis and Saya, his voice slicing through the noise. "What is it?"

A third officer leaned over the rail, eyes wide. "It's the water, sir. It's... boiling."

"Ridiculous," Ghan barked.

Suddenly, the ship groaned, its timbers creaking ominously as if an invisible hand had tugged on its underbelly. The two officers holding Kharis and Saya staggered, struggling to keep their footing as the deck tilted beneath them. An abrupt lurch seized the vessel when a massive wave crashed against it. The spray of water engulfed everyone, drenching the deck as the ship pitched and rolled.

"Sir?" The third officer wavered, soaked and clinging to the rail.

The salty scent of stormy seas invaded Rawiri's nostrils. *Tanganokai...*

"Return the girls to the palace," Ghan shouted, glaring at the turbulent waters. "There's no need for them to be here."

Aided by others, the officers descended the slick gangplank, cradling the girls in their arms, and hastened towards a carriage. More waves, like desperate hands, splashed against the ship and the quay.

Rawiri's ire mounted as the carriage disappeared into the fog, and the rhythmic sound of the horses' hooves gradually faded. The ship ceased swaying. The waters settled into an eerie calm. The infusion of sea salt in the air dissipated.

Soldiers dragged the ship's captain to the deck, his boots skidding against the planks as he twisted in their grip, his face flushing as he fought for breath. Words burst out of him, loud and uneven.

"Please, I'm innocent. I didn't do anything."

Ghan released an exasperated sigh, the scar on his face twitching, and padded over to the man with a grim expression. "What about this tells me that you are?" He gestured at the Kahurangi, now on their knees, wrists manacled, and surrounded by Zahari soldiers.

The captain gave the group a panicked look, his eyes frantically darting. "T—They requested passage back to their homeland and paid upfront. Is that a crime?" A nervous laugh escaped him.

"It is not." Ghan patted the man's cheek with an odd grin. "Why would I stop Kahurangi from going home? I'd rather keep them all there."

The captain's mouth twitched.

"But tell me, why was it so important to leave in the cover of night, bypassing the usual inspections?"

The man chuckled faintly, his eyes roaming the deck. "I

—I don't ask questions. They paid, and if they wanted to leave now, why not?"

"Hmm." Ghan fixed a hawkish stare on the captain. "Where's their cargo?"

"Eh?"

"You know." Ghan gave the man a wicked smile. "Their crates and barrels. I'm assuming they are returning to Kahurang for good." Looking over his shoulder, he addressed one of his officers. "Was there any below deck?"

"No, sir," was the answer. "Mostly empty."

Rawiri tensed. He wanted to trip the captain before Zahari soldiers, his loyal witnesses.

A blow to the liver sent the captain reeling, gasping as he doubled over in pain.

"The way I see it," Ghan checked his knuckles, "you have a group of Kahurangi desperate to flee in the middle of the night with two princesses of the realm." He glared at Rawiri with another smirk. "That alone makes me ponder." His narrowed gaze fixed on the captain, observing him for a long moment as the man coughed and wheezed. Ghan yanked on his hair to tip his head back and traced the left side of the man's face with a finger, from forehead to neck. "I wonder what a scar would look like on you." The High General tilted the captain's head sideways, pondering this with a curious glint in his eyes.

The captain swallowed hard. "I've done nothing." His voice quivered. "I swear."

Ghan hummed, unconvinced. "I wonder if General Mendi can help you remember why following the law is vital to our economy. Perhaps I'll bring you to him, and you can enlighten him? I'll enjoy watching your explanation."

The captain's eyes bulged.

"It should be entertaining if you know his reputation." Ghan scrutinized the Kahurangi prince with triumphant confidence, crossed the distance, and examined Rawiri's tattooed face. "And what about you? I could give you a scar, too."

Rawiri said nothing. The nick on his neck stung. Drops of blood had mixed with his sweat, causing an uncomfortable itch. Despite the urge to scratch it, he did his best to resist, his eyes never breaking contact with Ghan's.

"Yours could benefit from one, Rawiri. It would disrupt the symmetry of your facial markings and make them... interesting."

The high general caught the sudden gleam of metal and moved instinctively, avoiding the dagger that the captain would've otherwise sunk into his flesh. Ghan grabbed the man's wrist and twirled, effortlessly slamming him onto the deck. The captain gasped when the knife intended for Ghan sank into his stomach.

Blood swiftly pooled under him.

"Too bad," Ghan said, faking his regret. "I missed the heart."

The captain's eyes widened as pain shot through his body. His hands trembled as he tried to pull the blade out, but Ghan pushed it deeper with his boot. "It's disappointing that *someone* forgot to check this idiot for weapons. I'm not happy about this."

A few officers nervously shifted on their feet.

Ghan shook his head. "What was this fool expecting, anyway? A medal for bravery?"

His dark laughter floated in the air.

The captain took his last breath. His eyes glazed over, and his body went limp.

"And here I was, counting on returning to the festival." He turned to Rawiri with a face that revealed he'd enjoyed every moment. "It revs up at night, Rawiri. My men were hoping to enjoy it, too. It's when the whores come out. Some are fantastic, especially those with tattooed chins."

Rawiri could sniff the dare; how Ghan tried his best to incite Rawiri into attacking him. Mahaluika's warning hammered his head. *Never turn your back on him. Never let his hands touch you.* Ataahua's words danced in his head. *Don't utter any words, or he will use them to trap you.*

Rawiri stood silently, his hands clenched, facing Arjun Ghan.

Ghan huffed. He unceremoniously dragged the lifeless body by a leg, a trail of blood shimmering in the moonlight, and threw it overboard with an unhurried kick. "One more thief, dead." He dusted his palms with satisfaction and eyed his men. "I'm done here. You know what to do."

He walked down the plank with his generals and disappeared into the night, his cackles hitting Rawiri's ears like discordant music.

An officer approached with cuffs and chains. Rawiri saw an opportunity to fight back, but something hit the back of his head hard, and everything turned black.

CHAPTER 46
DEFEAT

Rawiri floated at first, his mind hazy, but then something slimy coiled around his ankle and yanked hard, dragging him into the inky abyss. The frigid waters wrapped him in an icy grip. A searing pain shot through his left arm. He flinched in agony. Panicked, he kicked wildly, desperate to reach the surface before his air ran out.

A shimmering ribbon of delicate silver bubbles swirled around him, guiding him upward. He broke through the surface, gasping for breath, just as the presence leaped from the water, its ghostly form glinting in the moonlight before splashing back down in a shower of liquid diamonds.

"*Rawiri,*" a familiar voice called out, warm with affection.

"Kora!" he shouted, looking for her. "Kora!" His left arm throbbed painfully as he bobbed in the cold water. He scanned the waves, but only delicate foam circled him while Sharan's silvery glow shimmered on the water.

Rawiri woke up with a loud gasp.

Distant voices lingered in his mind, gradually getting closer. His hand reached for the back of his head, where a swollen lump throbbed with pain. Dried blood and dirt caked in his hair. He was filthy from lying on the floor. Hay stuck to his face. The acrid scent of urine and human refuse choked the air. The swaying told him he was inside a ship. The feeble light confirmed they were under the ship's deck, transported like cheap cargo.

"Highness?" A gentle hand patted his arm. "Are you all right?"

Rawiri sat up slowly, his vision swimming. Pain throbbed in his skull. The lingering dizziness from the concussion made the world tilt around him.

"Manaaki, get water," said that familiar voice.

Rawiri recognized it, but formulating words took him some time. His mind was chaotic. Myriad images moved swiftly past him. The unbearable headache felt like a hammer had mistaken his head for an anvil.

Manaaki brought a cup while the men settled around Rawiri. A few worried faces stared at him. Rawiri's eyes landed on the most familiar one.

"Tawhiri...?" he asked.

The man heaved with relief. "Your Highness, are you well?"

Rawiri groaned, rubbing the back of his head. "I've been better." Assorted memories assailed him. "How long have I been out?"

"Almost three days."

Rawiri's eyes widened, massaging the back of his neck. "Was I out that long?"

"We were anxious, Highness," Tawhiri said. "We feared the worst."

Rawiri took the cup from Manaaki and sipped from it. The water went down his throat, the mouthful heavenly on his parched throat. Iron bit into his wrists and ankles, the chains pulling him down. His vision sharpened slowly.

"Is everybody here?" he asked.

"Highness, you must rest." Tawhiri's hand kept him from getting up.

Rawiri grunted, waving the cup. "I'll rest when I know what's going on." So many questions encircled his head. "Where are we?"

"On our way to Kahurang."

His head snapped back to Tawhiri. "What?"

"We're in a Zahari naval ship headed for Almarim, where a Kahurangi delegation awaits our arrival. We'll be released to them. They'll take us the rest of the way."

"Almarim." Rawiri took a moment to process the information, his brain still sluggish. "I see. Prince Bikram must be acting as a mediator." His cousin. *That makes sense.* The headache was formidable, which made thinking that much harder. Ghan's gritty cackle echoed in his mind, and more images emerged.

Panic surged. Rawiri gripped Tawhiri's arm. "What happened?"

Tawhiri's brow wrinkled. "They were waiting for us, Highness. Someone tipped them off. One of their officers knew the signal to lure us in."

Rawiri rubbed his brow. "Why aren't they keeping us as prisoners?"

"You're a prince of Kahurang." Tawhiri's laughter rang out, bitter and mirthless. "Tattoos also make it difficult to hide us. Soon enough, His Majesty would locate us, pay the ransom for our release, bring this issue to the Commonwealth, and persuade the other nations to declare war on Zahar." At Rawiri's grimace, Tawhiri added, "The situation is being dealt with diplomatically to avoid embarrassment on both sides."

Rawiri's eyes narrowed into slits, disliking what he heard. "What do you mean?"

"Kidnapping princesses is a serious offense."

"When did freeing slaves become kidnapping?" he shouted.

Every man around the prince stiffened. Tawhiri lowered his head. "It came out wrong, Highness. We all saw how the sisters were treated."

"And we heard it, too," Manaaki added. "I won't repeat the slurs—"

"*Tuhinga o mua,*" Tawhiri shushed him, eyebrows slamming into a withering glare that made Manaaki swallow hard.

Rawiri grunted. "What else?"

"The female monk interceded on our behalf," Tawhiri continued. "The envoys told us. She spoke about how we protected the princesses when a drunken mob turned on us, that what ensued was a huge misunderstanding, that we didn't kidnap them."

"Then why are we leaving Zahar?"

Tawhiri's lips thinned. "The Butcher also accused you of murdering the ship's captain."

That comment echoed in Rawiri's mind for a long moment, a pulsating collection of words that hammered his head relentlessly. "So, he framed me."

Tawhiri spat on the floor. "We saw him kill the captain and told our diplomats everything. They said it would become a game of finger-pointing that we were bound to lose since the Butcher holds sway within the Zahari court."

"*Peke* bastard." Rawiri balled his hands so hard they shook.

Tawhiri's lips pursed, forehead creased, before he said, "The Zahari will execute you if you ever return to Zahar."

"He did this." Rawiri cringed. "That man found out and set us up."

"Sir," Wiremu said, "we all saw what happened. The Butcher killed the captain—"

"It doesn't matter." Rawiri struck the floor with his fist

and loosed a loud, angry bellow. "It's his word against ours. He played his pieces well, destroying any semblance of the impeccable reputation I could bring to the table." He groaned, furious. Another exhale brought him the clarity he needed to remain calm. "The girls. Are they well? I must know."

Tawhiri shook his head. "We haven't heard, Highness."

Rawiri felt dizzy. "That they could believe I'm a murderer." It hit him the hardest, and angry tears pooled in his eyes. He looked away, didn't wipe them.

"Highness...?" Tawhiri broke off, swallowing once. "There's more." He gestured to Rawiri's left arm.

Only then did Rawiri register the pulsing pain coursing through him. He lifted his left sleeve, revealing raw, inflamed skin beneath. The wounds looked eerily like those left by a venomous jellyfish. Tendrils had wrapped around his chest and coiled tightly down his left arm. Angry red welts and swollen lacerations marred his flesh, the marks pulsing as if the creature's venom still lingered.

Faces turned toward the arm. No one spoke for a heartbeat.

"Tanganokai's curse," one of his men murmured.

Faces blanched. A few made warding signs without realizing it.

Rawiri's entire world came crashing down around him, the weight of such ruin driving the air from his lungs.

"*Betray him,*" Ataahua had told him, "*and you'll become his kanga. A walking curse. An empty shell holding nothing.*"

He stared at his calloused hands, letting those words sink in—what they truly meant—and clenched them.

Failure tasted bitter.

Rawiri choked on a sob.

"You made Kahurang proud," he addressed his men. "You stood for what was right and didn't falter when it counted. This will not touch you." He lowered his sleeve and took a deep breath. "This is all on me." His voice cracked with emotion. "I failed her," he stammered, that statement a searing truth. "I didn't listen to her when it mattered most. I failed my Teppe." He lifted his gaze, staring at his men. "And I failed you."

He'd lost everything, even Tanganokai's blessing. Now, disgrace awaited him in Kahurang—probably execution.

Defeat crashed over him like a suffocating wave, and he wailed without restraint. He made no effort to hold back his tears, letting them stream down his dirt-streaked cheeks. A raw ache opened in his chest and left him hollow. The awful truth settled like a stone in his chest—his eight children gone, their mother lost to the sea, and now... his beloved Teppe.

He had always been an empty shell holding nothing.

PART THREE

THE YOKE OF TIME

CHAPTER 47

SORROW

Kharis jolted upright on the bed. Blurry images that she'd fought her assailants before the world turned black played in her mind. Everything had happened so fast. She'd bitten a hand. Her boot heel had certainly met someone's head. She checked her hands and arms, revealing no cuts, scratches, or bruises.

She threw her covers off to check on Saya, who was still sound asleep. She examined one of her hands, careful not to wake her up. The purple bruises on her arm, where unkind hands had clamped onto her, and the abrasions on her knuckles confirmed they'd indeed struggled.

Her memories were fuzzy, as though a painter had brushed them with fog...

Rawiri!

Kharis hurried to the balcony, leaning over the marble balustrade to search for him. He wasn't in the garden, reading under the bougainvillea-covered pergola like he usually did when he waited for them. She ran down the long, empty corridor toward the sitting room and flung the doors open. He wasn't there either.

Before tears took over, she rushed down the stairs and past the stunned servants.

"Highness!" one of them yelled at her.

"You're barefoot," said another.

"You're wearing your night shift," a third shouted at her.

Kharis sprinted toward the palace, moving as swiftly as the wind. The soldiers stationed at the ornate iron gate watched her streak past and, for a heartbeat, stood still, processing the blur. Soon, they chased her. She advanced quickly, entering the palace, dodging servants and sentries, sliding past attendants carrying trays, and darting between nobles engaged in conversation. A cacophony of alarmed cries and hurried commands echoed through the grand halls.

"Stop her!"

"Move it!"

"Grab her!"

When she found herself before Rawiri's chamber doors, she steeled her resolve and pushed them open.

The sitting room was empty. No Kahurangi décor adorned the walls or tables. The floors were bare, and the bookshelves empty. She checked the other rooms in his apartment and found them in the same state.

Rawiri was gone.

As if he'd never been here.

A painful swell forced the sobs that had been trapped in her chest. She dropped to the floor and cried, each howl burning her throat.

Hala stood by the entryway, stopping the soldiers and dismissing the servants. When her watery gaze met her brother's, he entered the room and closed the door behind him.

Kharis wiped her nose, and her tired eyes gave Hala a long, deep stare.

"He's... gone?" Her words faltered, aware that voicing her question would imply an answer she wouldn't like.

Hala settled beside her, closing the distance without being intrusive. Her chest shuddered, and he wrapped an arm around her shoulder. His smile was soft—an older brother hoping to comfort his baby sister.

"I'm so sorry, Khiri."

That was the answer she dreaded most. The kind tone in his voice brought back that awful emptiness.

Her beloved tutor was no longer at the palace. A fresh wave of grief overtook her, and her mournful cry tore from her throat. She wept over Rawiri, her suffocating lack of freedom, and the overwhelming sense that there was no hope, not even a sliver to keep her going.

CHAPTER 48
THE FURY WITHIN

Hala never answered her questions.

"It'll be best if you rest, Khiri," he said. "We'll speak in the morning." He hugged her gently, a tender kiss landing on her forehead, and knelt to put on the slippers on her feet that a servant handed him. "Promise me you'll rest." He met her gaze, his forehead wrinkled with concern. "Yes?"

Kharis nodded, struggling not to cry all over again.

"That's a good girl." He rose and patted her head, wrapping a cloak around her. With his quick nod, imperial guards escorted her back to the villa.

Once she returned, servants hovered over her.

"Are you hungry?"

"Would you like a bath?"

Ignoring their questions, she climbed the stairs. Since Saya was still asleep, she headed for the private terrace.

The sun bathed everything in its warm, golden glow. A gentle breeze swayed the palm trees, their long fronds shimmering in the sunlight. Bees flitted from one bloom to another, the scent of lavender heavy in the afternoon air.

Glistening droplets clung to the lion-shaped fountains, catching the sunlight like liquid diamonds.

It should've made Kharis smile, but her eyes watered again.

Deep sobs racked her body. She folded into herself, burying her face in the crook of her arm. She muffled her cries to avoid waking Saya, concealing her pain to prevent it from traveling through their bond and alerting her sister to her side.

"It was all my fault." Her voice quivered.

"*Why are you blaming yourself?*" asked the silvery voice.

She straightened, turning around to look for the voice's owner. "Where are you?" With a sleeve swipe, she dried her cheeks. "Who... are you?"

"*I'll be whatever you wish me to be, whatever you need me to be.*"

His tender tone reached her like a soothing balm, touching the wounded corners of her heart. That gentility became a shaft of sunlight, parting clouds after a heavy rain. Kharis didn't want to face her pain alone. She couldn't. And she didn't want Saya carrying this burden on her behalf. Her chest cleaved with the weight of guilt, and new tears pricked her eyes.

"I need a friend." Her request came from deep within her soul—a call for help, for support, for a glimmer of hope.

"*Then I'll be your friend. What do you wish me to do? How do I comfort you?*"

"Comfort me?" It turned out to be a perplexing question. What would comfort her? Freedom was what she wanted. Freedom to make her own choices—good and bad ones. But when would she ever see her wish come true?

"Just... stay with me. Don't leave me, like my mother, like Rawiri."

Kharis slid to the floor with her knees pressed to her chest and cried again, her sorrow spilling out in silent waves.

In the realm of her mind, the voice's owner sat beside her like a silent guardian. His quiet strength met the fragility of her emotions, forging a connection that transcended the need for words. He waited with her, ready to fulfill any request she might have.

&.

Saya opened her eyes with heavy blinks. Her body was sore, and her mind a scrambled mess of thoughts and images. The inside of her nose and throat stung as if burned by heated smoke. A pulsating throb pummeled her skull ruthlessly. She rubbed her forehead, wishing for the ache to go away.

Outside, dusk had enveloped the sky, tinging everything in garnet and gold. The evening shadows had crept in, gradually cloaking the bedroom.

The bedroom...?

She sat up slowly. Her muscles screeched at the effort. A pained groan escaped her.

Thirsty, she got out of bed, spotted an ewer, and, bypassing a cup, gulped the water. Muddled recollections replayed in her mind. She'd been at the festival last night, then on a ship. *Right?* Her sense of time was off, as if she'd slept for days.

Her eyes landed on the other bed—the empty one.

Her gaze swiftly moved to the open balcony doors. Her sister stood there, conversing with someone. Her murmurs carried an unusual softness as if directed to someone standing beside her rather than a person in the garden below.

"Khiri?" she called out.

Kharis didn't move, focused on her quiet exchange.

Who's she talking to? With a furrowed brow, she crossed the length of the room. *Is it Rawiri?* Crossing the balcony doors, Saya settled beside her. A quick, furtive glance revealed an empty patio bathed in the last bursts of vibrant crimson and dark amber before the evening's indigo gobbled it up.

The hair on her arms lifted.

"Khiri...?"

Kharis slowly rolled her gaze toward her sister as if awakened from a daydream.

"How are you doing?" Saya asked.

Kharis's face was unusually blank, but her eyes were red and puffy.

"Is everything all right?" Saya insisted.

Her sister nodded, oddly quiet and somewhat disconnected.

"How long have I been out?" Saya asked.

With a narrowed look, Kharis looked up, studying a few passing clouds. "Servants will bring dinner soon."

"How long?" Saya insisted.

Kharis studied the wispy gray puffs, watching how they dissolved in the sky's violet. "A full day," she finally said. "I'm the Djinnshirukh, sister. I heal much faster than you."

Saya raised her eyebrows. Kharis's tone worried her. Anger and resignation resided in those words, but something else mixed in—dangerous, full of steely claws and fangs, feral and bloodthirsty.

"My apologies, Khiri. I didn't mean to—"

"Why are you apologizing?"

Saya stiffened at the atonal question. Perhaps it was better not to say anything. She remained beside the sister she loved above all else, but just in case, she scooted closer. Since Kharis didn't push her away, she wrapped an arm around her shoulders, heads touching.

"I love you, Khiri."

Her sister's tense body finally eased.

"And I love you more," Kharis said.

CHAPTER 49

THE WINDS OF BETRAYAL

The next day, Hala had breakfast with his sisters, but the three ate in uncomfortable silence.

Kharis barely touched her food, pushing it around with her fork. Occasionally, she took a bite, making a face each time. Hala had gone to great lengths to ensure that servants brought her favorite dishes: savory cornmeal sprinkled with crushed hazelnuts, potato-and-onion dumplings, and steamed fish. Kharis barely ate any of it, lost in thought.

Saya kept her eyes on her plate, rarely looking at him.

For his plan to work, he had to earn their trust and fix any severed hopes and wishes with bribes. He pondered what to offer them so they could put this fiasco with Rawiri behind them and move on. Their willingness to cooperate without resistance was the measure of his success.

Hala wasn't sure what to make of the awkward stillness, so he decided to speak first.

"I'll answer your questions." He regretted saying it once those words left his lips. It was out now, and he braced for the anger he expected, but none came his way.

Kharis stared at her food with the same blank stare,

picking at her steamed fish as if Hala's remark were no more than a breeze blowing past her.

Saya's lips twitched with questions, her eyes darting between him and Kharis until she couldn't hold them. "What happened to Nana?" Her voice was a tad too soft. "Is she safe?"

Hala was relieved that the grim silence had finally ended. "She's a remarkably strong woman, but her face found itself on the wrong side of a fist—"

"That's not funny." Kharis slammed her hands on the table, rattling cups and dishes.

Hala flinched.

An orange rolled to the floor.

"A mob overtook us." Her voice rose. "One moment, she was laughing with us, and the next, she was pushing Rawiri to get us out of there. And while we ran away, they attacked her."

Hala raised his hands in a conciliatory motion. "I apologize, Khiri. I just wanted to make light of a difficult situation. My joke was in poor taste. Nana is well and recovering nicely. We can visit her today if you wish." He hoped his smile would convey his desire to fix the rift.

"When can I visit Prince Rawiri?" Kharis demanded. "I want to speak with him and know he's well, too."

A muscle ticked in his jaw. "Khiri—"

"When?" Her voice boomed across the room, her tone sharp like a blade.

The fire in it stung Hala, but he couldn't allow her to assert herself in this fashion. The upper hand belonged to him—always him. He inhaled slowly, counting to ten in his head as he put his fork down. He reminded himself that he had to be the doting brother for his plan to work.

Keep your composure.

"Although we understand that he wanted to rescue you," he said, "he didn't take you back to the palace as agreed at our many meetings where we planned and organized this blasted festival visit." Fury was coursing through him now, trampling on his composure. "Instead, he took you to a ship, violating *your* water prohibition." His voice surged as he rose from his chair. "Last I checked, the palace's on the opposite side of the Ibaia quay."

"He was protecting us," Kharis shouted.

"Then he failed, didn't he?" Hala roared as his fist struck the table.

She wasn't relenting. "When can I talk to him?"

"You can't."

Kharis held Hala's glare. Her voice was low and controlled. The air around her became heated. "Why won't you let me see him?"

"Because we sent him away."

Her nostrils flared as her breath rushed through them. "We were at the festival two nights ago. Where is he?"

Hala averted his eyes. He paused, calming his breath and uncurling his fingers. "His ship has sailed for Kahurang. By now, they've cleared the delta and are on their way to Almarim."

Her eyelids fluttered in a few quick blinks. Her hands, flat against the table, shook. The wood under them began to smoke.

Seeing those wispy tendrils gave Hala some pause. Rage was a dangerous state for the Djinnshirukh—an emotion that could unleash the Akumi king. Hala had to avoid *that* at all costs.

"I don't want to discuss this any further." He sat, his back ramrod straight, and crossed his arms, hoping to end this conversation. "This bickering won't get us anywhere."

"Hala..."

He ignored Saya's warning tone. Unable to meet his sisters' gaze, he focused on the balcony instead. "Rawiri's gone, and that is that."

"That is that?"

Hala turned to Kharis.

Her eyes bulged as she clenched her hands. A dangerous smile flashed on her face as she cocked her head. "That. Is. That?" She enunciated each word with weighted scorn. Her piercing glare lifted the hair in his arms. Her deep, guttural growl was the last sound he heard before she stormed out of the dining room.

"Where are you going?" Hala threw his napkin on the plate and pulled himself away from the table, facing the door she'd exited. "We're not done with this conversation. Khiri, get back in here!"

When she didn't, he shouted with all his might, spit flying out of his mouth.

"Kharis Ghan, return this instance."

CHAPTER 50

THE PROMISE

Saya rose slowly, paying no attention to Hala's expletive-laden outburst.

The invisible bond between the Djinnshirukh and the Sorukhipa flickered desperately, like the line of a kite caught in stormy winds, its thread on the brink of snapping. She rubbed at her brow. Sweat traced her temples and slid down her spine. Her world was spinning out of control. She struggled to maintain her composure—to be kind, loyal, and dependable.

She drew a careful breath. Then another.

Shouts from outside cut through the room.

Saya stiffened. Her pulse surged, loud in her ears. She turned and bolted for the door, leaving a bewildered Hala behind.

***

Kharis ran, dodging people as a need beyond her drove her body. She punched and kicked the sentries blocking her way, leaving a trail of gasping bodies in her wake.

As a formidable weapon imbued with otherworldly

strength and speed, she effortlessly pushed past the palace's heavy doors, swiftly navigating through the bustling Zahar-Regia square. She ran, her pace intense, until one of the massive Zahar-Homa gates loomed ahead of her.

Behind her, palace guards yelled and gave chase. On the barbican, others hurried toward the levers to slam the massive gate shut. Soldiers appeared from all sides. Kharis pushed herself, her strides lengthening with each step. Her lungs burned, yet she surged forward as if propelled by the wind. She slid under the imposing iron gate, narrowly escaping its thud as it slammed shut and rattled.

A column of White Guard officers crashed against the bars, colliding with one another amidst a tangle of bodies and a flurry of muttered curses.

"Spear me!"

"Fires, get off me!"

Their angry fists pounded relentlessly on the formidable iron. Their barked orders cut through the chaos.

"Open the blasted gate!"

Kharis smirked and melded into the sea of people that filled the bustling capital.

🙎

Trumpets blared, sounding the alarm, and Saya halted. The zenka soldiers patrolling the neighborhoods stood still, waiting for the next set of signals.

An eerie silence hung in the air as shoppers and vendors exchanged worried glances.

The trumpets resounded again—loud and sustained—like the mighty waters of the Ibaia River. Standing on a tower, a zenka soldier used banners to signal a message.

"The docks!" Saya knew what that message meant. To her chagrin, so did the Zenka forces aiding the royal guards that poured out of the Zahar-Regia. She had to get to Kharis before they did. Saya turned, scanning the streets. The city refused to arrange itself in her mind. She'd never been out of the Zahar-Regia long enough to form a proper mental map of the city. But the festival paths surfaced, bright and recent, winding through the chaos like a promise.

She broke into a run.

"Where are the docks?" she asked frantically of passersby. "The docks?" she insisted, tugging on sleeves.

"That way," said one vendor, and she ran in the direction given.

Dread was pushing her, giving her feet wings.

Fully awakened, the bond between her and the Djinnshirukh vibrated like a thread held against a fierce gale, tugging and pulling on her.

Kharis was everything to her—the center of her world. And so, Saya, who loved Kharis above all else, rushed through the streets on her way to the docks, bumping into people, jumping over carts and crates, and dodging soldiers herself.

❧

Soldiers yelled, shoving their way through as the mystified crowds parted.

"There she is."

"Get her!"

"She's headed that way!"

"Move it!"

The imperial and zenka guards sprinted after Kharis, but she dashed through alleyways and streets with one goal—to reach the docks.

Curse the whole water prohibition. She would jump on any ship and wave everybody goodbye while at it. She was done with Hala, Zahar-Ghak, and this stupid Djinnshirukh nonsense that kept her from having a life. Once on a ship— any ship—she would make it to Kahurang.

I'll be free at last.

The river scent became more potent as freedom lit the way for her. The streets soon opened to the quay ahead.

The soldiers were also closing in. *Blasted trumpets.* Kharis was aware they'd announced her location.

She ran and ran. Then she spotted it—Stoneberry Bridge—and the ship approaching it. Hope smiled at her.

Her breath burst in and out as she ran. Her heart pumped blood with vicious efficiency. Every muscle tensed and released, pushing her forward.

I must reach that bridge.

The damp wind blew past her, whipping her hair. Her lungs were on fire, gulping air. Nothing else mattered but the ship ahead. But then, the scent of jasmine and orange blossoms embraced her with arms that carried a strong sense of the familiar. Deep affection colored the sound, calling her back.

"Khiri."

Saya's magical tendrils had found her, gently coiling around her, asking her to stop—begging her to reconsider.

No.

Kharis's body became heavy.

No, Saya. I beg you.

It took Kharis longer to move her legs. The world was slowing down.

"Please!" she screamed.

The pull was strong, yet Kharis fought it. She would make it to the bridge. *I must.* She clenched her jaw and strained to keep going, engaging every thought on a single focus.

I must reach Stoneberry Bridge.

"Khiri..."

Kharis ground her teeth and kept running, but her legs had stopped moving.

The world stilled. She felt like she'd been caught in a vat of honey. Soldiers hung suspended mid-motion, their feet descending in agonizingly slow falls. The screaming faces froze into eerie stillness. The grasping hands, mere inches from her clothes, became petrified.

"Saya, please. I'm begging you."

Trapped inside an invisible containment, her sister's magic had immobilized everyone around her.

Freedom dissolved like shards of ice on a hot day.

Saya, the Sorukhipa, had unleashed her power and stopped the flow of time.

Kharis lifted her tear-blurred gaze. The wall shimmered beneath her fingers. A gilded silhouette rippled toward her.

"Why are you doing this?" Kharis had been so close— had almost grasped freedom. "Why are you stopping me?" Tears jumped from her eyes. "Let me go," she begged. "Please!"

Saya's golden orbs glowed with the intensity of her magic. "I can't, Khiri. Think about it. Do you believe High General Ghan and the Regiazenka will sit idly while you sail away? And what will be Zahar's response to this?" Her forehead creased. "Khiri, you *are* the Djinnshirukh."

"Please!" The world around her blurred as more tears collected in her eyes. "I can't do this anymore." It was either freedom or life in a gilded cage. "This place drains the very essence of my being." She gazed at her sister's shimmering form with pleading eyes. "Please, let me go."

The ship's horn blared its last call before approaching the bridge. Kharis's hope was sailing away. "Saya, *please*."

Saya's voice turned rueful. "Khiri, we'll leave Zahar on *our* terms when the time is right, without causing a war between the two nations, without bloodshed or destruction, or an impact on our subjects."

Caught between duty and the pull of desire, Kharis felt torn, her emotions waging a silent war. "This life is exhausting." Her lips quivered. Every hope and dream was melting before her eyes. "Please, release me. If you love me, set me free."

The shimmer on the surface wavered. Gold light thinned

and stretched. It clung to the silhouette before letting go. Saya stepped through.

Her eyes glistened. A tortured look crossed her face. Saya clutched Kharis's arms tightly. "Running away isn't the answer."

"Then come with me," Kharis wailed, her voice cracking as she strained against the magic holding her. The desperation in her voice surprised even herself. "Please."

A storm flashed behind Saya's golden eyes. "No nation will dare oppose Zahar by welcoming us. As soon as we arrive, they'll send us back. The Crown will place bounties on our heads and punish anyone helping us." Her words cut like glass. "There won't be any freedom, Khiri. We will be persecuted, and life will be worse once they find us."

Kharis lowered her head. Tears burned her eyes, the fight draining out of her like water slipping through her fingers.

"Listen to me," Saya said. "We'll leave this place together, of our own accord and with the Regiazenka's blessing." She wiped Kharis's tears with a gentle thumb. "There won't be a war, Khiri. When we leave, there will be a celebration."

With a sharp intake of breath, Kharis accepted defeat. "You promise?"

Saya's kind smile never faltered. "Would I ever break my word to you?"

Kharis's howl splintered the silence between them. It was raw and unrestrained, brimming with despair and shattered hope. Her knees buckled, and she sagged into Saya's arms, giving up on her dream of being free.

※

Saya stilled when something tangled in the bond between her and the Djinnshirukh. A power as intense as a southern wind—hot, dry, and full of anger.

295

"*How could you betray her?*" This voice shrieked, rage consuming this other pair of eyes—a glowering stare that wasn't silver and sapphire but scorching crimson.

Saya threw her arms around Kharis, roaring her threat against the invisible intruder. "She's *my* sister! I'm the one who protects her. Do you hear me? Stay away from her."

Saya released her magic, and time unfroze.

Chaos resumed.

Gulls took flight, their panicked cries piercing the air.

Shouting soldiers surged forward.

Screams erupted from the dockworkers and fishermen, who scrambled to duck behind crates.

Then, a massive blast of gold light engulfed the quay.

CHAPTER 51

THE FORGE OF RESENTMENT

High General Arjun Ghan, donning his military regalia, stood before the imperial king of Zahar. Hröld's immutable gaze stared at him while the annoying crown prince settled to the king's right. Below the dais sat the Regiazenka—fourteen unfriendly ministers wearing luxurious ivory and gold finery.

Bloody royal protocol.

Faking his politeness, Ghan offered everyone a soft, pleasant smile and continued his report. "Once we found the princesses, we returned them to their residence."

"How did Princess Kharis breach the palace security?" Hröld's jaw was tight, his gaze accusatory.

Ghan kept his composure, forcing himself not to cackle with an "I told you so" smirk. "She's the Djinnshirukh, Your Majesty. No wall will ever be too high for her. Locks and gates can't keep her inside forever."

"Then how do we contain her?" the king asked.

"The answer is simple." He tried to suppress it, but the outline of a sneer crossed his face. "The best incentive for good behavior lies in keeping the sisters apart."

"I disagree." Hala jumped from his chair.

"I won't allow it." Hröld waved his hand to urge Hala to sit. "Not only are they sisters who care for each other deeply, but there's no point if the Sorukhipa is far from the Djinnshirukh she must guard."

"Your Majesty," Ghan said, "perhaps different chambers might—"

Hröld's features hardened. "I *won't* allow it."

"Your Majesty," Lady Khostuna said, "The Regiazenka supports your position. We can't fault the Djinnshirukh for the events that led to her failed escape." Her eyes slid to Ghan. "It appears security was lacking."

Ghan fisted his hands, maintaining a pleasant demeanor even as this meeting tested his limited patience. The metaphorical Silver Moon Festival fireworks were still exploding in his head. The headache was overwhelming.

Hröld exhaled quietly. "Arjun, what happened?"

"As you know..." Ghan let the pause stretch. "The Djinnshirukh bypassed our checkpoints—all of them—and made it to the quay."

"And why was she headed that way?" Hröld asked, eyes narrowed.

"We're unsure," Ghan said. "My working assumption is that she got lost. Stoneberry Bridge left a lasting impression on her when she visited with—" He paused, embodying the role of a Zahari still offended by the Kahurangi prince's failed kidnapping attempt. "Perhaps that's why she went there."

Hröld huffed audibly, making Ghan's inward smile much brighter. "I can share that a beam of light shot up in the sky, followed by a formidable blast of"—he read the report—"sunlight."

A roll of whispers traveled the chamber.

"It's how my men described it," Ghan added. "Sunlight and the lingering scent of orange blossoms. Other eyewitnesses corroborated it. The explosion rattled nearby buildings, cracked a few windows, and lifted a considerable cloud of dust. When everything settled, we found the sisters unconscious, clutching each other, and a ring of soldiers equally knocked out, spread around them."

Ghan waited for the next question, but when it didn't come, he continued.

"Your Majesty, the Djinnshirukh's magic—"

"What proof do you have that Kharis did it?" Hala cut him off, his tone harsh.

Ghan almost arched an eyebrow at him. "None, Highness, outside worrisome cracks on walls, broken cobblestones, and plenty of shattered glass." He relished the idea that his comment would fuel gossip and rumors.

"Our evidence," Prince Jordha swiftly added, "points to forgotten festival fireworks. An unfortunate coincidence, and nothing else. Thankfully, the engineers have deemed the quay safe and have allowed the port to reopen. Therefore, the arrival and departure of ships have resumed, and cleanup is underway." He glared at Ghan. "Normalcy has returned."

Hröld exhaled his relief. "How are the soldiers?"

"They are recovering," Ghan said. "Most have headaches or ringing in the ears. A few are still experiencing dizziness or vertigo. Overall, nothing of concern, according to Her Excellency Monk Yuna." Ghan almost tittered, aware of how she hated that title.

Hröld's face softened. "And the girls?"

"No harm came to them, according to Yuna's report."

"Thank you," Hröld said—a silent dismissal.

Ghan dipped his head, silently seething, and sat.

When the proceedings were over, Ghan exited with General Mendi trailing him.

"You're limping," Ghan said.

"Nothing of concern," Aghet Mendi said. "Yours truly is rather resilient."

Ghan frowned. "Where have you been? You were gone for weeks."

Mendi didn't reply, keeping his rhythm behind his high general, despite favoring one leg over the other.

Ghan drummed his fingers against his thigh. "You missed the fireworks."

Aghet chuckled. "So I've heard, but you handled it admirably."

Ghan halted and met Aghet's gaze. Held it. "Where were you?"

Aghet arched a brow. "I'm not accustomed to explaining my every move. You asked for the Djinnshirukh, so I've spared no effort to present her on a silver platter, as it befits you. Trapping an inconvenient yet cunning mouse takes finesse and patience, my prince." His gaze glimmered. "To achieve it, I must move freely—unencumbered." Then he leaned in closer. "But if you wanted to breathe down my neck," a cruel grin hinted at the corners of his mouth, "I could easily arrange it."

Ghan loathed dares and threats. He stared at Aghet for a moment longer, his temple vein pulsing. "You haven't answered any of my questions."

Aghet's gaze sharpened. "Would you answer mine?"

"Aghet." Ghan's voice took an ominous edge.

Aghet exhaled, and his face softened. "My prince, that power doesn't belong in the hands of a child, but you must decide if you possess the courage to take it from her—to do what you must. Your hesitation... doesn't become you." Aghet's eyes narrowed. "Where's the man I met *that* day?"

That day. On a bloody battlefield. Ghan glared at Aghet, huffed, and resumed his march.

The lack of footsteps announced that Aghet wasn't following. Ghan turned, only to find his lover observing him keenly. Ghan's nostrils flared. "What is it?"

Aghet eyed the servants scurrying past them with quick, nervous steps. Once they turned the corner, his gaze returned to the high general, studying him with an unreadable face.

"Nothing." An icy smile played on his lips. "Nothing at all, my prince."

Ghan's lips twitched. That "nothing" was a sharp dagger Aghet had just hurled at him.

It's only a word.

And yet, his hands clenched. He was back to being that lonely child in a corner of the room, surrounded by expensive toys, while his father showered Yuna and Aghuti with affection. *It's nothing.* Rage surged through him, not the scorching type, but slow and terrifying—cracking ominously like a sheet of ice over a lake.

He turned and marched down the corridor. If Aghet followed, he didn't care—tried not to care.

CHAPTER 52
CRIMSON EYES

Weeks slipped past, steady as the waves of the mighty Ibaia River.

On this particular day, Saya was performing her exercises with General Salazar. She emulated Salazar as he explained proper form and the principles of foot placement and winding, emphasizing body mechanics and cutting alignment. Sharp, one-sided metal blades had replaced their wooden swords—Ghan's coming-of-age gift.

"Now that you're using an actual blade," he said, "we'll go over the basics to ensure your safety."

Saya nodded with little else to say. They repeated the steps together, moving through different cut positions.

"Nicely done," he said. "Go ahead and take a water break."

She wiped the sweat from her brow and reached for her water, but a stern voice rose above the clatter of swords. Their uncle was drilling Kharis on a particular maneuver— the heart plunge. He expected her to leap onto the vertical dummy and drive her blade down, piercing the target until the sword tip struck the floor. Nothing out of the ordinary, except he barked his orders with scorn.

Saya frowned, but the thirteen-year-old knew better than to speak up. Questioning the high general publicly came with punishment, princess or not.

Kharis repeated the drill over and over, but it didn't satisfy him. *Nothing ever does.*

"Once the enemy is down, you must finish them." Ghan forced Kharis to redo the steps. "Again. Again. AGAIN." He struck the floor with his staff to keep the rhythm.

The knuckles on Kharis's sword hand whitened. That gesture worried Saya. Dark emotions surged through her bond with Kharis. *Do something*, Saya told herself. *But what?*

"Wrong! Do it again."

The officers exchanged wary glances. A few whispered among themselves, flinching when Ghan yelled at Kharis. The high general was in a particularly foul mood today.

"You're useless," he roared. "Do it *again!*"

Saya clenched her jaw. Kharis's form was accurate. Her moves were precise, her speed otherworldly. Kharis *was* the embodiment of perfection. However, High General Arjun Ghan expected his definition of it. And so, he banged the wooden floor with his staff, the gold fittings atop it jangling. Kharis gritted her teeth each time, clearly unnerved by their sound. Rather than stop, Ghan continued, seemingly pleased with her distress. His verbal assault continued as he made her repeat the same tedious drill nonstop.

"You're *nothing* but a monster."

"Useless."

"You can't do anything right."

The bond tugged on Saya, demanding something from her—action, interference, courage. It sensed her hesitation, so something else coiled around that filament when she did nothing.

"You are worthless if all you do is watch."

Saya froze, questioning her sanity, and turned around, looking for the one who'd spoken to her.

"Highness?" Salazar asked.

She snapped out of her shock and offered Salazar a quick bow. "My apologies, sir."

Salazar didn't say much, but his glimpse in Ghan's direction conveyed that the ongoing abuse bothered him, too—that it was painful to watch. The tension in the room thickened. The officers murmured among themselves, some frowning as they watched how Ghan pounced on a hummingbird.

"Ready to continue?" Salazar asked.

The Sorukhipa got into position, but her mind was no longer on the exercise. Behind her, Ghan yelled at her sister, his gravely voice echoing against the walls.

The thread connecting the sisters pulled, tugged, then jerked—hard.

"*Where are you?*" that voice asked with growing urgency. "*Where is her protector?*"

Saya halted, desperate for air.

Salazar's brow creased. "Are you well, Highness?"

A sudden jolt flooded the bond as though lightning had struck her. She swiftly pivoted on a heel.

"You're wasting my time," Ghan shouted at the top of his lungs. "Do it again! You useless thing."

Kharis lunged and plunged her sword into the intended target with such force that the flooring shook and cracked. The dummy shattered. The sword's tip snapped off, hurtling across the room. It embedded itself into the wall, perilously close to an officer's head. The woman froze as she studied the sharp metal that could've speared her skull.

Everyone froze, wide-eyed faces watching Kharis. That unexpected show of power had stunned the entire room into silence. Even Ghan had clamped his mouth shut.

The Djinnshirukh crouched beside what remained of the shattered wooden dummy, her fingers white-knuckled around the sword. Her shoulders rose and fell with ragged breaths. Her sister's eyes glowed crimson, and through them, another presence looked back at her. Ancient. Ravenous. Not Kharis.

Goose bumps prickled across Saya's skin.

"*You didn't help her,*" said the silvery voice that traveled through the bond. "*She is mine now.*"

That word echoed in Saya's mind, accompanied by the ghost of an unkind smile.

"*Mine.*"

CHAPTER 53
THE HAWK AND THE BIRDS

Saya jolted upright, drenched in sweat, gasping for air.
A nightmare.

She patted her chest with a trembling hand, slowly regaining her breathing rhythm. It was hot and muggy. Her night shift stuck to her skin. She wiped the sweat off her forehead and flicked the plastered hair strands off her face, but couldn't shake off the guilt gnawing at her.

Why didn't I stop Ghan yesterday?

Saya shook her head to erase the question from her mind.

Awake and unable to return to sleep, she got up. She strolled down the corridor and stopped by one window, observing the millions of stars. They twinkled, oblivious to the toils of men or sisters.

The Silver River commandeered the night sky—a luminous flow across the black sky. Sharan, the ivory moon, was rising in the east, crowning the mountains with its light. Tung, the tiny red moon, was already midway. The celestial sisters chased each other, battling for a place in the starry canopy. Soon, Tung would catch up with Sharan. As it crossed over the ivory moon, it would give Sharan its curious red eye for three days.

"Who am I?" Saya wondered. "Am I Sharan or Tung? Do I lead or follow?" Lately, she'd felt like neither. Guilt was eating her from the inside out—a bite here, a taste there, leaving holes in her soul.

"Why didn't I help her?"

Why didn't she let Kharis get on the ship or stop Ghan's abuse? Saya pressed her hands against her eyes with a grunt. *Why?* She leaned her forehead against the window pane only to find it warm.

Her gaze traveled to the bedchamber doors.

"Khiri's all I have," she said to the empty corridor. "I'm an orphan. A royal decree made me a princess. Another could take it away. What do I have to call my own?" The Djinnshirukh defined the Sorukhipa's entire existence. "Without her, I'm nothing." Saya heaved a sigh. "So why didn't I help her?"

With sunrise a few hours away, her thoughts wandered to the books on the sitting room table. "There has to be a way out of this." A road out of being the Djinnshirukh and the Sorukhipa. A path to a different life.

The crimson thread connecting her to her beloved Khiri fluttered, always present—delicate, like a silk filament, but it sometimes carried thorns and sharp barbs.

❧

Tender arms wrapped around Saya, pulling her from the quiet world of her book. A soft, sisterly kiss landed on her cheek.

"What are you doing up so early?" Saya asked.

"Early?" Kharis gave her sister another tight cuddle. "The sun's already out." Her breathing tickled Saya's ear. She sat beside her, fingertips grazing over the spines of books before plucking one off the pile. "Is your insomnia back?"

Saya breathed out. "It never left."

"That's it." Kharis struck the table. "I'm taking you to Nana."

"It's nothing—"

"Insomnia isn't nothing." Kharis's voice softened with concern. "What bothers you?"

Saya groaned. Kharis took the hint and opened the book, lazily flipping its pages until she paused on one. "You know...?" Her gaze never left that page. "I still dream of the festival."

Saya's heart lurched.

That night.

Hala and Jordha had questioned them endlessly, repeating the same inquiries in different forms. No matter how hard they tried to trip them, Kharis's and Saya's retelling of the night's events had remained consistent. The Zahari soldiers had been excessive in their force to part a crowd. A few drunks had taken offense at that, and the mob had turned. Rawiri had dragged them away in the ensuing mayhem, got lost in the narrow alleyways, and ended up by the docks. They had climbed onto that ship, the safest spot beyond the ruckus.

Ghan had been in the room, leaning against a wall with arms crossed, studying them with sore eyes.

Ghan...

"We must get dressed," Saya said, putting her book down. "The servants will be coming soon with breakfast."

Kharis grimaced. "Do we have to attend class? It's so hot."

"We're princesses of the realm, with duties and obligations."

"Then you go and tell me how it goes."

"Khiri?" Saya's voice sharpened.

"If you are not seeing Nana, I'm not going," Kharis said. "I'll visit the Royal Library instead."

"Fine!" Saya hissed.

Kharis flinched, her head snapping back in surprise.

"Sorry," Saya said. "I'll ask Hala if we can go this afternoon. Nana will perform a thorough check-up to show you there's nothing wrong with me."

"If you can't fall asleep—"

"Get dressed and stop wasting time."

Kharis's eyebrows lifted.

Saya huffed, mad at herself. Here was Kharis, concerned and seeking to help her, yet Saya hadn't helped her the day before. Guilt took another bite.

"I'm truly sorry." Saya took a deep breath and offered Kharis a playful smile. "I'll race you."

With the incentive to move away from this subject, both girls sprinted for the door, dashing down the hallway.

Kharis sat in the lovely garden at the Royal Academy of the Healing Arts. A giant willow tree provided shade, its cascade of branches embracing her. The luxurious scent of roses filled the air everywhere. Across the patio, the koi fish swam in the pond, one occasionally jumping out to catch an insect. *Hungry little things.*

It didn't help that *her* stomach was growling, too.

Kharis sat on a bench, bored while she waited for her nana to finish her sister's check-up. The Djinnshirukh smoothed her ivory linen gown, the layers of fabric adding to the day's heat. *Stupid dress.* The guards wore summer uniforms. *Why can't I wear something like that?*

She shaded her eyes to watch small birds fight off a red-tailed hawk. They swooped in and out, brave little soldiers, pecking their enemy without mercy. The hawk did its best to avoid them, dodging and twisting in the air, flapping its wings, and flinging its talons. The chickadees, a fierce and relentless mob, continued their attack. A blur of copper feathers hit the willow tree and fell to the ground. The hawk's wings fluttered. Its body spasmed.

The mob landed on the tree, chirping and cawing angrily. Kharis pulled her underskirt off and threw it over the hawk. She scanned the garden, but no one else was there.

"Of course. It's too hot."

She approached the bundle and uncovered it, mindful of the bird's sharp talons. The animal didn't fight her; it gasped for air instead. Its eyes were half gone. Death was wrapping itself around it.

"Life's so unfair." She knelt beside it, caressing its feathers gently and wondering why life gave only to take it away. "I'll keep you company as you enter Andaheimur."

Kharis closed her eyes and summoned her power. The world in her mind turned black, except for her and the hawk. A silver thread unraveled from the bird, stretching endlessly to connect to something past Andaheimur's veil. The filament was frayed in the middle and was soon to snap. Yet, as she studied it, another idea popped into her head. Sewing and darning fixed rips and tears in fabrics. Tiny knots kept stitches from reopening.

Determined, she focused on that filament. It was soft, pliable, and somewhat slippery, like handling butterfly wings, but she managed to pull it together and tie a knot. As other filaments appeared in the fringes of her vision, she used them. One by one, she grabbed them, coiling and twisting them around the hawk's thread. The strand now sparkled with tiny silver flashes as if a universe of stars resided in it.

Pleased with her work, Kharis opened her eyes. The bird remained motionless, its sharp beak open. Disappointed, she sighed. "Death always wins." She sat back, leaning against her hands. The other birds preened.

The hawk twitched so subtly that Kharis thought she was imagining it. When its wings shuddered, a few blackbirds chirped their dismay. The hawk jerked, gained control of its body, and took flight.

Stunned, Kharis followed it with her gaze as it became a tiny spot in the distance.

Kharis self-healed, one of the Akumi king's gifts, but what if she could use that power to nurse others to health?

It was her moment of triumph, an earth-shattering discovery.

She lingered on the epiphany when something soft and warm landed on her head—a dead blackbird. Then another, and another. The bodies of chickadees and blackbirds surrounded her, some quivering until they went still. She froze, afraid to count how many lay on the ground. An icy shiver traveled down her back.

When a final bird fell from the tree, struggling in agony, Kharis screamed and ran away.

CHAPTER 54
THE PULL OF FATE

Yuna sprinted toward a bhiksun, her heart caught in her throat. "Where is she?"

"This way," the woman said, gesturing to a room guarded by imperial officers.

Kharis sat inside, trembling, half in tears, with her knees drawn to her chest. Yuna wrapped her arms around her little butterfly. "Gutxi, are you well?"

Gasping sobs and a shaky head were the Djinnshirukh's response.

Yuna glanced over her shoulder, but the bhiksun only shrugged and shook her head.

"What happened?" Yuna insisted, her voice soft.

"They're dead," Kharis finally managed to say.

Bewildered, Yuna's gaze moved from Kharis to Sanvi, one of Yuna's apprentices, who entered with a cup. "I made her chamomile tea and added honey, Your Excellency."

"Thank you." Yuna quickly gave it to Kharis. "Please drink this and promise me to finish it all."

Kharis bobbed her head and sipped.

"What happened?" Yuna whispered to Sanvi.

"Her Highness was in the garden, then she ran in,

screaming. A few soldiers dashed out, but besides dead birds..."

"Dead birds? How?"

"We aren't sure," Sanvi said. "We've never seen anything like it. The workers removed the carcasses. Someone's already looking into this, checking for disease. We should know in a few days what caused it."

"It was me," Kharis said.

Yuna sighed. "It wasn't you, Gutxi. You were in the wrong place at the wrong time. It must've been scary, and I'm sorry it happened to you."

"Nana." She put her cup down, sounding more determined. "It was me."

Yuna pursed her lips.

"Why don't we go to my office?" she said. "I haven't finished Saya's check-up, but you can sit with us while I do. Plus, I got a new shipment of aljaicin, and I know how you love them."

Still sniffling, Kharis held Yuna's hand and followed.

⚬

Back in Yuna's study, Kharis sat beside Saya, shoulders touching.

"Why do you think it was you who did it?" Yuna asked Kharis.

"A hawk crashed into the tree, trying to escape a group of birds," Kharis said. "It looked like it was dying. I thought it was unfair how the small ones had attacked it just for flying past the garden."

"A few bird varieties will do that," Saya said.

"That's right." Yuna dipped her chin in agreement with Saya. "What happened next?"

Kharis offered a dispirited pout and lowered her head. "I healed it."

The bhiksun raised an eyebrow, momentarily speechless. "How?" she heard herself asking.

"I tied a knot."

Yuna sat before Kharis with an encouraging smile. "Gutxi, I wasn't there to see it. Will you paint the scene for me?"

Kharis's forehead creased. "I don't know why I thought of it, but I had to do something, so I grabbed it and tied a knot."

Yuna narrowed her eyes. "Tied... what?"

Kharis shrugged. "The thread that connected the bird's body to Andaheimur's door."

Saya gasped.

Yuna blinked. "W—What happened next?"

"I didn't think it worked because the hawk didn't move, but then, it flew away."

"What about the dead birds?" Saya asked.

Kharis shook her head. "I don't know. They fell off the tree like raindrops."

"Hmm." Yuna cupped her chin, thinking. "Self-healing. It's one of the four powers the Akumi king grants its vessel. Yet, there's no mention in our records of a Djinnshirukh ever healing others." She leaned back in her chair, bewildered. "Tell me, why did you want to save the hawk?"

"Why not?" Kharis replied.

A rueful smile shaped Yuna's lips. "The universe has rules we shouldn't transgress, and death is one of them."

Kharis frowned. "You work daily to cheat death."

Yuna flinched. "My darling girl, I fight disease, not death. I can mix potions into the water to keep cut flowers alive a little longer, but eventually, they'll wither. Death is woven into the fabric of our universe. Without it, life can't exist. Life and death are opposing forces, constantly in a state of balance. When we disrupt that harmony..." She paused, her voice dropping to a grave whisper. "We pay a heavy price."

Kharis glanced away with an angry pout.

Yuna exhaled, aware that she needed—*no, deserved*—a better explanation. "The Akumi king heals you to extend *your* life. He cares for his vessel, but that power, Gutxi, is for you."

"Why?" The Djinnshirukh drew her eyebrows together. "If I can heal beyond myself, why not do it? You do it. Why can't I do the same?"

Yuna studied her for a long moment, letting those words sink in. Her fingers drummed the armrest; then she wetted her lips. "It sounds as if you want to become a healer."

"Yes, I do."

Yuna's eyebrows went up. "You continue to surprise me." An inward smile added to her mounting pride. "It'd be an honor to teach you. You could be the first Djinnshirukh in history to undo tradition, defy the expected, and redefine the role of the Keeper of the South Wind." Yuna turned to Saya. "I can train both of you and—"

"We aren't discussing the birds." Saya's voice deepened.

It took Yuna aback. "What do you mean?"

Saya locked eyes with her sister. "You mended what was beyond repair. You re-tethered a soul to a body that should've died." She turned sharply to Yuna. "You said there's a price when we disturb the balance between life and death. My question is *when*, as in, when does Khiri pay it?"

Yuna frowned, pressing her lips into an angry line.

Saya ignored Yuna's stern warning. "By saving your hawk, you sentenced those birds to death—"

"Saya, that's enough."

"—And their lives became the source that allowed your hawk to fly away."

Kharis sat still, her face devoid of color. Yuna squirmed in her chair. "Darlings, why don't we retake this conversation later?"

"No," Saya insisted. "We can't ignore the truth. Khiri

doesn't heal, Nana. The Djinnshirukh can feed on the souls of those they've killed to strengthen themselves."

Kharis's gaze shimmered with fresh tears.

"Khiri used that power not to fortify herself but to save the hawk," Saya said. "She sacrificed the birds—"

"Saya Ghan!" Yuna's face hardened. "Enough of this."

She still disregarded her aunt, facing Kharis. "Do you have what it takes to decide who lives and dies?"

"Saya, I said that's enough," Yuna snarled, rising from her chair.

The Sorukhipa grimaced. "I'm sorry, Nana. I don't want any more lies or half-truths. Khiri has the right to know and choose for herself. We must grant her that, at least."

Yuna sat, her heart still thudding hard, but let the exchange play out.

Saya took in a deep breath and held her sister's hands. "I'll walk this path with you, no matter what. Even if we must travel to the Netherworlds of Ifran, circle its lake a thousand times, and fight our way back. If you wish to heal, let's learn it together."

Kharis lowered her head with a sorrowful exhale. "Three words fly around me like vultures. *Useless. Djinnshirukh. Monster.* I stand behind an invisible line that others drew for me. I wish to redraw it. I want other words to describe me. I want to be useful. I want to be loved." She took a deep breath. "I want people to see me." She tapped her chest. "Not the Akumi king, but *me*."

A slow smile blossomed across Yuna's face.

"I want to become a healer," Kharis said, a tear rolling down her face. "I want to save lives, Nana. Not end them." She wiped her eyes with the back of her hand. "I wish to change my fate."

Yuna's chest puffed with endless pride as tears welled up in her eyes. Her niece's pieces, once part of a jumbled jigsaw puzzle, had finally clicked into place.

"A healer." Yuna's heart drummed inside her chest with

unbridled joy. She'd dreamt of this day, and now that she faced it, warm drops trickled down her face. She wrapped her arms around her beloved Gutxi, taking in her small form.

"So be it, my darling. If you wish for this, I'll make it happen."

THE DINNER

As the king, Hröld chewed slowly, allowing the other three to eat at their own pace. Once he finished, everyone else did too.

He eyed Yuna discreetly since she'd requested this meal. She put her fork down and sipped from her water glass.

Hala ate. Well, it was more like he forced himself to eat. Things were always more complicated when Yuna was involved. Kharis and Saya had not joined them, so Hröld suspected it had to be about them.

Ghan ate with gusto, either too pleased with himself or because he enjoyed every tense moment at the table. The misery in others made the high general giddy.

Hröld glanced at their plates. When the three had finished eating, he set his fork down and gestured to the servants, who quickly took the dishes away.

"Thank you for the lovely dinner, Hröld." Yuna's stare assessed Arjun Ghan. "It's been quite a while since we had a nice *family* meal together."

Ghan huffed, as if he hated breathing the same air as her.

"If you weren't so busy, we might have more," Hala said.

"Funny," Yuna remarked. "I was about to say the same about you, *nephew*."

Hala half-smiled, aware that her sarcasm extended to him as well.

"So," Yuna pursed her lips. "You look well, Arjun."

Ghan flicked his eyebrows, surprised that she was actually talking to him. His head pivoted slowly in her direction, sporting one of those smiles she hated. "So do you, *sister*. Always *delighted* to see you."

"I aim to please, *brother*."

Sister, brother, nephew—words wrapped in sarcasm and cynicism. Hröld sighed silently. It was going to be a long night. "Shall we retire to—?"

"I want to train Kharis and Saya in the healing arts," Yuna blurted before Hröld rose.

Hala coughed.

Ghan's mouth thinned.

Hröld studied Yuna, hiding his shock. "You haven't changed." He kept a neutral voice. "Always direct."

"It's the best quality I have," she said. "Clear and direct."

"Why do you wish to do this?" he asked.

"Why not?"

He met Yuna's intense gaze. "I expect you to provide arguments to back your request."

Servants stood by the wall, bewildered that the four were still sitting at the dinner table. Hröld noticed it, too, and with his subtle nod, they exited.

"Disposition," Yuna said.

Hala coughed again. Ghan sat silently.

"Care to explain?" Hröld asked.

"The girls possess the disposition to become healers. They are conscientious, empathetic, curious by nature, and collaborative."

"You're describing Saya," Hala said.

"I'm describing both of them." Yuna's voice turned

slightly sharp. "They're compassionate, honest, courageous, committed—"

Ghan scoffed.

She scowled at him. "Do you have an opinion, or are you here to irritate me?"

His smile widened. "If I have, I've achieved my goal."

"Pfft, you wish." She stared at Hröld. "They're *your daughters*; therefore, the decision is yours. I'm here to make the request, for I believe they are ready for this responsibility and will excel at healing. I'll tutor them and—"

"It's a bad idea," Ghan said.

Yuna gritted her teeth and studied her brother for a long moment. "Why?"

Ghan exhaled loudly, dramatically pausing to irk Yuna, and faced Hröld. "Saya possesses discipline and commitment. She's a reliable child with the qualities needed to become an exceptional healer." He turned to his sister. "She would be like you, Yuna. Perhaps even better. The Regiazenka would approve the request. I'm sure of it. But Kharis is a different issue."

"Why, Arjun?" She scrunched her nose at him. "Because she's the Djinnshirukh?"

"Precisely. You're so caught up in her humanity that you forget she's *not* human."

"She's *your* niece, Arjun, not a monster—"

"Enough." Hröld's hands fisted on the table.

Yuna's voice turned icy. "Aghuti would've blessed this decision—"

"But she's not here, is she?" Ghan snapped.

"I said, enough!" Hröld rose, and the immutable face raged with anger. "How could you bring Aghuti into this?" Emotion stung his eyes as fury coursed through his body. He flexed his fingers, struggling to calm down.

Yuna got up. "I've made my request. Now you must decide." Her stare locked on Ghan. "I take my leave. The company has gone... stale." And like that, she bowed and left.

Ghan exhaled slowly, the red along his scar darkening. Hröld could almost hear him counting to ten.

"It was a lovely dinner," Ghan finally said, "and I'm thankful for the invitation. However, the reason we don't do this often is clear to all. I stand by what I said. Saya would be an excellent healer. Kharis, I'm afraid, would not. You both know why." He dipped his head to Hröld and exited the room.

Once they were alone, Hröld sat. "You didn't speak."

A puff of air escaped Hala's lips. "With those two, one can't say a thing."

Hröld didn't comment. Without Aghuti to buffer the two siblings' constant quarrels, their bickering had become worrisome. "What do you think about your aunt's request?"

Hala hummed. "I hate to agree with Ghan. I truly do, but Kharis's unpredictable temperament is already a prickly issue. I wish Yuna's training could temper her behavior since we have the Crown to consider. We've resolved a few disputes connected to her, but we can't keep doing this every time her anger flares and she strikes someone. It erodes the Regiazenka's trust in us. When the king's child is involved, favoritism is a bad political move."

Hröld grunted, rubbing his forehead. "Your mother was the Djinnshirukh, and the Regiazenka adored her." He'd held onto the hope that this body would eventually come to love Kharis.

Hala pressed his lips. "Mother was unique, Father. Khiri isn't. I have no issue with Saya learning under Yuna. As the Sorukhipa, it makes sense. The Regiazenka wouldn't question this decision."

Hröld heaved a sigh. "And Khiri?"

Hala rasped his fingers against the table. "Everyone fears her, Father. And while I could argue Ghan's ideas about her and find fault with all of them, the training he provides her is what she needs—what keeps the Akumi king sated."

Hröld glanced away, fixing his gaze on a portrait that Aghuti had commissioned long ago.

Hala pulled his chair closer to him. "The immortals created the Djinnshirukh as the ultimate weapon against the Akumi," he added. "When unleashed in battle, this weapon decimates armies. In times of peace, it overstays its welcome."

Hröld tilted his head, studying the ornate cornice and elaborate ceiling tiles. He never felt as useless as he did at this moment. "Then what do we do?"

"Allow me the time to think."

"So be it, but don't take long." Hröld pinched the bridge of his nose. "Yuna will hate my answer."

"Let me handle her. I'll speak to her and appease her. She loves them dearly, and she wants what's best for them. She'll understand."

He rested his hand on Hala's shoulder. "Thank you. You're a good son."

CHAPTER 56
ONE MORE PROMISE

"A good son—?"

Saya slapped a hand over Kharis's mouth, cutting her off. "Be quiet." She tugged her sister along the hidden passage toward their old chambers.

"I'm glad we weren't found out," Saya said. Once inside, they pushed the heavy furniture to hide the fake wooden panel. "I told you to keep your mouth shut."

"I know." The conversation had deflated Kharis. She slumped on the floor, fidgeting with the tip of her braid. "What are we going to do?"

"We'll prove them wrong," Saya said. "And we start when you accept responsibility for your actions and stop being so reckless."

Kharis's face twisted with anger. "Is this my fault?"

"Yes."

Kharis pinched her lips, staring. "Do you see me as they do?"

"Of course not. Don't be ridiculous, but Hala made a point I can't argue unless your behavior shows him otherwise."

"Hala said—"

"I know what he said, and he was wrong on every count except one. You tend to resolve disagreements by punching people in the face. That has to stop."

Kharis huffed and lowered her head, more disheartened than before.

Saya sat beside her. "It's like playing xakea, Khiri. We move pieces carefully, following a plan."

The Djinnshirukh lifted her gaze, open to listening.

"To win a game, we anticipate attacks and plan accordingly to take over the opponent's field," Saya said. "Sometimes, our opponent may surprise us with an unexpected move, so we adapt our plan and move forward."

"Hala said I lean toward violence."

"Everyone feels anger," Saya said, "but the difference is what happens next. I let it pass. You don't." Her hand closed softly against Kharis's palm. "You hold onto your pieces until it's right to use them to overtake your opponent. You don't attack right away. You wait for the right time to sweep the board."

Kharis assented with a wicked grin. Xakea was something she understood well. Saya got up and dusted her hands. "Come, we must return to the villa before Hala does. I suspect he'll be visiting to check on us tonight."

"Saya?" Kharis remained on the floor, her eyes on the rug. "Do I overstay my welcome?"

Saya poked her sister's cheek. "If you keep those comments up, yes." She squeezed Kharis's waist, tickling her.

Kharis rolled away, choking on chuckles. "Stop!"

This time, Saya gave her a dangerous smile. "Listen to me, Khiri. I'll learn everything from Nana and teach you. I'll make it happen if you want to become a healer. And if you wish to become a conquering, bloodthirsty warrior, we'll do that, too."

Kharis furrowed her brow, shooting her sister a sharp glance.

Saya stifled a chuckle. "As long as we conquer *together*."

Kharis still frowned at her.

Once Saya was sound asleep, Kharis tiptoed from the bedroom and into the garden. She eased the thorned bougainvillea aside, revealing a small, forgotten gate, and slipped through as an owl fixed her with lucent eyes. The moon hung low, silvering the cobbled path. She waited behind a thicket, listening until the patrol voices faded, then moved again, keeping to the shadows.

Soon, Sharan outlined the towering Royal Archives. A key jingled softly in her pocket.

A flickering torch led her to a haven filled with ancient knowledge, savoring the thrill of her clandestine visit. She reached for the stolen key and opened a side door, slipping inside like a ghost. The quiet welcomed her with the musty scent of aged books. With a candle in hand, she traversed the aisles, fingers tracing leather-bound tomes as she made her way to the map room.

Once there, she opened a cabinet and pulled out maps, spreading them on a table.

"I'll find this place," she whispered into the dark, "and when I do, I'm headed there to find the spell to break the Akumi king's curse."

She leaned over the maps, tracing unfamiliar borders, searching for a place that had long eluded her—Hegra.

"Hang on, Saya. Soon, we'll be free."

CHAPTER 57

WHISPERS OF THE HEART

Kharis's breath misted in the morning's frigid air. Her nose, reddened by winter's kiss, dripped nonstop. Her sleeve was damp from frequent wiping. Frost covered the grass, but the sun's warmth slowly melted its delicate, lace-like shapes.

"There you are!"

Kharis flinched and turned toward the voice.

"You missed breakfast," Saya said.

The Djinnshirukh lifted a shoulder.

Saya tapped her boot on the ground. "Did you go to the archives again?"

Kharis didn't answer.

The Sorukhipa narrowed her eyes as if trying with her intense gaze to have Kharis confess to something. "You certainly like that place."

A snort escaped Kharis.

"Why do you go there?" Saya asked.

Kharis shrugged. "Looking at maps."

"There's one in our—"

"I'm studying *ancient* maps, Saya."

The Sorukhipa hummed thoughtfully and lowered herself beside Kharis. "Why?"

Kharis groaned softly. "Why not? At least I'm learning something."

Saya arched an eyebrow. "By looking at ancient maps?"

"The world was different a thousand years ago," Kharis said. "Did you know that? Even the names of places were different. The One War also changed the landscape. The Ghasmanoör Chasm wasn't a wasteland. It teemed with lush forests, thriving under the Forest Kin's care. Magic fueled the world back then. The Zahar-Katea mountains weren't as tall, having three known passes. Did you know that?"

Saya let out a low whistle, impressed.

"After the One War," Kharis continued, "a mysterious power wrenched those mountains from the earth to meet the sky. Those passes no longer exist; the only way to access the Chasm is by sea. What tutor is ever going to teach us that? The immortals forged a weapon using formidable magic a thousand years ago, and here I am today. If I learn about the past, I could fix my present."

Kharis leaned back on her hands, observing a passing cloud.

"Maybe I'll never leave this place," she said after a pause, "but I can't let go of the idea that there's someone out there waiting for me to step over this line others have drawn for me. So, just let me find the answers I need. No one else will give them to me."

Saya chewed on the inside of her cheek. "You shouldn't miss your lessons. Hala will lecture you."

"Let him. What will 'the good son' say that he hasn't?"

Saya made a face. "But your lessons—"

"Why should I care?" That twisty sensation returned. "Why bother with mathematics or astronomy if I'm a weapon?"

"You aren't a weapon, so stop it. You're my smart, clever

sister, and if you let me in, I'll help you find whatever you're looking for."

"I want freedom," Kharis shot back. "I almost savored it. Now my chains are heavier."

The glistening in Saya's eyes conveyed how deeply that comment had wounded her.

Guilt sank its teeth into Kharis. "I'm sorry. That was mean of me to say." She glanced away, biting her lip, remorse gnawing at her. She hugged her knees, too afraid to look at Saya. "Don't be late on my account... please?"

The pause felt endless.

Afraid to talk or look at Saya, Kharis returned to creating misty clouds, wondering how to make them larger, hoping to blur the entire world permanently.

"I know you didn't mean it," Saya finally said. "But I stand by my decision. One day, you'll understand why I stopped you."

Kharis lifted her head, and Saya pulled her into a firm, heartfelt hug. The storm of emotions in her mind dissipated. A profound sense of relief replaced her guilt. Saya was everything to her, and freedom meant nothing without her by her side. "I love you," she whispered into Saya's hair.

Saya tightened her grip, her voice soft. "We'll get through this together." She pulled away to poke her sister's cheek, her smile broad and bright. "I promise." She rose and brushed off her trousers. "Come. We must head for the palace."

"Lucky you," Kharis uttered with sarcasm. "You'll follow Nana everywhere while Ghan yells at me."

Saya gave her sister's shoulder a gentle squeeze. "Soon, he'll ride for the Zahar-Katea region to drill his battalion in winter warfare."

"I hope the cold claims him," Kharis muttered.

"His blood's like ice," Saya said, lifting her to her feet. "He'll thrive in the frost—and likely plunge into some half-frozen lake with that general of his, Mendi."

Kharis chuckled.

"Soon, Ghan will be gone." Saya patted her sister's shoulder. "And we'll spend time together."

"I should make it into a song." Kharis dusted her trousers, humming a catchy tune. "Ghan is gone, we giddily grin. Ghan is gone with his grouchy grapes and gall."

Saya, already walking toward the gate, laughed.

"Who'll be training me in his absence?" Kharis asked.

Saya opened the iron gate, and the sentries saluted. "I'm unsure. The Regiazenka floated a few names, but you know how Ghan is. No one's ever good enough to train you but him. If there's no selection, you'll enjoy time off while I follow Nana everywhere."

Kharis pouted, still mad at the Crown for refusing Yuna's request to train her.

Saya gave her a tight smile. "Hala hopes Ghan won't select anyone so we can enjoy a little time together while he's away."

"Oh, the good son?"

Saya shushed her, looking behind her. "Khiri, let it go. First, no one must know we overheard their conversation. I can't believe I agreed to eavesdrop on them. Second, he gave Father an honest assessment. I won't fault him for that. And that brings me to the third point. You must work to change the Regiazenka's opinion of you. I would add Hala to that task because he has extraordinary sway with Father."

"Fine. I'll let it go." Kharis glanced away, wondering whether to ask. "Hey, have you gotten any letters from Koa?"

"No. You?"

Kharis shook her head. "I've written a few but have received none from Taika."

Saya shrugged. "Kahurang is far."

"It's been a year, Saya. Don't you think it's odd that it would take this long to receive one?"

"I'm sure they're as busy as we are. Don't let it worry you."

"Pfft. Who said I was worried?" She tried to sound casual.

Saya gave her a wry look. Kharis's cheeks heated despite herself. Saya burst out laughing. Kharis rolled her eyes, nudging her sister forward. No secret tunnels led to Hala's study, sadly. Otherwise, she would head there tonight and take a peek.

"Would Hala intercept the letters?" she asked.

Saya halted and turned. "That's an odd comment." She resumed her walk, their Guide Guard escort never far. "He's annoyingly overprotective, but I don't believe he would do that."

Kharis still pondered whether to sneak into his study.

Mindful of their escort, Saya leaned closer to her sister. "Nana and I have an idea."

"Have you figured something out about the birds?"

"Possibly, but you must fake being sick so I can bring you to her."

"Saya." Kharis heaved an exaggerated sigh. "I'm the Djinnshirukh. I never get sick."

"Make it something"—Saya snapped her fingers with an idea—"womanly."

Kharis deadpanned. "Womanly?"

Saya bobbed her head a few times.

"Hmm." Kharis scratched her head. "I have yet to start my bleeding—"

"Perfect. That'll do it." She locked arms with Kharis. "I'll take you to Nana to discuss my theory." Saya gave Kharis a mischievous grin, and the Djinnshirukh replied with a funny little frown.

CHAPTER 58

THE TIES THAT BIND

Hala accompanied his sisters to the Royal Academy for the Healing Arts.

Kharis had mellowed out, which surprised him. It had been months since the Silver Moon Festival incident and her failed escape attempt. It seemed winter had cooled his sister's anger. The Djinnshirukh trained diligently, tempered her mouth, and didn't get into fights. *Blessed Mother, she's behaving for a change.* He wasn't sure if he liked this child or the other. Missing the feisty sister who gave him so many headaches was odd. Kharis never mentioned Prince Rawiri, but he occasionally found her absorbed in a book written in the Kahurangi language.

"Poems," she'd explained. "A gift from the king and queen of Kahurang."

He should've taken it away, but couldn't bring himself to. Permitting her to hold onto this item felt like a small, permissible indulgence.

He sighed—loudly.

In a few months, his sisters would turn fourteen, and his thoughts meandered to gifts that could turn the currents around. "You haven't said what you wish for your birthmark."

Both girls halted and stared at him.

He stared back, hands on his hips, waiting.

Kharis tapped her lips. "Hmm. He gifted us a villa for our coming-of-age."

"He can give us a castle next." Saya grinned at her brother with sass. "Or a kingdom, with soldiers we would command."

"Oh, yes." Kharis clapped her hands with fake excitement. "Urrun sounds like a good place to me."

"Add pink horses and blue dogs," Saya said.

"Yes!" Kharis raised her fist in victory. "We'll proclaim honey cakes the official dish, and everyone will eat them for dinner."

Their cheeky sarcasm flustered him. "Urrun, eh?" He narrowed his eyes at them, tempted to send them there.

The sisters chuckled and sprinted toward the ornate entry doors.

"Blue dogs," he mumbled under his breath.

❦

Saya spotted her nana in the foyer, and a swift smile parted her lips.

"Ah, my darlings!" Yuna approached, arms open, and hugged the sisters. She ignored Hala entirely. "So, Gutxi, what's the issue?"

Kharis flicked her eyes toward her brother, lips pinched.

"Oh!" The bhiksun understood perfectly well.

Hala cleared his throat. "I trust you can manage from here."

"I can," Yuna replied. "In fact, leave them with me for good, and you'll never need to trouble yourself with returning."

Hala frowned. "Ha-ha. Truly, you're in fine spirits today, Auntie."

Yuna smirked.

"You two, behave," Hala said. "Your escort will return you when you're ready."

"May the girls stay for supper?" Yuna asked.

Hala wrinkled his nose. "Only if you feed their guards."

"Them?" Yuna glanced at the five stern-faced White Guard officers, each one easily twice her size. "Consider it done." She chuckled. "Come, my darlings. We have *girl* matters to discuss."

Hala rolled his eyes but said nothing.

Saya beamed as Yuna nudged them along. Her plan was going on swimmingly.

❦

Kharis entered and swiftly sat on a chair, eager to get started. Yuna closed her office door. "Did Saya explain things?"

"Not a word."

"In my defense," Saya said, "I wanted us to tell her together."

Yuna waggled her eyebrows. "You were so excited that I'd assumed you told her right away." She grabbed a fistful of aljaicin from her glass jar and dropped the candies on the small table between the sisters. With a greedy look, Kharis reached for one.

"Your sister Götrid sends them to me."

Kharis quickly withdrew her hand. Yuna noticed, but Kharis didn't care. She folded her hands in her lap and stared straight ahead.

"I don't know how she manages the time," Yuna said after a beat, "but she found the hazenka that handles these lovely confections and has them shipped to me directly.

These arrived yesterday. A gift for the winter solstice, she wrote—"

"How nice," Kharis said. "That she writes to you."

Yuna's warm smile vanished. "It's disrespectful to interrupt."

Kharis swallowed, but resentment pecked at her like a crow.

"One day," Yuna said, "you'll eat your words. Learn to temper your assumptions about others, especially Götrid, and avoid passing judgment until you have *all* the facts."

Kharis lowered her head, but her anger still swirled inside like an unbanked fire. If Götrid ever got lost in Ifran, Kharis wouldn't lift a finger to find her, but she loved her nana, and Yuna's impression of the Djinnshirukh mattered.

"I'm sorry, Nana."

Yuna huffed unhappily. "Never mind, Gutxi. Here, have some. Be thankful I'm sharing them with you. These are exceptionally good." She unwrapped one and put it in her mouth, the hard candy blowing up a cheek. "Anise. My favorite flavor. So, the idea. Saya, explain it." Yuna sat back to enjoy her aljaicin.

"It may sound crazy," Saya said, "but it's worth a try. All life is connected—plants, animals, us. We perceive everything as separate entities, but that's not the case. The force that created life shattered itself endlessly to create everything we see. Since we come from the same source, we are all linked. My Sorukhipa training focuses on reaching a higher level of perception that allows me to see these connections."

"Why?" Kharis asked.

"Because I'm your guardian. If we're ever separated, this higher level of consciousness, my third sight, allows me to find you no matter where you are."

"So, that's how you did it." Kharis frowned. "I lost every game of hide-and-seek."

Saya chuckled. "You can't hide from me—"

"Saya's ability," Yuna cut in gently, "is *not* a skill to play with. There are inherent risks associated with using her third sight."

"Nana." Saya's eyebrows slammed down. "You interrupted me."

"Just saying." Yuna raised her hands, signaling that she'd delivered her warning.

Saya glared at Yuna. "Back to the subject, shall we?"

The monk offered an innocent smile.

"You drew from the life force around you when you healed the hawk," Saya said. "It's what we know the Djinnshirukh does. However, there's a moment when all connections disappear, and you can't pull on any because everything ceases to exist."

"Eh?" Kharis quirked an eyebrow.

"Remember at the quay?"

Kharis's curiosity faded. "How could I ever forget it? You stopped me that day."

Saya grimaced. "And I'm still sorry about that. I relied on my Sorukhipial magic to stop you. When I unleashed it, I removed you from reality."

"Huh? How?"

Saya scratched her cheek, thinking. The glint of an idea widened her eyes. "It's like this." She unwrapped a piece of candy. "Imagine you're this aljaicin. The candied ball inside is your soul, and the wrapper is your body. When I release my magic, I can take you out." She popped the candy in her mouth and folded the paper back into shape as if the aljaicin were still inside it. "The wrapping looks full but empty because I pulled you out. My magic can remove you from this reality because I can bend time to my will to achieve this."

Kharis blinked rapidly. "You can do... *what?*"

"I told you we'd get sidetracked," Yuna said.

"Saya's magic is extraordinary," Kharis said. "Mine only makes me strong and fast."

Saya patted Kharis's head. "The full extent of your magic is yet to awaken."

"Oh, right. But when will I—?"

"No more questions," Yuna said. "Pay attention to your sister; we're about to reach the good part."

Kharis frowned. "Nana, you interrupted me."

Yuna sighed. "Accept my apologies, Gutxi."

"Can we get back to the explanation, please?" Saya glared at both women. "When I summon my magic and time stops, there's nothing you can draw upon because nothing exists within this bubble."

Kharis raised an eyebrow, skeptical. "Then how do I heal?"

"You draw from your life force."

Kharis's eyes narrowed into slits. "Won't I die if I do this?"

"Your Akumi king won't let you."

Kharis studied her sister for a long moment. "You sound *preeetty* confident about this."

Saya scratched the back of her head with a nervous chuckle. "Testing this theory is risky, but if you are willing, we could try it."

Kharis's squinted gaze surveyed Saya. "Try... how?"

"Ah! At last, my part." Yuna shifted the hard candy in her mouth to speak more clearly. "Gutxi, are you willing to try?" Her tone held an almost scholarly air. "If so, an opportunity presented itself this morning. If not, we shall forget this talk and enjoy Götrid's aljaicin."

Forget it and eat candy? For a moment, Kharis wanted to slap her aunt. Or maybe she should slap herself? Or both? She wasn't sure. "Fine. Let's do it."

"Very well," Yuna said. "Girls, follow me."

Yuna and Saya shared smug smiles. Kharis pursed her lips. Yuna and Saya walked ahead, chatting and giggling, while Kharis shuffled behind, aware that those two had formed a secret bond that excluded her. She blamed "the good son" for it.

They walked past hallways and corridors, greeting apprentices, monks, and patients. Some even called Saya by her name, not her title. They exited through a back door and headed for the stables. There, a young man was caring for a bundle of fur lying on the ground.

"Monk Efram, how's our patient doing?" Yuna crouched beside the young man and a medium-sized dog.

"Not well, Master Yuna. His injuries are severe. He may not live past the night. Therefore, I would like to ease his pain."

She gently stroked the dog's brown fur. The animal didn't move but stared, whimpering weakly. The tail's tip fluttered. "Even in this state, he's glad for the tender pat."

"What happened?" Kharis asked.

"A stray dog," the young man replied. "Struck by a carriage. I brought him here in hopes of healing him, but it looks grim."

"What's the damage?" Yuna asked.

"Broken ribs, a punctured lung, likely damage to other organs. He's in great pain, and moving him might worsen it."

"Your judgment?"

"Not a hopeful one," Efram said. "He won't take water. I fear his liver and kidneys are failing."

"And the course of action?"

He hesitated, then spoke softly, "Ease his pain. Perhaps a merciful death."

"Death?" Kharis blurted out.

Saya raised a finger, quietly urging her to hold her tongue.

Yuna remained focused on the animal, her expression grave. She rested a gentle hand on the dog's side. "I agree with the treatment," she said at last. "See it done. Prepare what you need."

"Yes, Your Excellency." Monk Efram bowed and stepped out.

Kharis turned to Saya. "What's happening?"

"The dog is dying," Saya said. "Rather than let it suffer a slow, painful end, Monk Efram will ease its passing—likely with valerian, so it slips away in sleep."

A jolt coursed through Kharis. "You're speaking of it as if it were nothing."

"Gutxi." Yuna rose to her feet, her gaze steady. "A healer must set aside emotion when faced with death. What we feel doesn't change what must be done. Right now, this creature suffers—and mercy is all we can offer. However, before Monk Efram returns, would you like to try Saya's hypothesis?"

"Now," Kharis said. "We do it now."

Yuna nodded once, then turned to Saya. "Darling, you know what must be done. And let me say—I'm proud of you both. May the Blessed Mother guide your steps there and back."

"I don't know how long I can sustain my magic," Saya said. "It may be dangerous. So when I call you back, you must return—without hesitation."

Kharis nodded, even when fear flickered in the pit of her stomach. What if she didn't return?

CHAPTER 59
THE WONDREOUS VÄLISSA

Kharis felt the air still before she understood why.

Saya's magic surged outward, swallowing sound as it swept through the stables. Gold dust spiraled around Kharis, sealing her inside a shimmering sphere. Everything beyond it froze. Yuna. The dog. Dust hung suspended in the air. Sunlight stopped mid-flicker against the glass. Even the shadows refused to move.

The Sorukhipa had stopped the flow of time.

Saya's voice drifted toward Kharis, a siren's call nudging her sister to be ready. Kharis slowed her breathing as Saya's magic gently coiled around her. Gradually, the stables dissolved into an otherworldly mist.

With a gentle tug, Kharis soon glided upon the dunes that rimmed the endless black ocean of Välissa—the in-between for the souls and the bridge to Andaheimur.

The beach, bathed in midnight moonlight, stretched out with sands that glowed softly under the star-studded sky. A gentle breeze, cool to the skin, blew hair strands off her face. The waters glistened like liquid obsidian, each wave catching the dim light. Their rhythmic lapping at the shore was both haunting and comforting, calling to her.

As Kharis walked, the fine sand cradled her feet. When she reached the shore, the threads connecting every soul to the spirit world shimmered into existence, appearing like silken strands in the air. They swiftly encircled her, glowing faintly. Kharis swatted them away with care until she found the dog's weakened tether among them. Her fingers brushed against it, feeling its fragile pull. It wasn't unraveling yet, unlike the hawk's.

"How am I going to do this?" Doubt crept into her. She'd found the dog's soul tether, but couldn't use the others to strengthen this one.

"Let me help you," said that familiar voice. A shadowy presence stood close enough to her that his body provided warmth. *"Allow me to guide your hands."*

She assented with a nod.

"First, summon your soul tether. Imagine it appearing before you."

She did, imagining it to be a long thread of vibrantly colored yarn. It emerged from nothingness—not a single diaphanous silver filament like the ones floating about her, but deep crimson and made of countless strands coiled around each other.

"Why doesn't it look like the others?"

"Every Djinnshirukh's fate is tied to yours. Rather than one, it will resemble a skein of yarn," the silvery voice said. *"Now, rub on it until you pull a fiber."*

Kharis did until one came out, curling it around her forefinger.

"Wait until it turns silver." The thread pulsed in sync with her heartbeats until its deep red color dissipated. When it matched the dog's tether, the voice said, *"Now, coil it around."*

Kharis released it. The filament twisted around the dog's tether as if it were endless, strengthening it. Little bursts of light threaded and repaired it as they interacted. When the work stopped, she ran her fingers over it to ensure it wouldn't come undone.

"I think it's finished. How did I do?"

"*You did well.*" Those words made her feel taller. "*The connection is strong.*"

Saya's voice drifted through Välissa like a gentle breeze. "Khiri... Come."

"Time has run out," Kharis said.

A sad hum vibrated in the air. "*Brace yourself, please. The return won't be pleasant.*"

She lifted her chin. "I'll be fine." Then, "Thank you for helping me."

"*We are friends, are we not?*"

A curt nod. "Forever."

She closed her eyes and braced herself for her retreat.

The shadowy presence dissolved in the wind.

Phantom hands pulled her out of Välissa on a vertiginous journey back to the stables, turning her stomach. The enchanted bubble popped, the gold dust vanished, and chaos drowned her vision. Sound flooded her ears—loud and strident. Bright and sharp silver light pierced her eyes, bursting inside her head like an eruption. The world spun violently, and a dizzying swirl trapped her body.

Viciously ill, she vomited up her breakfast.

Yuna shrieked her name before Kharis keeled over and fainted.

CHAPTER 60

IROH, THE DOG

Familiar voices echoed in Kharis's head like an endless roll, all speaking at once.

"What happened, Yuna?"

"Why is *that* on her bed?"

"When is Khiri waking up?"

Kharis was still nauseous, but the world spun less forcefully. The ringing in her ears had lessened, but the constant chatter worsened her headache. She had every intention of shutting everyone up, but an invisible weight sat atop her body, pinning her to the bed.

Something warm and moist licked her cheek. She opened her eyes with a groan. The weight moved, and a pair of arms wrapped around her. Tears landed on her neck and trickled down.

"What happened?" Kharis asked, her voice soft to keep her headache from worsening.

"You're awake!" Saya sobbed. "Father, she's awake."

The bed shook, and a second body embraced her. A low growl warned the king to back off or else.

"Why is there a dog in here?" Hala joined the choir of voices asking Yuna questions simultaneously.

Kharis wanted to kick everyone out. The dog, too happy to have her back with the living, licked her face, keeping her from uttering a thing.

"Everyone!" Yuna said. "You're in a hospital, please."

Silence flooded the room.

"Now, one question at a time."

The bed shook once more. Her father's tender hand touched her forehead. "How are you doing?" His eyes were overly bright, his forehead creased.

Kharis smiled at him. "I'm fine, but unsure how I got here. Nana will explain if you let her."

"Yuna?" The father and the king spoke at once, and neither sounded happy.

Yuna exhaled, resigned. "We were caring for a dog in the stables when Khiri fell ill, threw up, and lost consciousness. We—"

"What made her sick?"

"Hröld, if you let me finish, you'll learn the cause."

The king grunted. Loudly.

Yuna took a deep breath to collect herself. "She likely ate something that had gone bad."

Kharis was quietly impressed. That woman had an answer for everything. She'd just lied through her teeth— calmly, convincingly, and without so much as a stammer. Kharis loved her all the more for it.

"Was she poisoned?" asked Hala.

All eyes turned to him.

"What?" he said with an angry shrug. "It's a reasonable question. Both ate the same food, yet Saya isn't in bed with her sister. That dog is, and why is it on her bed?"

"May we keep him?" Saya asked.

"That mutt?" Hala glared at the fur ball.

"Iroh's so cute." Saya wrapped her arms around the grateful companion.

"It has a name?" Hala rubbed his forehead, scowling at Yuna.

"I like it," Kharis said of the name.

"Can we keep him?" Saya insisted, showering the pup with plenty of neck rubbing and scratching behind the ears.

"When can we take Khiri home?" Hröld insisted.

"You can do it now," Yuna said, with her matter-of-fact attitude. "She's doing much better and—"

"She should stay," Hala said. "And someone better take that dog out of here. This isn't the place for an animal."

"No," Kharis said. "Iroh stays with me."

Kharis, Saya, and Hala argued over the dog, raising their voices to be heard over one another. Hröld tried to appease the three while cute little Iroh barked his opinion. Yuna, exhausted by this mob, sat down to massage her temples.

The door flung open, almost slamming against the wall. "Where is she?"

Yuna scowled. "Arjun, she's fine."

"Was it poison?" he asked.

"See? I'm redeemed," Hala said. "I told you it was a reasonable question."

Ghan closed the door behind him, sneered at Yuna, and bowed to Hröld. His eyes bulged when he saw the dog on the bed.

"Why is that on her bed?" He reached out to grasp the mutt by its scruff, but Iroh heaved a menacing snarl, snapped its fangs, and lunged in an attempt to bite his hand. Startled, Ghan swiftly withdrew it.

"Yuna!"

"I'm right here, Arjun. No need to shout. Let me check your hand." She huffed, mortified. "Not even a scratch. You'll live. You wear so much armor. I'm surprised Iroh isn't asking me to examine his teeth."

Ghan grunted and snatched his hand back. "I want a full report—"

"Or what?" She crossed her arms. "Send me to the dungeons?"

Anger twisted his features.

"Enough, you two." Hröld's voice was soft, but everyone familiar with that tone knew to stay clear.

Kharis and Saya lowered their heads, their arms gathered around Iroh.

"The Djinnshirukh unexpectedly ended up in the infirmary," Hröld said. "Therefore, a report will be due to the Regiazenka. We can't avoid that. Yuna states this is a case of spoiled food, but it's best to be safe. Hala, ensure the soldiers thoroughly check the villa's pantries and food storage areas. I want all servants questioned."

Ghan's scowling eyes traveled to the dog nestled in Kharis's arms. "What about the mutt?"

"Let the dog be," Hröld said. "We'll figure out what to do with it later."

Ghan let out an exasperated huff. "Our mastiffs will kill it."

"There's been enough arguing for one day," Hröld said. "Let's worry about it tomorrow. Yuna, could Khiri stay overnight?"

"She's fine, Hröld."

"Can she stay?" His voice dropped an octave, deepening and becoming more penetrating.

Yuna held Hröld's hard stare, her voice clipped. "Yes, she can."

"Can I stay, too?" Saya asked.

Her face softened right away. "Yes, both of you can stay." Then her semblance hardened as she eyed Hröld, Hala, and Ghan. "Everyone else leaves."

"I want their residence swept," Hröld told Hala and Ghan, ignoring Yuna's comment.

Kharis sucked in her teeth. Her candy stash would be confiscated by day's end, for sure. And her bag of cookies. And the cake slice she stole from the kitchens this morning. Thankfully, she'd hidden her map of the palace tunnels under her bed's floorboards.

"And the dog?" Ghan asked again, throwing Iroh a glare.

"It stays," Hröld replied. "If it had the sense to bite *you*, of all people, then it's earned its place."

Kharis suppressed a victorious grin. Iroh sat proudly at her side, tongue lolling, tail wagging, wearing the most satisfied expression a dog could manage.

"I'll ensure guards are at the doors."

Yuna balked at the command. "Arjun, this is the Academy."

"That's an order—"

"Last I checked," Yuna snapped, "I give orders here."

And while the four adults resumed their arguing, Kharis and Saya petted their new friend.

"You did it," Saya whispered. "You healed Iroh."

A cold sweat invaded Kharis. "Don't get attached."

"Huh?" Saya cringed at the unexpected advice.

"Did you see how Ghan kept staring at him?" Kharis tightened her grip on the dog. "He intends to kill him, and knowing him, he'll do it in front of us, so he gets double the enjoyment."

Saya paused, throwing Ghan a cursory glance. "What do we do?"

Kharis petted Iroh, scratching the back of his neck. "Let's ask Jordha. He may know of a good family willing to take him in. If we keep him, he'll face Ghan's sword. I didn't save Iroh so that Ghan could kill him."

Saya pressed her lips together, wary. "But Iroh attached himself to you. Don't you want to keep him?"

Kharis shook her head. "Wanting has nothing to do with it. This is Rawiri all over again. Before Ghan takes him away from me, Jordha will find him a home."

Her loathing of the man had settled deep, a dark presence beneath still waters, coiled and patient. She would wait. She would bide her time. And she would make him pay for what he had done to Rawiri.

Ghan threw her a glance over his shoulder.

Kharis could have sworn his eyes glinted black. Anyone else would have missed it, but her Djinnshirukh sight didn't. Iroh quietly whimpered beside her.

PART FOUR
THE RIVERS OF FATE

CHAPTER 61
THE RIVERS FLOW

Jordha found a good home for Iroh—his.

"So you can come and visit him," he added, rubbing Iroh's neck. "Any time you want."

The girls bid Iroh farewell, hugging him one last time, their fingers numb from the chill. The cold winter air bit at their damp cheeks as they watched Jordha take their beloved pet away.

Spring's embrace soon replaced winter's blanket, warming the soil and inviting blooms to grow. Kharis sat in the villa's garden, quietly observing hummingbirds flitting between the orange and lemon blossoms and the lavender shrubs.

With the coming of spring came another birthday ceremony—a modest ritual to mark another year in the sisters' lives. Now fourteen, Kharis and Saya recited passages from their sacred book with steady voices. Yuna, Hala, Jordha, and their father were present. Ghan, thankfully, was not.

At the ceremony's end, the guests showered them with aljaicin. But something had changed. It wasn't the same.

Saya's eyes crinkled with joy as she dodged aljaicin and hid behind her father and brother.

Kharis forced her smile, but she didn't go after the candy. She looked for Prince Rawiri's face in the crowd, a preposterous hope since he was gone from her life. She missed him, his absence lingering after all this time. The hollowness in her chest, which Yuna told her would vanish with time, grew like those lovely blooms in her garden.

The events that led to the explosion at the quay faded with time, feeling more like an episode in a worn fantasy book. The weighty concerns and pressing matters of running a significant Empire diverted the Regiazenka's attention from the Djinnshirukh: construction projects, tax collection, the harvest season, road repairs, and floods in the west after unseasonably heavy rains.

At the palace, rumors returned to being mundane, the usual gossip never faltering or easing. Kharis kept abreast of it all with her midnight strolls through the palace's secret tunnels.

Under the guise of getting regular check-ups, Kharis practiced her healing magic while Yuna kept a watchful eye. When the fifth attempt, as the others had, ended with Kharis fainting, the bhiksun halted the training.

"As long as this happens, I can't allow it," Yuna said. "First, I don't know why it happens or how it affects you in the long term. Could this process shorten your lifespan, for example?"

Kharis brushed the concern aside with a hand flick. "The Akumi king will keep me alive."

"It's the Akumi king, Gutxi," Yuna insisted. "Eventually, he'll want to bargain with you and keep you alive in exchange for something, so we must be on our toes."

Kharis shrugged. "He hasn't asked me for anything."

"Ask you?" Yuna stiffened like a board, exchanging a glance with Saya. "Does he speak to you?"

Kharis had never mentioned the mysterious silvery voice, but her comment had slipped out. Now, she had to cover her tracks.

"No fire, brimstone, or whatever he's supposed to do," she said. "That's what I meant."

Yuna studied Kharis for a long moment. "The king of the Akumi burned and broke our world. Therefore, don't underestimate his power."

"Nana?" Kharis sank into her chair. "How was he sealed into a human?"

"That we don't know unless you ask an immortal."

Kharis pouted. "Would that answer be in the Archives?"

Yuna gave Kharis a pointed gaze. "Is that why you go there? Officers told me of your visits."

Kharis's lips drew into a thin line.

"Your *many* visits," Yuna emphasized.

Kharis huffed emphatically. "My tutors are boring, and I want to learn"—she searched for a word—"faster."

"Is that so?" Yuna arched an elegant eyebrow, not entirely convinced.

"How can Saya wield magic?" Her question came before the one Yuna was about to ask.

Yuna heaved a sigh, pinching the bridge of her nose. Kharis suspected the archives topic would return later, now that her aunt had figured out these visits weren't random.

"The Spirit Kin queen," Yuna said, "gave half her soul to the Sorukhipa so they could protect the Djinnshirukh from the Akumi king."

"Did she die?" Kharis asked. "If the queen gave up her soul?"

"Gods don't die, Gutxi."

"And what about me? Will I ever wield magic like Saya? Stop time and all that?"

"Is that why you go to the Archives?" Yuna glanced at Kharis meaningfully. "To find out?"

Kharis heaved a grunt of annoyance. She didn't expect "later" to happen so soon.

The monk exhaled slowly. "Saya's magic shields you from the outside, while the Spirit Kin queen's soul within tempers the Akumi king's power. Perhaps it takes all that magic to keep him in check."

"It's not that great," Saya said. "I can only use mine briefly to find you and come to your aid, not stop time so you can heal. I may also have to pay the price."

"Enough with the somber talk, you two."

Kharis frowned. "You started it, Nana. You said you didn't know if using my healing magic would have a long-term effect."

"Ah, yes. You ask so many fine questions, I lose my train of thought. Loss of consciousness is harmful to humans, so it's best to avoid anything that causes it. Until we understand the reason behind it, the practice must be limited."

"How often could we do it?" Kharis asked.

Yuna pursed her lips, thinking. "Never."

"Nana!"

"Gutxi, I don't know what effect this may have on Saya, either. You lose consciousness, a very visual and physical manifestation of this power, but I can't assess what happens to your sister."

"She appears to be fine," Kharis countered.

Yuna squinted. "Is she, now?"

"Whatever happens," Saya said, "it affects Khiri alone. As the wielder, my magic bars her from drawing from my life force. Thus, I'm fine."

"Well, we can't risk worrying your father—much less letting him find out. And if Hala were to learn what we're doing... well, it's Hala. You know how he is." She drummed her fingers on the table. "But Arjun..." A pause. "I fear what he'd do with this knowledge. He wouldn't ask you to stop. No." She shook her head, lifting a finger. "He'd press and press—until the door gives way."

"Was he always like that?" Kharis asked.

A hint of sadness sparkled in her gaze. "He was certainly different from the rest of us, consistently unhappy—a child without a sense of belonging."

"How come?"

Yuna's gaze fixed on a distant place. "Under other circumstances, I'd suggest talking to him. But since this is Arjun, stay away. Once you finish your training, leave. Do *not* linger. There's a darkness about him that I dislike. Promise me to keep your distance."

"If that's the case," Kharis wrinkled her nose, "why must I train under him?"

Yuna turned to her sharply. "Has he crossed a line? Has he asked you to do something that makes you uncomfortable or jeopardizes your safety?"

The Djinnshirukh shook her head. "He yells a lot, always seeking perfection. He isn't nice about it, but is that way with everyone."

"If he crosses *your* line," Yuna said, "you must tell me. I'll slap him so hard his eyes will end up on the wrong side of his head." The fury in her voice took Kharis by surprise.

"Kharis." Her nana hardly ever used her given name. "I mean it." She tipped Kharis's chin toward her. "If he ever— ever—crosses a line with you or Saya, he'll have to deal with me."

"And you'll slap him?" Kharis asked.

"Precisely, my child. I'll ensure *everything* ends on the wrong side of his head."

The knocks on the door interrupted the moment, and Yuna released Kharis. "Enter."

Suri stepped inside, her forehead creased. "Master Yuna…"

"You worry me, Suri," Yuna said gently. "What is it?"

Suri drew a breath. "It's the dowager queen."

Yuna lifted her chin. Her voice came out thin. "What about my mother?"

"A messenger," Suri began. "The palace just received the news. Queen Naya has passed. I... I'm so sorry for your loss. My thoughts are with you and the royal family during this difficult time." She held out a sealed parchment. "This came with the messenger. A letter from Princess Götrid."

Yuna broke the wax seal and read in silence. "She went to sleep... and never woke up. She didn't suffer." Her gaze met Suri's. "Please arrange for my travel. I'll depart for Almarim this afternoon."

Suri bowed her head. "At once, Master Yuna."

As the door closed behind her, Yuna sank into her chair, still clutching Götrid's letter. "My darlings," she said softly, "I must leave for Almarim soon, but stay with me a little longer, will you?"

Kharis and Saya wrapped their arms around the monk. "For as long as you need," Kharis said.

At that, Yuna burst into tears.

CHAPTER 62

THE WEIGHT OF WATER

Arjun Ghan walked past the regal portraits that displayed the glorious past, but his steps faltered as he reached one in particular. The ornate frame held a painting commissioned by his mother, Queen Naya. Before him, a younger version of himself sat on Naya's lap, a mere toddler. He clutched a long-forgotten toy in his tiny hands, and a wide, joyous grin adorned his cherubic face while the queen gazed at him with endless affection.

The artist had skillfully captured a moment between a devoted mother and her beloved son, etched in brush strokes and a magical play of light and shadow. Ghan could almost feel the warmth emanating from the canvas—a cherished fragment of a time when life was simpler, and ignorance was bliss.

His fingers gently traced the outline of his mother's face, so young and beautiful. He adored her, often seeking her counsel to understand his father's indifference.

"Patience and time, my son," she'd assured him gently. "Be patient, and allow time to do what it must."

Ghan never questioned why this painting was placed on

this wall, far from others, or why his father chose not to appear in it.

But now, his mother was dead. He held onto a sealed letter delivered to him by imperial messengers. A letter that bore Queen Naya's signet—a swan. A private letter.

Ghan wavered in the silent hallway, a shaky hand covering his mouth to suppress the whirlwind of emotions threatening to engulf him.

Back in his chambers, he paced frantically, glad Aghet was gone. He clutched the letter tightly, its weight intensifying with each footstep. His thoughts raced as he contemplated its contents—the last words his mother would ever utter to him. He paused, his hand still gripping the letter, and took a deep breath. He hesitated opening it. *Her last words.* Yet, he steeled himself and broke the seal.

My dearest child, the letter started.

Ghan dropped his body on a settee.

The words unfolded before him. His gaze moved across the parchment, absorbing each line. It was as if, by reading it, he could almost conjure the soft, sweet cadence of his mother's voice. His mother's prose embraced his soul.

He continued to read until his brow furrowed on a word. "Olhan?"

Puzzled, he retraced the paragraph, reading and rereading it to convince himself that he wasn't dreaming.

Aram wasn't your father.

His entire being shuddered.

His gaze lingered on that sentence, the world utterly still.

A storm of emotions churned within him—disbelief, betrayal, and a yearning for the familiar. The letter didn't unravel his life. It had reshaped the entire narrative of his existence.

Olhan is the man who sired you.

Ghan remained fixed on that damning sentence, no longer reading the rest.

The parchment slipped from his fingers. With that cursed revelation came another.

True blood seals the spell.

A memory circled his mind like a vulture. When Yuna had eloped, King Aram had named Aghuti his Heir Apparent. He was next in line, but Aram had chosen Aghuti. She then married Hröld and no longer qualified to be the Djinnshirukh, but his father never selected him as Lord Larek's replacement.

"He knew." An icy shiver rippled down his back. "Father always knew."

His indifference. The aloofness with which he treated him. Why he didn't pose for the portrait. Everything now made sense.

Djinnshirukh. That title once promised power and purpose. Now, it was a distant mirage. His mother's truth had severed his ties to the lineage that had defined him. As the reality settled, it lay before him—his dreams, scattered on the floor like fragments of a broken vase.

CHAPTER 63

THE AKUMI AND
THE REWERA

The palace was in mourning, but Ghan hadn't relented on her training.

No prayers. No quiet time for reflection.

Despite the black ribbons hanging in the training hall, Kharis still stood with her sword drawn, sparring with three officers. One, Ren Azdaha, hesitated with his task, exchanging concerned glances with the other two now and then. Kharis had been at it so long that her breath came heavy, sweat dropping from her nose and chin.

The officers were no better. The woman, Officer Hina, could barely swing her sword. Officer Omaru swayed and blinked excessively, his dark brown skin glistening with sweat. Officer Azdaha faltered more often, his gaze darting to the black ribbons. He looked away just as quickly, lips pinched, fingers brushing the black band on his upper arm.

The heavy doors creaked open.

Steel slowed. Breath rasped. All eyes turned.

General Ghan entered, dragging Saya along by the arm.

Kharis stopped. Her nostrils flared. She squared her shoulders and closed the distance, gaze narrowed on the man she despised.

"Why is she here?"

Saya shook her head, lips thinned, eyes silently begging her to return to her station.

"Are you looking for a more challenging exercise?" Ghan asked Kharis.

Kharis gritted her teeth. Threats wouldn't work today. "Saya's expected at the Academy."

Ghan leaned in closer. "Her job isn't to clean urine from the floor. She's a princess of this realm, not a bloody servant."

"Saya wants to be a healer like Nana."

"The Sorukhipa must also train." The general glowered at Kharis, then turned to the three White Guard officers standing not far from him. "You haven't finished your exercise."

Her hand tightened on the hilt. He'd taken advantage of Yuna being in Almarim for Dowager Queen Naya's funeral to pull Saya out.

"Saya isn't supposed to—"

"Are you done?" Ghan's face mottled.

He hated her, now more than ever. Still, she held his gaze.

Ghan cocked his head, staring at the Djinnshirukh with a wicked grin. "You know what happens when you disobey my orders."

Kharis swallowed hard, pondering what punishment he would come up with, but she clicked her tongue. "As if I would be afraid to—"

"Saya!" His voice boomed. "I have a treat for you, courtesy of your sister."

Kharis blinked in confusion. Ghan's eyes landed on a heavy wooden beam with her carved name.

Her eyes bulged. "You can't—"

"Finish your exercise," Ghan's eyes darkened as he leaned closer to the Djinnshirukh, "and you can take her back to the Academy. I won't even stop you." He straightened, jerking his chin at Saya to follow.

To punish her disobedience, Ghan forced Saya to hold the beam over her head. It barely cleared the floor before it crashed down again. He smacked Saya with his staff and made her pick it up.

Bastard.

Kharis gritted her teeth. Heat stirred beneath her skin. One flash of her fire magic would end this, and then she would be executed. Worse, Saya would be forced to do it.

And so, Kharis sparred.

Her muscles shook. Sweat ran down her back. Where it slid along her neck, it hissed away, leaving a thin veil of steam in its wake.

Ghan shouted, striking his staff against the floor. The gold rings at its head clanged and rattled, the sound crashing into her again and again, each blow sending her to the edge of madness.

When Saya dropped the beam again, it hit the floor with a loud, resonant thud, sending a wave of tremors through the flooring. Ghan struck her sister with the staff. Kharis flinched at the sound of wood hitting flesh. Like a feral beast, her magic shrieked, clawing at the walls Kharis had created. It hissed, demanding to be let out, and growled at her for being such a coward.

Burn him, it screeched at her.

Kharis twisted aside just in time, Omaru's blade skimming past her ribs. Fabric tore. She cursed, not at Omaru, but at the man torturing her sister. This darkness inside her was growing and urging her to give in. Her focus snapped back to her sister.

Saya's arms trembled. Her legs shook as the beam's weight became intolerable. When she dropped it, its loud thud sent another roll of vibrations through the flooring.

"You've grown soft," Ghan berated her. "Training with Yuna has made you weak."

Ghan struck her again.

"A disgraceful Sorukhipa," he snarled. "Pick it up. Again!"

Saya did.

Officer Hina swung her sword, steel ringing. Kharis turned the blow and drove forward. Hina's sword flew from her grasp and skidded across the floor. She staggered back, then collapsed, limbs slack against the stone.

Two more.

Kharis moved before finishing the thought. She dropped low, swept Omaru's legs out from under him, and sent him crashing down.

Azdaha fell, his breathing hard. He tried to rise, using his sword for leverage.

Omaru dragged himself to the wall, shot Ghan a look, and limped for the door.

Kharis got into position. *A kick ends this.*

Saya gasped. The timber crashed onto the floor. Kharis spun around. Saya lay crumpled on the floor, unmoving.

"You're nothing but a disgrace." Ghan loomed over her. "Get up."

Officer Omaru steadied against a wall and limped out of the chamber.

A darkness stirred in Kharis.

Thunder rolled through her skull. Wings beat the air. The horizon vanished beneath vast, moving shadows. Lightning split the dark with potent silver streaks, outlining their massive forms. The heat became intense—all-consuming.

"I said, get up," Ghan screamed.

Dragons slammed into her.

Scorching magic speared her mind.

Ghan raised his staff.

Kharis moved, hurling herself between them. Her steel flashed. The staff split. Ghan went down hard, the impact ringing through the hall.

"How dare you hurt her!"

Kharis planted herself over Saya, feet wide, blade raised.

Heat poured off her in waves. Sweat hissed into steam along her skin. The room's heat intensified.

"You stupid child," Ghan said. He pushed himself upright, one hand braced on his knee, rising slowly, vertebra by vertebra, until he towered over her.

"How dare you?" Spit flew out of his mouth as he screamed. His temple veins engorged. His face turned an angry red. His knuckles whitened as he gripped his staff piece.

"You... Raven spawn. I should've dropped you into the water myself." His face twisted. "Watch you drown and be gone for good."

Fragments of memory came to her. A hand at her mouth. The rag's overwhelming scent. Darkness had surged, but the Akumi king had fought it. The deck had pitched. She had stared at the water. Then, Rawiri's voice.

"Stand down."

Metal had clattered—

Pain exploded through her.

Bones snapped. Her sword flew out of her hand. Her scream filled every inch of the room. Ghan punched her face. The world spun. Her back crashed against the stone wall. She slid to the floor, her right hand a mass of limp flesh. Her face throbbed. The taste of blood, hot and metallic, flooded her mouth.

"*Get up*," the silvery voice urged. "*Get up.*"

Kharis lifted her gaze. Saya lay unconscious, her bloody vomit pooling on the floor. Everything inside her tore loose. Her vision flashed red.

Ghan's boot connected with her ribs, and she curled into a ball.

"Cursed raven spawn," he bellowed, unleashing kick after kick. "You shouldn't even be here. Die already, blasted Djinnshirukh."

Djinnshirukh.

The monster that fed on souls.

Pressure flooded her chest. Heat coiled tight, no longer contained. Something vast shifted inside her. Dark. Impatient. Awake.

Magic surged—no longer willing to wait.

"*This ends now.*" A low, resonant voice rattled her skull. The stench of molten metal and sulfur churned her stomach.

"Sir, please," Officer Azdaha shouted, putting all his weight on the sword to rise. "Stop this. They are children."

Ghan whipped his head toward him. "Who said *you* could speak?" Crossing the distance, he struck Azdaha with the staff, and the officer collapsed to the floor. "You, insolent filth," Ghan screamed at him, each word emphasized with a savage blow.

Kharis clutched her torso and crawled to where her sword had landed.

The Akumi king roared. His power gushed through her. Heat enveloped her right hand. Needles burned beneath skin. Bones snapped together. Tendons and ligaments tightened with a vicious pull.

It was painful. It was exquisite.

Her fingers curled, then clenched, strength slamming back into them. She tightened her grip on the sword. Her gaze locked on the man who'd hurt her sister.

Iridescent scales shimmered into existence across her skin.

All her senses sharpened at once. Every heartbeat became a loud, jarring blast in her ears. Every scent floating in the air invaded her nose—sweat, fear, rot. The flames on the torches flickered. A tapestry lit on fire, burning quickly and turning into ash. The room's temperature soared, hitting the chamber like a surging wave.

"No one hurts Saya."

Kharis raised her sword, already seeing it in her mind: to plunge it deep into his back—again and again and again.

She took one step, and another—

Fingers closed around her ankle.

Kharis hissed and looked down.

"Khiri, no," Saya begged, her voice now a breathy whisper. "Resealment." She held on with a shaky hand. "Please... don't."

Her golden eyes flared. Kharis could almost taste her fear, bitter like endives. Saya sagged. Her grip slipped away.

Kharis turned slowly.

"You," she said.

A breath.

"Hurt."

A step.

"Her."

Heat surged, coiling tighter. Words pressed at the back of her teeth—

"Stop!"

The command cracked through the hall.

Prince Hala stood in the entryway, a column of White Guard at his back. Omaru led them.

CHAPTER 64
REVENGE

Soldiers poured into the chamber, some restraining Ghan and others offering aid to the downed officers while the rest encircled the girls across the room.

"Your Highness!" One soldier called out, his voice frantic. "Princess Saya's injuries appear to be severe."

Hala stiffened. "Alert Monk Yuna. Quickly." Some of his officers ran out. Then he glowered at Ghan. "Take him away."

The soldiers struggled to restrain an enraged high general, dragging him away as he yelled and ranted.

The Djinnshirukh, however, stood her ground to protect her sister, keeping the officers from reaching Saya.

"I'll handle her." Hala inhaled sharply.

"But Your Highness—"

"On my signal." Hala removed a dagger from his leather armor and gave it to his officer. He gritted his teeth, and before the officer could protest, the crown prince took unhurried steps toward his sister. Using hizkuntza, a signed language, Hala instructed the soldiers to grab Saya at his signal.

"Khiri, it's me," Hala said softly. "Your brother."

More beast than girl, Kharis growled back.

Blood trickled from her nose, but a large scab was already crusting on her split lip. Behind her, Saya lay unconscious, her body covered in red-colored welts and bruises.

Hala's breathing caught. *That bastard did this.* He clenched a hand and did his best to keep calm, approaching Kharis with cautious steps, mindful of her speed and the sharp blade in her hands.

"Khiri?" His voice seemed to break the dark spell. The crimson in her eyes faded, revealing silver and sapphire. The intense heat in the chamber dissipated.

"Hala?" She cocked her head, squinting with her good eye. "Is that you?" The purple bruising on her face shifted from a deep purple to green, the swelling around her left eye subsiding.

Her self-healing ability is uncanny.

"Yes," Hala said, his smile soft and kind. "It's me. I'm here to help you." He gestured to the soldiers. "We're all here to help you."

She wavered for a moment, then dropped the sword. It clattered on the floor, its sound refusing to die. Kharis's knees folded under her. Hala grasped her before her body hit the ground.

"Now!"

The soldiers placed Saya on a stretcher. "Take her to Monk Yuna," Hala ordered. "Immediately."

Kharis focused on his face as if confirming it was him before her body went limp.

"Bastard." Hala scooped his sister in his arms, her body small and delicate like a hummingbird, and headed for the door behind the officers transporting Saya. *You'll pay for this, Ghan.*

CHAPTER 65
TWILIGHT

Kharis was in and out of consciousness.

Yuna called on her, trying to keep her awake. Conversations, instructions, requests, and prayers floated around her. A parade of familiar and unfamiliar voices and faces filed before her. Then everything faded. She found herself on the shores of a dark ocean. Golden threads materialized before her, but she ran away from them, fearful of touching them.

Then the voices returned, calling for her to stay awake.

It was a back-and-forth between dreams and semi-lucidity.

Kharis wasn't sure how long this lasted. She wanted to find Saya, but a phantom hand gently pushed her back onto the bed.

"*Rest,*" the silvery voice said, melodic and breathy whisper in her mind. "*You must recover your strength.*"

She closed her eyes and slept.

CHAPTER 66
A BALL OF CRIMSON YARN

The pain woke her up.

It was dull but persistent, like a pebble inside a shoe. Kharis opened her eyes, and light pierced them. She grunted weakly.

"Close the curtains," said a familiar voice.

"Nana?"

"I came as fast as I could from Almarim." A gentle hand caressed her forehead, and Kharis knew all would be well in the world again.

"Gutxi, how are you doing?" Yuna asked, her voice unsteady.

"Everything hurts."

"Could you tell me where?" Yuna's voice was soft, her breath catching on the last word.

"Generalized pain in the torso and extremities."

Yuna's face lit up with a grin, tears trailing down her cheeks. "Spoken like a true healer."

Kharis managed a small smile. "I learn from the best."

Yuna sagged with a gasp, shoulders dropping. With her help, Kharis sat on the bed as the bhiksun fluffed a few pillows behind her, propping her up comfortably.

"Where's Saya?" Kharis asked.

Yuna froze.

Goose bumps broke out along Kharis's arms. "Nana, where's Saya?"

The bhiksun settled into her seat, rigid as stone. "We're keeping her in a different room."

"I want to see her."

Yuna's eyebrows knit together. "You need your rest, my darling, and so does she. You have both been through a lot."

"Nana?" Kharis's voice came out thin, words crowding behind it. "Did you slap him? I hope his eyes are on the wrong side of his face now."

A tiny wisp of sound escaped Yuna's throat. She turned away, shoulders drawing inward. More tears followed. Her hands gripped the armrests as if they were the only thing holding her upright.

"Nana?" The fog in Kharis's mind thinned.

Yuna broke. She folded forward, her arms wrapping around Kharis. Wails tore out of her. Kharis closed her eyes. The pounding in her ears drowned everything. An edgy, twitchy feeling enveloped her body. Fire flooded her mind—scorching, relentless.

❦

Kharis opened her eyes again, trying to inhabit the realm of the living, but her sense of time was off. The closed curtains darkened her room. She had no idea how long she'd been asleep or at the Academy.

Yuna slept in an oversized chair beside her. Her cheeks were hollow, dark shadows pooling beneath her eyes. She looked smaller there, as if the chair had swallowed her.

"Nana?"

Yuna's eyelids fluttered, and she sat, slow at first. "Are you all right?"

"I am, but are you? You look tired."

Yuna shook her head. "Oh, darling. This is nothing," she said with a warm smile. "But until you return to being my bouncing butterfly, I'm not leaving yours or Saya's side. I can't help it. I love you both too much."

"I love you, too, Nana."

Yuna got up, only half awake, and handed Kharis a glass of water. "Your father came by to see you."

Kharis stopped drinking. "You didn't wake me up."

"He insisted on letting you sleep. Now that you're awake, I'll send a messenger. He will rush over, I'm sure."

"When can I see Saya?"

Yuna exhaled softly, her chin quivering. "What about today?"

Kharis's chest tightened. "Nana... what's the matter?"

"Sweetheart, as the Djinnshirukh, you heal swiftly. The Akumi king's magic protects you fully. Some say it's a curse, but it's a blessing to me because it keeps you safe and sound. For that, I'll forever thank him. Never forget that."

"Nana." Kharis frowned. "What's going on?"

Yuna took a deep breath. "Your sister doesn't have the same protection. Her injuries were severe, and she will take longer to—"

"I must see her now."

Yuna's lips thinned into a white line. "Very well. Before we proceed, you should be aware that Saya's recovery has been slow. You must be brave for her. Do you understand?"

She didn't, but nodded, anyway.

Yuna helped her out of bed. Kharis grunted with the effort. Her legs trembled with each step, a hollow weakness settling deep in her bones.. Healing herself this way— drawing on her own life force instead of taking it from others—had left her weak and vulnerable. With wobbly steps and Yuna's help, she inched toward Saya's room.

Yuna opened the door, and when Kharis walked in, Saya quietly rested on her bed. She didn't stir or move. Her eyes didn't open.

Kharis turned to Yuna. "Nana?"

Yuna's eyes glistened. "Your sister lost consciousness and hasn't regained it. Her injuries, especially her internal ones, were quite severe. Despite all our attempts"—she swallowed hard—"she has yet to awaken."

Something inside Kharis snapped. "He did this." She snarled. "He—"

"Gutxi, don't do anything rash."

"Rash?" Her eyes bulged. "Oh no, Nana. It won't be. It will be slow. Glacially slow."

Kharis limped toward her sister's bed, leaned in, and caressed Saya's face, brushing strands of chestnut hair off it. Her glossy hair was dull and limp. Her lips didn't curve into one of her bright smiles. Her golden eyes didn't open. Kharis took a deep breath. The crimson thread of destiny—their bond—pulsed faintly, its presence so distant it seemed to belong to another world entirely.

"Nana, this is the royal wing, right?"

Yuna blinked at the question. "Yes, of course."

"Saya and I are the only patients here, right?"

"Yes."

"Good." Kharis straightened and turned toward her. "I need you to walk out and go as far as you can from this room."

Yuna's lips twitched. "What are you going to do?"

"Tell the monks and guards to do the same. I want you to empty the entire floor, and you have a little time while I collect myself."

"Gutxi, I forbid you to—"

"Start walking."

Yuna's face paled, her body still for a heartbeat, then she dashed out.

Outside the door, her aunt was shouting at people to move out.

Kharis took a deep, cleansing breath, summoning all the energy in the universe to support her.

Saya slipped between worlds, always carrying Kharis along. Alone, she would have to find another way.

"How do I cross into Andaheimur?" She prayed silently to the gods above and below. "I need your help, please."

"*I'm here,*" said the silvery voice that had become all too familiar. "*I'm always here.*"

"Thank you." Kharis stifled her tears and held Saya's hand. "I'm coming, sister, and bringing you home."

"*Once you settle yourself, I'll start.*"

Kharis climbed onto the bed and lay beside her sister. "I'm ready."

Magic washed through her—hot and immediate, sinking deep into her muscles and bones. All sounds dissipated—the city hum creeping through the windows and the swift footfalls shuffling past the door on their way out.

"*I will guide you, but to do that, you must trust me and let go.*"

Phantom arms gently wrapped around her. Kharis focused on her breath. In, then out. With the exhale, she loosened her grip on herself and yielded to the pull. Weight abandoned her. She drifted through a vast, lightless expanse, the world falling away until only motion remained. Below them stretched the endless black seas of Välissa—the bridge between worlds.

A voice rose from the depths. Sweet. Familiar. A siren's song. It wound through her like a hook.

"That's Saya," Kharis said. "She's down there."

"*Good. Now we know where she is.*"

Together, they plunged into the black waters.

Giant fronds loomed in a vast kelp forest, swaying with the tides. Kharis swam among them, grasping them to propel herself forward, seeking the one she needed—her sister's soul. The long, billowing towers glimmered and flickered, shifting in the dark currents, each the same as the others. She glided past them, searching until she found one unlike the others—a thin, weakened one calling for her sister's help.

Saya.

Kharis reached for it and smoothed the loose strands between her fingers, holding fast to her sister's lifeline as gold dust gathered along her skin.

"I'm going to make you shine," Kharis said, "and when I finish, your radiance will shame the sun."

Silver gossamer threads connecting every soul to Andaheimur now surrounded her. More materialized before her, tugging insistently for her attention. They poked and coiled around her to get her attention. Kharis kept pushing them away.

"I'm only using mine," she told them.

It didn't matter. They still demanded to be chosen, twisting around Kharis's arms and legs, relentless with their prodding and jabbing.

"Only mine." A burst of fire erupted from her, its force pushing the tethers away from her. This time, they stayed away.

"*Are you ready?*" the silvery voice said.

"Yes."

A shadowy presence settled close enough for her to feel an arm brush her shoulder—a tangible, hazy body radiating warmth in this cold world. The silvery voice no longer felt like a whisper in the dark. Here, in Andaheimur, it was something else entirely. The Voice.

"*Let's begin. Summon your tether,*" he said. "*Let it unfurl from you.*"

Kharis envisioned her soul as a flame lighting the darkness before her. It appeared before her, pulsing in rhythm with her heartbeats, slowly taking shape. Yet, her thread wasn't a single diaphanous one like those surrounding her. Hers was a ball of crimson yarn, thick with countless strands wound tightly together.

"One for every Djinnshirukh that has lived before you," the Voice said.

She stilled, letting the realization wash over her. The gods had tied all those fates to hers, collecting them into this massive skein. Kharis unraveled it carefully, letting a solitary strand break free.

"This is the one for her," she said.

"As before, wait until it tells you it's ready."

The deep red softened into sparkling gold, matching Saya's tether. Kharis released it. The strand looped, curled, and spiraled, reinforcing her sister's tether until it shone so brightly that she couldn't look at it directly.

"I've finished," Kharis said. "How did I do?"

"You did well," the Voice breathed, the ghost of a grin dancing in his words. *"Exceedingly well. Now, you must return. However, you used your life force to repair it. This will weaken you."* He paused, hesitant. *"You must rest to recover."*

"I promise."

"Good."

A gentle hand pushed her from that vast space. Kharis tumbled through wind and darkness, then struck something hard. Her soul slid back into place, settling into her body. She was in her chamber again. Her eyelids became heavier as exhaustion pulled her under, but she held on a moment longer.

Not yet.

When Saya coughed—a soft moan, a slight shift—Kharis smiled in quiet relief. She nestled close, and a pleasant haze carried her into sleep.

CHAPTER 67

THE WHISPERS OF AN IMPENDING STORM

By the next day, Kharis stormed down the long corridor, boots striking stone hard enough to echo. Servants scattered from her path. Courtiers pressed themselves against the walls.

"Gutxi!"

Yuna's voice chased her, frantic and close, but Kharis did not slow. Her eyes were already locked on the ornate doors at the far end of the hall.

"Gutxi, return this instance."

Kharis strode forward, headed straight for the King's Chamber. There, her father held a private audience. Ahead, imperial guards repositioned themselves to bar her entrance.

"Let me through," she shouted.

Their spears crossed against the doors.

"I said," she roared, "let me through."

The men exchanged fearful glances and uncrossed their spears. Before they could move, Kharis flung them open.

The conversation stopped.

Every head turned.

A gust of wind tore into the chamber with her, scattering

papers and nearly ripping the legal assessor's cap from his head.

Her father sat upon the dais. At his left stood the king's jurist, while two scribes, not one, recorded the proceedings. That detail slowed her step. Hala sat at a nearby table with two junior jurists, conferring in low voices.

High General Arjun Ghan had dropped to one knee in the center of the room. He glanced over his shoulder, a brow arched at her, his lips tight. Upon seeing him, heat surged inside her, but she tamped it down, hands clenched, and forced her face to remain neutral—unreadable.

Chin lifted, she stopped several steps ahead of Ghan, enough to make the point.

"I didn't summon you." Her father's voice carried warmth, concern lining his gaze. "Shouldn't you be resting?"

"I'm well, Your Majesty." Kharis met his eyes. "I hope to be heard just as he is."

She glanced over her shoulder. The flicker of fury in his face was satisfying.

Her father studied Kharis for a moment, pondering something. Then his eyes landed on her nana. "Monk Yuna, come forward."

Kharis stiffened, not expecting this, and threw Yuna a questioning glance. Yuna patted Kharis's shoulder. "Patience," she whispered. She then bowed to King Hröld and waited for his questions.

"How are the children?" the king asked.

Her attention shifted to the scribes, lingering a fraction longer than necessary. The smile she offered Hröld made Kharis's hair stand on end. It wasn't about comfort.

"Your Majesty, Princess Kharis arrived with some facial lacerations, remnants of trauma to her left eye from a punch, and a fractured rib, matching injuries received from being kicked. Princess Saya sustained internal organ damage. In addition, her body bore multiple bruises—signs of being repeatedly beaten with a blunt object.

"Both princesses were unconscious and severely dehydrated when they arrived at the royal infirmary. Princess Kharis recuperated quickly, as expected of the Djinnshirukh. Princess Saya miraculously awoke and is no longer in a coma. Her recovery, however, will take longer." Yuna held her chin high. "Your Majesty, if I may be so bold. I recommend having a healer monk at their defense arts training to ensure everyone's safety."

"So be it," Hröld said.

Kharis breathed out in relief. Her aunt would select someone loyal to her. A monk's presence would temper Ghan. Soldiers wouldn't speak against a high general. Monks would.

"Thank you." Yuna bowed. "I will forward a list with my recommendations as soon as possible."

Kharis expected the king to address her next, but her father rested his chin in his hand, elbow on the armrest. His forefinger tapped his right temple as he thought. Then he gestured for the royal assessor to come to his side.

Eh?

They spoke in hushed tones. The scribes didn't stop writing.

Kharis kept her composure, reminding herself of the importance of convincing everyone she could control herself and be reliable and predictable, as Saya had asked. She eyed the scribes, writing everything down, and squared her shoulders, playing her part.

***

"Your recommendation," Hröld said.

The legal assessor shifted. "The best option is to downplay and resolve the issues via simple disciplinary action—for example, a demotion for the officers involved. I would suggest reassignment to a different unit, but nothing beyond that to send the right message. After all, one stood to protect the princesses while another sought help."

"And for Princess Kharis?"

The royal assessor exhaled. "That's a more difficult question, Majesty, given the accusation against her—namely, that she defied a direct order and attempted violence against the high general. No one believes the high general was a victim here. Princess Saya remains under Monk Yuna's care. That alone speaks to the severity of what was done to them. However, to keep this a family dispute, you must exercise restraint and avoid bringing it up. Disciplinary action against a general of his caliber will undoubtedly involve the Regiazenka."

"He injured my children," he said through gritted teeth.

The assessor raised his hands in a conciliatory manner. "And one of them is the Djinnshirukh, Your Majesty. Initiating legal proceedings against the high general would inevitably entangle him with your daughter, making the Regiazenka the ultimate judge in this matter. And that is precisely what you wish to avoid."

Hröld exhaled quietly, letting the information sink in. "Your suggestion, then?"

"At fourteen, the case could still be made that her age played a part. I recommend emphasizing how her desire to protect her sister drove her actions. Everyone knows how close the sisters are." The assessor side-glanced at Ghan. "And I would keep the high general out by handling this as a parent dealing with a disobedient child."

Hröld frowned. "So bringing one down inevitably drags the other."

"Yes, Your Majesty. A most unfortunate turn of events."

"Anything else?"

The royal assessor shook his head.

To protect Kharis, he would have to let Ghan walk free. *Is justice even possible?* The burning in Hröld's stomach turned into a blaze.

CHAPTER 68
ANGER, HATRED, AND REVENGE

The king's legal assessor bowed and returned to his chair.

Good. My turn. Kharis steadied herself.

But her father instead said, "This is a family issue. It is never a simple task when the family is my own." He turned to her. "Kharis, you disobeyed an order from your superior—"

"Father!" Hala rose. "She was protecting Saya."

Her father's glare dropped him back into his seat.

"Kharis," her father said, "you disobeyed an order from your commanding officer during training, even to help a fallen comrade. This must not happen again."

Realization struck her like a bolt of lightning. This wasn't justice. It was containment. One wrong word, and her fate would be resealment.

Across from her, the scribes furiously jotted every word.

Kharis clenched her jaw and nodded. "It will be as you ask."

Behave. Behave. Behave.

Her thoughts drifted to the man still kneeling behind her, and she swallowed the curse burning on her tongue.

"However," the king said, "you were aggrieved. Therefore, you can demand justice. What would you ask for?"

Kharis lowered her gaze, observing the gold veins crisscrossing the marble floor like the bruises on Saya's body. *He did this to her.* She gritted her teeth to collect herself.

In their quiet corner, the scribes wrote and wrote.

"I've come to request justice," Kharis spoke slowly, giving them the time to record every word. "Not for myself, but for Princess Saya."

"Proceed."

Kharis paused, her chin trembling as she struggled to restrain her tears. She took a deep breath.

To protect her sister, she swallowed her pride.

"With my behavior," she lowered her head, "I've brought shame to the House of Ghan."

A collective gasp swept the chamber.

Hala's chair scratched sharply against the floor.

Someone coughed.

Her father gripped the armrests, his knuckles whitening.

Kharis dropped to her knees, and her muscles flared in protest as the Akumi king fought her choice. He screeched inside her head like an angry beast.

Yuna protested, settling beside her. "Gutxi, please," Yuna whispered, hands hovering, ready to lift her. "Stop this."

Kharis shook her head and bent slowly, wincing and grunting, until her forehead touched the cold floor. Dizziness washed over her. Her breathing hitched.

Blessed Mother.

The Akumi king hissed in protest, sharp and relentless.

"I ask for forgiveness." Her voice cracked. "I hope His Majesty will continue to light my path. I will abide by whatever punishment fits my transgression, but as I said, I'm here for Princess Saya."

The chamber's silence was overwhelming. Kharis held

her breath to curb the agony and kept her forehead pressed to the floor.

"What do you desire?" the king asked, his voice revealing a subtle uptick in pitch.

"Please remove Princess Saya from High General Ghan's supervision."

"So be it." His command thundered in the room, but to her ears, it was music. "The crown prince and I will discuss her tutelage today."

Relief bathed her body. "Thank you, Your Majesty."

"Now that you've made your request for Princess Saya," the king said, "is there one for yourself?"

That question gave her pause. What could she possibly request that she hadn't already asked for?

I'm the Djinnshirukh. I'll never get what I want.

However, people would regard her as pliable and obedient if she didn't ask for anything. *This is like playing xakea.* She would sacrifice pieces, like her pride, to take over the opponent's side. Her goal was High General Arjun Ghan, and he would never see her coming.

"No, Your Majesty."

Her father's lengthy silence grated on her. It was an eternity. Yet, Kharis kept her head down. For Saya's sake, she would behave. The scratching sounds on parchment brought her solace. *Write how the Djinnshirukh bent her knee and submitted to the Crown.* She squeezed her eyes shut, grinding her teeth to hang on. The pain was making her nauseous.

"So be it," her father said. "Sit up."

Kharis exhaled quietly and straightened with Yuna's help. It felt divine to give her lungs the space to breathe again. Her body slowly adjusted as the waves of pain dissipated.

The silvery voice in her mind paced like a wild, untamed beast. *"Never do this again. Ever."*

Hröld glared at Ghan. "General Ghan, what punishment do you seek for White Guard Officer Ren Azdaha?"

"Your Majesty," Ghan's voice was deep and nasal. "For disobeying my directive, I ask that Officer Ren Azdaha be exiled to a battalion in the northern territories."

Kharis wanted to punch Ghan, who would've asked for his execution if he could.

"So be it." Hröld rose from this chair and gestured to the scribes, signaling the end of this proceeding.

Kharis breathed a sigh of relief. *Good. This is over.*

"However," Ghan said, his voice modulated and cloyingly pleasant, "with Princess Kharis, exile isn't an option."

Kharis stiffened.

Yuna snarled at him, her fists shaking.

The scribes stopped writing, mouths opened. The king's legal assessor glanced away and lowered his head.

Hröld froze, glaring at Ghan. Speaking after the king had ended a proceeding was an appalling breach of protocol and a blatant act of defiance against the imperial king of Zahar.

The silence in the room was overbearing.

Taking the silence as permission, Ghan said, "I know the imperial king of Zahar would never favor his child over the laws of the land." A pause. A faint smirk. "In the same manner that Officer Ren Azdaha is punished for going against a direct command, so should Princess Kharis. Therefore, I ask that Princess Saya and Princess Kharis be separated." He squared his shoulders. "Keeping them together undermines the Sorukhipa's ultimate task as the Djinnshukh's executioner."

Kharis stopped listening.

No. No. No.

An icy trickle rolled down her back. All voices became distant, muted noises. Her world cracked. When it finally shattered, the strident sound stole her breath.

"Let me ask again," her father, his voice calm yet resonant, "so we properly state it for the record. You, High

General Arjun Ghan, want Princess Saya and Princess Kharis to be separated."

General Ghan replied swiftly. "Yes, an accurate rendition of my request for the record."

"So be it." Hröld's voice boomed like an eruption, unequivocally ending the proceedings this time.

Hala pounded his right fist on the table. "Father, I—"

The king whipped his head toward Hala. "My chambers —now."

Her father departed in a sweep of bows. Hala followed, rigid with fury. Guards escorted Ghan out. Jurists and scribes fled the chamber.

Kharis remained where she was, still on her knees, breath shaking. Cold seeped into her limbs. Yuna whispered in her ear, rubbing slow circles against her back, but the words never reached her.

Behave. Behave.

Where was the value in behaving, following rules, and being obedient? Sparks arced through her fingertips.

Behave?

It was a ridiculous assumption now.

Rawiri had been sent away in chains. Now, Ghan was taking Saya. She could endure his training. His humiliation. But not this.

"No." A new clarity came to her. "He's not taking her."

"Gutxi?" Yuna raised her eyebrows.

Kharis rose slowly, every muscle coiled tight. She wanted blood. His blood. When she stared at the marble floor, its veined patterns twisting beneath her vision, something else took hold.

Revenge.

She would sit quietly and be an obedient Djinnshirukh.

High General Arjun Ghan would never see her coming.

CHAPTER 69

THE KING'S ORDER

Höld hurried back as everyone bowed in his wake and entered his chambers.

"Your Majesty?" Arman, so small against Höld's height, stared at the king with worry written all over his face. Höld glanced away to hide the tears pooling in his eyes. Arman nodded, knowing, and helped him out of his royal garb—the sash with the medals, the official empire emblems, the heavy ermine robe, and the heavy crown he was required to wear for these.

When Hala walked in, Höld glared at him.

"Leave us," Höld told Arman.

Arman took the items, bowed, and closed the doors behind him. Höld slumped in a chair. His stomach was ablaze. He tried to breathe, but his chest was too tight.

"Father—"

Needing a moment, Höld raised his hand to silence him, but Hala grabbed and examined it. His nails had left bloody crescent moon marks on his palms. "You're bleeding—"

Höld snatched his hand away. "Yuna will take care of it. Sit."

Hala pursed his lips, staring at his father, then dropped his body on the closest chair.

"Hala," Hröld said. "One day, as king, you'll have to make difficult decisions based on law. You can't see brothers, sisters, or even children. As the king, they become subjects, no different from any other."

"But Father—"

"Make peace with it," Hröld said sternly, "or would you rather have the Regiazenka decide Kharis's fate?"

"No, never." Hala clenched his jaw. "But how do I make peace with what he did to them?"

"Do you think I don't see it?" Hröld was breathing hard. "That it hurts me less?"

Hala didn't answer.

Hröld stood, clutching his abdomen, the burning in his stomach overwhelming him.

"This is what we'll do—first, the officer. Ren Azdaha. I want him and his family sent to the northern territories, not as a punishment but as a promotion—make it Tulaä. He did what he could to protect them and took the brunt of the abuse. His role in this new post must match our gratitude for his sacrifice.

"Second, I want the other two officers equally compensated. They might've chosen not to speak against him, but I can't blame them. Send them to a post in Almarim. Götrid and Bikram will see that they're protected there.

"Third, identify the best individuals to assume Saya's training. I want Officer Edurne Salazar to be at the top of the list. We'll provide it to the Regiazenka, and Arjun's vote will be diluted accordingly. Further, it removes us from the decision-making process, eliminating any appearance of favoritism he could later use against us.

"Fourth, I want you to handle Saya's move." Hröld winced in pain, clutching his chest with a soft groan.

"But Father, without Saya to guard Kharis—"

"Ensure Saya's at the palace. We'll keep Kharis at the

villa. If Ghan files a grievance, show him the record of the proceeding.

"And last," Hröld paused, "I want you to identify new trainers for Kharis."

Hala sat up, shocked. "What do you mean?"

"Ghan may supervise her training, but never train her again." Hröld doubled over and stumbled back to his chair. "Have Arman bring Yuna." He shut his eyes, gritting his teeth as sweat beaded his forehead.

Hala flung the doors open, yelling for Arman to get help. Then he raced to his father's side.

Hröld gasped, clinging to Hala's arm. "If Arjun ever touches them again, I'll kill him myself."

CHAPTER 70
A DEFIANT WIND

Kharis stared at nothing, quietly pondering scenarios.

A dagger? Poison? A poisoned dagger? A fall down a long set of stairs? Falling out of an open window?

She worried her lip.

Public shaming? That could work.

Her silence worried Saya, who was already giving her "that look."

It was odd being back in their old palace chambers. When Yuna allowed them to leave the royal infirmary, their father moved Saya into the palace to visit her often. Kharis missed the villa's quiet but refused to return each night, staying by Saya's side through thick and thin.

Servants will start the move tomorrow. Kharis shook her head. *No power on this earth is going to rip Saya from me.* If it came to it, they would escape, but before that, she would make Ghan pay for the misery he'd imposed on them.

A heavy piece of the rock wall falling on his head? Crushed by a horse? Disgracing him?

As Prince Rawiri had once suggested, she would walk on horse manure and make Ghan lick her boots clean.

"If you share your thoughts with me," Saya said, "I'll share my aljaicin."

Kharis snapped out of her pondering whirl. "Sorry."

Saya wrapped her arm around Kharis's shoulders. "What are you thinking? I can see that head of yours planning something."

Kharis turned to Saya. "How are you feeling?"

"Much better. Nana believes I'll be hopping and skipping soon enough, not that I want to." Saya's nervous chuckle failed to elicit Kharis's sisterly smile.

Her sister had almost died. Had she died, Kharis's world would've ended with her.

Kharis's gaze swept the room.

"Khiri?"

Saya stopped fiddling with a loose thread on her sleeping shift. Kharis jumped out of bed, wearing a wicked grin.

Saya stiffened at the sight. "Khiri, what's going on?"

Kharis locked the doors and placed the thick wood planks across the metal brackets. She walked over to a tall armoire, pressed her back against a side, summoned her otherworldly strength, and pushed.

"W—What are you doing?" Saya's voice went up a pitch higher.

The Djinnshirukh grunted with the effort to slide the wooden goliath in front of the door.

"Khiri, you're blocking the—"

"Precisely." Kharis wiped the sweat off her forehead.

"But Khiri—"

"I made the foolish mistake of not fighting for Rawiri," Kharis said. "I lowered my head and behaved. I accepted the king's decision and didn't dispute it. And for what, sister? For what?" she shouted. "I miss him. Every. Single. Day. And yet, here we are again."

She inhaled sharply.

"No one's taking you away from me." Fire coursed through her veins. "That's final."

Kharis rolled her sleeves, scanning the room for more heavy furniture. She eyed the long dresser, and another dark grin tugged at her lips.

CHAPTER 71

THUNDER AND LIGHTNING

Yuna and Anong followed the servant in silence, their steps quickening with each turn of the corridor.

"Why all the secrecy?" Yuna asked. "What's so important that you interrupted our dinner?"

A blush crept across Roha's cheeks. "My apologies, Highness, but we didn't know what else to do."

Yuna winced at the title, but now wasn't the time for lectures. "Do what?"

"Look." Anong tilted his chin toward the gathering ahead when they turned the corner.

A cluster of servants huddled in front of the princesses' chambers, engaged in hushed conversations. Upon spotting the couple, their expressions shifted from tension to relief.

"Roha," Yuna asked, "what's going on?"

Before Roha could answer, the servants surrounded them.

"Your Highness," Roha said, "they won't open the doors."

"They've locked them from the inside," another servant said.

"We've tried everything," said a third.

The monk pursed her lips. Her gaze settled on Anong, who adjusted his glasses along the bridge of his nose with his forefinger, his telltale thinking gesture.

"Very well," Yuna said. "I'll have them open it."

A quiet chorus of thanks floated in the air.

Yuna knocked on the door. "Kharis, Saya, please open the doors." Silence was the only reply. She knocked again, harder, the sound echoing. "Girls?"

Nothing.

Yuna huffed, leaning into the door before facing the servants. "How long has this been going on?"

"Today's the second day, Highness."

Yuna frowned. The hallway felt narrower than before. "Is the crown prince aware of the situation?"

"Not yet. We came to you first."

Relief stirred in Yuna's chest. Loyalty among the palace servants was no small thing. She and Anong had earned it not with coin or threats, but with poultices, steady hands, and long nights spent tending wounds that would never be mentioned at court.

Coming to her first carried risk. Positions could be lost if the wrong ears heard of it.

"What about His Majesty?" Yuna asked. "Has he come?"

"He doesn't know, either," Roha said, lowering her head.

Yuna exhaled, twisting her plain gold necklace. "I'll see what I can do."

The servants sighed in relief. Yuna drew in a breath and met their eyes, as she did with her patients. "For now, go on with your tasks and leave this to me." A pause. "Please."

Everyone bowed and scattered, leaving Yuna alone in the hallway with Anong. She reached for the door with a hand pressed against her chest. "Girls?" She knocked again. "It's Nana. Please let me in."

Not a single sound came from the other side of that door.

The sisters never answered. The doors remained closed.

Ghan's name rose unbidden, sour on her tongue. Visions of the retribution she would inflict on him played vividly in her mind. She swallowed it back, fists curling until her nails bit skin.

Anong squeezed her shoulder. "Focus on the girls," he said, his voice soft and comforting. "Perhaps they need this time away from everyone. They've endured a lot."

Yuna wrung her hands. "Anong, they've never lived apart. Add that their bond is otherworldly, divine, and this decision could explode in our faces."

Anong clutched her arms. "We'll protect them no matter what. Our promise stands."

"Oh, Anong." A sense of foreboding made her shudder. She clasped her hands, taking a deep, steadying breath to stop trembling. "He's going to listen to me," she muttered. "By the Netherworlds of Ifran, Hröld will listen to me."

A different fire lit her resolve as she headed straight for the king's chambers.

She gathered speed with every step.

Anong barely kept up with her.

৶

Kharis climbed through the window, entering the room like a stealthy shadow. "I'm back." She dropped a bag on the floor and, with a swift motion, closed the window behind her.

"They've stopped trying," Saya whispered.

"Who?"

"I couldn't make out the voices. Maybe they've given up?"

Kharis shook her head. "I'll believe it when the king stands on the other side of that door and agrees to keep us together. Until then, we sit here and wait."

"Do you think Father will relent?"

Kharis smiled at her sister as she walked to the bed with

the bag in her hand. "Is the sky blue?" She took off her boots and sat cross-legged, dumping the contents of her bag on the bed: honey biscuits, a loaf of rye bread, half a round of hard cheese, a large piece of cured meat, apples, and a waterskin. "Dinner is served."

Saya assessed the loot with a frown. "Someone could've seen you."

"Pfft. Doubtful. I'm the stealthy Djinnshirukh, remember? It's dark, and I know the patrol routes. The servants' corridors are empty at this hour." A smirk. "And not all the tunnels are sealed."

She sliced cheese and meat with a knife and placed them on a slice of bread.

"Here," she said. "You must eat to keep your strength. Not as fancy as eating with Father, but quite tasty anyway."

"What will happen if Father doesn't change his mind?" Saya asked.

Kharis waved a dismissive hand. "I'm not entertaining failure." She settled against the headboard and crossed her ankles.

"There's no world where you aren't with me." She bit down on her food hard enough to hurt.

Saya leaned in with a satisfied sigh, resting her head on Kharis's shoulder. "I love you, Khiri."

Kharis patted Saya's head, mouth half-full. "And I love you more."

Saya laughed. Kharis didn't. Her gaze flicked to the door. Every piece of furniture she could move—chairs, tables, washstand, even the small bench from the foyer—was stacked there, wedged tight, braced to hold. She had made sure of it.

Kharis had taken enough from the kitchens to last them days. This was a siege, she decided. They would endure it and emerge victorious.

CHAPTER 72

FATE STIRS

On the third day, word reached Hala, who added his voice to those imploring the sisters to reconsider. He pounded on the wood, each blow splintering what remained of his patience.

"Open this door." He punctuated every word with a heavy blow. "Open it now or else."

"Hala, please, halt this move," Yuna pleaded.

Hala's headache pounded behind his eyes as he cocked his head, casting his aunt a withering look. "You've been at the palace long enough to know I can't overturn a king's order," Hala snapped. "Not without starting something worse."

"You can stop it for now," she said. "Where's Hröld? Why is he not here—?"

The sound of harsh footfalls resounded along the hallway. A shadowy figure stepped from behind the corridor's gloom, taking a familiar shape—tall, broad, imposing. The Wall of Zahar-Ghak was approaching with a column of his soldiers. His eyes gleamed as he smirked, too satisfied with what he intended to do.

Yuna's voice sharpened, scowling at him. "What are you doing here?"

Arjun Ghan exhaled, dripping in sarcasm. "Ah, Yuna, you're always so delightful."

"Arjun." Anong frowned with his warning.

The high general gave Yuna's husband a scrutinizing look. "Remind me... Who are you?"

"Arjun!" Yuna raised her voice, hands fisted at her sides. "We don't need you—"

"Oh, I beg to differ, *sister*," Ghan interjected. "A little bird told me that the princesses have been holed up in their rooms for... let's see... three days now?" Ghan glanced at Hala. "It appears our crown prince can't follow a simple royal directive."

"Leave," Yuna hissed. "Now!"

Ghan crossed his arms. "And what will you do if I don't?" He sneered with delight. "Send me to the dungeons?"

Before Yuna could go for his throat, Anong grabbed her waist, pulling her back. Utterly uninterested, Ghan curled his hand in a come-hither gesture, ordering his soldiers to approach. The first row parted to let the soldiers in the back move forward. They quickly closed the distance and lowered a heavy-looking iron-tipped battering ram onto the floor.

Yuna froze in Anong's arms.

"This is warfare at its most basic," Ghan told a stunned Hala with a smile as broad as his shoulders. "Too bad you forgot all my lessons." He tapped his cheek. "Oh, wait. You hardly ever came to them."

Hala curbed his urge to choke his uncle.

The scar on Ghan's face twitched as his sinister grin dimpled his right cheek. "We treat this like a siege. Break the doors and get Saya out. Today." He gave Hala a triumphant sneer. "Otherwise, I'll ask the Regiazenka to intervene since you can't manage your sisters."

Hala went still. The Regiazenka. They would strip what little authority Hala had left in this.

Ghan jerked his head at the beam, smirked at Hala, and walked away, too bored to stay and watch the door break. Aghet Mendi stole a look, eyes shining at the ram, and trailed behind his high general, both figures gradually fading into the corridor's gloom.

Hala imagined a dagger between Ghan's shoulders and hated himself for lacking both the blade and the freedom to use it.

"Your Highness, we are ready," the captain alerted.

Hala flinched. The order lodged in his throat.

He stared at the wooden doors, his stomach churning relentlessly.

One day, he would be king. The Regiazenka would expect him to be fair and objective. To choose law over love.

"Hala, please, I beg you. Don't do this." Yuna's frantic eyes landed on the battering ram. "Send that thing away. Let me talk to them. Convince them." Anong released her, and Yuna bowed low before Hala as her tears collected on the floor, her voice shaking. "Please."

"Your Highness?" The captain awaited his orders.

Hala's head spun. Saliva collected in his mouth, but he found it hard to swallow. Nausea made his stomach roll. He studied the massive monster made of wood and iron, and an icy hand scratched his back.

All eyes pressed in on him. Soldiers. Servants. The captain.

Yuna's sobs echoed off the walls, leaving no space to breathe.

His chest clamped. The king had thrust him into this predicament, unable to face his daughters. If his father were here, he would defy his own decree, and Arjun Ghan would seize the chance to spark a civil war.

Hala took a deep breath, but the decision weighed on him like an unrelenting burden. His heart thumped against his ribs as uncomfortable drops of sweat rolled down his back. He hated Ghan, who had ordered the battering ram to spite him.

One day, I'll be king. Spots danced in his field of vision. *One day, I'll be forced to make decisions solely on the basis of the law.* His heart thudded harshly against his chest. An invisible hand gripped his neck and squeezed. This was how his father lived. Choked.

Khiri, Saya, please forgive me.

Hala studied the sizable battering ram again, took a deep breath, and released it.

Curse you, Ghan.

His right hand clenched, clutching a fistful of his embroidered kurta. Hala stepped back. "Proceed."

CHAPTER 73

FIRE AND BRIMSTONE

The pounding on the door jolted the sisters awake. Saya shot up, startled, while Kharis let out a snore, groggily wiping the drool from her mouth.

"Khiri?" Apprehension twisted Saya's face.

Kharis scratched her head, her eyes half-open, and wrapped an arm around her sister. "It's fine, Saya. Calm down. We've reached the negotiations stage." She smiled, certain.

The furniture muffled the sounds. The girls heard a few words, but that voice belonged to Hala. There was no doubt about it. "Open… Now… Else…"

There were others in the background, people Hala spoke to or who spoke to him. The sisters picked up Yuna's voice among them. There was an inaudible back and forth, dampened by all the furniture piled against the entrance.

"Khiri, what's happening?" Saya asked.

"Hang in there. The peace treaty is coming." Kharis focused on the heap of furniture blocking the door. "I bet Father's with them."

Saya wrinkled her forehead. "I hope you're right."

Kharis clutched her sister. "No one's taking you away from me, Saya. No one." Then she flashed her usual grin. "Together, remember?"

Saya nodded. "Forever."

An explosion rattled the doors. Kharis's heart slammed against her ribs, and she jumped out of bed with a wooden sword, the only weapon in the room since all else was at their villa.

The silence was short-lived. Without warning, something brutal and violent struck the wood again. It sent shockwaves through the floorboards, causing the windows to quiver in protest.

"Khiri?" Fear laced Saya's voice. "What's that?"

Kharis's breathing hitched, and her heart galloped at full speed. Something significant rammed against the doors once more. Its thud echoed in the room, shaking the walls. The windows rattled, and the tapestries and portraits shook with the vibrations.

"A battering ram?" Kharis mumbled under her breath. Her legs faltered at the realization. She lowered her wooden sword, tilting her head. "They brought a battering ram?"

Shock quickly gave way to disbelief. *We're being treated like enemies.* Her hands curled until the wooden blade creaked in her grip.

"Khiri?" Saya's voice cracked. Her face had turned ashen. She sat stiffly on the bed with her back pressed against the headboard.

The ram pounded the wood without mercy. The furniture piled against it rattled, and the smaller items fell and crashed to the floor.

THUD.

The blow echoed loudly in their ears.

THUD.

The sound bounced off the walls, impossible to ignore.

THUD.

Kharis jumped on the bed. "We're going to fight."

"But Khiri—"

"We've done this hundreds of times, Saya. We've trained for this."

"But we have no weapons."

"Yes, we do," Kharis said. "You have me. I'll tackle this as if *that*," she gestured to the door, "were a horde of Akumi." A sharp, unwanted clarity snapped into place. "And when I tell you to run, you run. Do you understand?"

"Kharis, please—"

"Listen to me." Kharis cupped Saya's face in her hands, her voice low and urgent. "I will fight. *You* will run. Don't turn. Don't look back. Just—run."

"But Khiri—"

"Promise me, Saya." Kharis's world shimmered with unshed tears. "I can't fight them with everything I have if you're still here. Swear to me—you'll run and save yourself."

Saya gave a trembling nod, words lost to the knot in her throat. Her breath came in shallow bursts.

"When it's over," Kharis whispered, "find me—like you did when we played hide-and-seek."

"Khiri..." Saya choked.

THUD.

The doors cracked and splintered. The furniture blocking the door shook, jangled, and clattered. More items crashed to the floor. The battering ram kept its rhythm, its sound growing louder with each strike.

THUD.

"Get ready, Saya."

THUD.

The wooden planks gave way, bursting into a cloud of splinters and sawdust.

THUD.

The ram broke through the door.

THUD.

One door shattered and fell apart, and eager hands and staves appeared through the gaping hole to push and shove the furniture away, making it tumble and crash.

"On my mark, Saya," Kharis said, her tone commanding. "Get ready."

A mob of soldiers ran into the room to grab them.

"Run!" Kharis yelled at the top of her lungs and lunged forward with her wooden sword, hitting, striking, and whacking bodies without care or fear of consequence. She headed for the door. Ghan had to be out there, and she would end him once and for all. With her free hand, Kharis punched and beat indiscriminately, driving herself toward the door.

A firm hand grabbed her shoulder. Kharis pivoted quickly and bit it hard. She grabbed the soldier's wrist and twisted, using their weight against them. Both soldiers went down in a tangle of limbs. The Djinnshirukh jumped over bodies on the floor and dodged the hands attempting to capture her, moving like a dangerous blur.

Saya screamed and yelled, throwing objects at the soldiers to escape them, but more soldiers poured in—ten, twenty, thirty.

They swarmed Saya before she could break free of the room.

"Khiri!" she cried, thrashing in their arms.

Kharis turned and ran to her, shrieking. She jumped in, punching faces to free Saya.

The Sorukhipa kicked and flailed, striking everywhere she could reach. More soldiers spilled into the room to restrain the sisters apart. Kharis met Saya's desperate gaze, who couldn't fight them off anymore. Exhaustion had claimed her, and the soldiers swiftly pulled Saya away. When she disappeared behind a wall of white uniforms, Kharis snapped.

A fire-infused scream escaped her throat.

Utter blackness encased her.

The scent of pungent smoke and sulfur enveloped this space as a resonant bass voice filled with anger and profound resentment vibrated through her.

"*He took my beloved.*" A tendril of smoke twisted around her like a caress that offered support and understanding. "*He took the ones I loved like they are taking the one you love.*"

"They can't take her away." Her words sputtered between sobs. "Not her. Not my sister." Her desperation turned into something dark and dangerous. "I must save her."

"*Then we do it together.*" The Akumi king's deep voice rattled her bones. "*I failed once. I will not fail again.*" Heat radiated from the void, dry and searing, as though the fires of Ifran loomed just beyond her reach. "*I shall battle with you until the very end.*"

His oath boomed in the ethereal darkness that embraced her, fueling her power.

"*Do you consent?*" the king demanded.

To save her sister, Kharis would even go to Ifran. "Yes," she shouted. "May the Fires burn me. Yes, yes, yes."

The Akumi king heaved a delighted hum. "*Together then.*"

Her body shuddered with the force of the Akumi king's power. The darkness that overtook her mind was absolute.

"Together!" the Akumi king and the Djinnshirukh shouted in unison.

Magic flooded in, barbed and merciless, forcing her muscles to lock and her breath to shatter. Her heart slammed again and again until it felt like it would burst apart. Always invisible, the magical seals on her skin now flared, no longer holding. Something ancient and furious surged through the cracks.

Stardust sealed around her, hard and blinding. Iridescent scales tore through her skin. The last containment holding the Akumi king in check dissolved.

A flash of red overtook her vision.

When she screamed again, fire answered.

Kharis seized a sword from a stunned soldier. Moving like a bolt of blazing lightning, she attacked, slashing and cutting indiscriminately.

CHAPTER 74
DEFYING FATE

The soldiers dropped Saya and surged toward Kharis, swords drawn.

Saya had promised Kharis she'd run, but she froze, horrified. Kharis, her beloved sister, was gone. The weapon the immortals had created to destroy Akumi demons now fought Zahari officers.

Kharis's magic slammed against everybody like a moving wall. It exuded extraordinary heat, singeing hair and skin. The ceiling smoked, sending black clouds creeping across the room. The wood under her feet smoldered. The air grew thick and acrid. Sparks and embers fluttered like fireflies, landing on curtains and tapestries and setting them on fire.

"Khiri, stop!" Saya yelled, but the Akumi king's magic sustained Kharis's deadly rhythm.

Her sword was a gleaming blur as it cut everything in its way. Some servants ran from the room, but others, not so lucky, got caught in the melee. More soldiers rushed in, shoving servants out of the way as the massacre continued.

The screaming multiplied. Blood sprayed the walls, turning the room red.

And in that terrifying chaos, Saya's power stirred. She rose from the floor and unleashed a formidable wave of magic. It burst from her body in a blinding explosion of light. The swell inundated the room in glimmering gold dust, sealing the space around Kharis.

Her skin pricked, her spell ready. Delicate filaments, fragile like cobwebs—the fabric of time—emerged from nothingness. She grabbed as many as she could in one hand and pulled on them at once, bringing them toward her.

A vacuum sucked all sounds out of the room. The objects flying in the room were suspended in mid-air. The flames halted their destruction. Smoke stopped billowing.

Saya had stopped the flow of time.

Here, with time held still, Saya conjured her magic unencumbered. Her Firegrazer sword materialized—a blade that cut through everything.

Magic had coated Saya's throat, and she sang.

"*Khiri...*"

As Saya's voice steadied, she pressed forward, using her sister's name as a beacon to end the possession and bring her back.

The Firegrazer sent tremors through her arm, demanding to fulfill its task.

Saya kept her song, her voice soft and irresistible like a siren's.

"*Khiri...*"

Kharis spun around, crimson eyes finding Saya in the frozen chaos. Her pupils widened at the power Saya exuded.

In that moment of clarity, the sapphire and silver in Kharis's eyes returned as if her sister were fighting the Akumi king. She dropped her sword and whispered, "End me." She opened her arms and tilted her head to expose her neck. "Let me be free." Kharis closed her eyes. "Do it."

Saya shuddered. Her magic sputtered. "I can't do this." She let go of her Firegrazer, and the sword turned into a drizzle of gold dust.

Kharis's blue-gray eyes turned crimson once more. The Akumi king shrieked through her.

"I'm bringing my sister back," Saya said.

The Akumi king recoiled, fury tearing through Kharis's voice, but the darkness protecting him slowly retreated. As Saya's voice gained its footing and advanced, the Akumi king struggled, clawing at Saya's light.

Saya kept her chanting. Step by step, she closed the distance, using her voice to remind Kharis of her endless affection.

"*Khiri*," Saya sang softly, lovingly.

Her magic, like a gilded wave, crested over Kharis and rippled through her body, pushing the Akumi king back.

Saya drew her sister into a fierce embrace. Her touch chilled Kharis's furnace. Flames guttered and died. The iridescent armor vanished. Kharis sagged. Saya caught her, lowering them both to the blood-soaked floor. She rocked Kharis gently, whispering comfort in her ear.

With her sister held close, Saya released the threads of time the way one let a kite slip free. They drifted away and vanished.

Time unfroze. Chaos rushed back in.

The floor creaked under the heavy footfalls of soldiers and healer monks as they rushed in. Wood crackled. Steam hissed as sweat drops hit hot spots. Horrific screeching, moaning, and wailing flooded the room again.

❦

Light dispelled the shadows. Despite her blurred vision, Kharis made out the bodies—so many of them. Crimson slicked the floor and walls. Turmoil thundered all around her—moans, wails, cries, shouts.

"Saya?" Kharis's voice trembled. "I'm scared."

"I'm here, Khiri," Saya whispered. "I'm not leaving you."

"You should run."

Saya held her tightly, as if trying to shield her from the world, from everything.

"I... I killed them." Kharis's voice cracked. "I... did this."

"Look at me," Saya said firmly. "That wasn't you."

"Leave—"

"No," Saya said, her voice steady. "I'm not leaving you. Ever."

Kharis gazed into her sister's golden eyes. And in that gaze, she found shelter, but how long would it last?

She closed hers and let go of the world.

CHAPTER 75

THE NEWS

"Sir, someone's coming."

Arjun Ghan turned on his saddle. His eyes narrowed on the shadow approaching his cavalry.

"Who?" Ghan asked.

"General Mendi," was the answer.

He'd stayed behind to spy and report. How Aghet galloped told him he was the bearer of important news—good news. Ghan smiled and urged his horse forward to meet him.

"My prince," Aghet Mendi said in that seductive voice Ghan enjoyed, "it happened as you planned." He dismounted swiftly, his brown eyes gleaming with excitement. "I saw it all." Flecks of darkness floated in them.

"And?" Ghan swung a leg and got off.

"Tails, my prince. Not heads, but tails, tails, tails." Aghet's fingers brushed the scar on Ghan's side, reverent. "You'll finally have what should've been yours."

The irony burned Ghan. That annoying little voice echoed in his head: *True blood seals the spell.*

"After this," Aghet said, "the Regiazenka will call for her execution. The Akumi king will be yours at last."

"How many dead?"

"So many, my prince," Aghet said with utter pleasure. "Her death warrant is all but sealed."

Ghan pursed his lips.

"I behaved," Aghet confessed. "The urging was so explosive, so painful. I craved to tear and cut and slash as she did." His gaze gleamed. "She was formidable. Fire and death embodied." His grin was broad. "The way she moved with the blade. Like a dancer."

A black spark glinted in Aghet's eyes.

"I can't get it out of my head." His gaze widened. The shadows in them twirled with frenzy. "The screaming, the sound of metal piercing flesh, the spray of blood in every direction. I wanted to join her—"

"Aghet."

Aghet flinched as if suddenly awakened. His brown irises refocused, gazing once again at the high general. The madness in his eyes had capitulated to Ghan's commands.

Aghet smiled. "What does my prince desire?"

The Silver Moon Festival had been partly successful, having at least gotten rid of that meddlesome Kahurangi prince. The Djinnshirukh spell could still work, even if his father had been a nobody. With her execution, a new vessel would be needed.

All that power would finally be his.

"There are a few prisoners to execute," Ghan said. "You can torture them first if you want."

Aghet's eyes widened again, framing a toothy smile.

"Would you enjoy that?" Ghan asked.

"I thought you'd never ask."

CHAPTER 76

THE DUNGEON

Saya jolted awake in the dead of night, drenched in sweat, her heart racing.

In a few more days, her sister would face her sentencing.

Her body ached. Bruises and scratches mottled her arms and legs. Ghan had put her here weeks ago. Now the massacre had brought her back again.

A bhiksun sat across the room, quietly reading a book by the light of a single candle.

Saya turned her head. The bed beside hers was empty. Kharis should have been there, except that, as the Djinnshirukh, she healed faster.

The Akumi king's gifts came to haunt her. Strength. Speed. Fire summoning. Self-healing.

Gifts? No. They were a curse.

Twenty-one officers and six servants had died at Kharis's hand. The number of injured and maimed was even higher.

Officers came and took her to the dungeons days ago.

Rumors about the fire that had blazed through Prince Rawiri's chambers reawakened and ran rampant in the palace and beyond. Those murmurings had shared the same theme: Kharis had started the fire in Rawiri's rooms just as she'd done in hers.

But it was worse. Now the Regiazenka knew her sister could fire-summon. Nothing would sway them now. The thought hollowed her out. Now, an underground cell held Kharis while the Regiazenka deliberated.

Saya lay still, her chest tightening, until the bhiksun rose and slipped from the room.

Swiftly and quietly, Saya placed pillows under the covers to mimic a resting body and tiptoed toward the door. She found a closet and donned the expected uniform at the royal medical wing: a long cotton tunic with ties on the sides, trousers, and the blue kashaya that healer monks draped over a shoulder. Nobody would question one of Monk Yuna's apprentices checking on sick prisoners in the middle of the night. Covering her head with the kashaya would complete the disguise.

The sentries guarding the royal infirmary didn't look at her when she exited it.

Kharis's call traveled through the bond, tugging at Saya. Harkening to such a power, Saya hurried through the corridors until she stepped outside. *Another foggy night.* Guards on patrol ignored the monk in dark blue robes as she crossed the central plaza.

Ahead loomed the massive doors to the Zahar-Regia's prison.

"Blessed be the earth and sun," Saya said, lowering her voice to mask it.

"May they sustain us," the sentry replied. "Hey!" He knocked on the door to signal the soldier inside to open it. "A monk is here to check on prisoners." Once opened, Saya quickly crossed it.

"Where are you headed?" the soldier inside asked her.

"I'm tasked with checking on the princess."

The man scoffed. "Well, better you than me. Good luck with that."

"May the earth and sun sustain us both," she said, playing her part.

The soldier jerked his chin at a guard seated across from them. "Zahir, escort the bhiksun to the Djinnshirukh's cell."

"Must I?" Fear tightened his voice.

"It wasn't a request, soldier."

Zahir let out a low, unhappy groan, then rose and motioned for Saya to follow. They descended a narrow spiral stair until they reached the lowest floor. Several empty cells lined the corridor, but at the end of the hall, the largest cell held Kharis.

"Why is it so dark here?" Saya asked.

The soldier shrugged. "She hasn't requested light."

Saya's shoulders tightened. "Has she requested anything?"

"Nope," Zahir said. "She stays quiet, and that makes our job easier. I—I have a family waiting for me." The man scratched his cheek, glancing at the stairs. "But a few officers would love to spend time with her." He drew a finger across his throat.

"Has anyone come to check on her?" Saya had hoped her father or brother would.

"No one," Zahir said. "Bhiksunim, like you, but that's it."

Saya did her best not to show how her heart shattered.

"No. Wait. General Mendi also comes to interrogate the prisoner."

Interrogate? Her hands fisted. "What does he want?"

"I don't know." Zahir threw a cautious glance up the stairs and lowered his voice. "But if you ask me, it can't be good."

"Why is that?" Her hands were shaking, nails digging into her skin.

"That man." A shudder ran through his shoulders. "I'll never break the law just to avoid his punishment." He leaned in closer as if sharing another secret. "I've heard he enjoys torturing prisoners. We... We stay out of his way. When he comes, he sends us away. However, I lingered by the stairs one evening, lacing my boots. He unsheathed his sword and dragged it across the floor on his way to her cell. That sound sent me running."

"Has he touched her?"

Zahir lifted his hands, his tone conveying a desire to appease. "No one can. High General Ghan's order is not to open the iron gate to anyone other than him. We may fear General Mendi, but High General Ghan scares us even more."

Saya took a calming breath. "I'll head over. Stay here if you wish."

"Thank you," Zahir bowed, hands pressed flat against each other. "Holler if you need anything." He handed Saya the torch and sat on a nearby chair, his hand resting on the sword's hilt.

"I'll need the keys."

"That I can't do," he said. "Our orders are to keep that cell locked at all times, remember?"

"Then how am I meant to check on the prisoner?"

Zahir shook his head, a hint of remorse in his expression. "I'm truly sorry, but no keys."

Saya bowed, schooling her face, and marched toward the end of the hallway.

The cell was generous. The jailers had placed rugs under a comfortable-looking bed. A few books rested on a desk, and on the far end, behind a shade, was the night pot. Outside the torch Saya carried, the place was dark. She placed it on a bracket, and once her eyes adjusted, she made out the outline of a small body crouched in a corner.

Kharis sat on the floor, hugging her knees with her back to the bars. At the other end of the corridor, the soldier fidgeted with something, not paying her any attention.

"Khiri?" Her voice was soft.

Kharis remained motionless, facing the wall.

"It's me, Saya."

Nothing. Kharis didn't move at all.

Saya eyed the ring of keys on Zahir's belt. Her power stirred, summoned by the need to protect her sister. She strode purposefully toward the guard, channeling magic within her clenched hand. Her fist shook.

Zahir got up, smoothing his jerkin. "Ah! You done?"

"Please accept my apologies."

"Eh?"

Saya drove her fist into his side. The air left him in a wet gasp. Before he could cry out, she struck again, harder, and he went down. Swiftly, she snatched the keys off his belt and returned to the cell, unlocking it.

"Khiri?"

Saya approached slowly, her hand resting on Kharis's shoulder. The Djinnshirukh's head swiveled slowly. A crimson gaze stared at Saya. A shiver coursed through her. Those were the Akumi king's eyes.

"You're not him." Kharis's voice was sharper and more ominous. "Who are you?"

She drew a quiet breath. "It's me. Saya."

With a flutter of blinks, the fiery storm retreated. Silver and sapphire gazed back at her. "Saya?" Kharis's muted voice tugged at Saya's heart. "You came?"

"Of course. Why wouldn't I?"

Kharis looked away. "Because I murdered them."

Saya's breath broke. "That wasn't you." She pulled her sister into her arms. "I'm here because there's no world where I'm not with you."

&a,

Zahir wheezed, his vision still blurred after the strike.

His head throbbed from striking the stone floor. He pushed himself up, struggling to regain his breath despite the burning pain in his abdomen. He patted his hip only to find the keys gone from his belt.

His gaze snapped down the corridor. The Djinnshirukh's cell stood open. A sound tore out of him. Whimpering, he scrambled for the stairs, stumbling as he screamed for help.

❧

Bells clanged loudly from the upper floors. The commotion announced that a column of soldiers was descending quickly.

"You should leave," Kharis said, her gaze fixed on the wall.

"I'm not leaving you." Saya clutched Kharis tighter, her heart beating so fast she feared it would jump out of her mouth. "They'll have to lock me in with you." Her body trembled, but she held onto her sister.

"Then I'm not leaving you, either." Kharis released her knees and hugged Saya, enveloping her sister in a protective embrace.

The harsh footfalls grew louder, rattling the wooden stairs. Shouts followed, closer now.

"Khiri?" Saya whispered, trying to control the shakiness in her limbs.

The Djinnshirukh snapped her head toward the gate, crimson eyes flaring, and hissed.

The torches sputtered out, and darkness swallowed the hallway.

Chaos erupted in the stairwell. Footsteps faltered. Men stumbled blindly, crashing into stone and each other. Expletives rang out as bodies tumbled down the narrow steps, groans and grunts echoing in the pitch-black dungeon.

Yielding to an edict born a thousand years ago, Saya unleashed the full force of her Sorukhipial magic.

CHAPTER 77

THE EXPLOSION

Outside, the clanging of bells plunged the Zahar-Regia into chaos. Orders were shouted. Soldiers flooded the plaza, clustering near the prison gates. From windows and balconies above, hundreds of watchful eyes peered down, trying to make sense of the uproar.

High General Arjun Ghan cut toward the command center, officers scrambling behind him with the rest of his uniform.

He seized a White Guard officer by the collar and hauled him close. "I want a full report."

He never received one.

Light tore through the plaza, not hot but cold. For a heartbeat, there was no sound at all. Then, a concussion flung bodies across the flagstones. Ancient sigils flared and failed. The blast ricocheted through the Zahar-Regia, hammering walls and colonnades before collapsing in on itself. Stone and metal sheared apart.

The palace walls shuddered. Windows burst. Glass rained down as a rolling cloud of dust swallowed the square.

CHAPTER 78

THOSE LEFT STANDING

Yuna and Anong led the healers as they poured into the plaza, their arms laden with stretchers and satchels of salves and bandages. All around them, soldiers scrambled to pull the wounded from the wreckage.

As the cloud dust began to settle, the damage revealed itself.

Men and women lay with broken limbs, their bodies slick with blood, skin torn by jagged stone and splintered wood. Boots pounded across the flagstones, orders barked and lost beneath cries of pain.

Yuna moved swiftly among the injured, calling out instructions as she vaulted over stretchers to reach the gravely wounded. Apprentices scattered at her command—bearing blankets, applying tourniquets, or pressing herbs to open wounds to dull the pain.

Even so, her attention kept slipping. Kharis lay imprisoned in the deepest dungeon floor. Worse still, Saya was gone from the infirmary. Yuna had not yet told Hala.

Her hands faltered on a bandage.

Had Saya gone to Kharis? The thought lodged in her chest. She forced herself to keep working even as her gaze kept straying toward the entryway. The air reeked of scorched timber. Grit clung to her tongue.

"Yuna!" Anong called out, gesturing sharply.

She was going in the wrong direction.

She reached for a salve and stopped, hand shaking. Tears blurred her vision. It took everything to control the urge to rush into the wreckage herself to look for the girls.

The explosion had sealed the prison's entrance in a tangle of heavy rocks, jagged rubble, and splintered wood. Yuna closed her eyes. *Breathe*, she told herself. *Just breathe.*

Arjun sat nearby, one of her apprentices tending to the cuts and scrapes on his face. By right and rank, it should've been her. She turned away.

He had brought this upon them—all of it.

Had the choice been hers, she would've reached for arsenic, not astringent.

Rage kept her steady. Sharp. Ready.

May the Blessed Mother forgive me. Brother or not, she wanted him gone from this world.

§

Arjun Ghan returned to command, his face and hands wrapped in fresh bandages. He cast a glance over his shoulder, eyes narrowing at the blur that was Yuna. Even in the chaos, her innate leadership radiated—and the thorn of envy pricked at him.

Turning away, his gaze swept the crowds, scanning for a familiar face—Aghet. He was nowhere to be seen.

Just then, an officer approached at a brisk pace.

"Debris is being cleared, sir." He gestured to the horses now pulling heavy beams out of the way. "We're working to reach the soldiers and prisoners below."

"Dead?" Ghan asked.

"A few, sir—but it's too soon for a final number. The

work is slow. We won't know the full toll until we reach the lower level."

Ghan spotted Hala approaching and greeted him with a thin-lipped smile. "Good evening, Highness."

Hala's gaze flicked from the officer to his uncle. "What happened?"

Ghan shrugged. "You know as much as I do. I've requested a full report. When I have it, I'll share it."

"And *her*?" Hala asked.

Ghan arched a brow as if Hala had inquired about a sack of onions. "Her?"

Hala glared and turned, striding toward the shattered entryway, his White Guard escort close behind.

"Good," Ghan muttered under his breath. "I've work to do."

He curled and uncurled his hand, a silent command for reports to be presented, and swiftly scanned their contents. The initial list of dead included both soldiers and prisoners. The lower levels remained sealed off, buried beneath rubble. One note raised a troubling concern: the secured dungeon might have collapsed entirely.

This was inefficient.

"I want to know what caused this blast," he said, his voice carrying. No one could give him a definitive answer. Aghet Mendi remained conspicuously absent.

Yuna quickly caught up to Hala. They exchanged words, her gestures sharp and unrestrained. Then they broke into a run, monks hurrying after them.

Ghan watched. Yuna only flailed her arms like that when something had gone wrong.

"Sir?" one of his generals asked.

Ghan turned away from the spectacle. "Continue clearing the debris."

He paused. "And bring me tea."

CHAPTER 79

UNBROKEN

The brigades worked throughout the night.

Throughout it all, Ghan barked orders and skimmed reports thrust, his gaze returning again and again to the prison's entrance.

Soldiers, monks, and volunteers worked together, passing buckets of rubble hand to hand in a slow, grueling rhythm. Bit by bit, they cleared a path into the bowels of the dungeons. At last, as the first pale light of a cloud-veiled dawn broke over the royal city, the teams reached the level where the Djinnshirukh had been held. A long, harrowing night had come to an end, but its toll remained unknown.

When the crew cleared the final stones blocking the way, they quickly braced the ceiling with thick wooden planks. Soldiers and monks surged inside, stepping over rubble to reach the wounded.

As workers cleared the last of the rubble from the stairwell, Ghan thrust out an arm to halt Hala and Yuna.

"Stay here and let me do my job."

Without delay, he took up a lantern and began his descent, a handful of officers following close behind. The shadows swallowed them whole. The deeper they went, the thicker the air became, clinging to them like damp wool. The lantern's flame wavered but held.

"The place is stable," Ghan murmured, voice low, and his officers nodded in agreement. He turned sharply and made the climb back up. Reaching the top, he addressed Hala and Yuna with clipped finality.

"It's safe—for now. Do not linger."

Hala turned to his retinue. "Let's go."

"Make it quick," Ghan said. "This was the epicenter—"

"Out of my way." Yuna shoved past him.

He stumbled, catching himself against the wall. With a grunted curse, Ghan followed. They entered the corridor. Here, the stone walls stood untouched.

"As if nothing had happened," Ghan murmured.

Golden motes drifted lazily through the air. The sweet scent of orange blossoms and jasmine lingered, thick and cloying.

Hala ran a hand along the stone, tipping his head. "No damage indeed."

Ghan said nothing. This confirmed what he'd warned them about. Now, they couldn't deny the danger any longer. The group stepped carefully until they reached the end. Hala raised his lantern to illuminate the cell's interior.

Inside, Saya sat curled around Kharis, her sobs quiet but raw. Her eyes glowed in the gloom with a dangerous intensity.

"She's my sister," she said. "No one's keeping her away from me."

Yuna stepped forward, speaking softly. "We're here to help you, darling, but we must leave quickly—before this section collapses."

Saya bared her teeth. "No one touches her." The gold in her gaze flared as she fixed it on Ghan. "No one."

Ghan raised his hands. "Fine by me."

Saya eased Kharis to her feet, holding her close. Her sister leaned into the embrace, unsteady but alive.

Ghan stepped aside as they passed, watching the Djinnshirukh's slow steps, her presence still defiant. That old bitterness stirred in his chest, the weight heavier than ever.

Blasted child. She even survived this.

Behind the sisters, Yuna followed, eyes glistening with tears.

"I'll inform Father she's alive," Hala told his group, exhaling in relief.

Not for long. A cruel smile tugged at Ghan's lips.

Weeks. That was all it would take.

CHAPTER 80

THE THRONE ROOM

Hröld couldn't even breathe.

Three weeks after the explosion, the Regiazenka convened to decide the fate of a child—his daughter.

He sat on the imperial throne, the ancient Zahari symbol of authority and secular rule, except that he had none on this day—no power, authority, or control. Today, hope was a frayed thread barely keeping him together.

The Throne Room was a massive rotunda with high, vaulted ceilings, marble flooring, and a raised dais where a lavish chair resided under a large, embroidered canopy. Seven steps, like those leading to spiritual enlightenment, led to the throne. Exquisite stained-glass windows lined the tops of the walls, and the sunlight filtering through them painted the space with colors.

Hröld tilted his head to curb his tears. *Please, Blessed Mother, save her. Guide her steps. Embrace her in your mercy.*

Above, detailed frescoes depicting the rebuilding of the world after the One War decorated the vaulted ceiling. It displayed the theme of eternal hope everywhere: the sun rose from behind lofty peaks, the wheat fields swayed under a summer breeze, and lovely lotus flowers surrounded the glorious Mahabhal. Herensuge, the great silver dragon, slumbered on one end, the world resting on its back. At the other end, the regal phoenix took flight, for the Empire of Zahar was born out of its ashes. Brilliant strokes of silver and gold depicted the world. Those frescoes filled the eyes and fueled the imagination, reminding everyone that there was always hope.

Hope. The lack of it scorched Hröld's insides.

Lady Khostuna, High Minister of the Regiazenka, sat to the king's left. Hala, as the crown prince, settled to Hröld's right. The Regiazenka members sat below the dais. Armored soldiers lined the walls. Archers packed the balcony.

The heavy wooden doors creaked loudly as the sentries pushed them open. Their sound echoed through the chamber, and goose bumps ran up Hröld's arms. Advancing in a disciplined formation, two long rows of White Guard officers marched into the room. Hröld flinched at the rhythmic clicking of military boots on the marble floor. They saluted the imperial king, moving in unison. Swiftly turning, they assumed an attentive stance, facing each other with swords unsheathed. The archers nocked their arrows.

The sound of boots and metal chains dragging against the polished floor broke the eerie quiet. Six White Guard officers led the prisoner. Six more followed with their spears angled at her. Moving slowly between the two rows, a barefooted child entered this revered place. They had shackled her ankles, impeding her stride. The manacles kept her wrists clasped together in front of her. Chains connected her wrist cuffs to the iron choker around her neck.

Hröld choked on a sob and gripped the armrests so tightly that the wood carvings imprinted on his palms.

Hala heaved.

Lady Khostuna drew in a quiet breath, unsure of where to look.

His daughter appeared so frail and tiny against the weight of the chains she bore that it was hard to process.

Every Regiazenka minister was suddenly more interested in the stained-glass windows or the frescoes above. Some fidgeted in their chairs, crossing and uncrossing their legs as they pulled on their ceremonial robes.

Only one minister sat still, the ghost of a smile dancing on his face—High General Arjun Ghan.

The hands of a few officers shook with forced restraint as if itching to sink their blades into her body. On the balconies, all archers aimed at her. Every set of eyes in the crowd glared at her, demanding one thing—her death.

The pungent scent of revenge choked the chamber.

Hröld's world crumbled.

CHAPTER 81
THE PRISONER

Kharis moved slowly, her steps hindered by the short chains binding her ankles. It had been a long, agonizing walk of shame toward the Throne Room.

Her father looked exhausted, the bags under his eyes more pronounced. His royal regalia couldn't hide how gaunt he appeared. *Is he eating?* His face was thinner, his eyes more sorrowful than ever. *This is all I do. I make those who love me suffer.* Guilt was eating her alive—guilt, remorse, and regret.

When Kharis reached the center of the room, the two rows of officers formed a circle, creating a barrier between her and the Regiazenka. She stood quietly, a lonely figure cloaked in leather and chains.

"On your knees," was the loud command. Kharis slowly dropped herself to the floor, her shackles making it challenging. She winced when her knees hit the hard floor, lowered her head, and waited.

"Kharis Ghan of Zahar," a woman's voice boomed across the chamber. "You stand accused of murder."

Her heart jolted.

A roll of murmurs struck her ears.

"We laid twenty-one White Guard officers and six servants to rest. The number of injured was staggering."

Kharis gulped.

"Fifty-four soldiers were seriously injured. Some lost fingers or hands," the woman continued. "Others lost arms, legs, eyes. Thirty of them were severely burned. A few will be disfigured for life."

The murmurings intensified. Vile comments met Kharis's ears.

"We can't calculate the damage with currency; the loss is irreplaceable. Children lost their parents. Spouses were gone in an instant. Siblings died that day."

Kharis drew in a breath. The tears that had clung to the corners of her eyes leaped away.

"We've gathered on this somber day to determine your sentence."

The unbearable silence dragged on for five, ten, twenty heartbeats until the sound of a heavy cape falling to the floor hung in the air. Gentle arms wrapped around her, and bitter sobbing came with them.

"I'm sorry," her father barely whispered. "So sorry for everything."

Kharis knew what he meant—sorry that fate had chosen her as the Djinnshirukh. His chest heaved with each ragged breath, his voice never finding a way out. She met her father's eyes. His brow wrinkled as he caressed her face with the utmost gentleness. He opened his mouth to say something, but grief overtook him, and his shoulders shuddered. He held her tightly against his body as tears spilled down his face.

This is all I do.

His weighty ermine robe lay on the floor while the scepter and crown rested on the throne chair. The man hugging her wasn't His Imperial Majesty, Son of the Sun, but Hröld Aren of Cecchio, the doting father of Kharis Ghan of Zahar.

"Your Majesty?"

At the sound of that call, Hröld wailed softly and tightened his grip.

"Your Majesty, we must start the proceedings."

"No," he whimpered softly—anguished. "I can't do this."

His shaky voice wrung Kharis's heart.

"Your Majesty—"

A cacophony of screams and yells from beyond the closed doors interrupted the moment.

Outside, the shouting between sentries and the people clamoring for access intensified. The Regiazenka ministers straightened in their seats, their eyes fixed on the ornate doors—archers turned and aimed at them. Officers faced the entry with their swords drawn.

Kharis braced herself for the chaos, for those outside had to be more people demanding her execution.

Her father, pressing her against him, quivered with the stress. He whimpered softly. His tears landed on her neck, and the grief they carried burned her skin and soul.

CHAPTER 82

THE DEFENSE

Yuna stood outside the Throne Room doors, her chin high, her spine locked, her hands steady at her sides.

Voices rose from both sides, orders snapping back and forth. Sentries blocked the threshold, spears raised—but the line wavered. One woman shifted her grip. A few hesitated, eyes flicking to Yuna and away again. Another looked to his captain. He never gave the word. No one wanted to be the one to touch her.

"Enough!"

At Yuna's word, monks in deep purple surged forward. They shoved the sentries aside, armor clattering, and drove the doors open with a crash that echoed through the hall. Yuna stepped through with Saya at her side.

When Saya saw her father and sister kneeling before the throne, she tore free and ran to them, dropping to the floor and wrapping them in her arms. She held them there, murmuring fiercely, heedless of the murmurs rippling through the chamber.

Twenty warrior monks closed ranks around them, spearheads lowering in unison—their call for justice. The shafts struck the stone floor as one.

The sound rang through the Throne Room.

Saya rose.

She faced the ministers, breath sharp, hands shaking. Yuna moved to her side.

The hall fell silent.

"I'm here to beg for mercy for my sister," Saya said, her voice clear.

Lady Khostuna glared at the monks, then at Yuna. "What is the meaning of this?"

"What about this isn't clear?" Yuna strode forward, her azure robes billowing. "I'm here to advocate for my niece, a child of the Morning Star. What would Her Imperial Majesty Queen Aghuti say if she were here today? I'm sure she would look you in the eye and call the Regiazenka a travesty."

Lady Khostuna rose. "It was Her Majesty who created the Regiazenka—"

"To curb the power of an absolute monarch," Yuna said. "Let us not forget who my father was. King Aram ruled without restraint, and the Empire paid for it in blood, famine, and ten years of war. My father believed power justified everything. His attempt to assassinate my uncle, Prince Narayan, and his wife, Princess Hahana, led us to the last war—"

"A war we won, Yuna."

Yuna's fists shook. "Tell me again, Arjun. How many Zahari soldiers died in the attack against the Kahurangi army?"

Ghan stiffened, glowering at her.

"Ah! Quiet, aren't we?" Yuna's voice took on a dangerous lilt. "We lost three thousand soldiers in one day." She raised three fingers. "Three thousand, and I know because I was there, tending to the wounded," she told the crowd. "Let that number sink in."

She drew a breath.

"My sister created the Regiazenka to prevent a repeat under a different name," she said. "It was never meant to punish the powerless. It was meant to restrain the power-ful." Her gaze shifted to Hala, who bore his share of the blame in this. "It was about maintaining a balance of power."

She clasped Hröld's shoulder in silent support.

"Our imperial king is neither cruel nor selfish. Princess Kharis didn't ask to be the Djinnshirukh. The monarchs didn't select her. She didn't undergo training before it. There wasn't even a proper resealment ritual."

Her scowl landed on Ghan and Hala.

"And let us not forget the ones who bear the blame for this terrible incident. Had patience and compassion led us that day; if kindness had stopped an unfair decree, rather than force the king's hand, we wouldn't be here."

Yuna's chest heaved as she met every minister's gaze.

"My sister ruled with compassion and decency. Hröld has honored her wishes. Arjun Ghan has not. Or must I remind you that his abuse of the girls got us here in the first place?"

"Yuna." Ghan rose, his face mottled, his extremities shaking. "She killed twenty-seven people. Twenty-one of them were White Guard officers—"

"And what would you suggest?" She cocked her head. "Tell me, Arjun, what? That we reseal the Akumi using *you* as the vessel?"

He stilled, his guard down for a moment. Then his scowl returned. "She killed—"

"You already said that." Her voice boomed in the cham-ber, bouncing against the frescoes on the ceiling. "But it wasn't she who did it. It was the Akumi king, and I know because I was there. I tried to stop the insanity, but you, Arjun, fed it with your abuse, your cruelty—your battering ram." She stared at every member of the Regiazenka, her nostrils flaring. "Who among you has the mettle to execute a child?"

"She's already an adult." Ghan's voice rose, his neck corded. "She's fourteen—"

"Arjun," she shouted. "At what age can a woman marry in Zahar?"

"This has no bearing—"

"At what age?" Her voice thundered. She planted her feet, her fingers curling and uncurling as she faced her brother.

Ghan's lips thinned into an angry white slash. "Eighteen," he said through gritted teeth.

"Then she is *not* an adult."

Yuna breathed hard, hands clenched so hard that her knuckles hurt. She met and held Khostuna's gaze.

"I warned you." Yuna jabbed a finger at Khostuna. "But you dismissed me. I begged you to keep the girls together and to overturn the king's decision. You had the power to avoid this, but you chose to ignore me. 'It's a family dispute,' you said. I warned you that the magic binding the girls is forbidding and that we shouldn't play with what we don't understand."

Yuna faced the Regiazenka with a slow shake of the head.

"I warned all of you."

She moved slowly and deliberately toward the ministers.

"Instead of admitting your failure," she said, "you refused to accept accountability for the error in your thinking, quickly blaming a child." Her voice bellowed. "You taunted the Akumi king. You dared him to come and show you how wrong you were. So here we are, *all of us*. We shouldn't blame this child but the adults who led to the Akumi king's awakening."

"Please!" Saya dropped to her knees before the Regiazenka, arms open. "I'm begging you. Please allow my sister to live. Don't take her away from me." She got on all fours and prostrated herself to them. "I'll do whatever you ask," she said between sobs, "but please allow her to live."

Hröld straightened, releasing Kharis slowly, then turned on his knees to face them.

"Please," he managed, his voice breaking with sobs. "Please."

His forehead touched the floor, tears pooling beneath him.

CHAPTER 83

THE ILUNA FOREST

An icy shiver ran down Kharis's back as her sister and father humbled themselves on her behalf.

I should've died that day.

Hala studied the empty throne with a look Kharis couldn't define. The crown prince rose slowly and stiffly, almost reluctantly, walked over to his father in measured steps, and knelt beside him.

"Please," he said before his forehead met the floor.

Yuna lifted her chin. "Let the scribes enter into the records of these proceedings that on the fifth of Ynith, his Imperial Majesty, King Hröld of Zahar, his son Crown Prince Hala, and his daughter Princess Saya begged the Regiazenka for mercy to save the life of one of Aghuti's children, Princess Kharis, who just turned fourteen. A child, according to Zahari law. Let it be known that Yuna, sister to Her Imperial Majesty, Queen Aghuti, may she rest in peace, also asks for the same mercy to save the life of a child who was never allowed to live like one."

Breathing hard, Yuna knelt, and her head rested against the marble.

Her beloved family groveled at the feet of these men and women, and her chest tightened, her breathing thinned.

Curse you, Kharis.

Tears jumped out of her eyes, and she looked away, tilting her head to take in frescoes depicting hope and renewal.

Blessed Mother, how do I fix this?

Twenty-seven people were dead. Many more were injured or maimed. And this turmoil had swallowed up everybody she loved.

Ghan sat in his seat, breathing hard and glaring at the four prone on the floor. *He will never stop. I should die already.*

"The Iluna Forest!" A voice yelled out.

Kharis flinched.

Lord Miresma, minister of the Interior, sprang to his feet, his eyes alight with urgency—as though the answer had struck him like divine lightning. "Send her to the Iluna Forest."

Kharis frowned.

Hala lifted his head on a quiet gasp. He glanced over his shoulder, then at the Regiazenka. "Weren't you sending her to the prison fort in Dulaä?"

"The Iluna Forest?" Prince Jordha rose to his feet, his shoulders tight. "That place is cursed. Nobody in their right mind goes there unless they want to die."

Kharis stopped breathing.

"Those foolish enough to enter it," Jordha said, "never come back. You *cannot* send a child there."

"Monsters roam those woods now," Lord Garrantzi, another minister, muttered, his eyes wide and stricken. "It's where the Forest Kin lived before the Akumi came."

Lady Khostuna opened her mouth to speak, but Lady Karitza spoke first. "That forest was *much* larger back then, but the Akumi burned most of it, driving the Forest Kin out—"

"Enough." Khostuna thundered, her expression pinched. "We haven't gathered here to share children's tales."

"These are not children's tales, Khostuna." Miresma shook his head, gaze locked on her. "Everyone knows of the magic still inhabiting that place. The demon inside the princess once burned all the forests of Zahar," Miresma said, "but the Iluna's magic defied him and survived the onslaught. It played a role in defeating him. Let that magic decide his fate."

"Wait, no." Hala sat on his knees, his voice shaky. "Dulaä is the best option."

"Yes," Jordha agreed, eyes darting. "Let it be Dulaä."

Lord Garrantzi said, "No. Let the Iluna handle this. Let it be the judge."

"You can't send a child there," Hala almost yelled. "Send her to Dulaä, I beg you." He turned to Khostuna. "Please stop this. It must be Dulaä. We'd discussed it."

The ministers shouted over each other, their commentary quickly turning into a chaos of hissing and bickering. Khostuna called them to order, banging the gavel to no avail.

"I'll do it," Kharis said, but the mayhem drowned her voice.

The ministers jabbed fingers at each other. Their arms flailed, hands balled into fists. As if enchanted by the same dark emotions, the muttering in the crowd intensified. Some angrily shoved a few, while others raised their voices and waved their hands in protest.

"I'll do it," she roared.

Everyone stopped, the silence in the room suddenly unnerving. All eyes turned toward the Djinnshirukh.

She lifted her chin. *One dies, so the majority live.* She found it ironic that a man who only thought of himself had taught her about the ultimate sacrifice.

"I'll do it," Kharis said. "I'll go to the Iluna."

"Khiri, no." Saya's voice wavered, forehead creased. "That place is cursed."

A rueful smile tugged at the corners of Kharis's lips. "Then I'll fit right in."

"Khiri, please. You can't do this." Saya wrapped her arms tightly around Kharis. "You can't," she whispered in Kharis's ear, her body trembling. Then she pulled away. "Father, please, you can't allow this." Her eyes glistened. "You can't do this."

Kharis said nothing. There was no sense in defying fate any longer. Her gaze slipped past them all, already fixed on the path ahead—already walking into the forest alone.

CHAPTER 84

THE VERDICT

Hröld stiffened. How Saya looked at him broke him into so many pieces that an eternity wouldn't be enough to put him together.

"A decision has been reached." Lady Khostuna cleared her throat. "Your Majesty, if you will."

Hröld shuddered at the woman's voice, and the invisible weight of his role and responsibility crushed him. He swallowed an anguished sob as his shoulders sagged.

"Father, please!"

Hröld avoided Saya's gaze.

"Please, Father, you must send her to Dulaä," Hala, still on his knees, clamored. "The Iluna Forest is madness. *This* is madness."

"Hröld." Yuna's voice carried an ominous threat. "Don't do this."

Hröld got up slowly, stone-faced, ignoring how Hala and Yuna yelled at him or how Saya's anguished wails tore his soul. He glanced at Kharis, who knelt quietly, resigned, and guilt punched him in the gut. Feeling hollowed out, he shuffled toward the dais. Arman, his valet, approached him with a knitted brow.

"Your Majesty." Arman clasped his hands before him, pleading with his eyes to end this and walk away.

Arjun Ghan seethed, his presence looming like a predator, watching, waiting for blood. The king glanced back at his daughters, swallowing a sob. His breathing faltered.

He met Arman's damp eyes and gestured to the ermine cape on the floor.

Arman stilled for a heartbeat, then bowed his head. He picked up the cape with shaky hands and fastened it on Hröld. He lifted the crown from the throne chair but hesitated to place it upon the king's head.

Hröld knew why.

Once I wear it, I stop being a father.

Hröld gave him a slight nod, but Arman stared at him for a moment longer, hoping perhaps the king would change his mind.

Hröld took a deep breath, sat, and signaled to Arman for the crown again. Arman fought back tears and did as commanded.

With the unbearable weight of the crown upon him, Hröld swallowed hard to tamp down the rising bile burning his throat. He squeezed his eyes shut, hands clamped on the armrests until it hurt.

Forgive me, Aghuti.

He rose, holding the long royal scepter, and thumped it against the floor. "Kharis Ghan of Zahar," he said, the pain in his voice sharp, "I hereby send you to the Iluna Forest to meet your fate."

"No!" Saya wailed, carrying such suffering that it broke the last of him. She clutched her sister, unwilling to let go. Her eyes accused him of everything. She begged and pleaded, but Hröld no longer heard any of it because his internal screaming was deafening.

Kharis kept her head down, hardly moving, as if quietly saying her goodbyes.

"Take the prisoner back," Khostuna told the officers.

The White Guard escort pulled Kharis from the floor and dragged her out while another set of officers restrained a screaming Saya.

"Let go of me!" she shouted, flailing and kicking as she struggled to free herself from their grip. "Khiri!" Her shouts reverberated in the room. "Khiri, don't do this."

When the doors closed, Saya slumped to the floor, crying, and Yuna cradled her in her arms as she wept. The purple-robed monks kept their protective fence around the women, their wary eyes on the guards.

Hala, still agape, had remained on his knees, stunned and speechless.

I failed her, Aghuti, and I failed you.

Hröld closed his eyes and shoved all sounds and images out of his mind.

CHAPTER 85

THE PANGO CLIFFS

The king of Kahurang reached Rawiri's estate with his warriors. It had recently rained, and the gentle pattering of droplets filled the air. Leaves of all sizes and shapes glistened with moisture, drops pooling in stems and dripping off them.

A lush canopy shadowed the two-story mansion. The calls of exotic birds echoed through the foliage. Heavy banana bunches in bright yellow clusters hung from nearby trees. Not far away, fig tree branches brimmed with fruit. Perched on one, an emerald iguana lazily nibbled on a fig.

A blare of conch horns broke the stillness, announcing his arrival and sending a flock of cobalt and crimson parrots soaring from the trees. Servants poured from the mansion, gradually lining the shaded veranda that wrapped around its broad front. Others emerged from the gardens and fields, hurrying to take their places.

Kiwa waited atop his horse, still pondering his decision.

Any other would've been dead by now.

That had been his initial judgment, but diplomats and envoys had intervened, lending their voices to a plea for clemency. Letters also arrived fast, overwhelming palace staff. Even Yuna Chantarasang had penned a heartfelt missive that was read aloud in Court. The Kahurangi, who loved and highly respected their prince, advocated for Rawiri with such passion that it prompted the Crown to reconsider and mitigate the severity of his punishment.

"Your Majesty." Atarangi, tohunga to Prince Rawiri, stepped before all the rows of servants and workers. Upon thumping his staff on the wooden floor, everyone bowed low to their king.

Kiwa studied the sizable crowd, and a frown wrinkled his brow. "Where is he?" he asked.

Atarangi approached, formal and dignified, a hand pressed over his chest. "He's at the cliffs, Your Majesty."

Kiwa's voice turned sharp. "He's under house arrest."

Atarangi bowed lower still. "Please, Your Majesty, allow him this small mercy, for it dispels the clouds that otherwise cast long shadows in his heart." The tohunga kept his head down, a supplicant figure pleading for his master. "Let us receive you properly," he added. "Come inside—I shall send for him at once."

Kiwa narrowed his eyes, studying the lush vegetation covering a gravel path. After a long exhale, he dismounted his horse.

"No," he said. "I shall go to him."

Parting the colossal rubber plant leaves, Kiwa headed toward the cliffs. A monkey hooted in the distance, and another replied. Kiwa stepped over roots and ferns until the sound of crashing waves greeted him. Not far, Rawiri sat on a long bench watching the ocean.

Kiwa halted, pursing his lips.

His brother would remain here until the Crown saw fit to release him. Rawiri's actions in Zahar had brought the two nations to the edge of war—and had shamed Kahurang in the process, especially after Zahar's welcoming gestures and hospitality.

The king of Kahurang was disappointed.

The brother was proud. Only a fool would ignore how Zahar treated the sisters, especially the Rangatira.

Kiwa sat beside Rawiri, shoulders touching.

His brother had lost weight and looked gaunt. Given his body odor, it didn't appear Rawiri had changed his clothes in days. Atarangi had bandaged Rawiri's left arm, but Kiwa could spot the swollen red and purple skin under it— Tanganokai's curse. The waves crashing against the rocks below had captured Rawiri's gaze, but the specter of defeat lingered in that empty stare.

The salty spray mist kissed their faces.

"Your Majesty." Rawiri gave him a quick nod. "What brings you here?"

"Do I need an excuse to visit my brother?"

Rawiri shook his head, smiling ruefully. Kiwa huffed, unhappy with the situation, and gazed at the horizon. "Ataahua is worried about you."

"I'm sorry," Rawiri said, lowering his head. "Please tell her that I'm..." His voice softened. "That I'm fine."

Kiwa puckered his lips. "The kids want to visit. Taika, especially."

Rawiri nodded, still avoiding his brother's eyes. "It would be an honor to host them, Your Majesty."

Kiwa drew in a breath, frustrated by everything, and handed Rawiri a sealed letter. Rawiri turned it over in his hands, then looked up, confusion clouding his gaze.

"It arrived yesterday," Kiwa said. "A letter that went through many hands to reach us. Given the current climate, it's a dangerous one. I wondered what to do about it, but Ataahua, always wise, reminded me that I'm not the letter's addressee."

"Thank you, Your Majesty." Rawiri's hand shook.

The sight of it broke Kiwa's heart. His brother, the mighty Prince Rawiri, now looked like a hollow shell of his former self. Defying Tanganokai had broken him, and now, something essential had been stripped away—something Kiwa did not know how to restore.

The brand along Rawiri's arm twisted beneath the bandage, a living reminder that his brother now bore Tanganokai's *kanga.*

"This other letter," Kiwa continued, "contains a report our ambassador in Zahar-Ghak, Lord Kauri, sent. Its content is…" He paused, choosing his words with care. "It's deeply concerning. I understand that the issue presented in this report is being handled as an internal Zahari affair and, thus, will never rise to the level of the Commonwealth's Council. As a result, Kahurang may never ask about this or use it to inquire about the girls' well-being and share our concerns over their treatment."

Rawiri's hands shook. Kiwa understood the gesture well. Rawiri was still angry. The question was whether at The Butcher or himself.

"Which letter should I read first?" Rawiri asked.

Kiwa paused for a long time, pondering how best to answer. "Read the first one," he finally said. "I'd rather you didn't read Lord Kauri's report, as I have my concerns, but I brought it and am giving you a choice."

Kiwa took a deep breath of salty air.

"However, if you choose to read Lord Kauri's report," Kiwa went on, "heed this warning—not as your brother, but as the king of Kahurang. I share it with caution and against my better judgment. If you act on it—on any of it—and break the terms of your house arrest, my blade will find your neck. Is that understood?"

"Yes, Your Majesty."

"Then read the letter," Kiwa said, patting his brother's shoulder. "Many took untold risks for you to receive it."

Rawiri offered the king an embarrassed nod. He broke the seal and opened it, and, recognizing the handwriting, his breath caught.

"Teppe." His voice cracked with emotion.

The lettering was small and compact, as if the writer had wanted to use every inch of space on the parchment. Yet, it was a well-balanced script, slightly slanted to the right. There was something whimsical about how some letters were gently rounded, with a circle, not a dot, over all the Is. She'd drawn a flower on one margin with colored ink. The word under it, written in Kahurangi, read "tiare." At the bottom was a drawing of a large man holding the hands of two girls. She'd written "whānau" under it.

He read the first line, his voice barely above a breath.

I finally figured out the peke curse. It's like "spear me," right?

Rawiri squeezed his eyes shut. A broken sound tore from his chest as he crushed the letter against his heart..

Kiwa struggled to keep his emotions in check.

"Rawiri," he said, "I have always trusted your judgment. You've been my right hand and voice of common sense for as long as I can remember. Whatever possessed you that night—I will not condemn it, nor you. Any man with half a heart would've done everything in their power to take the sisters away. Know that your brother is proud even if the king of Kahurang is angry about the measures I must take to smooth the tension with Zahar."

Rawiri bobbed his head, and more tears flooded his eyes.

Kiwa squeezed his brother's shoulder, a gesture of steadfast support despite everything, before walking away. He paused by the tree line, glancing back over his shoulder.

His brother read the letter, his body shuddering with emotion. He pressed the letter against his chest one more time, and an anguished howl escaped him—loud and filled with endless pain.

PART FIVE
TRIALS AND RULES

CHAPTER 86

AFFECTION AND COMMITMENT

The morning light filtered through the windows in the makeshift cell. The scents of Kharis's breakfast—cinnamon tea, freshly baked herb bread, and sheep's cheese—lingered in the air. She closed her eyes and pictured her garden. It helped her forget that for three weeks, she'd slept on a thin pallet on the floor and that chains restrained her to the walls.

She'd made peace with the undeniable truth that, one, the Regiazenka wouldn't pardon her for the massacre, and two, they had assumed she'd caused the explosion.

That display of power had shaken the ministers to their core. Fear, not reason, ruled them now. Akumi or not, twenty-seven lay dead, but the destruction wrought upon the palace grounds only deepened the scandal. The Crown's debt was a heavy one. She couldn't sleep, these thoughts tormenting her day and night.

I should've died.

The man hiding inside the king—her father—became a broken shell. He came to visit, but his gaze, damp with unshed tears, broke everything inside her. She imagined his

451

hand shaking as he pressed his signet into the wax that sealed her sentence, the Regiazenka watching.

And now, she was headed to the Iluna Forest—to her death.

And yet, she smiled anyway. If all blame was placed on her, Saya, who had unleashed her explosive power that night, was safe.

Saya will live.

The Regiazenka had overlooked one tiny detail. The Djinnshirukh was a formidable weapon, yes, but the Sorukhipa, as its sheath, had to be equally powerful.

Kharis half-laughed. "Such fools."

"*Idiots, all of them.*"

Kharis jumped to her feet. Her gaze darted, nervous. "Hello?"

The silence stretched uncomfortably, punctuated by the distant drone of the city.

She heard soldiers approaching and recognized the voice of one of them. *Ghan.* Swiftly, she dried her tears, determined not to allow him to mock her despair.

He opened the cell door, and guards moved in, aiming their swords at her.

"Time to meet the Iluna." Ghan's smile lit his eyes with a sinister glint. "You, undo the wall restraints." He threw a set of keys to one of the soldiers. Before the high general walked out, he turned around. "Be careful," he told his officers with a hint of fake concern. "She's the Djinnshirukh, a vicious monster. Blink, and she'll eat you whole."

❧

Saya watched the activity in the bailey from the palace's rooftop. Her sister, chained from head to toe, endured the guards' prods, guided by staves as if she were an animal. The sight was a wrenching blow, and she inhaled sharply.

"They didn't let me visit her."

Yuna wrapped an arm around her shoulders and drew her close. "None of us were allowed."

Saya flexed her fingers, and wiped her eyes. "I'm never forgiving Father for this."

"Saya," Anong said. "This wasn't Hröld's doing." He tilted his chin toward the bailey. "Don't lose sight of the real culprit."

Below, High General Arjun Ghan was barking orders and mounting his steed.

"That self-serving bastard—" Yuna clamped her lips, glancing away.

"He's taking her away." Saya's muscles quivered. "He can yell all he wants, but I'm coming along and waiting for her at the other end of the Iluna because Khiri will make it. And when she crosses the tree line, I'll be there to hug her."

Anong embraced the two women, holding them close. "We'll all be there to greet her, and if I shove Ghan by accident and he falls flat on his face, please don't help him up."

Saya burst out laughing, but tears still collected in her eyes.

"Darling," Yuna said, tilting her head to the activity below. "It's time."

Kharis had climbed into the covered wagon, and soldiers were locking the doors.

I will find you, wherever you are.

Saya closed her eyes, and after inhaling all the air she could to calm down, she released a wave of magic through the bond. It coursed along the invisible thread until it reached Kharis.

The tug in response told Saya her message had been received. A familiar, impish cackle rippled back through the connection—mischievous, defiant, and unmistakably Kharis. What followed was a surge of affection so vast it nearly stole Saya's breath, bright with rainbow hues and dusted in sweetness, like powdered sugar on festival cakes.

"I love you, Khiri," Saya said.

"And I love you more."

CHAPTER 87
SHADOWS AND MOSS

Two small windows, each no larger than her hand, flanked the covered metal wagon, letting slivers of light spill inside. Kharis let their light warm her face. As the wagon lurched forward, a gentle golden glow crept along the metal walls. The air quickly bloomed with the scent of orange blossoms and jasmine.

Then came the tug—faint but certain—along the magical thread that bound her to Saya. She was near, steadfast as ever. No matter the distance or danger, Saya wouldn't falter. Not while she still had breath to guard her beloved sister.

"I love you, Khiri."

Saya's tender voice drifted through the bond, and Kharis smiled through her tears, cherishing the moment and breathing in the scent that always reminded her of Saya.

The convoy rumbled on, the road long and uneven, each bump making the wagon jolt and creak.

Rawiri had once told her that *not doing* was, in itself, a kind of doing. She held on to that now. And so, Kharis let herself simply be. She inhaled deeply and closed her eyes to meditate.

There was no need to pay attention to the road. They would arrive when they arrived.

&a.

Some two and a half weeks later, the wagon rolled to a stop —this time not for rest or repairs. The days had blurred into breath, chains, and silence.

The air was cooler, the scent of pine and damp earth stronger than ever.

When the door creaked open, a shaft of bright light struck Kharis's face. She winced, her eyelids fluttering open as her eyes slowly adjusted.

The end of the road had come at last. The long stretch of waiting was over. What came next—she could only guess.

Kharis overheard the soldiers arguing over who would unshackle her. None had volunteered, so they drew lots. The unfortunate loser—a slight woman—climbed into the wagon without a word. She moved quickly, unlocking each chain with a speed that betrayed her fear. With a sharp jerk of her head, she signaled Kharis to rise.

The soldier tried to mask her terror with a glare—a brave attempt at defiance. In response, Kharis flashed her a sweet, angelic smile.

The woman flinched as though struck by lightning.

As Kharis descended the wagon, a hummingbird fluttered before her. She smiled at it. The tiny bird hovered a moment longer before it flew away.

An impressive ribbon of teal, jade, and olive colors opened before her eyes: an endless sea of lush forest, shadows, and moss. There was magic there, and hers stirred in response. Whatever resided in those woods studied the contingent with interest, its hushed whispers drifting toward her ears.

The soldiers quickly gathered around her. Archers

nocked their arrows, officers drew their swords, and guards angled their spears in her direction.

Ghan twisted in his saddle. "They should've executed you on the spot." He groaned, the smile bitter, and swung down from his horse. "Let's be done with this."

Aghet Mendi didn't speak a word but met her gaze as if seeing her for the first time. His eyes shimmered with an eerie intensity—a monster eyeing another monster. His face, usually indifferent, now showed a flicker of respect.

Kharis lifted her chin, leveling Aghet with a questioning glare. The general huffed and turned away, fixing his gaze on the forest ahead, his eyes tracking the shadows that clung to the ancient woods. Unlike the soldiers around them, fidgeting, Aghet's still expression spoke of an inner conflict brewing beneath the surface. Not fear. *Longing? Guilt?* It gave Kharis pause. *What secrets does he carry?*

Ghan marched over, glowering at her. Kharis smiled at the man. This was as good a time as any to annoy him. Her gesture, as if this were a game, flustered him further.

"Welcome to the Iluna Forest," he said. "I trust you'll behave?" He studied her chains and smirked. "I'd rather keep them on. Add to the challenge."

Kharis shrugged, no longer caring, her gaze drawn to the dandelions beneath her boots.

Ghan barked at someone behind her, who approached with the keys to her restraints.

"Well, hello?" said a familiar voice.

Kharis lifted her gaze and faced Lord Korshak.

"Imagine seeing you here," he whispered as he took his time removing chains and shackles. "I still owe you for your garden picnic stunt since the fire didn't work."

Kharis's eyes widened.

"Unfortunately, you escaped that blaze," Korshak clicked his tongue, "but perhaps today's my day." He grinned, that mouth like a slash across his face, and slowly unfastened the iron choker around her neck. "I'm going to enjoy this, raven spawn," he said softly, his breath warm on her ear.

"Are you done?" Ghan grumbled. "We don't have all day."

"Done, sir." Korshak turned and bowed to Ghan.

Ghan huffed, sending Korshak a displeased glare over his delay.

"This place is cursed." Ghan turned to Kharis. "Nobody dares go in, and those foolish enough to enter it never come back. Some say monsters living in it enjoy eating mortal flesh." His eyes traveled to the tree line. "Personally, I don't believe a word of it. It's an ancient forest with plenty of bogs in the most unexpected places. Get stuck in one, and you'll slowly sink to your death. A fitting end, don't you think?" He sneered. "Bears and wolves also call it home."

She raised an eyebrow as though he bored her, even when fear flickered in the pit of her stomach.

"You have three days to reach the other side." His eyes danced with dark pleasure. "The Regiazenka has deemed this to be your punishment. Not a single member dared to call for resealment. Aghuti's star still shines upon you."

Kharis crossed her arms, uninterested. "I've been told that you worshiped Mother—"

In a flash, his hand shot to her throat, gripping hard. "Don't you ever call her that, you filth."

A moment later, he recoiled with a choked groan. His palm blistered, skin scorched by sudden, searing heat. The stench of burned flesh curled in the air.

Ghan gritted his teeth, fighting the pain.

"Resealment would've been the merciful way to end your life." He clutched the wrist of his injured hand. "You have three days to cross this blasted forest. I'll send my best men after you to ensure you don't escape. The Regiazenka may have balked at the idea of executing you, but I won't. And, as the lore goes, the Iluna Forest is dangerous. Things... can happen."

She could almost see him drooling at the possibilities—at what those *accidents* entailed.

"Too bad I can't go with you." He leaned in closer. "I must be at the other end—waiting."

He straightened and gave her a wicked smile.

"You'd better get going," he said. "I'll give you a head start, but my men will go in when the afternoon shadows fall behind them."

He gestured for zaldunak to come forward, and the men settled beside him.

Kharis knew them well—Korshak's group.

A dark chuckle tumbled from Ghan's lips. "I believe you had a pleasant encounter with Lord Korshak when the Kahurangi visited us."

Korshak, standing beside General Ghan, grinned from ear to ear. "I'd be delighted to repay the honor, Your Highness."

His men snickered.

Kharis was glad to see their true colors finally showing. With the fire mystery in Rawiri's wing resolved, things were looking up. She would enjoy telling Saya and Yuna who the culprit was.

"Three days?" She eyed the forest as if utterly bored with the task. "Very well, what weapon do I use?"

"Weapon?" Ghan cocked his head, wearing an evil grin. "You receive none—no weapons, no water, no food. Oh, and I almost forgot this part. Injure any of my men," he shared a grin with Korshak, "and my orders are to kill you on the spot. Now, get the fires out of my sight."

She locked eyes with Ghan. "You'd better hurry, then. It would be a shame if you missed my arrival." Then she faced Korshak. "What a sad day it is for Zahar that your dream is to come after me because that little brat Rudra didn't know when to shut his mouth, a trait you share with him."

Korshak moved toward her, but Ghan put out his arm to stop him.

"Hate me all you want," Kharis said, "but your brother, who insulted one of King Hröld's daughters, branded your family permanently. No matter what you do, that is now your fate."

Kharis turned and marched toward the forest, grumbling under her breath. Anger made the tips of her fingers glow like embers.

"*Listen to me.*" That soft, silvery voice in her mind carried a tinge of concern.

"Not now."

"*The Iluna Forest is much older than me, and if you wish to survive, you will listen to me.*"

"Fine. What must I do?"

"*Stop.*"

"What?"

"*Let it welcome you. Do not trespass.*"

Kharis could feel all those eyes boring a hole in her back. "They are looking at me."

"*Let them. Your focus is ahead, not behind you.*"

"Fine." She took a deep breath to calm down. A tendril of magic slowly approached her, evaluating this creature that stood before the ancient woods.

"*Let it welcome you,*" the Voice said, always pleasant and modulated. "*The Iluna Forest is alive, and you can only enter when it allows it.*"

"How will I know?"

There was no need for an answer. The gossamer magic coiled around Kharis, and pleased with this child, it pulled her in.

CHAPTER 88
THE GENERAL
AND THE FOREST

Ghan watched her, and a smile pulled at his lips when he realized she was probably hesitating whether to enter the woods. If he could taste or smell fear as she could, what would hers feel like? Ghan's mind lingered on that thought with dark fascination.

Aghet didn't look at him. His gaze was fixed on the forest, drawn to it with the same fierce devotion he had once reserved for him. After thirty years together, that cursed woodland now held more of Aghet's heart than he ever had.

"What's she doing?" Korshak grumbled, shoving Ghan out of his ruminations. "We're wasting time—"

Ghan struck him across his face, sending him to the ground.

"Never question my orders," Ghan said.

Korshak sat up, his face pale as he rubbed his jaw. "It won't happen again, Your Highness."

Ghan fought the urge to crush the young man's skull. He despised Korshak's kind—cowards cloaked in finery, all swagger and bravado, hiding behind polished cuirasses and gilded swords while striking from the shadows like vermin.

His niece had entered the forest, and shadows swallowed her form. His attention then shifted to the rich, verdant expanse, where an alluring presence called him. At first, it was a sweet whisper—a lover's call tempting him to enter the woods. He was about to succumb to its pull when a sharp, discordant sound shattered the moment, wrenching him back to himself. Only then did he realize it had come from behind him. Korshak was whimpering to his friends—a shrill, pitiful noise, like the pampered child he'd always been.

Ghan wondered if he was the type to squeal when skinned alive. If he were to pull his fingernails out, would he scream or endure it? His gaze lingered on Korshak's face, cutting and slashing it in his mind.

"My prince?"

Ghan turned slowly.

"We must march out." Aghet smiled, seductive and wicked—his eyes finally on him. "Your destiny awaits. The time for legends to be born is upon you."

The high general beamed. Aghet knew what to say and how to say it. His sultry voice had a melodic texture that trailed off suggestively. It rolled inside Ghan's mind like a hot wind rushing through the steppes.

"Tell me, Aghet." Ghan's gaze returned to Korshak. "How would you get a man to squeal like a pig?"

Aghet Mendi arched a single brow, his brown eyes shimmering with intrigue. "It depends, my prince." An evil smile teased at the corners of his lips.

Ghan gave Korshak a calculating stare. "We should put it to the test."

Korshak shuddered when Aghet cast the zaldun a look equally hungry. The young man's face blanched, dread twisting his mouth as his breathing hitched. Aghet's lips curled into a sinister grin, throwing Korshak an unblinking stare.

"My prince always amuses," he said, his voice low and

sensual, how Ghan liked it. "Those are good conversation topics when on a long journey."

"Heads, then?"

Aghet's eyes glinted. "It was 'heads,' but for you, my prince, I could flip again."

Ghan wanted to kiss that mouth and get lost in it. Instead, he turned away, jaw clenched, gaze snapping to Korshak with barely veiled contempt.

"To the horses," he said sharply. Then, casting one last glance at the forest—where desire, resentment, and duty tangled within him—he muttered, "I'm expected at the other end."

CHAPTER 89

THE SILVERY VOICE

Kharis stepped carefully over roots and rocks, lifting low branches and sidestepping shrubs and bushes. The forest pressed close and ancient, its towering trunks swallowing the light as she moved beneath them.

"Well, we are in," she said.

"*Getting in is the easy part. Getting out is another.*"

She stopped. "What do you mean?"

"*If the forest likes you, it may want to keep you.*"

"Great." She threw her arms up. "Now you tell me."

"*I wouldn't worry.*"

"Why?"

"*Why would a forest want to keep a fire-wielding child?*"

She frowned for a moment. "Hmm, you make a good point."

"*I'm glad you agree.*"

"If I could see your face, would you be smiling?"

Silence followed her question, but she suspected the Voice grinned.

"I don't even know your name."

"*Why must you know it?*" A curious tone colored his question.

Kharis shrugged. "It creates a connection."

"*We are already connected.*"

"Not like that. My sister calls me Khiri, and my nana calls me Gutxi. Even Prince Rawiri had a nickname for me, Teppe. His little badger." She beamed at that memory. It was warm, like the sun, and colorful, like a rainbow. "We use names to create special bonds with people we love."

Silence again.

Kharis pinched her lips. "I mean, you know my name."

"*Do you know your name?*"

Kharis blinked. "Now, that's an odd question. Of course, I do."

"*Hmm.*" There was a long pause after that. "*I thought you had many.*"

Kharis tittered at the comment. "How many names do you think I have?"

"*Ten thousand,*" the Voice said without hesitation.

Kharis burst out laughing. This had to be the craziest moment ever—conversing with herself.

"Now that we are here, what do we do?"

"*You're going to do three things. First, you'll keep your eyes on the ground. Do not look up or stare, regardless of the circumstances. Second, you'll walk, even when you want to run. Do you understand?*"

Kharis nodded. "Loud and clear. What's the third thing?"

"*You'll listen to me and do as I tell you.*"

Kharis's gaze sharpened. "In exchange for what?"

The Voice didn't respond.

Kharis thought of Saya, Yuna, her father, Hala, and, even though he was across the ocean, Prince Rawiri, too. To see them again, she had to survive this place first. "Fine. I'll do as you ask for the next *three* days."

"*It's a smart choice.*"

"I must succeed because blasted Ghan expects me to fail.

I'll triumph and live, and by the Netherworlds of Ifran, after this, I'll be free."

"*Good,*" said the Voice with utter satisfaction. "*Very good.*"

"So, what do you get out of this?"

"*Why do you ask?*"

Kharis vaulted over a fallen log. "Yours is the voice I've been hearing for a while—at the Archives, the day of the fire, after the quay event, and even back in the cell." A chuckle spilled forth. "You thought they were fools."

"*Are they not?*"

She stopped in her tracks. "Not all of them." She thought of Officer Ren Azdaha, who had protected her from Ghan and was exiled to a northern battalion. "A good soldier always follows orders. It doesn't mean they like them."

"*He who follows a fool is foolish.*"

Kharis resumed her pace. "I suppose that's the case, but if I follow your commands, how do I know I'm not a fool?"

"*A fair question.*"

She hopped over shrubs and skipped around exposed roots. "If you're the Akumi king, that makes me the queen of fools."

Kharis expected confirmation. None came.

Resuming her pace, her gaze wandered, forgetting to blink at times. She was farther from the palace than she'd ever hoped. Now, trees towered over her. Their sunlight-dappled leaves quivered in the breeze. Birds chirped, preening on swaying branches. A small, elusive critter rustled the underbrush, briefly revealing a furry face with curious violet eyes before darting away.

Her steps lightened without her meaning them to. A sense of adventure surged within her, igniting the curiosity that only the wilderness could kindle. She caught herself smiling.

"This forest is lovely," she said. "Why would anyone fear it?"

"There's nothing to fear, I assure you."

"And why is that, oh, king of fools?"

"Because nothing will touch you while I am here."

"You promise?"

"I already did."

Kharis scratched her head, a narrowed gaze studying the space to her right. Or should it be her left? She wasn't entirely sure where the Voice stood.

"Now, if you stick to my three rules, we will reach the other side swiftly. The Iluna is a lovely place, as you say, but we mustn't delay if we are to focus on your task."

"Right." She maintained her stride, arms casually folded behind her head. "Three days to cross this place," she mused. "Will you stay with me?"

"Forever, if you wish."

She couldn't quite explain why his offer filled her with joy or why the Voice's presence felt so comforting, like a cozy blanket on a chilly night. "So you thought they were fools?"

"I still do."

"You know what?" she said. "You're all right."

And so, the Djinnshirukh kept her pace, occasionally chatting with the owner of the enigmatic voice or humming a tune to pass the time.

❧

The creatures in the forest, noticing the ominous shadowy figure who strolled beside that tasty little morsel, maintained their distance, quietly observing the two—waiting.

CHAPTER 90

THE GENERAL AND THE PROPHECY

Ghan rode, encased in dark thoughts and silent mutterings, engaged in a conversation as old as the years on his body.

It didn't matter that he kept a healthy distance from the Iluna Forest or hid in the palace. He could hear it all the time—the irresistible whisper that beckoned him. It was as if the trees and creatures inhabiting this place were calling out to him, their voices like a mermaid's song. They promised him power and spoke of untold wonders hidden beneath the ancient evergreens. They sang of the forgotten history and the unimaginable beauty that lay within. They chanted about love and freedom from the harsh realities of his world.

The temptation consumed him. His mouth went dry. His grip loosened on the reins.

"*We will celebrate your triumphs,*" the soft, enticing voices said.

"*Come and join us.*"

"*Here, we will cherish you.*"

For a moment, he almost felt the cool shade of the trees on his face and the soft moss underfoot. The peace that constantly eluded him came to tempt him, and he wavered. The forest was so close, and this sensation of *home* and belonging overwhelmed him.

He clenched his reins, his knuckles white under the strain, struggling to anchor himself to the reality of this world. His resolve stiffened, but the whispers persisted. Phantom hands stretched out to him, their touch so tantalizingly sensual that he found it hard to fight.

"*You belong with us.*"

The throbbing pain in his right hand shoved them all out of his mind.

Aghet Mendi rode beside him and occasionally glanced at Ghan's hand. When he caught him staring at it, Ghan scowled at him. Aghet frowned and refocused on the road ahead, his face revealing nothing else after that.

Ghan returned to his silent grumbling and cursed Kharis under his breath. The pain was unbearable, and the sensation of his skin still burning haunted him. The blisters opened and oozed, and the skin turned splotchy. His hand became a swollen mass of red and white flesh.

Throughout the march, the battalion kept to the open terrain, steering clear of the forest. Now and then, Ghan glimpsed flickers of movement between the trees. He told himself it was nothing—shadows playing games, testing his resolve, coaxing him to step closer, to surrender.

His soldiers were uneasy. Some stole wary glances at the forest's edge, while others fixed their eyes ahead, trying—and failing—to ignore the shifting shadows that seemed to trail them. The high general began to wonder if the forest haunted his men as it haunted him.

Behind him, a few soldiers muttered tales of the cursed woods, but the stories brought them no comfort. Ghan cast a sidelong glance at Aghet. Though his eyes remained fixed on the road, Ghan could tell he was listening closely.

"There are shapeshifters in there," a burly soldier said.

"The *dangu* live in there, too," a wiry one said. "Monsters with greedy little eyes and long, spindly fingers." He wiggled his fingers. "They'll catch you and suck your blood."

One scoffed. "That's a forest, not the marshy banks of the Ibaia. The *dangu* live near water, you idiot."

"Water's everywhere," the wiry soldier muttered, his tone oddly prophetic. "You can't see it, but it's there—and the *dangus* know."

An older soldier, silent until then, finally spoke. "My great-grandfather told me of the Forest Kin immortals. In the old days, they dwelled in the Iluna. The forest was much vaster then, alive with wild magic that fed the land. The immortals tended it, and in return, the forest gifted them its blessings. It was a sacred balance that kept the world in harmony." He paused. "Then the Akumi came—and set it all ablaze."

"And your point is?" asked the soldier who'd scoffed earlier.

"We never vanquished all the Akumi," the seasoned soldier said, his voice laced with warning. "And not all the Forest Kin returned to their realm." His eyes drifted toward the tree line. "There's still danger in those shadows. The immortals who remained in the Iluna went mad when they beheld the ruin the Akumi left behind. That madness seeped into the forest itself. Step within—and it'll seep into you too."

The older soldier only said, "When you do, the Iluna will claim you as its prize."

"Nothing but tales," the bold soldier scoffed, yet his voice now wavered.

Ghan kept the battalion well clear of the tree line, but even distance offered no protection. The forest's shadows stretched across the open land like grasping fingers. Eerie lights flickered in the dark, like blinking eyes. A chill settled over the march. Unease slithered through the ranks, quickening steps. No one wanted to linger near the Iluna. All they wanted was to move on—fast.

While Ghan's commanders kept his soldiers marching, Kharis stole every waking moment he had, distracting him to the extent that it angered him. And right now, he needed to direct his men, not grumble over an insolent fourteen-year-old.

That child rattles me.

That impudent girl was dangerous—far more than people thought. As the ancient prophecy had stated, she was the end-bringer, so why couldn't anyone see this about her? As the vessel for the Akumi king, she possessed the power to raise his army and burn the world again.

How do I stop her?

A storm of conflict raged in his mind. He'd long coveted her power—but he also had to stop the Akumi king from rising again. For years, he'd scoured the verses, chasing fragments and riddles to uncover the key. The words returned unbidden, as they always did.

> *All that was wrong will be righted,*
> *When the immortal vessel dies.*
> *Tear asunder the seals that contain it.*
> *Let its flames roam with might.*
> *Let it all be destroyed so freedom finds its light.*
> *Let the world revel in fire.*
> *Let it be consumed again,*
> *So the spirits join and transcend,*
> *And all the writings end.*

He shifted in his saddle and rubbed his forehead, as if pressure alone might force the meaning out.

"Sir, should we camp for the night?" a commander asked.

Ghan snapped out of his mental torture. While pondering options, his eyes returned to the woods and their taunting. "No. We march on. The sooner we clear the Iluna, the better off we'll be."

The wind carried mocking laughter, and Ghan caught another glimpse of movement. He gave the forest a narrowed look and scowled. He hated her, but he hated this blasted place even more.

CHAPTER 91

KORSHAK AND HIS ZALDUNAK

Korshak paced back and forth, appraising the forest with a frown. That *txakurra* was in there, and she was within reach. His fingers anxiously tapped the long dagger strapped to his thigh. The shadows, however, wouldn't lengthen for another hour.

"We've waited long enough," he grumbled, facing the commanding officer.

General Salazar gave him a lazy glance. "High General Ghan left precise orders to wait until—"

"So what?" Korshak spat on the ground.

Salazar drew his sword, and his officers followed suit. Korshak gulped, aware that Salazar's men outnumbered them, but scowled because, for someone like him, posturing was about hiding his fear. He faced the forest, cringing with impatience. He would repeatedly sink his dagger into her flesh and leave her body for beasts to feast on.

He glanced at his men, seeking their support. They subtly nodded, and that gesture tugged at a corner of his lips. With his mind made up, he turned to General Salazar.

"We are going in."

Salazar scrutinized the forest, tilted his head to assess the sun's location, then stared at the young zaldun. "Suit yourself, but my men are following His Highness's order."

Korshak shuddered with rage and turned away. "Let's go," he said, and his zaldunak followed.

❧

General Salazar watched their shapes blend with the forest shadows.

Officer Ranit, his second-in-command, settled by his side. "What would you like to do, sir?"

Salazar hummed, contemplating options. "Typical Zahari nobles. They rise in the ranks to become zaldunak, not by merit or skill, but by the depth of their parents' pockets and noble lineage. That group is the worst, lacking discipline and aptitude, yet when given a sword, they believe they own the world."

A third man, a younger one, approached. "Sir, the men await orders."

Salazar pursed his lips, his gaze still on the forest ahead. "Captain Aram Zhad, what would you do?"

Zhad pondered his words, as if to select them carefully. "Patience is a virtue that only the brave possess."

Salazar chuckled. "Spoken like the xakea master that you are. One of these days, I'll win a round." He exhaled, glad for the laughter. "What about you, Ranit? What would you do?"

Commander Ranit didn't mince his words. "If we are done babysitting, join High General Ghan."

Salazar sighed. "Patience and discipline reward us with a long life." The general's gaze returned to the forest, feeling no sympathy for the zaldunak.

His gaze lingered on the forest, silent and patient like a predator.

"Let's go," he said. "I'd like to report this to the High General."

With that, the cavalry cantered away.

CHAPTER 92
APPLES AND MOSS

Kharis sat with her back against a tree, watching as sunlight filtered through the canopy, like a cascade of gold, illuminating the bushes. She marveled at the idea of being in this place, so different from everything the palace offered. Wild and quiet, and away from judging eyes—a taste of freedom, even under these circumstances.

But she also missed her sister and sighed deeply, wondering how Saya was doing. It didn't help that her stomach growled, and that she was thirsty and cold.

"Are you there?"

The Voice didn't reply.

"I wish Nana were here. She knows everything about plants I can eat. Or Saya. She would know what to do." She heaved a sigh. "I miss her." She stretched her legs and stood up, ready to continue. "Hunger makes for an awful companion." She looked up. Recalling the Voice's rules, she swiftly lowered her gaze. Given the amount of light, the sun had set. The night was imminent.

She flexed her hand. "How do I summon fire?"

Dusk deepened, and soon she wouldn't be able to see past her own nose. Rawiri had once mentioned a fire goddess—one of many in the Kahurangi pantheon. "Maybe I could call on her?" she muttered, scratching her cheek. "Stupid. I don't even remember her name." She groaned in frustration. "Better to keep moving."

In her map-seeking excursions to the Royal Archives, she'd learned that the Iluna Forest abutted a small range of mountains, a natural border between the Ibaia and Ghetu Plains. The Ibaia Sea was to the north, and the Sarvalla Valley to the south. It hit Kharis that she didn't know where "the other side" was.

"Ghan never told me."

Wide-eyed, she slapped her forehead.

"He doesn't expect me to make it. That's why he didn't bother to tell me." She groaned again, disappointed in herself. "I'm so hotheaded that I didn't even ask him. Oh, no, not me. I had to open my big mouth and call his bluff."

She dropped her body under a tree, feeling dejected.

"*Moss grows facing north,*" the Voice said. "*If you need to go north, look for the direction in which it grows.*"

"Oh, now you speak." Kharis rolled her eyes.

"*I sense frustration.*"

"You sense hunger and thirst and exhaustion."

"*Have you looked up?*"

"Huh?" Kharis pinched her lips. "You said to keep my eyes on the ground."

"*This time, I'll allow it.*"

Had there been a face, she would've punched it. But curiosity was her vice, and even though she tried hard not to give the Voice a chance to boast, she tilted her head... and stared at apples.

The Voice didn't gloat.

Kharis mumbled her thanks.

She climbed the tree, picked as much fruit as she could, sat back, and bit into one, its crisp crunch, sweet and juicy. She devoured it and reached for another.

With her belly full and blackness enveloping the forest,

all sorts of sounds awakened—crickets, owls, frogs. Kharis didn't bother with any of it. Exhaustion was claiming her, her eyelids growing heavy. Fog blanketed her mind, but rather than fight it, she lay on a lush carpet of moss, her back pressed against the tree trunk.

"I'm so sleepy." She fought it, urging her body to obey and keep going. After all, she was on a timeline—three days to reach "the other end." But her body didn't move, grateful for the pleasant spot and meal.

"Traitorous body," she grumbled. "I'll get you for this."

"*Rest,*" said the Voice. "*You need your sleep.*" A gentle hand caressed her face—a timid touch, yet full of affection. "*I'll keep watch.*"

With that, her eyes closed, and the world vanished from her view.

In the middle of the night, Kharis awoke.

Her teeth chattered. Her body shivered. She curled into a ball, trying to stay warm. Her uncle had given her nothing. *Blasted man.* Her breath misted before her, not that she could see anything. Woodland creatures chittered in the underbrush. An owl hooted nearby, waiting for a chance to swoop down and catch its meal. The forest's darkness was overwhelming. And she was tired, caught between slumber and lucidity, half awake and half not.

She closed her eyes, too tired to think, when warm fur settled beside her.

"Iroh," she whispered, delighted. At the hospital, he'd lain with his paw resting over her, like he was doing now, protective of the one who'd saved him. Knowing Iroh was with her, she fell back asleep.

Kharis forgot that she was in the middle of the Iluna Forest, not a royal infirmary, or that the massive creature full of fur and claws was much, much bigger than her beloved mutt.

CHAPTER 93
THE LAKE AND
THE GUARDIAN

Kharis didn't have the nightmare where she ran down a dark tunnel looking for an exit.

Instead, she sat on the shores of an alpine lake, surrounded by the Iluna. The soft wind blew. The tip of her nose reddened with its kiss. It carried the scent of pine and birch, along with the sweet aroma of almond blossoms. A pile of apples lay beside her. She selected a plump one, taking a crisp bite that released a delectable crunch.

All her worries melted away.

"Now, where am I?"

This place was oddly familiar. She rose, stretched her arms, and planted her hands on her hips as she took in the landscape. A soft breeze teased her hair, yet the lake remained unnaturally still, its surface unbroken—a perfect mirror reflecting the distant mountain peaks. In the silence, flocks of birds suddenly took flight, all veering in unison toward that distant range. Even the trees leaned toward the peaks.

A smile bloomed between her cheeks as realization dawned on her. "The Lerra Mountains. That's where Ghan's headed." She let out a chuckle. "I can't wait to see how disappointment twists that smug face of his. I'll commission one of our court painters to capture the moment—and hang it in my chambers."

Kharis meandered to the shore, removed her boots, and dipped her toes in the water, the gentle waves lapping at her feet.

"*Come*," she heard a whisper that wasn't the Voice.

She'd imagined the silvery voice to be a tall man, wise and elegant. One who never got angry—always composed and regal, with a smidge of sarcasm thrown in for good measure. And handsome, since someone with such a beautiful voice had to be.

The voice from the lake was different. Kind and affectionate, almost... *Brotherly?*

"*Kharasdir, come,*" this voice said again.

If only "they" could get her name right.

She tilted her head and had the wild idea of climbing on a boulder and jumping into the water. Maybe her body would dissolve, and she would become like the dancing silver sparkles.

But the sensation didn't last long.

A hand nudged her awake—a timid yet anxious hand.

"What?" she grumbled, thinking it was Saya. "Let me sleep."

"*Stay still,*" the silvery voice said. "*And no matter what, do not look up or stare.*"

Still curled into a ball, her eyelids fluttered open to an eerily quiet forest. Trees, dense bushes, and morning mist concealed a massive creature, its shadow creeping past her. Every muscle in her body tensed.

Kharis fought the urge to gag when the pungent scent hit her nose. The giant figure looked like a bear. At least, she hoped it was one. It snarled and growled, low and guttural. Its snout huffed, lifting wispy clouds of dust and plant matter. A flash of silver peeked through the thick shrubbery as it meandered, snorting and pawing at the ground and sniffing the air as if searching for something—or someone?

Blessed Mother...

Whatever the thing was, it was bigger than anything she'd seen. Those jaws would eat her whole, no question about it—like popping an olive into its mouth.

Kharis didn't move a muscle and barely took a breath. She shut her eyes, for it was better not to see. Eventually, the growls and snarls dissipated—the creature was moving on. Soon, the dawn's quiet enveloped the woods once more.

"What was that?" She sat, brushing leaves off her hair.

"*That was the Iluna's guardian.*"

"Was it looking for me?" She lowered her voice, glancing over her shoulder.

"*Perhaps.*"

Kharis gaped, eyebrows arching. "Is it safe to move?"

"*Yes.*"

She rose. "What a way to start day one." A shudder rolled past her shoulders, and she picked leaves and twigs off her clothes. "Thank you," she said, wondering whether her sanity was at stake. "Are there more of those?"

But the Voice, which sometimes could be stubborn, didn't answer. Perhaps it was better not to know.

She dusted her hands and eyed her pile of apples. "I'm not leaving these beauties behind." She tucked her tunic inside her trousers, tightened her belt, and stuffed apples down her collar.

"*Don't take them all,*" the Voice advised.

Kharis halted, counting the few left on the ground. "Why?"

"*The Iluna provides. There's no need for gluttony.*"

She heaved a sigh. It was hard not to, but she did as told. Perhaps the Iluna's guardian was looking for apples, too; if it focused on those, it wouldn't stalk her. Kharis patted the tree gently and pressed her forehead against its trunk.

"Thank you," she said, grateful for the fruit. "May the earth and sun bless and sustain you."

"I had a wonderful dream." She folded her arms behind her head as she began her trek. "I was here, in the Iluna, but a lake was in the middle. The funny thing is that the dream also told me to veer toward a set of mountains." She pulled on her lower lip, thinking. "I sometimes see this lake in my dreams. I wonder what it means."

The Voice didn't reply, but she knew he was listening.

Comforting musical whispers filled the forest. Sing-song chirps and tweets greeted them as she strolled through the woods, chatting about her dream. Their melody was sweet and ethereal, yet even more so as if nature had been perfected. It made the place bright and airy, dispersing the shadows around her. It enticed the tree branches to open up and let the sun in, and when its warmth kissed Kharis's face, it was divine.

"This is day one, I suppose. But given my uncle's *charming* disposition, perhaps yesterday was it." Kharis frowned. "I should run."

"*No*," was the Voice's stern reply. It was like thunder, rattling her mind uncomfortably.

Kharis raised her eyebrows, surprised. "Fine," she said. "We'll continue our stroll." She gave the Voice a cheeky grin. "Look! To our left, we have a lovely copse of elm trees. To our right, oh yes, more trees."

If the Voice had eyes, he would roll them with annoyance.

That image tickled her.

"I hope we run into a creek. I'm thirsty." She considered having an apple and patted the treasure inside her shirt. And so, the Djinnshirukh kept walking, prattling about this or that, peppering her comments with her laughter. Ah, she could be so clever.

❧

The leaves rustled, but Kharis was unaware that the forest's magical creatures were moving closer, gathering with gleaming eyes. Their otherworldly music filled the air, but those murmurs traveled even further into the forest, announcing that a human had entered this ancient forest. More leaves quaked in the phantom wind, tree branches bouncing with their invisible weight. Many assembled around her, studying the child and the tall shadow walking beside her with interest.

The Iluna creatures jumped from tree to tree to follow her, curious about the child with a familiar scent. Their twittering and chirping intensified.

The child's shadowy companion stopped for a moment. A pair of glimmering indigo eyes, filled with the power of the stars and the moons, glowed from inside the mass of billowing black smoke. That intense gaze glowered at the creatures—his only warning for them to stay far away from her.

The creatures halted their advance—for now.

CHAPTER 94

THE VISITOR

An otherworldly sound, like a high-pitched sigh, pierced the stillness of the night, jolting Aren awake. He realized he'd unintentionally fallen asleep instead of remaining vigilant during his assigned shift.

He slowly turned to survey the slumbering figures of his comrades. There was Korshak, his snoring more like an annoying faint whistle. Narek lay wrapped in his cloak, his chest rising and falling rhythmically. The feeble flickers of their dying campfire illuminated Davit's face intermittently, creating a grotesque play of light and shadows on his features. Samel, Bhazat, and Andrik huddled close together, their forms almost indistinguishable in the gloom.

The dying embers clung to life, casting elongated shadows against the trees. Beyond them, the inky blackness stretched and twisted.

Aren strained his ears, trying to locate the source of the noise that had awoken him, and stretched his back.

The haunting sound drifted toward him again. It echoed like a woman's soft, melodic sigh, its sweetness tinged with an unsettling allure. It captivated him immediately, his gaze flitting from shadow to shadow.

"Hello?" he asked, hesitantly.

A quiet outline glided before him, moving with a graceful, almost ethereal movement.

"Who's there?"

The figure stilled, and another one of those whispers floated in his direction.

"Are you lost?" Aren asked, getting closer.

The feeble moonlight, barely strong enough to pierce the thick canopy of trees, unveiled a woman. Her long chestnut hair cascaded like a river of darkness down her back. She wore a flowing ivory dress, its fabric shimmering as if woven from moonbeams.

She tilted her head to the side, assessing Aren with an intense, appraising gaze. "You're looking at me." It wasn't a question. "Not averting my eyes."

He frowned, confused.

"Wrong choice," she said.

Aren failed to register the swift blur of movement as the woman settled before him, her warm breath tickling his face. It caught him off guard. Before he could muster a word, she pressed her lips against his, her tongue parting his.

A bitter, acrid tang assaulted his mouth first. Then, a searing sting sent a shockwave through his tender palate. His chest seized. His breath refused to come. A numbing sensation spread to the rest of his body, like icy tendrils creeping through his veins. His muscles froze, limbs betraying him, and his paralyzed form collapsed to the ground, leaving him helpless.

His wide-eyed gaze darted toward the outlines of his comrades, blissfully asleep under their cozy blankets, unaware of his panic. He strained to summon their aid. His eyes bulged with mounting terror, but his voice remained trapped in his throat.

The woman caught his gesture, and a sinister curl

framed her mouth. "I'm glad I'll enjoy you by myself. Once my brothers and sisters learn of you, they'll come like a swarm. I should take advantage now since I dislike sharing."

Her fangs gleamed. She licked her lips, her low growl rumbling in her throat.

"Liver is my favorite."

Aren struggled to move, scream—do something.

A sharp claw tore the fabric on his tunic, leaving a thin line of blood on his exposed skin. The woman licked it and moaned, utterly pleased. "It's so sweet."

With hungry eyes, she ripped the rest of his tunic, exposing his muscled torso.

With deliberate slowness, she opened her cavernous mouth, revealing rows of glistening, razor-sharp teeth that sparkled in the faint moonlight. Her eyes locked onto his abdomen, and with a lightning-fast motion, she lunged forward, her jaws clamping down with a bone-chilling crunch as she tore into muscle and bone.

❧

The morning air was thick with fog, its damp embrace settling on everything: blankets, capes, hair. Droplets of crimson dew glistened like scattered rubies on the grass, each catching the faint light of dawn.

Korshak studied the splatter on the ground, almost sick to his stomach.

The other zaldunak, pale-faced, surrounded him. Whatever it was, it had killed and dragged off Aren in the middle of the night. There wasn't a body and no sign of a struggle, but the trail of blood left no room for assumptions.

"Should we follow it?" Narek asked. "He might still be alive—"

"Are you daft?" Korshak's raised voice startled them. "And do what? Walk into its lair to save someone already dead?"

"But his body—"

"Aren's gone," Korshak shot back. "There's nothing we can do about it now."

Narek frowned.

"We're in the middle of the Iluna," Korshak remarked, glancing at the trees. "It's a cursed forest full of ancient things, and one of our own is dead, probably killed by one of those things. Whatever is out there will return. Our best option is to keep moving and leave this place." Korshak faced north. "But first, we find her." He spat on the ground. "She'll pay for this."

Narek and the others exchanged worried glances but followed Korshak anyway.

CHAPTER 95

THE THREE RULES

"This is day two." Re-energized this morning, Kharis munched on a few apples as she strolled, leaving a few inside her tunic for later. The sound of water made her jump with glee. "A creek!" A thrill radiated through her, her whole body practically buzzing with excitement. "It must be close."

"*Wait for permission—*"

"Yes, yes." She waved her hand in the air. "The forest is alive. I must wait for its approval. No room for gluttery—"

"*Gluttony,*" he corrected her.

She chuckled. It was good to have company, in a way. She was unsure if her mind was playing tricks on her. Yet, if it was, it sure was pleasant to have someone to talk to, even if that someone was herself.

The outline of the Lerra Mountains was now visible—a two-day trek, if her calculations were accurate. She would make it "to the other side" by tomorrow afternoon.

She slowed her steps.

Leaving the forest to meet her uncle didn't appeal to her. She scratched her cheek.

"What will Ghan do if I don't show up?" She snorted.

"Burn the place?" She finished her apple, then placed the core near a tree so birds could peck at it later. "If I don't turn up, he'll assume I'm dead, this madness is over, and Saya is finally free."

"*It's a terrible idea,*" the Voice said after a lengthy pause.

Kharis wrinkled her nose at the air beside her. "Why?"

"*Because your sister will come looking for you.*"

That comment was a punch to her stomach. "Blasted fires. I must make it back. No more games." She needed to reach her destination by tomorrow afternoon. The time for musings dissolved, replaced by the urgency of her journey. Korshak and his men were coming to capture or kill her— definitely kill her.

"It's too quiet." She paid attention to her surroundings. "And I have no weapons." A puff of air rushed past her lips. "I wish I could summon my magic—"

"*No.*"

She gave the forest a long, sideways stare since there was no face to glare at. She wanted to ask, but the Voice must've seen her "why" lingering on her lips.

"*Magic calls on magic,*" he said, his voice low and resonant. "*Summoning it can be dangerous, given you can't control who answers it. Besides, you're in the Iluna, and yours is fire magic. How will the forest react when you use it?*"

"Good point," she said. "I hate it when you're right."

This time, the Voice tittered.

Kharis approached the creek with reverence, waiting for the forest to grant permission. Oddly enough, those magical tendrils scrutinized her, then pulled her along with a welcoming tug. She cupped her hands and drank.

"Korshak and his men must be half a day behind us, and they mustn't catch up to me. Are you positive I can't, you know, pick up the pace?"

"*The Iluna has rules that you must obey. Your zaldunak are not exempt from them.*"

Kharis sighed and sipped some more.

Then she noticed a blueberry bush she swore wasn't there a moment ago. She picked a few and ate them. The flavor explosion was outstanding—a juicy, floral flavor with a sour after-bite that provided a perfect balance.

"You've been helping me with these rules, but the zaldunak are unaware of them."

"*Worry about your goal, and let the Iluna handle trespassers.*"

She stood still, weighing scenarios.

"*Do you remember my rules?*" the Voice asked, curious.

Kharis raised one finger at a time. "Eyes on the ground. Don't run. Listen to you."

"*Good.*" If he had a face, he would beam with pride.

CHAPTER 96
THE ZALDUN AND THE FOREST

Korshak let out a piercing scream, the sound like shards of glass scraping his throat. The bodies of his comrades, or whatever was left of them, surrounded him.

Narek, Davit, Samel, Bhazat, and Andrik were dead.

Murdered while he slept.

Korshak dropped to his knees, stunned by the gruesome sight, his eyes darting everywhere. Sweat beaded on his brow and rolled down his temples.

Something had ripped his comrades to shreds.

His breaths came shallow and fast. Panic flooded his veins. His senses peaked. His entire body jumped at every sound around him. A storm of thoughts invaded his mind, each becoming darker and ghastlier. He scratched his head compulsively, his eyes zipping from corpse to corpse.

"She did this," he shouted.

Darkness slowly gripped his mind.

"She bloody did this." His chest heaved with each ragged breath. "She killed them all."

The signs of struggle were everywhere. Broken branches. Ripped clothing. Slashes on the tree trunks. Desperate hands had dug the ground, overturned rocks, and pulled grass clumps in an attempt to escape. Their mangled bodies were torn apart, parts everywhere. Narek's eyes were open. He'd seen what attacked him before it shredded his throat and abdomen. And whatever creature did it, it left the carnage for Korshak to find.

"She did this to me." Korshak's mind went wild with frenzy. "I'm going to kill you, *txakurra*." His gaze darted over the bodies. "I will avenge you."

Then he ran as fast as he could to catch up with her.

CHAPTER 97

THE PRINCESS
AND THE ZALDUN

"This is it. Day three." Kharis stretched her arms with a loud, obnoxious yawn.

"I slept well," she declared. Rising to her feet, she dusted off her pants, plucked pine needles from her clothes, and a stubborn twig that had tangled in her hair. Her body was coated in grime, and her hair likely resembled a bird's nest. Yet, none of it dimmed her spirits. She flashed a radiant smile, daring the world to outshine her cheerfulness.

"By day's end, I'll be on the other side." She bowed to the trees. "Thank you for your help. May the earth and sun bless and sustain you."

She closed her eyes and took a deep, cleansing breath, letting all that fresh, crisp air fill her lungs.

In the stillness of that moment, a tender tug pulled on her.

Her eyes popped open. "Saya!"

A jolt ran through her body. "She came for me." Kharis's eyes misted. Saya *was* at the other end of the Iluna. Waiting. "I'm coming, sister."

With renewed purpose, she stepped forward.

"That fool," Kharis mumbled. "Ghan didn't tell me she was coming. Ha! As if I wouldn't sense her." She laughed, and given her happiness, she decided to sing, making up a song on the spot.

"Mighty trees of the Iluna, such a towering grace,
Guardians of the forest, standing tall in your space,
Sharan's gentle glow bathes you in silvery lace,
And Tung, with a playful wink, adds to the chase.

Mighty trees of the Iluna, in your shelter I'd reside,
Grant me a moment of peace by your side,
Let me enjoy this bliss, our secret to hide,
In your shadowed embrace, your wisdom is my guide."

The forest listened, every leaf standing still. Even the birds paid attention. Her silent companion—that cadence of silvery sounds—remained quiet, but if he had a face, he would grin and perhaps even sing with her—if he were the type.

As Kharis neared the rendezvous point, the pull of her sister's magic grew stronger. She glanced around, excitement coiling in her chest. "Are you absolutely sure I can't run?"

"*Sprinting through the forest won't get you to your destination any faster. As I have instructed you, walk. Do not run.*"

"Could I whistle?"

There was a pause. "*Why not sing?*"

Kharis giggled at the comment. "You've been paying attention. I don't know many songs, but if you don't mind that I'm making up a few, I can come up with another one."

"*The forest won't mind.*"

Kharis raised an eyebrow, wondering if he wanted her to sing but wasn't coming out to say it. *I guess the Voice is shy.* "Very well, what would the forest want?"

"*It wants to hear your voice. The lyrics are irrelevant.*"

"So, I could sing nonsense, and the forest would be happy?"

"*Music is never nonsense.*"

"There's some logic to that." She sang and whistled, keeping her pace.

"In the quiet of the night,
His voice, so silvery,
Is a gentle whisper in the dark.
He sings to me so sweetly."

"Well, actually, you don't," Kharis said. "You should give it a try."

The Voice hummed.

Was he annoyed? She couldn't tell.

"Though stubborn in his ways."

The Voice made a grumbling noise.

"He's a warmth I can't deny,
A kind and soothing voice,
Beneath the starry sky.
Through the trials we face,
He stands his ground, unwavering."

She raised three fingers, referencing his three rules, while waving her hand high in the air. *Would he be rolling his eyes now?*

"A steadfast companion in times of need,
He's always there to lead.
Like a river, calm and gentle,
That flows through every bend,
This silvery voice's my trusted friend."

Eventually, Kharis noticed how the trees thinned enough to show the end of the forest. Banners and flags fluttered in the distance. Gold and ivory—the Empire's colors—streamed through them. Ahead, the Zahari battalion awaited. The tug was intense, pulling her along until it went taut.

"I made it!" Kharis threw her arms up in victory. "So, no running, right?"

"*No running.*"

"I can't wait to see Saya."

Fast footfalls approached behind her. Kharis turned, and Korshak smirked, panting. "I found you." Darkened eyes stared at her as he drew his sword. "Time to say goodbye."

"You ran?" Stunned, Kharis stood still. "He ran," she told the Voice, hers turning high-pitched. "What happens if one runs?"

There was no need to answer. The ground shuddered beneath her feet, the tremors rolling upward through her legs. Overhead, the canopy stirred, and a flock of birds burst skyward in a frenzied flight. Something vast was coming, and its weight rattled the earth.

CHAPTER 98

THE ILUNA'S GUARDIAN

A phantom hand pushed Kharis to the ground. "*Do not run, no matter what,*" the Voice said urgently. "*And do not lift your eyes.*"

Korshak's boot connected with her ribs. With a pained grunt, she rolled away from him. When a second kick came her way, she grabbed his ankle and twisted his foot in the opposite direction. Korshak cried out, losing his balance and rolling onto the ground, screaming in agony. Kharis struggled to get up, her hand clutching her ribs. *Eyes down.* She dashed and crouched behind a bush, waiting for his boots to appear at the edges of her vision. *Blasted, he has a sword.*

Kharis reached for a fallen branch. "Please, forgive me," she begged the forest.

Rawiri had taught her well. "*A spear is far more dangerous than a sword and has better reach,*" he'd instructed the sisters. "*Your odds of survival are higher with one of these in your hands.*"

The branch didn't resemble a Kahurangi spear by any stretch of the imagination, but it would have to do against Korshak, whose eyes flared with madness. She swung the branch when she spotted his boots, striking his legs hard.

497

The stick shattered. Korshak shrieked and crashed to the ground.

As a giant shadow emerged, Kharis lunged for the ground, her body hitting the earth with a thud. She pressed herself flat onto her stomach, her eyes facing down. The scent of damp soil and grass filled her nostrils.

A low, ominous rumble surged through the air. The earth trembled beneath her, sending tremors up her spine.

Don't run, she reminded herself.

But she wanted to.

Keep my eyes down. She would've told stupid Korshak the same, but he was moaning loudly as he slowly got to his feet, his body tottering, unaware of the colossal shape looming over them.

Don't look. Don't look. Don't look.

And it was hard not to since curiosity ran so strongly in her.

A massive reptilian paw—three times the size of her head—filled her gaze. It sported long, black claws and shining silver scales that resembled sharp little spear tips. Her mind halted all thoughts, including the urge to flee. Her heart was racing, nearly exploding, and her breathing caught in her throat.

The Iluna guardian.

Kharis squeezed her eyes shut, lying motionless as the monster sniffed her, inhaling her scent with deliberate intent. A warm, moist breath carrying an unpleasant odor reminiscent of rotten eggs huffed her nape, blowing strands of her black hair.

Blessed Mother. Kharis swallowed a scream.

Its deep growl made her insides vibrate. A wet tongue brushed one of her cheeks, and Kharis's squeal froze in her throat. *It's tasting me.* Kharis did her best not to whimper. Heavy drops of warm drool landed behind her ear, sliding down her neck. She stifled a gag. The creature nudged her flank with its snout, its menacing growl reverberating through her while attempting to roll her over.

Don't run. Don't run.

But Blessed Mother, how she wanted to.

And Korshak, the fool that he was, decided it was a good idea to challenge the Iluna's behemoth of a guardian.

"She's mine," he said, half-crazed. "I'm killing her." He swung his sword at the beast, the metallic whoosh cutting through the air. "Get away!"

The paw darted away from her.

The silvery voice whispered in her ear, his breath tickling it.

"Now you can run."

Kharis didn't argue the order, sprinting toward the ivory and gold pennons billowing ahead. The wind, howling past her ears, pushed her forward. That crimson thread connecting her to Saya tugged desperately, each frantic pull sending a jolt of energy through her.

Korshak's bellows and screams thundered in the woods as angry roars wrapped around him.

Kharis ran, not once looking behind her.

She lengthened her stride, the ground crunching beneath her boots. Air clawed at her throat as it filled her lungs, leaving a sharp, metallic taste in her mouth. Her heart raced like a wild mare.

And the massive beast, apparently done with Korshak, sprinted after her next.

The ground shook with each heavy footfall, her body jerking as she ran.

It was coming—fast.

Heat coursed through her veins as fear flooded every cell. The Voice had warned her not to summon her magic. But the Akumi king always protected his vessel. Even now. And the Akumi king obeyed no rules.

A sudden red flash shifted her vision, startling her. Her

senses heightened, and the monster's footfalls exploded in her ears. Its scent was strong. Loam, moss, and rain chased after her —a storm of wind and angry forest mist. But a different scent, orange blossoms and jasmine, was propelling her forward.

"Saya!"

The tree line was so close that her pulse quickened. Kharis ran, sure to cross it within a heartbeat.

But iridescent scales emerged on her skin, releasing a stardust haze. Sparks glittered around her. *No. No.* Flames arced across her exposed skin, itching to engulf her.

Alarmed, the forest roused, stirring to life.

"*Run,*" the Voice demanded. "*Faster!*"

And Kharis did.

Ethereal gold tendrils wound through the trees and found her, coiling around her tenderly.

The wave of magic her sister had released bathed Kharis in its light. Powerful. Overwhelming. A crushing force that slowed the world behind her. The beast roared in frustration, its deep, booming sound echoing. The monster no longer shook the ground.

The world around Kharis slowed. The flocks of birds that had erupted into flight were now suspended mid-air, the feathered chaos of beating wings and shrill squeaks silenced. A flying squirrel froze mid-leap between two trees. Sunlight stopped flickering through the canopy. Leaves no longer fluttered in the breeze.

Before Saya could stop the flow of time fully, the Iluna Forest answered.

A blinding flash of verdant light swallowed the forest. A piercing sound followed the blast, and a violent wave of force hurled Kharis through the air, flinging her clear past the treeline. She landed hard, tumbling across and leaving a trail of dirt and dead leaves until her body came to a jarring halt.

Pain lit every nerve, burning and relentless. Gasping and coughing, she lay there, stunned. Then, against all reason, laughter escaped her. Her jaw ached from the strain, but she laughed—at the madness, the miracle, the sheer absurdity of surviving.

"Khiri!" Saya jumped off her horse, dodging soldiers and officers, shoving past them, frantically calling her name.

"Khiri!"

That voice was heavenly. The scent of orange blossoms and jasmine grew stronger—richer and sweeter with each breath. Saya's sobs broke through as she flung her arms around Kharis, burying her face in the hollow of her sister's neck. Warm tears slid onto her skin.

"I made it," Kharis said between ragged breaths. The searing blaze rushing through her limbs told her the healing had begun. She felt the tugs and pulls—tendons drawing taut, bones snapping back into place. The heap of flesh she'd become returned to being a body honed for a divine war.

"I'll get you." A voice clawed out of the forest. "I'm not done."

Korshak's broken figure stepped out of the forest's shadows and limped toward them, bleeding profusely from nasty gashes. His sword hung from his left hand, and his right arm dangled precariously from his shoulder, bone and sinew visible.

Madness flared in his eyes. He was beyond pain now.

"You escaped me once, but never again, txakurra." His face was harsh. His crazed eyes glimmered with revenge. "Since that bloody fire didn't finish you, I'm going to kill you myself!" Korshak yelled at the top of his lungs. "I'm taking you both."

CHAPTER 99
THE SILVER DRAGON

Ghan clicked his tongue, mortified by Korshak's ineptitude.

Judging by his state, he seemed the lone survivor. Had he kept his foolish mouth shut, Ghan could've claimed Kharis had slain the zaldunak—violating the conditions set by the Regiazenka. The idiot—arrogant and eager for revenge—would've gladly upheld the lie. That would've paved the way for the resealment ritual. At last, he would finally be rid of her.

But now, with that imbecile bawling like a wounded ox for the entire battalion to hear, any hope of spinning the tale was lost. Worse still, if Korshak laid a hand on Kharis, she had every right to strike back—and no one would question it.

And Saya—proof of his broken promise to Aghuti—stood between them, quite literally, in the worst place possible.

Gritting his teeth, Ghan raised his arm in signal. "Sharp-shooters—position. Not a single arrow touches my nieces, or I'll kill you myself."

They swiftly nocked their arrows, sights fixed on Korshak.

Salazar and Ranit exchanged uneasy glances.

"The angle's bad," Ranit warned. "The archers can't make the shot without risking the girls."

Ghan didn't respond.

Salazar stepped forward. "Sir, the sisters are too close. The distance between them and Korshak is too narrow—the shot isn't clean."

Before Ghan could snap back, Captain Aram Zhad unsheathed his sword and broke into a sprint toward the princesses.

❧

"You're mine."

Korshak lurched toward them, dragging one foot, his sword now a crutch. "This is for Rudra—for what you did to him... and to my family!" He lifted the broken blade and slashed the air with a shaky arc.

Kharis rolled over Saya to shield her from Korshak's advance. Intense heat still flooded her limbs as the healing raged on, but she didn't care. She would fight him anyway. No one would ever touch her sister. Not while she still drew breath. And certainly not that fool.

She braced to rise, teeth gritted, ready to lunge—

A silver blur tore from the tree line like lightning.

A giant maw filled with rows of sharp teeth clamped on Korshak, who shrieked and thrashed to free himself. One savage snap. The monster ripped him clean in half.

Bones crunched and snapped. Blood sprayed across her face just as Captain Zhad dove over the sisters, shielding them with his body and forcing her back to the ground.

With a violent shake of its head, the beast flung Korshak's broken remains—one half crashing into the underbrush, the other disappearing into the trees.

The dragon loomed above, its shadow vast enough to swallow Kharis, Saya, and Captain Zhad where they huddled. Though its massive jaws hovered within reach, the beast paid them no mind. With a crackle of charged air, it unfurled its wings—immense, shimmering things that stretched wide enough to darken the clearing. Its silver scales thrummed with energy, buzzing like a swarm of hornets. Each step shook the ground, its weight splitting the soil with deep, thunderous tremors.

Then it roared.

Not as a warning. Or a threat. A challenge.

Come, it promised. *And I will flatten you.*

With a thunderous scrape of its claws, the dragon gouged the earth, sending up clouds of dust and debris that choked the air and staked its claim. The message was unmistakable—the Iluna was forbidden ground.

Its hide shimmered like polished silver, and beneath the harsh daylight, it glowed with a brilliance that rivaled the sun. That radiant gleam hinted at the ancient power coiled within the beast's massive frame.

The dragon's violet eyes—round, glowing, and seething with fury—swept across the battalion. Then they settled on the three figures at its feet. It huffed, the breath hot and heavy, stirring the dust around them as if urging the intruders to move along.

Kharis raised her head, shielding her face from the swirling grit. Slowly, she met the dragon's gaze. Its eyes locked with hers, and in that instant, something shifted in the beast—a flicker of recognition stirred in its depths.

Then came another roar—deeper, louder, and far more terrible than the last. A declaration of power. It shook the sky and echoed back through the forest. With a final snort, the dragon returned to the forest, melting into its dark shadows.

CHAPTER 100
THE GENERAL AND THE REGIAZENKA

Four weeks after retrieving the Djinnshirukh from the Iluna Forest, Arjun Ghan stood before the imperial king and the Regiazenka to provide the report.

He planted his feet wide, raised his chin, and confidently spoke of the march to the other end, how they met the rest of the battalion already camped there, and how they'd waited.

"We don't know what took place inside," he said, "but we witnessed the forest explosion that spat Princess Kharis out of the Iluna and how Princess Saya abandoned her assigned post to run to her aid—"

"Kharis was severely injured," an angry Yuna shouted.

Ghan groaned silently.

The order had been simple. If the Djinnshirukh could cross the Iluna and make it to the other side in three days, the Regiazenka would allow Kharis to live. The ministers, unable to draft the death sentence for a fourteen-year-old vessel, decided to let this cursed forest pass judgment on the Akumi king.

"Against my expressed orders," Arjun Ghan continued,

"a rogue group of zaldunak went after her to quench their thirst for revenge by killing the Djinnshirukh princess."

A roll of murmurs followed that statement.

Waiting for the crowd to quiet down, Ghan discreetly looked for Aghet but didn't see him anywhere.

Where is he?

Ghan cleared his throat and continued, "Unfortunately, Lord Korshak, the lone survivor, intended to kill the princesses, but the massive silver dragon emerged from the forest and slaughtered him."

His Serene Imperial Majesty, King Hröld, Son of the Sun, remained still and unreadable. Listening.

Crown Prince Hala shifted in his chair, crossing and uncrossing his legs. He bit his cheek, clearly annoyed by how long Ghan took to finish his report.

Meddlesome man. Ghan hated him as much as Kharis, so he took his time to irritate him.

The Regiazenka had settled on a sentence that absolved them from executing a child, but Ghan never imagined *she* would emerge alive from that cursed place. He'd hoped for the things living there to do the job for him. His fingers twitched because the annoying girl had succeeded, making it to the other end.

The Akumi king protected her. He studied the swollen mass of burnt and throbbing flesh that was his hand. *Blasted demon.*

Lady Khostuna exchanged a glance with the other members of the Regiazenka, their eyes speaking volumes in a silent conversation. A series of subtle nods passed between them, sealing their unspoken agreement.

"Your Majesty?" she asked, awaiting his decision.

Hröld pinned Ghan with a slow, appraising gaze. His forefinger slowly tapped the throne's armrest as his pause stretched between them. "Were all the conditions met?"

Khostuna cleared her throat. "The vessel made it to the other end of the Iluna alive. As per the report, the Iluna

Forest appears to have passed judgment on the Akumi king, allowing him to cross without much resistance. Therefore, the conditions stipulated in the decree were met." She looked to her right and left. "Members of the Regiazenka, where do you stand on the question?"

Lord Miresma, the decree's architect, stood swiftly. "The conditions were met. The Djinnshirukh is free."

Prince Jordha shared a relieved nod with Hala. "The conditions were met," he said. "The Djinnshirukh is free."

Lady Karitza rose next. "The conditions were met. The Djinnshirukh is free."

Lord Garrantzi repeated the exact words.

And so, every minister rendered their judgment, uttering the same rote answer until Ghan's turn came.

"The Djinnshirukh is the Empire's ultimate weapon—"

"No one disputes that fact," Lady Khostuna cut him off. "There's a motion on the floor that you must address. On this issue, as determined by royal decree, where do you stand?"

Ghan gritted his teeth. "If you allowed me to finish, my argument would be clear to all."

Khostuna narrowed her eyes, curling her lips slightly, displeased with his confrontation. She turned to Hröld, who flicked his hand to allow it. Miffed, she said, "Fine. The Chair recognizes you."

Ghan flattened his mouth, his demeanor radiating superiority, and projected his voice. "The Djinnshirukh is the Empire's ultimate weapon, forged by the immortals to be unleashed on the Akumi to raze and destroy their army. We must hone it carefully and sharpen it constantly." He spoke, full of bluster, as he paced the room. "In times of peace, unfortunately, it wears out its welcome."

He shook his head as he faced them.

"You see only a child—but that's your mistake. We've had a thousand years' worth of vessels. And through them all, the Akumi king has endured. Today, the vessel is a child.

But the madness will soon claim her. And when it does, we'll choose another. And another. An endless line of bodies to contain the monster. You're trapped in the present. But I see the long chain of vessels still to come... and the tireless labor required to bind the king of fire and ruin."

Hröld remained impassive, staring at Ghan while his finger tapped that wretched armrest.

That sound. It exploded in Ghan's ears.

Lady Khostuna raised a single eyebrow. "What do you suggest?"

"I'll train her—to ensure the beast within is kept sated, for all our sakes."

Hala shot to his feet, fury twisting his features. "The Regiazenka stripped you of that right, or have you forgotten how you sent two princesses of the realm to the royal infirmary?" His voice cracked like a whip through the chamber. "One of them nearly died from the wounds you inflicted."

Those final words, sharp and damning, echoed in Ghan's mind like a tolling bell.

"So be it."

"What?" Hala turned to his father.

"Your Majesty!" another voice clamored.

Hröld raised a hand, halting Yuna mid-stride as she advanced toward the dais. "Monk Yuna's terms remain unchanged," the king declared. "That will not be revised. High General Arjun Ghan shall not train her—only oversee the process. Every session will be held in the presence of monks, and the Regiazenka will appoint her instructors."

The ministers exchanged approving nods. "Very well," Khostuna said. "High General Arjun Ghan, where do you stand on the question?"

Ghan stiffened, almost choking on his words as he uttered them. "The conditions were met. The Djinnshirukh is free."

"The decision is unanimous," Khostuna said. "The Djinnshirukh is free."

Hröld rose, holding the long royal scepter, and thumped it against the floor with fire in his eyes.

"Let it be entered into the proceedings," his voice resounded across the room, "that on the fifteenth day of the month of Anar, Princess Kharis Ghan of Zahar, Djinnshirukh of the Zahari Empire, walked free on the charges of murder, and that the conditions set forth stand. Let it be known that Zahar can never hold the child accountable for the Akumi king's crimes."

The scepter struck the floor again, and Ghan flinched out of his thoughts. *Not all is lost.* After all, he'd successfully argued his position to become her overseer again. *I'll ensure the Netherworlds of Ifran are like a child's playground compared to what's coming to her.*

Ghan smirked.

She's mine. Again.

CHAPTER 101

THE NIGHTMARE

Arjun Ghan sat tall on his stallion, though he couldn't remember mounting it—or why the world around him had been drained of sound and color. Ahead, the fog parted, revealing the dark edge of the Iluna Forest.

He dismounted, reins in hand, meaning to keep his distance—but the voices whispered, coaxing him forward. He knew he was dreaming, but even here the forest called to him, sweet as a lover's breath. The wind traced his cheek with deceptive gentleness, luring him closer. He stood still, entranced. The forest loomed, ancient and alive.

He hated it—yet it wanted him.

A rumble startled his horse. The stallion reared, tore free, and vanished into the haze. Ghan cursed, but his attention snapped back as the mist shifted.

Two figures stepped through the fog.

The first was a bare-chested warrior with a broadsword slung over one shoulder, silver eyes gleaming with unshakable power, like a revenant of the old world. His face was handsome—familiar, even—though the shadows and distance blurred the finer details. But it was the second who stopped Ghan cold.

Kharis.

She strode forward, a wicked smile curling her lips, long black hair floating in the wind. Her crimson eyes gleamed like coals in a lake of fire. She wore the battle garb of the Ghasmanoör people—a red kilt, black fur-lined boots, and a lavish crimson cuirass embossed with a dragon wreathed in flames.

Black snake tattoos slithered across her bare arms—living seals of the Djinnshirukh. They pulsed, whispering secrets in her ear. Her smile widened. Her canines lengthened.

Ghan drew his sword.

"Stay back," he warned, voice hoarse. His sword hand trembled. "One more step, and I'll kill you."

Kharis just grinned.

Her skin shimmered—scales blooming like light over water. Stardust trailed behind her. Then she ignited—flames of gold and blood-red engulfing her body. Ghan shielded his face. The heat was unbearable. And yet, some bitter part of him hungered for her power. *Mine*, the thought echoed. *Mine. Mine.*

She grew. Shifted.

A silver dragon now stood where she had. Her roar shattered the air. Ghan stumbled and fell, the ground trembling beneath him.

On the dragon's chest glowed the sacred tree, inked in fire—roots etched into her haunches, branches unfurled across her wings.

Ghan's breath caught. "The Mahabhal..."

"We've been waiting for you," the warrior beside her said.

Before Ghan could utter a single word, much less use his sword, her maw opened—black, endless—and fire consumed him before he could scream.

❧

Ghan screamed, eyes shut and arms up to shield his face and fend off the fire.

He froze, realizing he was in his bedroom.

Sweat rolled off his temples. His heart thumped in his chest as the chamber's chilling darkness embraced him. He curled his fingers and cursed in frustration—the same dream every night since the Iluna.

"Nothing but this blasted nightmare."

Anger swelled inside him, and he gritted his teeth. "What does it mean?" Aggravation made his stomach burn. "The dragon. The Mahabhal. The blasted Iluna Forest. That warrior. Why do I keep seeing them in my dreams?"

He turned, but Aghet wasn't in bed with him.

His mouth tightened.

"Why isn't he here?"

Ever since the Iluna, Aghet had stayed away. Ghan rubbed a shaky hand over his forehead and wiped it dry. The scar itched, and his left eye twitched. It had been weeks since the Iluna incident, yet the image of the dragon and the warrior haunted him.

He groaned, struck the bed with his fist, and threw his covers off.

"Why?"

Massaging his temples didn't curb the nasty headache. He perched on the bed's edge, elbows resting on his knees. The pounding inside his skull predicted another awful day. The scent of burned flesh clawed at his nostrils like a threat.

"It was a bloody dream and nothing more."

Ghan studied the burn scars on his right palm—the ones he'd received from *her*—and huffed. A persistent thirst pricked his throat. He walked toward a large ewer and gulped its contents. Unable to rid himself of the heat clutching him, he poured the rest over his head. It didn't lessen the sensation of his skin on fire.

His mind returned to the prophecy, the puzzle that tormented him. Kharis, the Djinnshirukh, possessed the power to raise an army of Akumi and consume the world with her fire unless she died.

Old memories came to him. He learned of this prophecy and had spent thirty years deciphering it, reciting it from memory, searching for hidden clues about what he had to do.

> "All that was wrong will be righted,
> When the immortal vessel dies."

He wanted that power, yet this prophecy bothered him like a thorn trapped under his skin.

> Tear asunder the seals that contain it.
> Let the world revel in fire.
> Let it be consumed again,
> And all the writings end."

What does it mean? The rage ate him alive. It tore his insides and ripped him apart. It became a slow, agonizing burn that had no remedy.

With a violent sweep of his arm, he sent everything on the table hurtling through the air. Glass, porcelain, and metal tumbled to the floor, the sound of dissonant crashing and shattering echoing through the room.

Ghan could hear Kharis laughing, mocking him, running around him, and daring him to catch her. In his mind, he ran after her, clutched her arm, and raised a dagger to strike her, but she turned into water and slipped through his fingers.

Her sardonic laugh lingered, echoing in that hopeless black void of his.

PART SIX
THREE YEARS LATER

CHAPTER 102

THE MONSOON

Three years later, the atrium rang with familiar screams.

Ghan appraised his charge from the atrium's balcony with his arms crossed. His fingers tapped a broad bicep, pleased by what he saw: his niece's formidable power.

This arena was the only place she could let loose. If there were any displays of her magic outside the atrium, resealment would be her fate. He smirked, thrilled to grip her metaphorical neck and squeeze hard. He raised his right hand, its surface a tapestry of burn scars. Ghan huffed, clenching and unclenching it.

I have what I want. That brutal power would never be his, but Kharis was, and his training had paid off. She'd become a lethal weapon he could unleash on any enemy.

And with the appropriate stress, any weapon can break.

Ghan oversaw her training for three long years. Methodical, even in this, he fooled all security checks and bribed or blackmailed her trainers. He made her his executioner and threw the worst prisoners at her—none ever left alive. This creature of flesh and bone slaughtered them with a ferocity that impressed him.

The Djinnshirukh was a swirl of death, and Ghan fed that monster to sate it.

An endless parade of bodies to train her.

"When will you give me that?"

That voice jolted Ghan out of his wicked thoughts, and he swiveled to face Aghet, who appraised Kharis with an envious gleam. "I've asked you, yet you continue to deny me."

"I must train her first," Ghan said, "but I promise you the next batch."

Aghet cocked his head. A black sparkle danced in his eyes as he gazed at his prince. "I'm here, always at your side, ready to fulfill your every wish, yet you only have eyes for her."

Ghan grunted, annoyed by Aghet's jealousy. "The next group is yours. All of them." He caressed his face. "For now, allow me some fun, would you?"

Aghet leaned into the hand, but his longing gaze had locked onto Kharis. "Whatever my prince wants."

Pleased, Ghan smiled.

Aghet didn't.

§

Officers opened the iron-barred gate and dragged the body out, blood leaving a broad trail on the sand.

Kharis panted heavily, staring at the two men on the balcony, hoping to hear the words that ended this nightmare: "We are done for today." But they never came.

Her sleeve, already soaked, wiped the sweat and blood off her face. She'd lost count of how many she'd killed today, but Ghan kept sending more.

More.

Always more.

It had been three years of the same.

Archers lined the balcony in case the Djinnshirukh got out of hand.

"Why?" she asked the space ahead of her. "Why must I do this?"

She knew the answer.

Fire magic always got her in trouble.

It had branded her. At eighteen, she understood that she would never belong. The Empire would deny her humanity—Kharis of Zahar would live and die as a monster.

She closed her eyes, and a phantom hand caressed her face with endless affection. She knew it was him. Besides Saya and Monk Yuna, the Voice was the only other semblance of kindness around her. He was her constant companion and possibly a sign of the madness that afflicted every Djinnshirukh.

The iron gate rolled open again, and that sound pushed Kharis out of her reprieve. Soldiers shoved a young man into the arena.

His head was shaven, as with prisoners slated for execution, but he was so young it rattled her—eighteen at best. The fear in his eyes gleamed like that of a trapped animal. He walked in, gripping his tunic, and frantically scanned the butchery. When his gaze landed on Kharis, covered in blood and gore, he gasped, dread widening his eyes.

"Please, I'm innocent," he begged the soldiers. "I was framed."

One kicked him, and he stumbled to the floor, sobbing in desperation. "Please, you must believe me."

Two officers wheeled a cart. "Choose your weapon," one of them said, uninterested in his plea.

"Wait, no. You don't understand. I'm innocent," he shrieked, thumping his chest. "This must be a misunderstanding."

"Choose your weapon!"

The young man's head jerked back. He fixed his widened

gaze on the soldier, a moment of hesitation passing over him. Fumbling with the array of weapons on the cart, his fingers closed around the sturdy hilt of a sword.

The guards stepped out and rolled the gate down. Iron bars clanged as the gate locked into place, the sound echoing through the atrium. A low hum lingered in the metal. That gate had opened and closed so often that its sound almost shoved Kharis off the narrow mental ledge on which she stood.

The monsoon season had started, and it was hot inside. Kharis sweated profusely, beads rolling down her nose and chin, past her neck, and down her back, soaking the surcoat beneath her leather armor. The rain seeped through the ceiling's cracks, and cool water drops fell onto the arena. Some fell on her face, and that sensation was divine. Others mixed with the pooled blood, forming crimson mud puddles.

It had rained all day long. A salty scent had lingered, making the air inside muggier. Lightning flashed, and the windows atop the structure lit and rattled with the thunder. The droplets from the cracks above were unrelenting, hitting the floor like unbearable little explosions.

Drip.

Drip.

Kharis swallowed hard, wanting it all to be done. But the young prisoner was different. He didn't cackle or curse or give her nasty, vulgar gestures. He didn't strut like a peacock, convinced he would be walking out free.

That was Ghan's deal—kill the Djinnshirukh, and one was free.

The young man whimpered. He lacked the killer instinct, that thirst for murder that the other prisoners openly displayed. Unable to lift the blade, his sword arm shook hard, and it was pitiful to watch.

"I didn't do it." His knees wobbled. "I was drugged, and someone else stabbed her while she lay on my bed." His body shook. "Please, I'm innocent," he shouted.

Innocent.

That word rolled throughout the atrium. It bounced off the walls, unwilling to die out. Some people were judged without a chance at redemption, like the Djinnshirukh. *Guilty from the moment I was born.* Guilty, like the young man she now faced.

Kharis shouldn't have bothered with him. He was one more kill in an endless parade of prisoners for execution.

But he's so young.

She got into position and raised her sword. The man dropped to his knees and pressed his forehead against the muddy ground. "Please, *please*, I didn't do it. I swear it on my honor, on my mother's name."

She eyed him for a long moment and huffed, suddenly sick. "I can't do this anymore." She lowered her sword, exhausted by her fate and disgusted by her punishment.

The soft, silvery voice whispered in her ear. "*What do you wish to do?*"

He caressed her mind, flashing images of wild meadows and alpine flowers. She closed her eyes to savor them. For four long years, the Voice had accompanied her everywhere. His promise of friendship and comfort never wavered.

"He's marked for death," she said. "If I don't kill him, they will." Kharis surveyed the archers. Bows ready, their strings taut. Aghet, on the balcony, waited for his chance, his eyes dancing at the idea of torture.

"It's a mercy if I do it."

"*Then let me,*" the Voice said. "*Let me help you while you rest.*" His whisper was sweet and alluring, enveloping her completely.

She lowered her chin, defeated. "I should just die."

"*If you do, I'll be alone.*" His warm, comforting voice took on a pleading tone.

She threw Ghan a glance. "This will never end, will it?"

The Voice didn't reply, waiting to see if she would find her answer today.

Kharis stared at the ground. One day, she lost control of her power and killed twenty-seven people. She would live with that for the rest of her life. One day, she would forgive herself for the pain and sorrow she'd caused. One day, she would be free.

One day, but today wasn't that day.

Was it?

"There's nothing I can do about being the Djinnshirukh," she said, "or about this power inside me that's bigger than myself. But nobody else has to die because of it."

"*What would you do?*" The Voice sounded curious but also pleased.

She straightened. "I must take the first step. No one else will do it for me." She wiped the sweat off her face. "I can go on as is or..." She watched the young man pleading for his life. Was she any different? "I start by redrawing the line." She pushed her shoulders back. "From this moment on, there's no more killing. No more death."

"*Good. Then let's do this together.*"

"It could get ugly."

His hum rumbled through her mind, eager for the challenge ahead. "*We've hit the bottom. From here, the only way is up.*"

A fluttery feeling grew in her chest. "Will you stay with me?"

"*Until my very last breath.*"

Her lips curved. "Then... we climb."

Kharis thrust her sword into the dirt, where it lodged firmly, and advanced toward the young man. His words devolved into incoherent blubbering as she seized him by his collar. He let out a shrill shriek, but to his stunned surprise, she dragged him back to the gate as the heels of his bare feet left deep grooves in the muddy ground.

"Open this door," Kharis commanded. When the soldiers ignored her, she raised her free arm. The delicate scales covering her skin glimmered before crimson flames engulfed her hand. "I said, open this gate."

"Get back in position and kill the prisoner," Ghan shouted from the balcony.

She ignored him, focusing on the sentries behind the gate. "Are you going to open it?" Her flames now engulfed her arm.

The soldiers froze. One broke ranks and bolted.

"Kill her," Ghan shouted at the archers. "Kill her before she kills us."

The volley of arrows turned to ash before reaching her, fluttering like black snowflakes that landed on the bloody ground.

"Did you forget I'm allowed to use magic here?" Kharis said.

"You're a useless monster," Ghan hollered, pounding his fist on the balcony's rail with each word. "Useless, you hear me."

His vitriol turned to the archers. "What are you waiting for, you idiots? Kill her!"

The archers exchanged hesitant glances but readied again upon Ghan's strident command.

"*May I?*" the Voice asked.

Kharis swallowed her chuckle. "Enjoy yourself."

A sudden burst of black flames engulfed the bows, transforming the wood into smoldering embers and charred remnants. The archers hollered in pain and fear.

"Are you opening this gate?" Kharis gripped one of the iron bars, and the intense heat melted the metal under her hand. "I'm losing my patience."

"Where do you think you're going?" Ghan yelled, leaning over the balcony. His eyes bulged. His face twisted, turning an angry red. "Get back in position." Spit flew out of his mouth as he screamed. "And kill him." He struck the rail with each word. "I said, kill him, or I'll kill you."

Aghet, standing beside the high general, watched the

scene unfold with mild interest. He leaned against the wall with his arms crossed, a faint smile playing on his face.

Kharis gave Ghan a long, hard look. "You believe I'm a monster, but you were the monster all along. You belong in the Iluna more than I do."

Ghan's face contorted in stunned surprise, his eyes widening as if the metaphorical dagger she'd thrown had struck its mark.

"Hate me all you want," she said. "Hate me until you rot, but I'm done with you."

Rage replaced his shock. "Get back in position," he shrieked at her, "and kill the prisoner!"

Aghet keenly observed Ghan succumb to anger. Kharis swore she saw disappointment cast a shadow on his face. His sharp gaze met hers, hinting at admiration. He pushed off the wall and walked away, leaving a raging Ghan alone on the balcony.

"Aghet, where are you going?" he yelled, indignant. "Aghet!"

Kharis faced the iron gate. "I'm counting to three; if you don't open it, I'm burning you all to a crisp when I do."

The wheels and chains creaked and groaned as the gate slowly rose from the floor.

"Please, don't kill me," the lad whispered, his body still shaking uncontrollably. "Please."

"Who says I'm killing you?" She arched a dark eyebrow at him. "What's your name, by the way?"

"Gen." His voice was high-pitched and shaky.

"Gen, you survived the Djinnshirukh. You're a free man." She smiled. "Now, you and I are off to speak to His Majesty. I want you to tell him *everything* that brought you into this arena."

And like that, she dragged him across the gate, and both disappeared beyond the shadows.

CHAPTER 103

THE WILD OCEAN

Prince Rawiri, clad in his training leathers, brandished his weapon. His opponent, General Tawhiri, was lithe and agile and carried his like an extension of his body. The two seasoned warriors stood on opposite ends of the yard, each gripping their staff. The sounds of the bustling estate in the background filled the cool morning air. Servants, walking past, watched for a moment, smiling through their chatter, then hurried to their tasks.

"Ready for a little competition?" Tawhiri wore his teasing smile.

Rawiri grinned. "I hope my skills have improved since our last encounter."

Tawhiri chuckled. "I'm about to find out. Prepare yourself."

The sound of a conch announced the start of this round. Rawiri advanced first, lunging with the speed and power of a charging bear. His staff cut through the air with a low, menacing whistle. Tawhiri, quick as a falcon, sidestepped with grace and precision, the blunt end of Rawiri's staff narrowly missing him.

They circled each other, footwork deft and fluid. The clash of their staves echoed through the yard, wood clacking against wood. The men moved, demonstrating three years of disciplined training.

Rawiri's strikes were unrelenting, his staff wavering and flexing with each hit, while Tawhiri evaded his attacks with swift movements.

They traded blows and strikes, their skillful display earning a few claps from soldiers.

Rawiri executed each parry and riposte with calculated elegance as he pushed his body, energized by movement etched in his muscles. Beads of sweat trickled down his brow, stinging his eyes as he pressed on.

After a year of pitiful inertia, he was thankful for Tawhiri's jabs, forcing the reaction this general had hoped for. Rawiri had grabbed a weapon and lunged at him, letting go with each strike of the anger that had simmered in him for so long.

Three years later, he was here, immersed in the moment.

That relentless pain was gone, even if the hollow in his chest persisted. Training with his warriors again brought him perspective—brought him back to life.

Soldiers had gathered along the yard's edge, their attention locked on the two. The occasional murmur of appreciation punctuated the intensity of the sparring. In a swift change of tactics, Rawiri followed through with a feint, his staff swinging dangerously close to Tawhiri's defenses, who almost stumbled but managed to keep his footing.

"It's good to see your deadly self is back," Tawhiri shouted.

Rawiri forced his smile. "It's good just to be back."

But would he ever be back? After four years, he still thought of her—his Teppe.

Their staves met once more, and this time, Rawiri deftly disarmed Tawhiri with a sudden pivot, the staff clattering to the ground. The general lost his footing and lurched back.

A wince and an "Oof!" escaped Tawhiri when his body hit the arena. "Impressive move, Your Highness." He wiped the sweat off his brow. "This round is yours."

"You've truly challenged me," Rawiri said. "Thank you for believing in me."

A kind smile framed Tawhiri's crisp nod. Grasping the outstretched hand, he allowed Rawiri to pull him to his feet, his breath coming in measured gasps as he grinned. "You're as relentless as ever, keeping me on my toes."

"Your Highness?" a voice interrupted the exchange.

Rawiri turned toward the servant.

"Prince Taika is here."

Rawiri frowned.

Tawhiri sighed, knowing, and took Rawiri's spear. "Take his call. I'll see you later."

Pursing his lips, Rawiri headed for the house.

Clad in his leather armor, the twenty-one-year-old stood on the veranda, his gaze lost in the distance. A hint of stubble dusted his jawline. A tousled mane of dark chestnut hair fell in disarray across his forehead, framing Taika's angular features and accentuating his expressive brown eyes.

And this morning, they glistened.

"It's done," Taika said when Rawiri settled by his side. "Princess Mahini."

"It's a good choice," Rawiri said after a thoughtful pause. "She's smart, beautiful inside and out, and will be a good wife."

"Couldn't we try again?" Taika pleaded.

Rawiri stiffened. "Taika."

"Why can't Father ask?" Taika begged. "Wouldn't she be eighteen now?"

Rawiri inhaled, a jumble of memories replaying in his mind. "We've been through this before. The princess is *rahuitia*. Zahar will never allow such a marriage."

"She never wrote." Taika choked on a sob. "She promised she would, but never did."

Rawiri found himself at a loss for words. His contemplative silence hung in the humid air as he patted his nephew's shoulder reassuringly.

"I got one letter," he said, "and it took a year and countless clandestine exchanges for it to reach my hands." He gazed back toward the ocean in the distance, recalling that day. "Teppe mentioned you in it with great affection."

A sigh laced with regret and understanding escaped Taika.

"I suspect she didn't receive any of your letters because the palace intercepted them," Rawiri said. "And that her letters to you never left the palace, so please, don't blame her."

Taika let out a despairing moan, the sound heavy with resignation. "So this is it? I marry Mahini and forget her."

"No." Rawiri creased his brow. "You marry and love Mahini as if you were marrying and loving Teppe."

A ragged breath escaped Taika, carrying the weight of unrequited longing. "Mother said it wasn't written in the stars." He rested his head against Rawiri's shoulder. "Maybe I should defy the gods."

Rawiri knew about that. "Taika, I'm Tanganokai's kanga —branded as a failure. Don't utter foolish things."

A serpentine sea dragon—the indelible mark of divine retribution—coiled sinuously around his left arm. No fabric could conceal it; the magic that had shaped it turned sleeves into water. It was inked proof that Rawiri had defied Tanganokai and failed, and now he was his *kanga*—no longer blessed but cursed by the ocean god. The otherworldly tattoo stretched across his chest and snaked down his left arm as if a sea dragon had broken the ocean's surface, twisted around him, and was ready to pull him into the abyss.

"Marry Mahini," Rawiri said, his voice tender. "Get to

know her. See her as a friend, a companion; with time, it will blossom into love."

"But uncle, I'm still in love with *her*."

"I know, Taika. *I know*."

And with that, Taika burst into quiet sobs, his grief spilling out in waves, mourning Kharis as Rawiri had once mourned Kora. He wrapped his arms around his nephew and sighed.

He knew that neither man would ever lay eyes on Kharis again—that, besides the ominous tattoo etched on his skin, Tanganokai's punishment ensured that Rawiri would never again see the child he'd chosen to keep from the ocean god.

CHAPTER 104

A DAY OFF

Today, of all days, Kharis had left the villa before Saya. The spring equinox was upon them once more, announcing another birthmark celebration.

"I'll find her," Saya told the world, waving a triumphant fist in the air.

She dashed down the mirador's spiral staircase with a loud whoop, startling some servants.

"Sorry!" she shouted, waving her apologies as she headed toward the private passageway that connected their residence with the palace. Sentries saluted her when she opened the wrought iron gate. She returned the honor and took in the heady scent of rosemary and lavender lining the path.

Excited for the day, she rushed down the footpath, forcing her escort to sprint. She ran into Hala, who was on his way to meet with their father, grabbed him by the hands, and twirled with him in cheery abandon. His scribes watched, amused, laughing at the princess's antics.

"What's gotten into you?" Hala smoothed his embroidered kurta but didn't hide his smile.

Saya beamed, too thrilled for words.

"Ah!" He understood that gesture. "You found out about my surprise, didn't you?"

"Guilty," she said, "but my lips are sealed. When Kharis finds out—"

His eyebrows slammed into a stern frown. "You're sworn to secrecy, Saya. Don't spoil the surprise."

She curtsied, faking her seriousness. Then, with a glint of mischief, she winked at her brother, waved, and dashed through the corridor.

"Where are you going?" he hollered.

"Yuna!" was all he heard as she turned the corner.

☙

Kharis meandered through the palace, unsure what to do with her time.

"A day off," she mumbled to herself, still wearing a look of disbelief.

It was unexpected, but not having to train today was gratifying. General Salazar's instructions were simple. "You have a day off, so enjoy it." Before she exited his office, he added, "And happy birthmark, Your Highness."

Kharis stifled a beaming smile. It was good to hear. *Eighteen years of age now.* According to Zahari law, she was officially an adult.

"Thank you, sir." She saluted General Salazar, now officially her permanent training officer, before striding out.

The sound of conversation snapped her out of her mental wanderings. A few servants were bantering and giggling with each other about an upcoming wedding, unaware that Kharis was within earshot.

Mindful of her position at the palace and the fear she stirred in most people, she hid, pressing herself against the shadows of a narrow alcove, waiting for them to pass first.

The servants walked past her, uttering a name that made Kharis blink.

"I hear Prince Taika is handsome," one said.

"Dreamy," another added.

Kharis inhaled, the pulse in her throat. He would be twenty-one now. She still possessed the book of Kahurangi love poems he'd left her, but the letters he promised never came. She wrote a few but feared they were never sent, suspecting the palace had intervened to ensure a complete break.

"I love weddings!" That comment pushed Kharis out of her sorrowful nostalgia.

"Do you think the Crown will attend?" one servant asked.

"Doubtful," said another. "There was that awful incident with the Kahurangi tutor a few years back, but the Crown will certainly send a gift fit for the occasion."

"What will His Majesty gift the couple?" asked a third.

"I know what I'd like," a fourth one said, giggling.

"And that is?"

"A large bed!"

The women laughed.

Taika is getting married? Kharis wasn't sure whether her heart jerked or shattered in that instance.

She understood that Taika couldn't wait for her. Princesses and princes had duties to uphold, and their realms were always foremost. Still, she'd hoped—she'd longed for more than a xakea player. But the Djinnshirukh would never marry or leave Zahar-Ghak.

And yet, she wondered whether she would ever love and be loved in return. Would someone ever see her as a woman —a balanced array of sensual curves, dreamy eyes, and a gentle heart, not a dreaded monster?

The servants' conversation dissipated as they kept their pace down the corridor, sharing their dreams and wishes for handsome boys, marriage, and everything the Keeper of the South Wind couldn't have.

Kharis stepped swiftly into the open, and the bright daylight was a welcoming change. It soothed her heart and made her forget.

Just then, a lovely hummingbird flew into her field of vision. "Hello, little one."

The tiny bird hovered before her as if observing her. It darted left and right, then flew away. They were never far from her. It made her wonder why.

People filled the Zahar-Regia's central plaza. Servants crossed the square on their way to their assigned locations. Soldiers were changing shifts, and a few were glad for the relief after a long night. Farmers carted their produce, merchants transported their wares, and zenka vendors set up booths and tables for today's sales.

The sky was clear—perfect spring weather. It had rained the night before, and a few wispy clouds crossed the heavens here and there, pushed by the prevailing winds. The air was clean, heavy with the aroma of ripe strawberries, sun-warmed figs, and fried orea laced with orange and anise. From nearby stalls, the scents of cardamom, fennel, and ginger drifted through the street—spicy milk tea simmering in wide copper pots.

After three years of exemplary behavior, and with the Regiazenka's blessing, the king granted Kharis the freedom to roam the Zahar-Regia's inner ring. She still had an escort, but so did Saya. After all, both were princesses of the Zahari realm, daughters of the imperial king.

Kharis was about to start her stroll when a pair of hands covered her eyes. The familiar scent of orange blossoms and jasmine teased her nose, coaxing a grin to her lips as she sang out a playful greeting.

"Good morning, Saya."

Her sister's squeal rang out, high-pitched. Kharis

flinched, her ears protesting. "What did you have for breakfast?" She rubbed her ear but still managed to smile at her bouncing sister.

"Promise me you'll eat with us," Saya said.

The idea tickled Kharis—sharing the noon meal with Saya and Yuna. "I wouldn't miss it, but won't that spoil the dinner celebration?"

"Absolutely not," Saya said. "Come, but if you don't, I'll find you." Saya threw her sister a mischievous grin.

Kharis sighed. "I'm afraid you'll find me even if I hide in the Netherworlds of Ifran."

Saya's chuckle confirmed she would. The Sorukhipa took her job seriously.

"Hey! Where are you headed?" Saya asked.

"I didn't think that far ahead. I wasn't expecting a day off. Maybe the Iluna?"

Saya's smile vanished. "That place is full of monsters."

"Perfect! Would the dragon play xakea?"

Saya pursed her lips, leaned into her sister, and held her hands. "Khiri, please, be mindful." She glanced over her shoulder. "People fear you, and they won't understand your jokes or wry sense of humor. Don't say anything to make it any worse—think of the Regiazenka's ears. Please?"

Kharis put her hand up. "I solemnly swear to behave and enjoy this lovely day. After all, it's rare to get a day off—"

"Two!" Saya corrected. "Today *and* tomorrow."

"Tomorrow is our eighteenth birthmark, so it doesn't count. Today, however, is the treat. Hug Nana on my behalf. And yes, I'll meet you at noon. I wouldn't miss it for the world."

"Good!" Saya kissed Kharis's cheek. "I love you, Khiri."

"And I love you more," Kharis said to Saya's back as she took off running with a cheery wave. She sighed, warmed by the endless and unconditional love her sister had bestowed on her. Saya made her life bearable.

But Saya also deserved better—freedom, love, and

happiness. None of that was possible as long as she was bound to the Djinnshirukh.

Kharis exhaled, watching as she and her bodyguards disappeared into the crowd. "So much energy," she mused. "She'll exhaust her escort before the day's over." That thought entertained her the most. She glanced at hers—twice the number of soldiers guarding Saya—and exhaled, resigned. "Some things will never change."

Well... She tilted her head to observe a flock of birds.

Something did change in a matter of months.

Her uncle no longer commanded the Zahari armies, disgraced for his role in using the Djinnshirukh to execute prisoners over three relentless years—an act carried out without the required approvals. His violations of Zahari law were too numerous to ignore. The Crown, seeking to avoid public scandal, conducted closed-door disciplinary proceedings. Even Hala had been barred from attending.

Rumors swirled that Lady Khostuna remained composed throughout the entire process and finally broke into a grin when she uttered, "We find you guilty."

The judgment was severe: Ghan was stripped of his princely title, and his royal salary was revoked. While the title of High General remained his on parchment, it became a hollow designation; he no longer wielded power or held a seat on the Regiazenka. The honor passed instead to Lord Arush Mehta, signaling a profound shift in Zahar's leadership.

The tides were changing, and her uncle had become obsolete in Zahar.

It was fitting for a man who often called her useless.

Kharis noticed the people around her already directing sour looks her way. "Fear me?" She shook her head and huffed, stoic. "Nah! They hate me." Some days, keeping her chin up took a lot of effort.

In the Ghak, where people hardly ever forgot or forgave, the massacre would hang over her head forever. Nothing she did would alter how people felt about her. Her uncle, "High General" Arjun Ghan, eagerly fed that hatred.

"*Are you ready?*" The silvery voice snapped her out of her dark ruminations.

"Oh, I was born ready." She pulled her hood over her head.

"*Where shall we go?*" he asked with a hint of amusement.

She thought of the Royal Library to look at maps for this place called Hegra, but today was a day off, and perhaps "not doing" would lead her to the answers she'd been searching for four years.

The Voice was an odd companion—if he wasn't the madness that afflicted every Djinnshirukh. She beamed, pleased by the idea of "him."

"Why don't you choose today?"

A low, resonant hum caressed her mind, signaling approval.

If the Voice had a face, he would smile, charmed by the opportunity.

&

Nearby, a cloaked figure lurked in the gloom of a narrow alleyway, studying her with a sharp gaze.

General Aghet Mendi watched her. *She reminds me of her... and him.* He shook his head, shoving recollections from long ago out of his mind. *How long have I lived?* Life had become so dull for him—endless and unbearable until he met "his prince." And yet, the memory of the twins invaded his mind. *Him.* That one pained him the most. *I loved him, but he didn't love me back.*

With a shudder, Aghet refocused, back to assessing the Djinnshirukh. *I should take her for myself.* His shadows weaved in and out of his vision, relishing the idea of commanding all that power.

A fence of bodyguards surrounded her, but it didn't

matter. She'd escaped him at the tunnel, the clever little child she was. It had taken him weeks to recover from the burns she'd given him. Now, his claws were poised for the perfect moment to strike. *She'll never see me coming.* A wicked smile parted his lips. Then he stepped into the light to follow her.

PUBLISHER'S NOTE

Dear Reader,

Thank you for choosing this book. If you enjoyed it, please consider leaving a review on Amazon, Goodreads, Bookstrovert, or your preferred social platform.

Your review matters, and here's why:

- **Support for Authors:** Your review helps others discover new stories, giving authors the visibility they need to keep creating.
- **Guidance for Fellow Readers:** Your guidance helps others discover stories they'll love, creating a ripple of discovery and joy.
- **Inspiration for Writers:** Honest feedback helps authors grow and refine their craft for future books.
- **Community Building:** Your review sparks conversations and connects readers worldwide.

We'd love it if you could share your thoughts. Your feedback will help this book reach more readers who might cherish it as much as you did.

Thank you for sharing this journey with us. We hope this story captivates you as much as it did us.

Happy reading,

The Silver River Publishing Team

WANT MORE?

A soulful epic for those who love their fantasy with longing, lyricism, and knife-edged grace—perfect for readers of Tasha Suri, Alix E. Harrow, and Robin Hobb.

Her choices could set her free—or end the world.

Kharis longs for freedom from the curse that chains her to an ancient demon, a fate written long before she drew breath. But breaking the curse won't be easy—and she must do it before madness takes hold. Her sister's freedom depends on it. In a court steeped in intrigue, where her brother and uncle scheme and backstab to seize control of her power, she must survive treachery, manipulation, and the constant pull of a seductive voice whispering in her mind.

A Thoughtful, Immersive Epic Fantasy, perfect for fans of Jacqueline Carey and R.F. Kuang—a tale where intrigue collides with magic and existential dread.

Enter the world of The Dandelion Tree, Part One, a darkly gripping literary epic fantasy that unfolds with the patience of a well-told legend. It weaves a tale of intrigue, sacrifice, and the quiet strength found in the choices that shape our flawed heroine. This book is ideal for readers who seek depth over spectacle, layered storytelling over haste, and a flawed heroine whose journey is as much about understanding herself as it is about the world around her.

Reviews:

- An extraordinary hero energizes a measured but absorbing fantasy. - Kirkus Reviews
- Once again, A.S.R. Gelpi delivers a captivating and deeply moving journey between sisters Kharis and Saya. – E. Sappia - Reviewer
- A beautifully crafted fantasy that weaves together magic, destiny, and an unbreakable sisterly bond. – R. Vrábelová - Reviewer
- Beautifully depicted world with exceptionally well-done characters and rich storytelling that is so immersive. – A. Riddle – Reviewer
- "The Dandelion Tree: Part One" is a spellbinding meditation on power, grief, and the quiet defiance of a cursed soul. Kharis's journey unfolds like poetry etched in shadow—layered, deliberate, and full of aching humanity. With every choice, the stakes deepen, not just for the world she inhabits, but for the woman she's struggling to become. Darkly lyrical and emotionally fierce, this is fantasy for those who crave soul-deep stakes over spectacle, and

strength that looks like survival." — NewInBooks.com

Sign up for the author's **newsletter** and be the first to learn about special offers, including promotional offers, bonus content, sneak peeks, new releases, giveaways, cover reveals, and more.

Follow the author on Instagram and TikTok. The handle on all platforms is @asrgelpi_author

Curious? Scan the QR code to browse the series and grab your free samplers!

Learn more at www.asrgelpi.com

ACKNOWLEDGMENTS

From the bottom of my heart, thank you for giving your time, passion, and imagination to this story. Without readers, stories would remain only dreams. Your support enables me to bring this world to life on the page.

If this book resonated with you, I'd be deeply grateful if you could leave a rating or review on Amazon, Goodreads, or even your favorite social platform. Reviews are a small act with a huge impact—they help stories like this one stand out in the vast sea of books published every year. More than that, they help connect new readers to the tale you've just walked through.

Writing this book has been both a joy and a challenge, but if I had to begin again, I wouldn't change a thing. For years, Kharis lived only in my imagination, and sharing her story with you now is an indescribable gift. Thank you for being part of their journey—and mine.

But... equally important:

Although writing is technically a solitary endeavor, it rarely happens in a vacuum. I'm forever indebted to my parents, Ana and Carlos, who instilled a love of reading from a very young age and nurtured my endless curiosity and mischief.

I want to thank my sister, Pilar, one of my greatest supporters. But above all, I want to thank my daughter, who was instrumental during the development of this story. Night after night, I'd shared with her the tale of a girl not so different from herself, and I watched the way her eyes lit up.

In that moment, I knew I had to write it—so that one day, she could pass it on to her own children. As my daughter grew, so did the story, and the 12-year-old Kharis we first imagined together became the woman who now lives in these pages.

I'm deeply grateful for Michelle, my chosen sister, who walked this path with me. A dear friend, lunch provider, coffee-bringer, and the one who kept me on the straight and narrow when I felt like giving up on the idea of being a published author.

I also want to thank Alice Creswell, Ana, Deborah, Noelle, Nick, Margaret, and Robin for beta-reading the series and providing invaluable feedback that improved the story. I'm grateful to Poppy Kuroki from Kuroki Books and Sophie Huhn from Silver River Publishing for their thorough editing and proofreading.

To everyone who read *A Land of Shadows and Moss*, you've made my world shine brighter.

We write to share our stories with the world; you discovered mine. I'm forever grateful for your support and encouragement.

A.S.R. Gelpi

Glossary

A – pronounced like the "a" in apple.
E – pronounced like the first "e" in elegant
EE – pronounced like the first "e" in eve
O – pronounced like the "o" in honor
OO – pronounced like the "u" in utensil
G – pronounced like the "g" in generate
GH – pronounced like the "g" in get

The syllable in ALL CAPS reflects where the stress for the word is placed.

List:

Aghet Mendi	A-ghet MEN-dee	A Zahari general and Arjun Ghan's lover.
Akumi	A-koo-mee	A race of fire demons that attacked Zahar-Ghak a thousand years ago.
aljaicin	al-ha-ee-SEEN	Hard candies from the southern region of Zahar.
Almarim	al-ma-REEM	Important southern city in the empire; also, the name of the dialect spoken in this region.
Andaheimur	an-HAEE-moor	The Spirit world, a realm behind a veil only spirits inhabit.
Argi	AR-gee	A Zahari patrol guard
Arjun Ghan	AR-joon gan	High General and Minister of the Zahari Armed Forces
Aroha	a-RO-ha	Queen Ataahua's sister
Ataahua	a-ta-a-HOO-a	Queen of Kahurang
Atarangi	a-ta-RAN-ghee	A powerful tohunga (a healer and conduit to the gods).
bimah	BEE-ma	A raised floor or dais.
Checchi	che-KEE	Dialect spoken in the Westernland region of the empire; Cecchio is the main city in the Zahari westernlands.
dangu	DAN-goo	A monster that drags people into a watery grave with their long fingers
Djinnshirukh	GEEN-shee-rook	A demon's human vessel-prison; the Keeper of the South Wind.
Dulaä	DOO-la	A city to the north, twin city to Tulaä
ghak	gak	Suffix that means "city"
Ghetu	GEH-too	A river east of Zahar-Ghak; also the name for the Eastern Plains
Götrid	GO-treed	One of Kharis's siblings
Gutxi	GHOOT-chee	Term of endearment term that means "small butterfly"
Hala	HA-la	Crown Prince of Zahar-Ghak

Hatorisaita	ha-to-ree-SAEE-ta	Zahari term for The Enlightened One.
Hazenka	ha-SEN-ka	An assembly of guilds
hitzalkea	heet-zal-KE-a	Trained empire assassins
hizkuntza	heez-KOON-za	A signed language used in Zahar
Hröld	rold	Imperial King of Zahar
Ibaia	ee-BA-ee-a	A river west of Zahar-Ghak
idli	EED-lee	Thin rice pancakes eaten in Kahurang
Ifran	ee-FRAN	A mythical location where the Fires of Creation reside.
Jordha	JOR-da	A Zahari prince, cousin to Hala
Kahurang	ka-hoo-RANG	An island continent to the southeast of Zahar
Kahurangi	ka-hoo-RANG-ee	That which pertains to Kahurang
Karrakusi Square	kar-RA-koo-see	A large square in the Zahari capital
kashaya shawl	ka-sha-EEA	It's a large, regtangular shawl wrapped around the body seven times, and over one shoulder.
Kharis	ka-REES	The Djinnshirukh, vessel to the Akumi King
Khator	HA-tor	One of Kharis's siblings
Kiwa	KEE-ooa	King of Kahurang
Koa	KO-a	Middle son of Kiwa and Ataahua
magr	MA-gar	A southern plain's antelope
Mahabhal	ma-ha-BAL	The Great Tree or the Tree of Legends; also known as the Tree of Life
Mahazenka	ma-ha-SEN-ka	A body of Hazenka leaders
Mahuika	ma-hoo-EE-ka	Kahurangi goddess of fire
Mate-Mate	MA-te MA-te	It means *Black Death*, and references a powerful shadow demon in the Kahurangi pantheon
Nikau	NEE-ka-oo	Crown Prince of Kahurang, son of Kiwa and Aatahua
orea	o-re-A	Fried balls of flavored dough covered in powdered sugar.
rahuitia	ra-hoo-ee-TEE-a	Kahurangi term for *forbidden*.
Rangatira	ran-ga-TEE-ra	It means *dirty or grimy child* in Kahurangi.
Ranika Hill	ra-NEE-ka	The tallest hill in the Zahari capital
Rawiri	ra-WEE-ree	Kahurangi Prince and Kharis's and Saya's tutor
Raysänen	ra-ee-sa-A-nen	The name of an archipelago in the East
Regiazenka	re-jee-a-SEN-ka	The King's Cabinet, a body of fifteen ministers that balance the king's power.
rewera	Re-OOE-ra	Kahurangi term for a demon or ancient evil spirit
Ruk	rook	A Zahari patrol guard
Saya	SA-eea	Kharis's sister
Sharan	sha-RAN	The large ivory moon
Sorukhipa	so-roo-KEE-pa	The Djinnshirukh's Protector or Guardian; also known as The Sheath.
Taika	ta-EE-ka	Youngest son of Kiwa and Ataahua
Tangaroa	tan-ga-RO-a	Kahurang's god of the sea

Tawhiri	ta-WEE-ree	Prince Rawiri's Second-in-Command
Teppe	tep-pe	Term of endearment; It means *little badger* in Kahurangi.
The Ghak	gak	The term capitalinos/locals use to refer to the capital, Zahar-Ghak. For example: "I am from The Ghak."
tohunga	to-HOON-ga	A healer/seer from Kahurang
Tulaä	TOO-la	A city to the north, twin city to Dulaä
Tung	toong	The small red moon
txakurra	cha-KOOR-ra	A pejorative term that means "filthy bitch." Used for women.
txakurri	cha-KOOR-ree	A pejorative term that means "filthy dog." Used for men.
Urrun	oor-ROON	A remote region in the easternmost region of Zahar
Välissa	BA-lees-sa	An in-between space between the human and the spiritual realms
whānau	wa-a-NA-oo	A Kahurangi term that refers to family, close and extended, friends, neighbors, and members of the same tribe.
xakea	cha-KE-a	A popular Zahari strategy board game
Yuna Chantarasang	YOO-na chan-ta-ra-SANG	Royal physician; Kharis's and Saya's aunt
Zahar	sa-HAR	A vast empire that encompasses 2/3 of the known landmass in this world.
Zahar-Ghak	sa-har-GAK	Capital of the empire, it means City of Zahar; also the name for the empire.
Zahar-Homa	sa-har-HO-ma	A wall encircling the enclave that shapes the imperial city.
Zahari	sa-HA-ree	That which pertains to Zahar
Zahar-Katea	sa-har-ka-TE-a	Mountain range northeast of Zahar-Ghak
Zahar-Kayo	sa-har-KA-eeo	The southern ocean
Zaharregia	sa-har-RE-jee-a	The royal/imperial city located within the capital of Zahar-Ghak
zaldun	sal-DOON	A knight-like officer of the Zahari army, selected based on noble status and lineage.
zaldunak	sal-DOO-NAK	Plural of zaldun
zenka	SEN-ka	A single trade guild
Zherik-Umea	se-RIK oo-ME-a	The name for the independent tribes living in the Zahar-Katea region.

A LAND OF SHADOWS AND MOSS

A sublime introduction to exotic lands full of alluring characters and extraordinary magic.

— KIRKUS REVIEWS

A Land of Shadow and Moss is a beautifully written fantasy of spellbinding suspense and the powerful ties of sisterly love.

— POPPY KUROKI, AUTHOR, GATE TO KAGOSHIMA

THE DANDELION TREE, PART ONE

An extraordinary hero energizes a measured but absorbing fantasy.

— KIRKUS REVIEWS

"The Dandelion Tree: Part One" is a spellbinding meditation on power, grief, and the quiet defiance of a cursed soul. Kharis's journey unfolds like poetry etched in shadow—layered, deliberate, and full of aching humanity. With every choice, the stakes deepen, not just for the world she inhabits, but for the woman she's struggling to become. Darkly lyrical and emotionally fierce, this is fantasy for those who crave soul-deep stakes over spectacle, and strength that looks like survival.

— NEWINBOOKS.COM

"Destiny rarely asks for permission; it arrives dressed as duty and leaves with your heart." The Dandelion Tree, Part One, by A.S.R. Gelpi, is a fantastic novel that harnesses its fantasy elements to the truly complicated emotions of guilt, grief, and love. Kharis is and has always been portrayed authentically, but her reconciling of trauma and the desire for redemption feels so much more strikingly real here.

— READERS' FAVORITE

Once again, ASR Gelpi has woven a mesmerizing tale of magic, adventure, political intrigue, forbidden love, and powerful heroines. From the very first page, I was completely enthralled, and I cannot wait for the next installment!

— ERIKA SAPPIA, NETGALLEY ARC REVIEWER
@ERIKAREADSNOVELS

A beautifully crafted fantasy that weaves together magic, destiny, and an unbreakable sisterly bond.

— R. VRÁBELOVÁ, NETGALLEY REVIEWER

Spectacular world-building and wonderful character development.

— AMANDA ROCHELLE, NETGALLEY REVIEWER

A beautifully depicted world with exceptionally well-done characters and rich storytelling that is so immersive.

— ABBIE RIDDLE, NETGALLEY REVIEWER

THE DANDELION TREE, PART TWO

Dazzling characters navigate this magic-infused tale of gallantry and resolve.

— KIRKUS REVIEWS

This series still stands as one of my favorites. I absolutely love the way Gelpi writes emotions and relationships! The richness and depth of the characters is absolutely beautiful and the way the story just seems to unfold while completely enveloping the reader is just something that must be experienced.

If you want an immersive, emotional, and highly engaging story - this is the one for you.

— ABBIE RIDDLE, NETGALLEY

I absolutely love Gelpi's work–her storytelling is powerful, layered, and emotionally rich. The first two books were incredible, and Part Two only deepens the magic. Her world-building is vivid and grounded in a kind of mythology that feels both ancient and intimate. The character development continues to shine. Kharis's internal growth mirrors the epic scale of the story.

— ERIKA SAPPIA, NETGALLEY

Flew through this one. The Dandelion Tree, Part Two completely delivered on everything I hoped for—intense stakes, emotional resonance, and characters who feel heartbreakingly real.

— HOLLY COLE, NETGALLEY

This book was incredible. From the first chapter, I was completely hooked and couldn't put it down. The writing is beautiful and emotional, and the twist genuinely surprised me.

Kharis is a powerful and relatable character. Her struggle with the curse, her grief, and the choices she faces kept me fully invested. The world feels dark and mythic, but it's the emotional depth that really stands out.

If you love character-driven fantasy with rich writing and real stakes, I highly recommend reading this. I'm already looking forward to the next one.

— RACHEL CATER, NETGALLEY

ABOUT THE AUTHOR

A.S.R. Gelpi began writing fantastical tales to entertain classmates (and occasionally terrify teachers—sorry again, Mr. Cumbie). In college, storytelling became her favorite distraction during long lectures (*what if a monster burst through that door right now?*) and while waiting for the bus in 35ºF weather (*a unicorn would've been handy*).

Her dreams of dragons and doomed heroes eventually gave way to academia—earning an M.A. from Stony Brook University and a Ph.D. from the University of Southern California (go, Trojans!). But the magic never truly disappeared; it merely hid behind a mountain of grading, endless meetings, and that elusive quest for tenure (she got it!).

After years of scholarly pursuits and caffeine-fueled conferences, Gelpi returned to her first love: weaving worlds. The result? **The Dandelion Chronicles**—an epic fantasy saga brimming with intricate characters, lush mythology, and just the right amount of chaos.

These aren't merely books—they're what happens when a linguist with too many ideas finally lets the monsters out again.

When she's not lost in her literary worlds, A.S.R. Gelpi can be found devouring books, sketching out new story ideas (*do not give her more coffee*), indulging in anime, exploring hiking trails, battling the occasional dragon (aka grading), or soaking in the sweeping vistas of Yosemite National Park.

Join her on this enchanting journey—where every page invites you to dream.

ALSO BY A.S.R. GELPI

A Land of Shadows and Moss

The Dandelion Tree, Part One

The Dandelion Tree, Part Two

Kharis's journey is just beginning—stay tuned for upcoming books!

A Land of Mist and Loss (February 2026)

A Land of Fire and Ash (May 2026)

A Land of Salt and Mirth (August 2026)

A Land of Wind and Thunder (November 2026)

Curious? Scan the QR code to browse the books in the series, grab your free samples, and even bonus chapters!